BURNT OFFERINGS

by

Charles W. Newsome

Copyright © 2004 by Charles W. Newsome
All rights reserved including the right of reproduction in
whole or in part in any form

Published by Washington House
A division of Trident Media Company
801 N Pitt Street, Suite 123
Alexandria, VA 22314 USA

This book is for Connie and Patty, who lived the life with me. It is also for Chuck and Lorien, in hopes that they might better understand their father. But most of all this book is dedicated to the veteran street cops—the oft-disparaged 'dinosaurs'—of Detroit's southwest side. They should be remembered for the profound responsibilities they undertook, the devastating physical and psychological wounds they suffered, and the unrequited dreams they dreamed...

"Draw your chair up close to the edge
of the precipice and I'll tell you a story."

F. Scott Fitzgerald

PART I—WOLF IN THE FOLD

"Whoever fights monsters should see to it that in the process he does not become a monster. And when you look long into an abyss, the abyss also looks into you."

Friedrich Nietzsche

"From childhood's hour I have not been as others were—I have not seen as others saw."

Edgar Allan Poe

"We sleep safely in our beds because rough men stand ready in the night to visit violence on those who would harm us."

George Orwell

PROLOGUE

They drove past the stadium and the rookie smelled the aroma of steamed hot dogs mingled with the sweet, slightly burnt smell of roasted peanuts. The night was hot and sticky and these blended fragrances of summer wafted skyward with the clouds of cigarette smoke, past the light towers, and into the golden haze above. The rookie took in the odors and openly reveled at the sight of the old stadium at the intersection of Trumbull and Michigan.

There came a sound of faraway thunder and the rookie thought a storm had come up, squeezed out of the humid air. He twisted in the passenger seat of the scout car to watch for the flashes of lightning that would accompany the thunder out of the west but there was nothing. Then the deep rumble came again and he knew that it was not a storm but the crowd in the ballpark, cheering some feat on the field—the 1968 world champion Tigers.

The senior officer, his partner, looked at him with a sidelong glance, wondering what the kid was grinning about. The old-timer saw the love of the job on the kid's face. What would he give to love the damn job again? Excitement had turned to boredom for him. Tedium, crazy regulations, asshole bosses, and cold winters. He was forty-one years old. A cop's job in Detroit wasn't worth a red piss anymore. But he liked the kid, so he grinned back, and in a small place at the back of his mind he remembered how it was. It was a good job until the family trouble calls, the endless hours of traffic detail, and the dead friends that turned it all to hell.

The senior officer drove north on Trumbull past Tiger Stadium, away from the noise, the traffic, and the lights. The sound of the dispatcher's voice over the radio was merely a hum in his ear. Most of the chatter concerned crimes in other precincts, or routine reports of prostitutes and the like. The old-timer's mind unconsciously sifted through the monotonous drone, waiting for their own precinct and scout car designator, *2-1*, that would send them on another run. His eyes restlessly searched the dark streets, swept the plate-glass windows of the storefronts, and flicked over the license plates of passing cars that his sixth sense told him to check on the hot sheet.

His stomach was bothering him, his ulcer now consuming half a bottle of Maalox a day. He had a feeling that something wasn't right, that something was going to happen tonight. He couldn't shake the feeling. It was ten o'clock, six hours into the eight hours of the afternoon shift.

At 10:30 the dispatcher called them. "2-1? Radio 2-1?"

The unpracticed ear of the rookie didn't catch it and the old-timer looked at him. "Kid?" He pointed to the microphone nestled on its bracket on the dash.

"Oh!" The kid reached for the mike, retrieved it, and depressed the transmit button. "2-1, radio."

"2-1, make 16th and Myrtle. They say there's a fight in progress in the street. Several youths are fighting there. Unknown if they're armed."

"On the way, 2-1."

They were only four blocks away.

The old-timer turned west onto Myrtle from 12th and sped toward 16th. They went silently. One of the first things you learned about police work in Detroit was that almost everything you learned in the academy was crap. Overhead lights and sirens were reserved for only a small fraction of marked patrol responses. Responding to the scene of a gang fight was not one of them. When the shitheads heard the sirens or saw the blue lights they would scatter. All you'd find on arrival would be a baseball bat or a bicycle chain.

When they crossed 15th they slowed to fifteen miles an hour and the senior officer doused the headlights. They strained their eyes toward the next intersection, dimly lit by a single street light. They could see eight or nine teenagers, some in the middle of the street, some on the sidewalks, flailing wildly at each other with three-foot sections of two-by-four. The teens were so intent upon annihilating each other that they didn't see the scout car until it was almost in the intersection. By the time they realized the cops were there, the rookie and the old-timer were both out of the vehicle and running toward them.

The youth the senior officer went for spotted him a split second before he was grabbed. He swiveled aside, wheeled, and was gone, running like a deer. The others scattered almost as fast. The old-timer lumbered in pursuit, more offended at the little bastard for sliding away so handily than intent upon an arrest. The pursuer and the pursued disappeared between two old houses in the ghetto neighborhood south of Myrtle.

The rookie had better luck. He was younger and twenty-five pounds lighter than his partner. He grabbed the gangster's right arm and pried a ball-peen hammer from his hand, throwing it ten feet away to the curb. In nearly the same motion he spun him around, jerked the arm behind his back, and weaved his fingers into the kid's unwashed Afro. He pushed him forward, off balance. The kid went down onto his face, scraping his nose on the street. The rookie landed on top, sitting on the kid's back. He quickly retrieved his handcuffs and snapped them on the kid's hands. He sat for a moment catching his breath, his grey eyes scanning the shadows beyond the yellow glow of the street light. His partner was nowhere in sight, apparently still pursuing one of the other gangsters. He stood, reached down, and roughly hoisted the kid to his feet with a yank on the handcuffed wrists. The kid screamed and swore as the rookie steadied him, preparing to walk him to the scout car.

Then the rookie was struck a blow from behind. The force was so great it nearly paralyzed him. He stumbled forward a pace, gasping. His lungs wouldn't work. His eyes instantly went to the place where he'd thrown the hammer. Had another gangster picked it up and whacked him with it? No, the hammer was still resting there. He reached behind himself without turning and seized his attacker by the jacket sleeve. Hooking his own left arm around his assailant's left arm at the elbow, he deliberately fell back hard, throwing him off balance, carrying him down in a backward spiral. They landed with the rookie supine on top, both face-up. The rookie still held the other man's arm with his own, and the gangster's hand still gripped whatever weapon he had used, wedged now between their bodies.

The rookie felt no pain, but he couldn't catch his breath. He looked down at his abdomen and was startled to see four inches of shiny metal protruding upward through his shirt, just to the left of his navel. He had been stabbed from behind with a long steel rod, sharpened at the end. The rod had passed completely through him.

The gangster struggled beneath him, trying to push the policeman off. The rookie jerked his revolver from its holster, brought it across his chest, and jammed the muzzle against the soft skin beneath the attacker's chin so hard that it made a little hole. The gangster shrieked and tried to get away, twisting the rod through the rookie's body, wriggling it from side to side within the horrible wound.

Then everything slowed down to a surreal slow motion. The rookie's senses were heightened, but he felt no pain. He marveled at the way the rod protruded from his own body, spinning in the wound, and at how little blood there was. He supposed he would die, but was happy and surprised that there was so little pain. He gently squeezed the trigger of his revolver, almost as an afterthought. He watched fascinated as the hammer rocked back, was released, and then fell, all in the same surreal slow motion. The tremendous muzzle blast of the .357 magnum so close to his ear rocked him. If he weren't going to die this day he supposed he would always be deaf in his left ear. He felt tired and dreamy. He turned his head to look at the face of his assailant—mercifully, the wriggling had stopped. But the face was gone. He could make out a part of the gangster's right eye socket and a little bit of the right side of the bridge of the nose. The rest was gone.

He lay that way atop the dead man for what seemed like a long time, feeling quite comfortable. He was getting cold but the body felt warm against his back. He was sleepy. After a while he heard a voice. He realized that he had been hearing it for a while, but it hadn't registered. What was the voice saying? He focused his eyes. It was his partner, his eyes wide and full of fear. *What is he worried about? It's me who's dying*, thought the rookie. He concentrated harder.

"Okay," the old-timer said, as if from the bottom of a deep well. "You're going to be okay. I'll take care of you. You'll be all right."

The rookie was glad that his partner wanted to take care of him, though he thought he was lying about being all right. He wanted the old-timer's approval very much. He smiled. The old-timer smiled back, but there were tears on his face now, running down his cheeks, dripping off his face onto the rookie's shirt. The rookie thought that he, too, must be crying, though he didn't feel like he was. He felt something wet sliding down the side of his nose. A red-grey piece of his assailant's brain had slid down, dripping like phlegm off his chin, down his neck to the buttoned-down collar. As he looked up into his partner's worried face he heard the sirens at last. Sirens, sirens, sirens. They were coming from everywhere.

He smiled some more.

He was twenty-two.

CHAPTER 1

The name of the bar was Nancy Whiskey and it stood in the shadow of Tiger Stadium. Westonfield had been seated on a stool at the bar for three hours. He sat beside his partner John Rourke: Fat Jack, Black Jack. Both shoes fit. Rourke was drinking beer, Cinci on tap. Westonfield was drinking Puerto Rican Extra Fino rum and pineapple juice on the rocks. Rourke was thoroughly horrified, as usual.

"Why don't you have a kiddie cocktail, Bill?" Rourke said. "They're cheaper. A little Grenadine and 7-Up. Maybe even have 'em put a pink umbrella in it."

"Fuck you," Westonfield said absently. He gazed across the room into space. Jack had been saying the same thing for four years.

Rourke hoisted his huge frame and put some quarters in the juke box by the far wall. He returned to the bar, lifted his leg in Westonfield's general direction, and farted.

Westonfield looked at him, his eyes roving over the policeman's giant stomach. The banlon shirt barely covered the frame of the Sig Sauer 9mm pistol in the waistband holster and certainly did not conceal its shape. He laughed. "Good thing everybody in here's cops or Teamsters, Jack. Otherwise you'd likely get shot for carrying a piece—and what did you have for lunch? Jesus!"

"Not everybody's a cop or a truck driver," Rourke responded, ignoring his partner's comment on his flatulence. "Look at those ladies over there." He pointed to a table near the juke box. Three girls in their twenties sat there, drinking and talking. "Those aren't cops, Bill. Those are girls. G-i-r-l-s.

Remember them?"

Westonfield looked at them. They were pretty. Probably invited by a few of the guys to the shift party. They had arrived a few minutes ago; a little early, though not as early as he and Jack. He didn't answer Rourke, but looked instead at another woman, apparently alone, a couple of tables away. She was dark. Mexican? She looked about thirty. She was prettier than any of the others. The other three were wearing jeans and sweaters—she was wearing a dress, a casual, peach-colored affair. It clung to her flatteringly. "I remember," he said finally.

Over the next hour most of Westonfield's seven-to-three troopers (so called because they worked the high crime hours of 7:00 P.M. to 3:00 A.M.) trickled in. Several other girls arrived, some singly, some in twos and threes. The dark girl remained at her own table, sometimes talking and laughing with the others, or dancing with one or two of the guys; but he could feel her eyes on him when he wasn't looking. He drank with Jack until he was feeling pretty high. He turned down several requests to dance.

"You okay?" asked Rourke, his glassy eyes focusing on Westonfield's. "I mean—you know... You okay?"

"Yeah, I'm all right," Westonfield replied. But he wasn't okay. He went to the juke box and put in fifty cents. A moment later *Someone to Watch Over Me*, the Sarah Vaughan version, began playing. Westonfield returned to the bar and sucked down four ounces of his drink. Mary, the old Irish barmaid and a good friend of Westonfield, patted his hand and poured him another. "Wouldn't hurt to go home a little early, Bill. Sitting around here with these clods won't do you no good. Drink this one and go. I seen you like this afore. You look like my brother Tim when his little terrier died."

Westonfield took another drink and someone was standing next to him. He turned. It was the dark girl. "My name is Magaly," she said. "Would you like to dance?" She smiled. Her lips were very full, her slight Spanish accent immediately apparent.

Westonfield didn't want to, and certainly not to this song, but he nodded yes. They went out to the small, crowded dance floor. Westonfield was hesitant at first. But Magaly followed his lead patiently and perfectly. She looked into his eyes and smiled. He smiled back, ever so slightly, at the corners of his mouth. He held her close and danced.

After a while the girl said, "You must have loved her very much."

Westonfield looked at her in consternation. "Who?"

"I don't know. Someone."

He studied her black eyes, but they were guileless. He said nothing.

"It's okay," she said. "Maybe I don't know what I'm talking about. I just wanted to dance. You looked like you could use a friend."

"Got a friend," Westonfield said, motioning toward Rourke and the bar.

She grinned. "Yes, you do," she said. "I can see that you do."

As they danced Westonfield decided he liked her. And the more he decided he liked her, the more he decided he shouldn't. She rested her head on his shoulder for the last few strains of the song.

"Who are you?" he asked, as he walked her back to her table.

"I already told you," the girl said. "Magaly."

He looked at Rourke across the room. Jack raised his eyebrows. He motioned to Rourke that he was going to sit with the woman for a while. Jack nodded.

Westonfield sat across from her at the small table and looked at her closely. He had underestimated her looks at first. She wasn't pretty. She was beautiful. "You weren't invited here, were you?"

"As a matter of fact, I was." She grinned sheepishly. "Well, sort of. Tom Bacon over at Personnel told me about the get-together here tonight." She looked around the smokey barroom. "This is a nice place. It's sort of like a shot-and-a-beer place and it's sort of like a *posada* in Mexico. Do you come here a lot? I can see how you might. It's a place you could get comfortable in." When Westonfield didn't immediately respond, she added, "I think this is your kind of place."

"You don't know me," he said.

"No, I don't," she replied. "But I know a few things about you—from Tom."

"Tom talks too much."

"But not you. You don't talk much, do you?"

Westonfield looked at her silently.

"Actually, I think Tom's a good guy," Magaly said. "And he really doesn't talk a lot," she added.

"Who are you?" Westonfield repeated.

"Magaly Rodríguez," she said.

"And who is Magaly Rodríguez? And what does Magaly Rodríguez want with William Westonfield? And what did Tom-the-big-mouth tell Magaly Rodríguez?"

"Well, I really don't know Tom that well," Magaly said. "In fact, I just met him this week. The AP man in Detroit, Jerry Talmadge, helped me contact Tom about finding people in the Police Department I could talk to about a piece I'm writing."

Westonfield frowned, his suspicions confirmed. "I don't talk to reporters," he said. "Not no-how, not no-way. Ever."

"I bet you don't," replied Magaly.

"Then it's been nice," Westonfield said. He pushed his stool back from the table and stood up.

"I'm not a reporter," Magaly said, looking up at him. "And I'm sorry. I guess you're right. No—I *know* you're right. I *am* sorry. Please sit down. Please." Her smile was beguiling.

Knowing he shouldn't, he sat. "So, what do you want?"

"I'm a writer. For *Harper's Magazine*."

"And what does Magaly Rodríguez from *Harper's* want with Bill Westonfield?"

"You say my name like you speak Spanish," she said. "Road-ree-guess." She laughed. "And two trills of the Rs to boot."

"I do speak Spanish," Westonfield said. "Didn't my friend

Tom Bacon tell you that?" Resting his arms on the table and peering closely at her he added, "And you have an irritating way of answering questions with another question that has nothing to do with the first question."

"*Touché!* Maybe I should have been a reporter, huh? But alas, no. I'm a lowly feature writer. My editor wants a story on big city cops. Well, more precisely, on *a* big city cop. A profile. A look at a day or a week in his life. A look, finally, I suppose, at all of his life. I flew into Metro at the beginning of the week, talked to Jerry who told me about Tom, talked to Tom, who told me about you. And here I am."

"Tom's an asshole," Westonfield said. "I've known him ten or twelve years. He knows that I barely talk to my partners, let alone lady feature writers from *Harper's*. He steered you wrong, Magaly Rodríguez."

"He told me that in his whole career, you were the best policeman he'd ever known."

Westonfield chuckled. "That's ridiculous. And, anyway, like I said, he told you too much. It's none of his business—or yours," he added pointedly.

"He told me you've been hurt. A bunch of times. Something about a tool, being stabbed with this sharp pipe or something when you were a rookie."

The woman's perseverance was exasperating. Just wait till he saw that rat Bacon! "That was a long time ago," he said. "It's all in the past, Miss Rodríguez. No one is interested, anyway." He paused, studied her anew. Then, determined to make his point, he said, "Well, law enforcement groupies are interested, maybe. The hangers-on who like the ambiance of violence... vicariously, of course." He grinned viciously. "You know—like the people who read *Harper's*." He regretted his sarcasm as soon as he uttered it. The girl had done nothing to warrant such a personal attack. But, somehow, he couldn't help himself. Something about the way she attracted him was unsettling.

"You're bitter, Sergeant Westonfield," Magaly replied, sipping her drink, apparently not at all upset. "Tom Bacon told me you were."

Westonfield sat back in his chair, exhaling. "Is there anything he didn't tell you?"

"You tell me," she said, continuing apace. "Stop me when I'm wrong. He told me you're the best. He told me you're smart. He told me that you have two kids, a son and a little girl. He told me you're divorced. Twice. He told me you've shot a bunch of people. He told me you're a magician—an amateur magician. That you're really quite good."

Westonfield sighed and stood up. "I won't talk to you on the record, Ms. Rodríguez." He emphasized *Ms*. "I won't. No matter what." He nodded toward Rourke at the bar. "I've left my friend alone long enough."

Magaly nodded slowly. "Okay, Sergeant Westonfield. I'm sorry I got you upset. I truly am." She retrieved a ballpoint pen from her purse beneath the table, grabbed a bar napkin, and scribbled her telephone number on it. She handed it to him. "That's my number at the Pontchartrain Hotel," she said. "Think about it. Please? I'll be here in town for a couple of weeks." She paused. "And thank you for the dance. Especially thank you for saying my name right." She smiled a brilliant smile with her full red lips. Her teeth flashed very white against her dark skin. "It's been a while since I heard it right."

Westonfield took the folded napkin from her outstretched hand and put it in his shirt pocket. He nodded almost imperceptibly and walked away.

As she watched his retreating back she thought, you're a ghost, Mr. William Westonfield. You're a ghost. She gathered up her purse, left a tip, smiled at Mary, and left.

She walked into the early October night. The sky was clear, but a chill breeze rustled through the bare branches of the early shedding sycamores and ashes. The moist air carried the smell of burning leaves, though it was late at night. *Who would be burning leaves in the middle of the city?* she wondered. *And at this time of night?* Her shadow, cast by the bright moon, bobbed along behind her all the way to her rental car. Her footsteps on the cold pavement of the sidewalk came loud to her ears. An abrupt gust of wind sent a handful of leaves whirling round her feet, skittering in little circles. A feeling of being followed suddenly came upon her—something about the empty streets, the crisp fall night, the silver moon. A thrill ran up her spine and the fine hairs on the back of her neck stood erect in horripilation. She fumbled with her keys, got into her car, and shut the door, locking it. She breathed, peered out through the windows. Of course, no one was there. She was safe. Alone. She sat for a long time without starting the motor, thinking.

After a while she started the engine and drove the short mile from the bar to her downtown hotel. She took a shower and brought a yellow legal pad to bed with her, sitting upright, her back cushioned by a pillow against the headboard. Her thoughts turned immediately to Westonfield. What a remarkable man. What an intriguing life he must lead. His eyes... they were grey, the color of sea-foam. But there were tiny flecks of green in them. They were sad eyes; hard and sad. They were filled with curious, dancing lights. They were also a hunter's eyes. There was death in them. His own? Or someone else's?

She hesitated, pen in hand, her tongue flicking at the corners of her mouth as was its wont when she was concentrating. Finally she wrote, "I met Sergeant Bill Westonfield tonight. At a little bar called Nancy Whiskey near Tiger Stadium. I talked to a few of his co-workers and I finally talked to him. I danced one dance with him. I told him who I was and what I wanted to do. He turned me down."

She stopped again for a moment, then continued. "He's got a policeman's natural suspicion of media people. I expected that. But there's more. What else was in his eyes? Guilt, I think. Lots of guilt. They were haunted eyes, I thought. The eyes of a ghost, I remember thinking in the bar. But there was watchfulness in them: hyper-awareness. A cat's eyes. The eyes of a hunter."

She stopped writing. No. A ghost's eyes aren't a hunter's eyes. So he's no ghost. She mused for a moment then continued writing. "Haunted eyes and hunter's eyes: a witch. Yes, that's it. A witch. And he speaks Spanish. Why didn't Tom Bacon tell me that? *Es un hechicero*—a sorcerer. I wonder if he knows it?" She mused again. Yes, he knows it. He knows *everything*. I've got to find a way to reach him. This could be the most fascinating work I've ever done.

But her heart told her to be careful. Every fiber of her being shouted danger. Why? A line from J. R. R. Tolkien's *Lord of the Rings* came to her—*Do not meddle in the affairs of wizards, for they are subtle and quick to anger*.

Be careful, Magaly, she told herself. You're playing with fire.

CHAPTER 2

At six o'clock the next afternoon Westonfield left home for work. He walked out of his rented three-bedroom ranch house on Auburn Street, reached the public sidewalk in front, and turned, looking back at the house. It wasn't home. It was all right, but it wasn't home. It had been a month since he'd left home on Belton, over west of Rouge Park. That had been a nice home: a small bungalow when it was originally built, but a succession of owners had added a family room on the back, a two-bedroom dormer on the roof, and had remodeled the kitchen. He called it *Nouveau Detroit*, which wasn't far from the mark. The home on Belton sat in a small subdivision of Korean War-vintage homes nestled between the green strip of Rouge Park on the east and West Parkway Street—the city limits—on the west, a distance of about half a mile. It extended north to Joy Road and south to West Warren Avenue, about a mile. In this half square mile of land lived a large number of city employees. Locked into living within the Detroit limits because of strictly enforced residency clauses in their contracts, many of these employees, policemen and firemen mostly, had moved steadily outward over the years as neighborhoods deteriorated. Finally they had reached the absolute limit of this tiny enclave on the far west side. Almost all of these employees were white, in a city nearly 80 percent black. Black cops called it *the Alamo*.

The rented home on Auburn wasn't in the Alamo. It stood just off Warren Avenue, east of Rouge Park, in the mostly Polish neighborhood of Warrendale. The sort of landscaping on which he had labored so hard at the Belton house was conspicuously absent, as was the familiarity, the love of a home that ownership brings. Westonfield grimaced, shook his head to rid himself of the thoughts that obsessed him—loneliness, regret, doubt—got into the Ford parked at the curb, and headed for work. He reached forward and snapped on the radio, tuning to his favorite 50s and 60s station. After a while he was lost in the sound. The music made him feel better.

Westonfield had worked in precincts almost his entire career, with only a two-year hiatus at the Armed Robbery Unit at headquarters. He eschewed the ostensibly more glamorous *bureaus* for what Jack Rourke called the real world of the precincts. He had worked at only three precincts in all of his twenty-three years of service: the old Second (now the Third) on West Vernor; the old Sixth on McGraw (now moved to the far west side); and the Fourth. All of them were on Detroit's predominantly Latin southwest side. The southwest side was home to him. He knew the streets. He knew the business community. He knew the religious community. He knew the people. From the barrio spread along West Vernor Highway to the smokestacks of Del Ray by the River, he knew it. It was home.

He pulled into the mud lot on the east side of the Fourth Precinct police station, walked into the garage past the barrels of oil and windshield washer solvent, past one or two scout cars, and into the building through the back door. The commander's unmarked dark blue Chevy was parked in its designated spot. Westonfield looked at his watch—6:25 P.M. What was *she* doing here? His stomach churned once. He chuckled: the reaction of a guilty man.

He walked into the main lobby, around the front desk and behind to the platoon mail boxes. The desk lieutenant, a tall, pale man with clipped dark hair and black, plastic-rimmed glasses nodded and smiled. His name was Larry Runyon, an old friend and scout car partner from the days at the Second Precinct.

"Hey, Larry," said Westonfield. "Gimme the bad news."

Runyon silently pointed toward the commander's office only twenty feet from the desk. He raised his eyebrows.

"Yeah, I saw her car. What's she doing here?"

Runyon, still grinning, said, "Message in your box."

A hugely fat female officer rose from behind the desk and approached him. "How you doin', Sergeant Westonfield?" she asked. "You look nice today." She had one of the sexiest voices he had ever heard.

"Well, thank you, Monica," Westonfield said. "You look great, too." She didn't, but he said so because he liked her immensely. She had been a good, reliable worker for him when he was a patrol sergeant on that shift. She had a heart of gold. She also had a terrible crush on him.

"The commander," Monica whispered, coming close, her brown face sweating in the stuffy lobby despite the cool weather. "She's pissed at you."

"No doubt," Westonfield said. "What did I do now? I suppose one of the mindless wonders of the new Police Department has accused me of claiming that all black cops—especially you," he added, smiling—"are incompetent?"

She laughed. "Well, lately a lot of 'em are," she said. "But, I don't think so. Not this time." She leaned forward conspiratorially. "I heard it's about the other night."

"What about the other night?"

"That little thing over on Deacon Street."

A telephone rang behind the desk and Monica reached for it. "Fort and Green," she said into the receiver. She silently mouthed to Westonfield, "That's all I know..."

Westonfield nodded his thanks, reached into the pigeonhole, and retrieved his mail—a twenty-four hour major crime re-cap sheet, several leave day requests from his shift people for the next month, an L. L. Bean clothing and equipment catalogue, an assignment from the staff lieutenant to investigate and report on a citizen's complaint of excessive force against one of his subordinates—and there, on a yellow sheet torn from a telephone message pad, scribbled in the almost indecipherable hand of the commander's clerk, the message: "Commander staying late to see you. Talk to her before roll call."

Westonfield stifled a raw *fuck!* and looked up at Runyon, who continued to grin. Runyon despised the commander. "What's so funny?"

"Your turn, Bill," he said. "Don't sweat the small stuff. Maybe she just wants a date."

Westonfield displayed a ferocious frown, grabbed his genitals in a *this is for you* gesture, and walked away toward the commander's office. He heard Monica cackling like a lunatic behind him. He didn't wait to see whether Runyon admonished her or not.

He entered the staff lieutenant's office, an anteroom, through the open door. The room was empty. The staff lieutenant and the commander's clerk, who shared the office, had left at the normal off time of 4:00 P.M. The commander's door was closed. He knocked. A resonant woman's voice said, "It's not locked."

She stood up when he entered and offered her hand. "Hi, Bill," she said. She pointed to a chair in front of her desk. "Sit down. You want a coffee?"

"No thanks." He sat.

"All right," she said, looking him over. "I wanted to talk to you about that barricaded gunman the day before yesterday." Her tone left no doubt that she didn't like the fact that she'd just heard about it today. "I didn't know anything about it 'til George Smith in the Detective Bureau mentioned what a nice piece of work you'd done."

"Well, I'm glad George thought so," said Westonfield cautiously. Lieutenant George Smith wasn't usually one to compliment anyone.

"But that's not why I wanted to talk to you."

"Of course not," said Westonfield.

She studied him. "You don't approve of me, do you? You don't like me very much." She rubbed her chin absently. "In fact, I would say you loathe me." She swatted at a fly. "Be that as it may, sergeant, you *will* respect me. At least you will treat me with the respect due my rank." She didn't bother to wait for a response, but went on—"The book says you call me in a situation like that."

"It was three o'clock in the morning."

"So what? I get paid to haul my ass out of bed at three o'clock, just like you."

"Well, it wasn't necessary in my judgment," Westonfield said.

"In your judgment?"

"That's right, Commander." He hesitated, then launched into an explanation he had absolutely no doubt would fall on deaf ears. "Look, this old guy got drunk. He was mad at his daughter for sleeping around or something. So they had an argument. She told him to get bent. They were hillbillies, you know? We've got a lot of Appalachian transplants in Del Ray. Not bad people. They just do things their own way. Anyway, he grabbed his twelve gauge and blasted the refrigerator. It was a dumb thing to do. Where's he going to get the money to replace it? He's living on General Assistance. But no one was hurt. The neighbors called 911. We got there, figured out what was going on, blocked traffic, set up a perimeter and all that, just like the book says. We talked to the neighbors and found out what the situation was. I went up to the front door, under cover, and talked to the old man. He was drunk. He was scared. It took me about five minutes to convince him to let his daughter go. We got her out with no problem. He didn't shoot anymore and we didn't shoot at all. There were no injuries. After another ten minutes I talked him out. We got the gun and we took him to the Crisis Center at Receiving." He breathed. "That's about it. Pretty routine."

"Horse puckey," grunted the commander, sitting upright in her chair. "How the hell do you consider that to be routine?"

"Happens all the time," Westonfield said. "Nobody got hurt, unless you count the refrigerator."

"Sergeant Westonfield, routine gets people killed. When people in our line of work become complacent, when they cease to worry, they get themselves—or someone else—killed. I've only been to two or three barricaded gunmen—" she choked the words down, hating to concede that to him "—but I've reviewed dozens. Complacency, not believing that these situations are dangerous, can cause lapses. And that can cause deaths among both the good guys and the bad guys."

Westonfield watched her as she talked: about fifty years old, a big woman with mouse-brown hair turning grey. She'd spent most of her twenty-five years on the job in the old Women's Division. When they had reorganized the department and opened patrol functions to females, she'd gone up the ranks fast. She was now one of two female precinct commanders. Unlike Runyon, he didn't despise her. She wasn't willfully self-aggrandizing or incompetent as the lieutenant believed her to be. But she was defensive, unsure of herself in her role as the supervisor of a precinct, and she was afraid of the political powers that be, like almost everyone else nowadays. Detroit's mayor and police chief and their appointed underlings had so completely politicized the Police Department that the whole operation was virtually paralyzed from the top down.

No. Westonfield didn't hate the woman in front of him. But he didn't respect her, either. She was the top dog of an entire precinct, calling the shots, directing the minutiae of daily law enforcement operations of an urban police station, one of the busiest in the city, even the whole country, yet she'd never so much as written a parking ticket. And now she was questioning his judgment about how he'd handled a barricaded gunman.

"Ma'am, experience suggested to me that it wasn't that big of a deal. You know, Commander, with all due respect, it's all dangerous, isn't it? I mean, every traffic stop a crew makes may end up in a fire fight. That's the nature of the beast. Book or no book, we can't change that. We're on our own once we hit the street. No book can prepare you for the surprises." He searched for words. "Barricaded gunmen are dangerous. They're supposed to be dangerous. I've been to thirty or forty of these things, and this one, this particular one, felt okay. It just felt okay."

"Your experience told you it was okay?" It was all she could do to avoid telling him he was a member of an extinct species to his face.

He sighed. He should have known better than to try. "More or less," he said.

"Well, you were wrong, Sergeant Westonfield. The book says you were wrong, and I think you were wrong."

He stirred, his face flushing. He bit his tongue, looked out the window.

"No, hear me out," the commander continued. "You should have backed off once you set up the perimeter. Then you should have called the station. And they should have called me. That's the way it works and that's the way I want it to work."

He looked at her. They both knew that they were just talking at each other. "It was late," he said. "It *was* routine. It was over in half an hour. I didn't feel it was necessary."

"You've got your instructions, Sergeant. From this day forward you will call me to the scene of any barricaded gunman after normal working hours. Understood?"

"I understand."

"You will set up a perimeter, stabilize the situation, and make whatever notifications are necessary. When higher authority arrives, they will determine the course of action to be followed—to go in, to talk, or to wait 'em out."

"I understand."

She looked at him closely again, sensing the depths of his disapproval. "Experience isn't everything, Sergeant. Intuition... is that what you call it? Intuition is for 1950s television like *The Donna Reed Show*. That's why we have a manual. That's why we have procedures. The book was written to provide a logical and generally understood framework for action—"

Or *inaction*, thought Westonfield.

"—based upon exhaustive review of these situations. That, Sergeant, is invaluable experience. You old salts rely far too much on hunches. It's a changing world and a changing Police Department. You may not like the idea of women performing patrol functions; you may not like affirmative action when you take the promotional examinations; you may not like a lot of things." She stopped, watched him, sipped her coffee, tapped her pen on her desk blotter. "Bend with the wind, Sergeant Westonfield. Bend with the wind. If you don't, you're liable to break."

Westonfield was tempted to argue, but he fought down the urge. What was the point? The commander had no feel for the job, for situations like the barricaded gunman he'd handled, for what cops like him had been through. And if he argued she might take him off his Power Shift assignment. She was, of course, correct—by the book. He took his dressing down without further comment and went to roll call ten minutes late.

CHAPTER 3

When he walked into the squad room he saw that someone had found a dirty pillow and put it on his desk chair. His crew was looking everywhere but at him. He laughed. "Thought I'd need this, huh?"

"We couldn't find no Preparation H, boss," said Roberto Arena, one of his booster (plainclothes) crewmembers in his strong Spanish accent, "But it was the best we could do on short notice." He sounded like Speedy Gonzalez, and Westonfield called him that sometimes. Arena's observation got a general laugh.

"Word travels fast," Westonfield responded, shrugging.

The other Power Shift sergeant, his partner Jack Rourke, said, "I held 'em up, Bill, for a few minutes just to see if there was anything we should know about. Is there?"

"Not really. Just an ass chewing over Deacon Street the other night." He added with feigned resignation, "I fucked up. Overzealous, lack of caution, disregard of the rule book." He looked around the room, at each of their faces. "Not to worry."

"All right, then," Rourke said. "The guys are just a little nervous about their assignments. Any wind'll blow that bitch."

"Shhhh..." whispered Arena. "The walls have ears."

"The only thing in the walls around this rat trap is cockroaches," said Rourke. "But, anyway, Bill, I'm ready to set these wolves loose upon the community. Have you got anything for 'em before I do?"

"Yeah," Westonfield replied. "Give me ten minutes." He glanced around the nine-by-twelve office, faded blue paint flaking everywhere, plaster hanging loose in clumps from the ceiling, dried mud on the ancient tiled floor. The only neat spot was his own desk. It was as neat as a pin, the paperwork stacked in the "In" and "Out" baskets and the blotter free of clutter. A five-by-seven photograph of his two kids, Tracey and Bill, Jr., stood in its brass frame on one end. Rourke's desk fit more comfortably into the shabby surroundings. Papers were piled high on it and what looked like a jelly doughnut that a rat had chewed on lay in one corner.

"I don't want to say anything, Sarge," interjected Rupert Johnson, a raw-boned transplanted Alabaman with a red face like a ham. "But that dispatcher's gonna kick butt if we don't sign on our MODATs muy pronto. We're fifteen minutes overdue now." Johnson referred to the fact that the department had just converted its manual dispatching system to a computerized one. Every scout car, both marked and unmarked, was equipped with a MODAT—an acronym for *Mobile Data Terminal*—through which police runs were dispatched and acknowledged via video display. Other official communications took place on the system as well, including car-to-car message exchanging. The system was tied to Michigan's LEIN (Law Enforcement Information Network) system and hence to NCIC (National Criminal Information Center) in Washington, D.C., so that computer want checks could be run instantly on any individual, vehicle or gun encountered on the street.

Westonfield grimaced. "Oh, yeah. Shit!" He looked at Rourke. "Jack, while I'm talking to the troops, would you call downtown and tell them we'll be on line shortly?"

"Sure," said Rourke, smiling as he hunkered out of the room. "Let that whore of a double-dip sergeant down there take a bite out of *my* ass."

Westonfield looked them over. Eleven of them. All male. Two Mexican-Americans, one black, four WASP midwesterners, and one hillbilly. They were good. They were his. "What's going on with the Cobras and the Counts?" he asked, referring to two rival Chicago-based youth gangs, the Latin Counts and the Cobras, recently creating havoc all over the southwest side. The media had been all over the story. "Anybody?"

"Danny Villanueva has been hanging around Campbell off of Army," said Arena, naming one of the leaders of the Latin Counts. "The Cobras are mostly staying out by the Boulevard." W. Grand Boulevard was in the Third Precinct, about a half mile from its border with the Fourth Precinct. There was close cooperation between the Power Shifts of the two precincts.

"So what are we working on?"

"I got a source," continued Arena. "He tells me there's something spooky going on over by Junction and Merritt."

"Junction and Merritt *is* spooky," said Westonfield, raising his eyebrows.

The crew chuckled again.

"No, man," said Arena earnestly, ignoring Westonfield's attempt to keep the talk upbeat. "It's just warehouses and shit. Remember when we busted that chop shop a couple of years ago in the big warehouse on the northeast corner?"

"I remember."

"That's really what the neighborhood is like. Just old houses and old warehouses. And the railroad tracks. But this guy says there's been some new people coming and going late at night at a place on Merritt west of Junction. He don't know 'em. He don't *want* to know 'em." A few of the crew guffawed. "But he's seen them. They're Latin. He don't know if they're Cobras or what, but he don't think so. He don't think they're kids."

"New crack house?"

"That's all I know, boss. That's all he told me. But it's got me thinking." He paused, looked at Westonfield. The worry on his face was plain and very real. "It's got me wondering, you know? It don't feel right. This guy, my source, he was *scared*." He pronounced it with an "e" at the beginning: e-scared. "Real scared. I thought he was gonna shit right there in the parking lot where I was talking to him."

"Why, Bob? Why so afraid?" asked Westonfield. "Cubans maybe?"

"I sure hope not," said Arena, shaking his head. "They're some bad motherfuckers."

* * *

In the late 1970s and into 1980 Cuba was in crisis. The rigid central economy was coming apart at the seams. The island was completely dependent on the Soviet Union, which paid exorbitant prices for Cuban sugar and other commodities in the way of subsidies, and the U.S. economic embargo was, after decades, taking its full effect.

The island was over-populated. There had been improvement in the medical and educational systems since the days of Batista, but the policies of Fidel's government took their inexorable psychological and physical toll. Cuba, like Chile and Argentina, had a sizable population of *desaparecidos*—ones who had disappeared.

At first in twos and threes, later in groups, the hungry, the sick, the politically dispossessed, the dreamers, began to attempt crossing the ninety shark-infested miles that separated Cuba from Florida. They came in homemade rafts and in fishing boats, in pontoons and even on truck tire inner tubes lashed together. Some made it. Some died.

Eventually the plight of these people caught the attention of both the U.S. and Cuban governments. The U.S., under the Carter administration, protested the Cuban inattention to the matter, demanding that Cuba improve the living conditions of its people and that free emigration be permitted. Castro denied responsibility but saw in the Carter administration's exhortations a chance to humiliate and embarrass the U.S. while he unburdened himself of a huge economic and social headache. You want our huddled masses yearning to breathe free? Then here you are.

Castro promptly emptied his jails, his labor camps, and his insane asylums. Every murderer, child molester, narcotics trafficker, and lunatic he could lay his hands on was loaded onto boats and launched toward Florida from the north Cuba harbor of Mariel. Eventually, 125,000 were sent.

The U.S. was caught in the web of its own ill-considered words. There was no place to put them, there was no plan to deal with them, there was no way to provide for them. But the United States took them. These refugees out of Mariel Harbor became known as *Marielitos*. Had it not been for the simultaneous occurrence of the Iran hostage crisis, it would have gone down as the Carter administration's greatest debacle. But Cuba's great northern neighbor accepted every one of them— even the assassins.

* * *

"Yeah, they're bad," said Westonfield. He, like Arena, had a worried look on his face, but he forced it off with an effort. "They're not as bad as we are, though, now are they?"

Arena didn't answer.

CHAPTER 4

He was born in the town of Campechuela on the shore of the Golfo de Guacanayabo in southeast Cuba. His mother gave birth to him in a fisherman's hut in the spring of 1959. Her name was Juana Pompa. Her husband, his father, was dead; killed in the war of revolution against Batista. She bore him alone in the hut. When he came forth, red-clotted and red-faced, he did not cry. He lay upon her belly and to her surprise and horror opened his eyes immediately and gazed at her, black pupils dilated. She had borne six other children, all healthy and normal. But now her husband was dead and this child came, with its stare and its silence. She screamed. She screamed again, and she kept screaming until other women came to see what was the matter. She shouted at them to take the baby because he was accursed, borne of a dead father: he had opened his eyes at birth and he did not cry. Over the next three days they tried repeatedly to bring the baby to Juana to nurse. She would not look at him. She would not touch him. She would not nurse him should *Jesús* himself come to earth to implore her. At last they knew that she was crazy and they took him away to find a wet nurse.

A woman in a nearby village whose child had died at birth was found and she nursed the baby until he could be weaned. She loved him—he appeared to be normal in all respects, except that he was unusually quiet—but she, too, was poor and eventually she gave him to an old lady who came to the village one day out of the Sierra Maestra, the mountains to the southeast, between Campechuela and Santiago de Cuba. She came in search of certain herbs which could be found only in trade and which were not indigenous to the mountains whence she came. She was old, but childless, she said. The old lady bought her herbs and took the baby boy away with her to her hut in the mountains.

* * *

The *vieja*, the old woman, was of mainly Yoruba ancestry, her forbearers brought across the Atlantic in chains generations ago by Spanish slave traders to work in the cane fields of the Caribbean islands. The Yoruba, native to present-day southern Nigeria, and their brethren the Bantu to the south, were decimated. But they brought with them the threads of their religions. Over the centuries the old African beliefs became interwoven with mainstream Roman Catholic tenets. Eventually slavery came to an end, but the symbiosis of African and Spanish religious dogma endured. The Yoruba tradition melded with Catholicism into the cult of *Santeria*. The Roman Catholic saints were syncreted with the Yoruba gods into a combination of the two beliefs.

But the Bantu traditions were slow to assimilate and ultimately borrowed little from Catholicism. The religion of the Bantus went in different directions altogether, delving more deeply into the black arts. The Bantus in Cuba today are called *Congos*, a reference to the heart of their ancestral home. Their cult is known as *palo mayombe*: The Black Branch. Practitioners are feared by followers of the more benevolent cult of *Santeria* to the point of abject terror. The specialties of *palo mayombe* are necromancy, murder, and retribution.

The boy had been named Enrique by the wet nurse. But the old woman did not call him Enrique. She named him Gabriel, and she thought this was amusing; for she raised him in the way of the Congos. Though she was a Yoruba by birth, in her heart of hearts she was a Congo. Indeed, she was a *bruja*—a witch. She laughed because she would raise the boy to be a messenger. Gabriel was the messenger of God, was he not?

Gabriel grew big and strong in her keeping. His skin was

very dark and smooth. The *bruja* could feel that he was of Bantu ancestry, she could see it in his wonderful, curious eyes as he watched her at work. She taught him *brujería* from the beginning, almost as soon as he could walk. His strange black eyes, seemingly without pupils, would go round with interest when she made the green and black candles or dried her herbs like *yerba bruja*, ground her powders like *sal pa fuera*, or extruded special aromatic essences like *acéite de arrastrada*. She slept with him in the night and held him close and crooned to him about the ways of *palo mayombe*.

He learned quickly, better than she had dared hope. At twelve he knew all the simpler recipes for interactive herbs and potions; he knew the milder curses, spells, and conjures. But when she killed a beast—usually a chicken, red or white, but on important occasions a cat or a goat—he grew excited and wanted to learn more. If it were a goat he watched intently, his black eyes growing three shades blacker as the blood was drawn and the light, in stages, died in the animal's eyes. An absent smile would appear on the face as he watched the gasping animal flutter and twitch. When he was older still, he rubbed himself, the heat growing in his loins. The old woman noticed this and looked at his cock in his tenting white cotton pants and laughed and laughed and laughed, loving him and loving his purpose. What would she use him for? What?

When he was fifteen, and over six feet tall, he killed a shopkeeper who cheated the *bruja* out of a few pennies. Gabriel came upon the man as he walked home alone at night along a mountain track. The boy snuck up from behind with the stealth of a cat, despite his size, and struck the man in the back of the head with a mallet. Gabriel threw him over his shoulder and took him to his place, a clearing in the jungle at the base of an ancient ceiba, or five-leaved silk cotton tree: a kapok. He tied the man securely to the base of the tree with a rope of hemp. He lit candles, burnt powders, and said prayers. When the man came to Gabriel (his witch mother had given him no last name) plucked out his eyes with the hooked wires he had fashioned for just this purpose. The man screamed and cried, thrashing against the rope, his voice echoing across the hills. No one came. No one would come even if they heard; the ridge upon which the apprentice *mayombero* and the *vieja* lived was known to be haunted. The *Santeros* had warned everyone away. Few people lived nearby anyway, the foolish and hapless shopkeeper being one of the few. But he was tied securely and he could not escape. He screamed until his voicebox broke in a final high-pitched squeak. The boy worked on him, slicing slowly, deliberately, burning and sealing the bleeding wounds with hot black candle wax; slicing and sealing again. The man looked silly with his eyes jiggling low upon his own cheeks, dangling from red-grey threads. They reminded Gabriel of marbles on strings; they swung like pendulums with every jerk the man made. It took the man two hours to die. For the first time in his life Gabriel ejaculated without touching himself or being touched by the *bruja*. It was a good night. He breathed deeply of the tropical air and felt alive. Truly alive. It was a world of infinite possibilities.

In 1978, at nineteen, he was drafted into the Cuban armed forces. The Sierra Maestra were remote, but he went to school. The *bruja* was skilled in her trade but she was not worldly. The boy was destined for great things, she knew, and he would need not just knowledge of the soul but knowledge of the ways of the modern world. And the reach of Fidel was long. One day a fat army recruiter came calling, shouting the boy's name from outside the cabin. The boy went.

He adapted well enough to army life, used as he was to the discipline, in its own way, of the *bruja*. And far away though she was, she spoke to him still. She came to him in his dreams and whispered to him of wonderful things yet to come. Even in the day she would come to him, her lilting voice like the gentle chatter of running water over stones, droning peacefully in his ear. She murmured to him now to be patient, to accept the temporary restraints placed upon him as only minor obstacles to overcome.

But submitting to the authority of lesser men was humiliating nonetheless. Biding his time, he would usually find a way to exact revenge for his humiliation. Possessions disappeared. Hard luck came at the most importune times. Gabriel (the last name the army gave him was Flores) gradually earned a reputation as a man not to be trifled with. After a while this reputation earned him an invitation into an exclusive fraternity, the brotherhood of Cuban assassins—no sanctioned military unit, this—but a loose knit group of assassins-for-hire. Each member was branded in a different way with the sign of his calling. Sometimes a scorpion would be tattooed on one of the hands, on the web of skin between the thumb and index finger, or the image of a spider would be burned into the soft tissue on the underside of the tongue. Typical of his dash, Gabriel had a small dagger tattooed on the underside of the base of his penis.

Thus Gabriel Flores became an assassin shortly after reaching his maximum powers as a *tata nkisi*, a sorcerer of *palo mayombe*. And his fame grew. But in Cuba, Fidel controls everything and knows everything. Even the activities of the most clandestine of organizations do not go unnoticed. So it was that in 1980, after two years in the military, having reached the rank of staff sergeant in the service, and chief assassin in the Order of the Dagger, the security police came and took him to prison. They tortured him and abused him, but he bided his time. It was given to him to know many things and one of the things he knew was that it was not his lot to die in a stinking Cuban jail.

He was right. One night, after seven months had passed, they came for him. Along with a number of other prisoners in the security ward he was herded onto a guarded stake truck and driven to a nearby military airport. He and the others were then transferred onto a Russian-built transport plane and manacled to a long bench. They landed at another airport in an hour, were transferred again and driven in another truck to Mariel Harbor. The men were all uncuffed at the dock and marched and prodded onto an old trawler. They didn't know it then, but they were about to become residents of the United States of America.

CHAPTER 5

With the crews finally on the street, Westonfield sat alone in the dingy office, reflecting on the Merritt Street information divulged by Roberto Arena. On the surface it seemed minor, perhaps irrelevant—the idle fears of an informant, or the desire of the informant to ingratiate himself with the police by offering meaningless street gossip in the guise of hard information. Westonfield worked it over in his mind. Something about it didn't sit right. It left him uneasy. Arena was a pretty tough Joe, even if he was usually the first to make a joke. He, too, had seemed unsettled and agitated.

Cubans. One was occasionally arrested in the southwest side for one thing or another, usually narcotics. Some were more confused than criminally inclined, trying to survive in an alien culture, strangers in a strange land. They used the only skills they had, the ways of the street and of violence, to get from one day to the next. But a few were different: hard men with a black stare that looked clean through you. Westonfield recalled his first arrest of one of these in 1982. "You call this a jail?" the man railed. "This is a fucking hotel, man. What are you gonna do to me, huh? What are you gonna do? I was in a jail. You know what I mean? A real jail. Are you gonna beat me, cop? You gonna shoot me? Fuck you, Mr. Policeman! You ain't shit and this whole fuckin' country ain't shit." Most of the handful of true sociopaths he had encountered on the street were Cuban.

Rourke poked his head through the doorway and said, "You about ready to go out, partner?"

"Yeah, in just a few minutes. I have to call my kids."

Rourke nodded and went back out. His voice came floating

back down the hallway. "I'll be downstairs bullshittin' with the detectives."

Westonfield stood up and looked out the dirty window toward the Detroit River. The view was blocked by warehouses, factories, and bars. He gazed out idly for a few minutes and then returned to his desk, propped his feet up, picked up the telephone, and dialed.

A small girl's voice on the other end said, "Hello?" Tracey, his six-year-old daughter.

"Hello," Westonfield said cheerfully, an involuntary smile coming to his face as it always did when he spoke to her. "What's going on, Rosebud?"

"Hi, Daddy."

"Whatcha doin'?"

"Eating."

"You're always eating."

She giggled. "I know it."

"Is your brother home?"

"Yep."

"What's he doing?"

" I don't know, he's in the basement."

"Ahhh."

"Daddy, Mommie says we're gonna move."

"What?" He wasn't sure he heard right.

"Mommie says we're moving to a new house."

"When? Where?" He couldn't believe it.

"It's not too far, Mommie says."

He recovered a little. "When are you moving? Did your mother say?"

"She says when we sell the house," Tracey said. When he failed to respond immediately, she added, "She's getting married."

Westonfield's heart went instantly cold as ice. "I see," he said, his mind flooding with so many possibilities that for a minute he couldn't answer. "Do you like him?" he finally asked, not at all sure what answer he'd like best.

"He's nice," Tracey said, but the brightness had gone out of her voice. "He does things with us sometimes. He plays video games and stuff."

Another piece of Westonfield was torn away. He actually became dizzy. With another supreme effort he said, his voice hollow, mechanical, "Well, that's good, honey. I'm glad you like him. So, how's your mom?"

"She's good. She's doing dishes."

"Ohhh."

"Daddy?"

"What, angel?"

"How's Cindy?" Cindy was his one-year-old Siamese.

"She's fine, Rosebud. She misses you."

"I miss her, too."

"Well, I have to go now," Westonfield said. "Can I talk to your brother?"

"He just went outside with Glen."

"Oh, gonna play with his friend, huh?"

"Yeah, they went to the park to play football. With Mom's... with Derrick."

Westonfield hung up and sat as still as stone, the blood draining from his face. A pain rose in his chest so intense that it took his breath away. He took his feet down from the desk and stared unseeing at the wall. Tears welled in his eyes and the guilt rose within him like a great hand, seizing his heart, squeezing until the pain was unbearable. He gasped. His fingers and toes, and eventually his whole body, tingled as he breathed too fast, sucking at the air that wouldn't flow into his lungs.

After what seemed like a long time he gained control, the pain in his chest diminishing. He stood up, looked out the window, looked at the calendar on the wall, looked at the telephone. With a Herculean effort he shrugged it off, forcing it all into a secret compartment at the murky bottom of his mind. A secret voice said, "It's over, let her go."

He went to his locker in the drafty, makeshift locker room, removed the lightweight Colt from his waistband, and placed it on the oiled towel on the top shelf. He unclasped his belt and threaded it through the pancake holster he pulled from the shelf, sliding it around to a point forward of his right hip. He then slid his speedloader clip onto the belt, lining it up so that it was in front, to the right of the belt clasp. Speedloaders were cylindrical clips on which were attached six cartridges each, in a circle, so that a revolver could be reloaded with six fresh rounds in a fraction of the time it took to reload each empty chamber separately.

He snugged down the holster and reclasped his belt. He next retrieved his Smith & Wesson stainless steel .357 magnum from its oiled cloth wrapping. He pressed the thumb piece on the revolver's left sideplate and swung open the cylinder, rotating it smoothly, silently, confirming that each of the six chambers was filled with a hollow-point cartridge. He snugged it into the holster. It glided into the fitted leather like a glove, the weapon's cylinder forcing the top folds of molded leather apart and then the leather closing in again when the cylinder, the widest part of the revolver, slid past.

Westonfield was one of the old school who preferred to carry a wheel gun—a revolver. Many of the younger men and a good share of the older ones had long since opted for the increased cartridge capacity and ease of reloading of the semi-automatic pistol, the .40 caliber Glock. The shooter had only to press a small button, eject the empty clip, insert another, and continue shooting. These had become the weapons of choice of the narcotics trade. Finding themselves outgunned, police agencies across the country had gradually adopted the newer weapons.

Jack Rourke opted for the Sig Sauer semi-automatic pistol in 9-mm: not an approved weapon, but as usual, he didn't care much. Westonfield was more comfortable with the wheel gun. The .357 magnum was familiar as old lace and more powerful than the 9-mm pistol. It did not jam, as was an everpresent possibility with any semi-automatic weapon. If an automatic jammed, the cartridge had to be manually extracted by hand, wasting time and squandering priceless concentration. What if one of the shooter's hands was injured? How would the semi-auto's slide be racked; how would a misfired cartridge be extracted? With the revolver, a misfired cartridge was merely bypassed in its chamber after the trigger pull and a new cartridge was rotated under the firing pin with the next trigger pull. In the event of a hand injury, the revolver could be switched to the other hand instantly. Westonfield practiced left-handed shooting meticulously. As for the hollow-point cartridges he carried, the department expressly banned their use, but he felt he'd rather be written-up and alive than dead and rule-abiding.

Westonfield slipped on his light weight faded green fatigue jacket and was ready for the street. He went down the stairs in search of his partner.

Westonfield drove. They hadn't gotten more than three blocks, Westonfield quietly driving, when Rourke turned to him. "You look like a fellow that's had his balls in a vise for a while. Big one, for a long time."

"Do I now?"

"Yes, you do. You aren't going to let that bitch's lecture haunt you today, are you? Jeez, I hope not," he added expansively. "I feel lucky today."

Westonfield grinned despite himself. "Lucky how?"

"Aw, Bill," Rourke went on, "you know a bad boy getting away with a crime is like a day without sunshine. Any dummy knows a first rate arrest is better than the best blow job ever had—which reminds me, remember that barmaid at the DelRay Cafe with the false teeth?"

Not exactly being in the mood to talk about the girl with false teeth, Westonfield put in, "Well, I'm glad one of us feels good, anyway."

"Why is it, Bill, that getting you to talk is like getting a whore into church? Do I have to ask you to confess? I'm fat and Irish, but I ain't no fucking priest."

"It's nothing."

"It's *nothing*," Rourke mocked.

"Well, it isn't. It's just me being me."

"That bad, huh?" Rourke said flatly.

Westonfield sighed. "Millie's getting married. Tracey told me a while ago on the phone."

"Millie's getting married?"

"Right."

"That's it?"

"Yeah."

"I repeat: that's it?"

"Yes. That's it, Jack."

"Jesus H. Christ, Bill!" Rourke yelled. "You divorced the woman, what—four years ago? And if that isn't enough, you went through another one since then. My God! Are you starting up a stud service? Or maybe you're working part time for the Wayne County Friend of the Court? Do you like child support?" He guffawed. "By God, I think I'll trade you in for one of them affirmative action sergeants with four years on the job. They won't be smart, but at least they probably won't be crazy."

"Come on, Jack. Gimme a break."

"No, sir. I will not. You're fucking crazy."

"I'm not crazy."

"Yes, you are. Crazy as a bed bug. You still love that woman, don't you?"

"I don't know."

"Hell, yes, you love her. Why the hell else are you acting like you've got a four day constipation going?"

Westonfield was silent.

"See? You're a lover, Bill."

Westonfield looked at him blankly.

"No, now wait a minute. I mean you're a lover in the dictionary meaning of the word. L-o-v-e-r. Lover. One who loves."

"Now who's crazy?"

"No, hear me out. You love the women, Bill. You're a goddamned knight-in-shining-armor. Some of us love 'em and leave 'em. Not you. I remember this line from the movie *Viva*

Zapata. Remember that? Marlon Brando is in love with Jean Peters. I mean really in love. Anthony Quinn, Marlon's partner in the Mexican Revolution, is talking to another guy, and he's disgusted, see? He says, 'I've loved a hundred women with all of my heart—for a day. Then I don't want to see them again.' He's talking about Marlon, who's totally hung up on this fancy-pants Mexican señorita."

He looked at Westonfield who remained silent, slowly driving.

"Most men are like that," Rourke continued, grinning. "I'm like that. Least I was 'til I got fat as a warthog and the women wouldn't have me anymore. But not you. You're a regular sticker-wither. Love 'em 'til the bitter end, by God! You're in love with Millie. You're in love with Susan. Jesus Christ! You're forty-five years old. By the time you're fifty, you'll have to have a file card system on a Rolodex just to keep their names straight. But you'll be in a nut house long before that, shitting in a bed pan and bemoaning your lost loves. Of course you won't really be in a nut house. You won't have the money for a nice shrink in a nice institution. All of your ex-wives will have it, and your fourteen kids. And you won't know half of their names either."

Westonfield looked at him. "You're very helpful, Jack. I needed that. Thank you."

Rourke softened his tone, his jaunty grin replaced by a thoughtful look. "Well, Bill, it's true. You're a lover and a carer, too. You love everything and you care about everything. Everything matters to you. Everything. The rights and the wrongs of the world are your own personal province. Your duty is to make it better. Duty. That's you. Duty. Well, hell! Who appointed you? God? You don't know him on a first name basis, do you?"

Westonfield continued to drive silently. The sun was setting over the buildings to the west and dusk fell quietly.

After a while Rourke said, "Nobody cares much about anything anymore, Bill. Live and let live, that's the ticket.

Everything's too fucked up to help. That's why everybody's checked out. You can't do anything. The world's too big, too complicated. It's every man for himself. It's normal. It's sane." He looked at his partner again, reached over and patted him affectionately on the shoulder. "You love 'em all forever and you care about everything forever. That's crazy. That's certifiable. It'll be the death of you."

Rourke belched and peered out the window, scanning passing cars for any sign of the unusual, furtive glances on the part of occupants (it wasn't hard for an accomplished thief to spot an unmarked police car), tape over the steering column possibly hiding ignition switch tampering, dirty plates, anything which would justify a second look. After a few minutes he asked, "How's the kids?"

"Okay, I guess. They seem to like the guy."

"Is it this Derrick you mentioned?"

"Yeah."

"Well, dip me in sugar and call me a doughnut! She picks 'em, don't she? First she marries a busted-out Welshman street cop who can't make up his mind whether he's a Mexican or a magician, then she marries a wuss. Is this guy the ball of fire he seems to be? I get the impression there's more fire in my old dog Fred than in that guy. Hell, she'll melt that faggot in five minutes. She was smarter when she was two than he'll be at sixty." He thought for a while. "Maybe not, though. She sort of shopped for him, don't you think? Kind of like a bag of groceries. He probably isn't a bad sort, really. Just there. Plain, easy, predictable company. A break from you. You burn just a little hot for her, Bill—too happy, too sad, too everything. Derrick, there... Hell, now Derrick isn't too anything."

Westonfield shrugged. "You hungry?"

"Yes, I am a little hungry as a matter of fact," Rourke replied. "Let's go to Duly's. A dog would go down good right now." He farted. "Don't worry about your kids, Bill. They'll be just fine. They're not stupid, are they? They'll see old Derrick for what he is—safe, reliable, and friendly. Like a puppy. He won't mistreat them. He won't hurt them. He'll just sort of drift along with the flow. They could probably use that kind of stability right now, just like their mom."

"Maybe," said Westonfield as he swung the beige Caprice to the curb in front of the coney island. "Maybe so."

Rourke ordered three coney dogs with everything, a bowl of chili with onions, an order of chili fries, and a large Coke. Westonfield ordered two loose hamburger on buns, no onion, and a Diet Coke.

"Let's stop in and see Father Mark when we leave," said Westonfield. "I haven't talked to him in a while."

"See, I was right. You do want to confess your sins," Rourke said.

"Horseshit. You like him more than I do, you Mick motormouth."

Rourke grinned, took an enormous bite of hot dog, chili spilling out and dribbling onto his plate, a look of amused satisfaction on his face. Westonfield couldn't tell if he was amused about the hot dog or something else. He suspected something else. With Jack it was impossible to tell, and the less you asked the faster you found out what he had on his mind.

Rourke groaned with gustatory pleasure. He nodded out the window. "Yeah, sure. We'll go see Father if you want," he said through his mouthful of food, nodding out the moisture-covered window, wet from the steam of the boiling hot dogs and bubbling chili. "It ain't like it's far." He said it like a man who hadn't exactly had his arm twisted. He chewed contentedly and looked out across the street at the red brick facade of Holy Redeemer, the landmark church, rectory, convent, and school which had served southwest Detroit's Catholic community for generations.

CHAPTER 6

Westonfield and Rourke finished eating, paid the tab, and exited into the cool, dry October evening. Westonfield guided the car away from the curb and into the flow of westbound traffic the few yards to Junction and then turned south. In another few yards they drew abreast of a driveway on the right and pulled in, driving all the way to the rear of the parking lot where the Holy Redeemer activities hall stood. Rourke reminded Westonfield that Father Mark would be delivering the benediction at a class reunion this evening.

They found the priest at a table in the back, surrounded by an eclectic, if not bizarre, throng of Polish and Latin women, cleaning the last bite from what had no doubt been a substantial plate of food. Father Mark (Marko) Lewendowski was a naturalized American citizen, born and raised in Poland. His father, a butcher by trade, had pulled up stakes and emigrated to the United States with his wife and five children in 1956, after the Hungarian Revolt. Marko had been sixteen. His father found work in Detroit's Western Market on Michigan Avenue and young Marko had helped, learning English and studying at night. The family lived in a flat on Springwells and Marko attended Holy Redeemer. He graduated in 1958. He continued to help his father who by then had opened his own shop at Wagner and Tarnow. When he was twenty-two Marko was accepted at the seminary at Notre Dame University. He entered the priesthood and returned to Detroit, filling a number of assignments in the area until there was an opening at Holy Redeemer. He came home, full circle, in 1968, a year after the 1967 riot—and the year Bill Westonfield joined the Police Department.

He was a fixture at Redeemer now, a legend, having taught at the school for twenty-three years, conducted untold Masses, and presided over hundreds of weddings, funerals, and graduations. Rourke, a devout Irish Catholic and occasional Massgoer, had introduced Westonfield to the priest years before. Though Westonfield wasn't Catholic, he and Father Mark had become fast friends, almost soul mates. Father Marko cursed roundly, relished obscene jokes, ate hugely, and partook copiously of the grape (in excess of what was expected in the way of sacramental wine).

He spotted Westonfield and Rourke, beamed, and waved them forward. "Well, fellows, how are you two? Haven't seen you much lately." He studied them. He and Rourke passed a look between them which Westonfield took note of. "Sit down! Have a bite." He motioned for them to pick up a plate at the buffet table in front. "Lord, what a feast," he said. "Pierogy, kielbasa, kraut, homemade tamales, arroz con pollo." He named them all lovingly.

"We just ate," said Westonfield as Rourke debated the merits of eating two dinners in a row. "We just came by to see how you're doing." He glanced around the hall. "Is this a bad time? Any speeches to make? Souls to save?"

"There are always souls to save, Bill. Of needful souls there is never a lack." He stifled a belch with the back of his hand. "But fortunately for you who thirst for enlightened conversation this evening, I am done." He walked to a fat Mexican woman who sat at a nearby table, talked briefly, explaining his intention to depart, and returned to the policemen. "Gentlemen," he said in his still-detectable Polish accent, "Shall we go?"

Eat as he did, Father Mark, at fifty-one, was as thin as a reed. He had a thick mop of unruly black hair and a swarthy complexion that made him look more Georgian than Polish. They followed him as he went out through the same door they had just entered and walked quietly behind as he strutted across the parking lot toward the rectory.

They sat at a wooden table in the library surrounded at once with the familiar leather and old wood smell. It was a comfortable aroma. Predictable, safe, sane. The priest offered them a brandy. They accepted and he poured the amber liquor carefully into three small snifters, the bottle clinking musically on the tops of the glasses. Rourke smoked a cigar. This would have appalled most priests but Father Mark gave it no thought at all.

"I say again, boys, what's new?" He looked at Westonfield. "I hear you're getting a divorce again. Unable to keep your dick in your pants, is it? Or something different this time?" He looked at Rourke and winked. "Of course, as Church doctrine teaches us, you're still married to your *first* wife, so you can't, strictly speaking, have committed adultery against your second wife since she's not really your wife."

Rourke said, "I never thought of it that way, Father, but you're right. By God, after the first marriage you can sort of go on any way you want, fornicating at will! Not a bad way of doing things, in my view."

The priest looked at Westonfield and was suddenly serious. "Are you all right, Bill? Sorry. You looked like you could use a little humor."

"Well, I—"

"I know," the priest interrupted softly. He pointed to Westonfield's empty glass. "Another?" He poured. "Yes, a little bit of humor is good for the soul; that, and a *purpose*. A task."

Westonfield looked closely at the priest.

"I really miss you guys," the priest continued. "It's not like it was a few years ago, when all you cops were in here like clock work. I see you two once in a while; precious few others, though." He sighed. "So many changes, don't you know? The Church is changing, the school is changing, the city is changing." He looked from one to the other. "The Police Department is changing, too. It doesn't sit well with you fellows, either. I know how you feel. Fort and Green still takes good care of us in their way. We get help with traffic for our affairs and special attention to the parking lot when the car thieves get particularly rambunctious, but the new fellows are like... ever read one of those food labels? Processed, emulsified, bleached, and leached. Whatever the original tasted like, there is no hint of it in the new stuff. Where do they get these people? Or is it really their fault? When our illustrious mayor vowed to clean up the Police Department he used a fillet knife instead of a broom. Gutted the street force like a goddamn fish. That cynical bastard really played his cards, didn't he? 'I was whupped upside the head by the *PO-lice* when I was a young man.' What a damned crock! That man doesn't know anything. Instead of weeding out the few bad apples—a laudable task— he shut down every effective street operation the department had. Out went the baby with the bath water. I get so goddamned fed up with the phony shield of racism he and his cronies hide their dirt behind, I don't know whether to shit or puke. Now they've hired people that ought to be behind bars themselves, not on the outside looking in. They've promoted incompetents, cronies, and *yes* men. Lord! Our Police Department is getting to be a national laughing stock. Half of the in crowd has been indicted by the feds and the other half of them are so scared they're *going* to be indited they're shaking like dogs shitting peach seeds."

Rourke was watching the priest, smiling.

Westonfield, catching the look, said, "Okay. What's going on? We haven't been here five minutes and I'm getting so buried in shit they're going to have to pump oxygen to me. I've had a feeling something was going on since we were at Duly's. Something is going on, isn't it?" He looked at Rourke. "Well?"

Rourke remained silent, looked at the priest, grinning.

Father Mark beamed.

"A conspiracy," said Westonfield. "A goddamned conspiracy. You set me up, Rourke—'Yeah, we can go see Father Mark if you want.' Christ! You must have cum in your pants when I suggested coming over here."

Rourke chortled and raised his middle finger in Westonfield's direction. "You're easy, Bill."

Westonfield turned back to the priest. "What's your excuse, you conniving, devious Polack? You're a disgrace to your order. You should take off your cassock and burn it."

Father Mark raised his hands in a mea culpa gesture. "All right, all right." He chuckled and quaffed an ounce and a half of brandy. His eyes danced from Rourke to Westonfield. "Was the speech a little too familiar? Perhaps you've made it yourself?"

Westonfield sat back in his chair. "You don't want to know what I think. What the hell is going on?"

"I talked to Jack this morning," said the priest. "Then he stopped by." He poured himself another drink, warming to the conversation. He smacked his lips, licking a lingering drop of brandy from a forefinger. "He had a lady with him. A most interesting lady. She's a writer."

Westonfield's mouth dropped open.

The priest went on. "Mexican girl. Smart. Sharp as a tack." He beamed again. "Sexy as hell. Big ones." He placed his hands on his chest, cupping them. "She writes for—"

"*Harper's*," said Westonfield dryly. "Or did Jack neglect to tell you that I'd already met her?"

"He told me. I just wanted to give you my scholarly impression."

"You think I value it? Let's see," Westonfield went on, counting on his fingers, "she's sexy. She's smart. She's got big boobs. Are you sure you haven't left anything out?" He couldn't decide whether he was amused or disgusted at his friends' plotting. They were like wicked teenagers.

"Do you want more?" the priest rejoined.

"Let's cut to the chase," Westonfield said. "First she talked to Jack." He cast a sidelong glance at his partner. "Then she talked to you. She talked to everyone but me today. So, you two are her intermediaries. Her charms must be far reaching, indeed." He finished his drink. "Quit beating around the bush, gentlemen," he said finally. "Who do you want me to kill?"

"Well, Bill, this is how it was," began Rourke like a story teller, aware that Westonfield was moderately pissed off. "She called me at home this morning at about 10:30. She got my number from that idiot Tom Bacon. She called and wanted to talk. She said it was important. I agreed to meet her and I got up and went to Greektown and met her for lunch."

"Why?"

"Why what?"

"Why did you meet her?"

Rourke looked blankly at Westonfield. "Well, like Father said, she's—you know."

"All she's got to do now is teach you to sit up, beg, and roll over," Westonfield said. "After you're housebroken, you'll be completely trained."

Father Mark laughed.

Westonfield turned to him. "What are you cackling about? You had better quit laughing and start praying that it doesn't storm. A few well-aimed lightening bolts will probably be sent your way. You talk to a pretty girl for five minutes and you melt like a popsicle. What about your vow of chastity? Don't you take any of your vows seriously? You're worse than Rourke."

The priest made a timeout sign with his hands. "All right, Bill. Seriously. Will you listen?"

"I should walk out of here and drag this Irish cretin with me," Westonfield said. "I should leave you with the rookies to talk to." His look passed slowly from one to the other. "Okay," he said finally. "For the second time, what's this about?"

For a moment the priest's eyes roved thoughtfully over Westonfield's face. Bill was physically unremarkable, of medium height and build, his dark brown hair neatly combed and parted. His face still held a summer's tan. He had a large Welsh nose and a full mustache over thin lips. His eyes were grey and glittering, filled with lights. A quiet manner belied a mercurial personality beneath.

The priest said, "You're a dinosaur, Bill Westonfield. Just as surely as those fossilized bones in a natural history museum: you, Jack, some of the fellows on your crew. You're all dinosaurs. When someone wants to learn about dinosaurs they go to a museum, study the bones. Paw at them. But they don't *feel* them. They don't reach down deep into their hearts and really feel them. It's a hard thing to do when all you have is a lump of bone, hard as rock." He rubbed his rough hands over his face, making sandpaper sounds as his palms ran over the contours of his cheeks. He had shaved early that morning but it was getting late and his beard was very heavy. "Sad, isn't it, the dinosaurs?"

"So," said Westonfield, arching his eyebrows, "You want to put me on display like one of them. Lay me out on a slab for all the world to see."

"No, Bill, that's not it," Lewendowski said. "That's not right at all. My point is really quite the opposite. With this magazine article you have a chance to tell your side. The real story. The real you. All of the lies ever told about police work, the TV hype, the false glamour, all of it can be shown for what it is."

"I've done enough."

"For who?" asked the priest.

"How can you say that?" asked Westonfield, the pain apparent in his face.

"Now wait a minute, Bill. Don't misunderstand! For me? Yes. Too much. For your partners, yes. But what about you? Have you done enough for you?" He finished his glass of brandy and rubbed his face again, glancing at Rourke, then back to Westonfield. "Maybe you would feel better if you were able to tell the story finally. Like I said a moment ago. A task."

Rourke nodded his big Irish head. "It's like Father says. We're dying out, just like the dinosaurs. If we don't tell the story then it will never be told. Not right, at least. Not the whole truth."

Westonfield shrugged. "Okay, then *you* tell the story. I've done enough."

Rourke looked into his partner's lonesome eyes and felt guilty.

"I trust this woman," the priest said. "I don't know exactly why, but I do—part of being a priest, I guess. But a feature article, a series of feature articles, she says, in a national magazine, would be completely different from anything else you've done."

Westonfield slumped resignedly farther into the chair. "She could do the piece on Jack or ten other guys."

"She wants *you*," the priest said.

"Why?"

"She finds you interesting."

"Why?"

"The same reason I do. Or Jack here. Or anyone." He laughed. "You're one of a kind, Bill. Truly one of a kind. Didn't you know that?"

Rourke looked at him and nodded.

"I already told her no," said Westonfield. "Besides, despite your glowing confidence, I don't trust her. Why should I trust her? Why should you trust her? She could write anything. Would she give me control over what she writes about me and Jack, or anything else? What about the department? Christ, the brass downtown hate my guts. You don't really believe they would let her follow me around, do you?"

"Talk to her," the priest said. "Just talk to her. Maybe she will have something to say that will change your mind. Talk to her. For me." He reached forward and gently touched Westonfield's hand on the table. "And for you."

CHAPTER 7

When they left the rectory it was nearly eleven o'clock. The moon was nearing the full and was high in the cloudless sky. The air was cool, crisp, and dry, but as always on the southwest side there was a faint chemical smell, like boiling soap or wet paint, the signature of the foundries and refineries that lined the river. Neither policeman noticed it.

As he stood by the unmarked car Westonfield looked up at the sky. "A hunter's moon," he said.

"Uh-huh," Rourke responded. "A hunter's moon. We've dicked around enough tonight. Why don't we do some hunting?"

"I want to find Katy Marroquín," Westonfield said.

"Okay," Rourke said, "then let's drift down through the jungle."

They drove east on Vernor, studying the faces of teenage pedestrians, looking for the girl or anyone who might know her whereabouts. Katy Marroquín was the girlfriend of the leader of the Latin Counts. She was Mexican but she had natural blonde hair and blue eyes. While this struck most people as curious, it was not particularly rare. On occasion, by an accident of heredity, a child would be born of Mexican parents who carried the matching combination of recessive genes for blonde hair and blue eyes.

As they cruised slowly along the street, checking every pedestrian and every doorway, pausing in front of every teen hangout, Rourke said, "I hope you're not pissed."

"I'm pissed."

"Well hell, Bill, you're always pissed. I mean I hope I didn't really upset you. I know you've got your own shit to think about. I didn't mean to back-door you. I talked to the lady and Father Mark talked to her. If you still aren't interested then just tell her so. Hell, you don't even have to tell her. I'll tell her. We just thought it would be a good thing for everyone concerned. Christ, I don't know. You're good at that sort of thing. Better than anyone else I know." He held up his hands, palms up in surrender. "I'm sorry, if that helps."

Westonfield shrugged. "Don't worry about it. It's possible that it's not such a bad idea. Maybe I'll talk to her. I'll think about it, sleep on it tonight. It wouldn't hurt to feel her out on terms, get acquainted with her. I just get tired of the hassles, Jack. It bothers me that everybody seems to expect me to be the spokesman. Jesus, they can use the Lieutenants & Sergeants Association for this crap."

As they approached Clark Park on W. Vernor, virtually the front lawn of Western High School, Rourke gestured toward it. "Bet you she's there."

Westonfield nodded. "Dollar to a doughnut." He passed Clark Street and continued to Scotten, then turned south. The park, a large, sparsely wooded lot dotted with picnic tables, braziers, tennis courts, and a wading pool was one of the oldest in the city. It occupied a rectangular section of land running the short block between Clark and Scotten Streets and then south from Vernor Highway all the way to Interstate 75. In recent years the Latin gangs had virtually taken over the park, forcing children and their parents to abandon its facilities. They hid behind locked doors, afraid, watching the dope deals go down across the street, even in daylight. The sound of fist fights, drinking parties, and gunfire had replaced the ring of childrens' voices.

They cruised past the high school and all the way to the service drive. Westonfield then turned north onto Clark, skirting the part on its western side. When they drew even with the YMCA, just south of Vernor, Westonfield spotted Katy Marroquín, her blonde hair luminous under the shadows of the trees. She stood in a semi-circle of teenage boys.

Rourke and Westonfield exited their cruiser and walked across the uncut grass toward the group. All activity within a hundred yards of the policemen stopped, voices lowering, heads turning. When they had approached within thirty feet, Westonfield said quietly, "It's late."

City Council had passed a curfew in response to the gangs, making it unlawful for persons under eighteen to be on the street unaccompanied by an adult past ten o'clock. The boys with Katy Marroquín knew what Westonfield's words meant. They groaned in unison.

"Hey, man, we ain't hurting nothing," said one short boy, barely five feet tall. He looked a little comical in his leather jacket with silver studs, the words Latin Counts emblazoned in crimson across the back. He wore braces and they glinted in the lamplight. Westonfield wondered fleetingly where he'd gotten the money for the braces.

Rourke pointed a stiff index finger at the three boys. "Scram!"

The boy with the braces said, "What about her?" He pointed to Katy.

"What about her?" asked Rourke.

"What are you going to do with her?"

"Well, she's younger than you for one thing, even though she is a foot taller. I believe we'll just have to take her in for curfew," Rourke said.

"Oh, man, that's bullshit, man. We ain't hurting nothing."

"I thought I said scram. Get the fuck out of here!" Rourke growled.

The boys drifted off, mumbling. Katy Marroquín stood watching them, silent.

Westonfield pointed to the car. "Let's go for a ride, Katy."

They drove to the parking lot of a neighborhood bar, La Norteña, a few blocks farther east on Vernor. Rourke turned to the girl in the back seat. "What's cookin', sweetheart?"

"It's the same. Like always. Hey, we weren't hurting

anybody, you know, you guys. We really weren't hurting anything."

"Where's Danny Villanueva?" asked Rourke. Danny was the girl's known boyfriend and a stalwart of the Latin Counts. "He's wanted on an assault warrant by the Vernor detectives." He looked her up and down. "But you knew that, didn't you?"

"I heard something about it."

"Sure you did. Where is he?"

"I don't know. I haven't seen him for three days."

"Bullshit."

"No, it's true. When he heard about the warrant he took off. Maybe he's in Chicago. I'm not sure."

"That's probably true, Jack," said Westonfield. "It's usually what the kid does." He twisted in the seat to look at the girl. "How old are you now, Katy?"

"Sixteen."

"That's what I thought. How old is Danny? Twenty-two?"

"Yeah, that's right. What difference does it make?"

"Last I figure," said Rourke, "about six years."

The girl rolled her eyes. "You think you're so cool, Sergeant Rourke."

"I am cool," he said.

"Maybe you should find a new guy," said Westonfield. "A new guy and a new game. You're smart. Do you want to end up dying in the street in an argument over an order of fries? This is bullshit, Katy. For you, for your folks, for everybody." He paused. "For me, too."

She shifted restlessly in the back seat.

"I know, I know," Westonfield continued. "The gang is just a social club. You meet. You talk. It provides *stability*. I read that crap you fed the reporter in the article in the *Detroit News*." He watched her eyes. "But that's not really why you hang around. We both know the real reason, don't we? It's the excitement: the fights, the cars, the reporters begging for a story, the cops hassling you. That's really what it's all about, isn't that right, Katy?"

She sat silently. Westonfield watched the tears slowly build in her china-blue eyes. "Look, Sergeant Westonfield, my dad left home when I was eleven. He left my mom with me and three sisters and six brothers. I'm glad he left. He was a drunk and he beat my mom. But my mom had to raise us by herself. It's not easy living down here. It's down right hard. The teachers don't care, the cops don't care, nobody cares. The whole place stinks. What do you think kids are supposed to do in the *barrio*, play chess at the community center? It isn't like that, Sarge. Not at all. This is the real world. The real world, you know? The Counts is what I've got. It's all I've got. I'm not going to give it up. Not just because some cop—" she hesitated and then smiled a little at him, softening her tone, "—even a nice guy like you, can come in and change things."

Westonfield stared at her. Then a smile flickered at the corners of his own mouth. "All right, kid. You got me. You're a pretty tough customer, aren't you? You kinda remind me of somebody I used to know. She was a tough cookie, too. My fault, okay?"

Rourke glared at him.

"Okay," Westonfield went on, ignoring his partner. "Danny's in Chicago, right?"

She nodded.

"All right. To tell you the truth, what I really wanted to know about has nothing to do with Danny. There's word on the street about some odd goings on over on Merritt Street, over off of Junction. You heard anything about that?"

The wan smile faded from her face and she looked like she wanted to get out of the car. She shifted nervously in the seat. "I don't want to be seen talking to you guys, you know? It's not like it's good for my health."

"Pressed a button, huh?" asked Rourke.

Katy said nothing, looked down again.

"Tell us what you know about Merritt Street and you can go," Westonfield said. "It might be important."

The girl finally said, "My Aunt Lúz—she knows an old lady

over there. She does her laundry and house cleaning and stuff. She saw this man bring a box, like with slats, you know, into this abandoned house in the middle of the block. Like maybe a cage. She heard a sound coming from the cage. Her car window was down. It sounded like a chicken."

"Like a chicken?" Rourke looked at Westonfield and then back to the girl. "What the fuck do we care about a chicken? Do we look like livestock inspectors to you? We don't have time for your bullshit, kid. Get real! Isn't that what you shitbirds say? *Get real*? Or maybe, *get a life*? Tell us what you know about this Merritt house without all the crap. If you don't, maybe we'll just take you in for a while, let you cool off in the youth home for a day or two. I'm sure we can think of something that will get you there. It ain't like you're a virgin."

Katy gave Westonfield an *if-you-don't-want-to-listen* look.

"Wait a minute, Jack," Westonfield said. He reached back and placed a finger under her chin, raising her head. "Okay, niña, what's it all about? I'm interested in what you've got to tell us." He glanced at Rourke. "Very interested. What did your Aunt Lúz say? *¿Qué dijo?*"

She smiled her wan smile again, saying in Spanish, "I like it when you speak Spanish."

"I like it, too," Westonfield said, also in Spanish. "But when I talk to someone with my partner present, I use English. He needs to know what's going on, too. Speak English, okay?"

She looked at Rourke and frowned. "He talks a lot of shit," she said, still in Spanish.

Westonfield laughed. "He talks to me worse than he talks to you, believe me. English, okay?"

"Okay."

"You were talking about the chicken."

"Well, Tía Lúz—"

Rourke interjected, "What were they gonna do, cook it?" He was irritated at Westonfield for what he considered his coddling of the girl and he was in no mood to back down, at least not entirely.

She squirmed in her seat and shrugged her shoulders again, "*Cubanos.*"

"Cubans?" asked Westonfield.

"*Sí*, they're black, so they're not Mexican."

"Puerto Ricans, maybe?"

The girl shrugged again.

"Haitians?"

She shrugged.

"So what about the chicken?"

She looked out the car window, her eyes tilting upward to the bright moon. She shivered. "Cubans," she repeated, her voice barely audible.

"Why are you so sure?"

"I just *know*. Tía Lúz knows. Everyone knows."

"How do they know?"

"The chicken. Other things."

"What other things?"

"I don't know. Just a feeling. Everyone can feel it."

"What does it feel like?" He was onto something here. He could feel it, too. There were forces at work, connections between seemingly unrelated events that he could feel, but which he couldn't quite put his finger on.

"Like something's going to happen. They're bad, the Cubans. *Muy malos.*"

"What about the chicken?"

"They kill them." She made a motion of drawing a knife across her neck. The skin on her upraised throat was milky white and translucent in the dim light.

"Sacrifice?"

"Yeah."

"Voodoo?"

"Well, sort of."

"They kill chickens and take their blood?"

"I think so."

"What about dope? Crack?"

"I don't know."

"No word on the street?"

"We don't talk to the Cubans."

Rourke interjected again. "You've got to have heard something."

"They've got their own thing, Sergeant!" Katy protested. "Mexicans and Cubans, they don't mix." She looked at Westonfield. "Sarge knows that. Not even in the business, you know?"

Westonfield nodded thoughtfully.

The girl looked around restlessly, like a cornered animal. There was something pitiful and sad about it. She reminded Westonfield of his cat Cindy the time she was chased into a corner by a stray dog.

"I gotta go, guys," she said plaintively, a note of desperation there suddenly. "Okay? I get seen here and I'm dead, right? Let me out, okay?"

"Is that all you know?" asked Rourke.

"That's all I know," she said. "For real." She giggled self-consciously when she said *for real*.

They let her go. She looked small and vulnerable when she got out of the car. She glanced back at them briefly as she walked away in the moonlight, and then she was gone.

"*Cuídate, mija*," muttered Westonfield softly. "Be careful."

* * *

There was little conversation for the next couple of hours, both Westonfield and Rourke preoccupied with their own thoughts. They responded to three police runs in the north end of the precinct, one on an assault in progress which turned out to be two brothers fighting over a single duplicitous girlfriend, and the two others on silent alarms going off at business places. Both establishments, a pharmacy and a hardware store, appeared secure.

They stopped for coffee at a Yum Yum doughnut shop at Michigan Avenue and Wyoming, on Detroit's border with the city of Dearborn. Westonfield sipped his coffee reflectively while Rourke flirted with the waitress, a large-breasted girl with a bad complexion. It was two o'clock when they left the restaurant and headed back toward the precinct station, their shift over in another hour.

They went south on Lonyo, crossed the railroad tracks at John Kronk, and continued on to Lonyo's end at Dix Road. They struck Woodmere, a meandering street that took them past Vernor and finally to Fort Street, a mile or so west of the police station.

Westonfield took this route because, between Vernor and Fort, Woodmere Street skirted the cemetery of the same name. Woodmere Cemetery was established after the end of the Civil War, in 1867, and covered two hundred acres on the city's southwest side. Hulking granite crypts and marble monuments, some discreet, others towering, all grey with age and generations of industrial pollution, dotted the rolling green ridges and knolls. Elms, ash and oak, some older than the cemetery itself, spread their branches over the quiet ground. A six-foot wrought iron fence surrounded the land, the sharp-tipped black rods interspersed with posts of red brick, faded to grey with age.

"Two more vaults broken into and robbed last week," said Westonfield, nodding to his right, toward the cemetery. The clipped grass, so green in the daylight, and the manicured gardens alight with the pastels of chrysanthemums, were all various tones of black and grey at this hour.

Rourke shivered. "It gives me the fucking willies. Imagine the sick son of a bitch breaking into those old vaults and taking body parts. How many is that now, in the last few months, four or five? It's hard on the old people, finding out some dickhead broke into their loved one's last resting place. What a town. They even rob you after you're dead. When you're alive they take your jewelry and your VCR, when you're dead they take your fucking leg bones and your skull." He shook his head again in disgust. "Any idea who might be doing this shit? Kids, maybe? Pretty bold for kids, though. Usually they just knock over one of the monuments."

Westonfield trained a spotlight through the fence and out onto the acres of grass and markers. The light stabbed like a white finger far out onto the grounds, trees and monuments alternately flickering into view and then disappearing into darkness as the police car slowly passed by.

Rourke repeated his question. "What do you think?"

"I don't know, Jack. I really don't know what to think. But I can't help but feel..." His voice trailed off.

"Can't help but feel what?"

Westonfield looked at him. He finally said, "Nothing, Jack. Nothing. Just a feeling I can't put a finger on. You know how it is with me sometimes."

Rourke shrugged his shoulders absently and watched the wrought iron of the cemetery's fence glide past his window in silence.

They arrived at the station and went up to the Power Shift office. Westonfield tried to update his paperwork a little in the short time that remained but found he couldn't concentrate. He thought about his kids and about Derrick. He thought about Millie. And he wondered about the house on Merritt. He couldn't get the fear on Katy's face out of his mind. Was there some connection between the house on Merritt and the vandalism at Woodmere Cemetery? Was that what his sixth sense was trying to tell him?

The crews were all accounted for and checked in, their daily log sheets submitted, by 2:55 A.M. Rourke sent them home. He said good night to Westonfield, but his partner didn't hear him. He was looking out the window again. Rourke didn't know what he could see. It was dark.

CHAPTER 8

They came in from the east, across Biscayne Bay, having skirted the Keys on the south. An American Coast Guard cutter had intercepted them only two hours out of Mariel and had shadowed them ever since. The trawler captain knew the routine. He had plotted a course straight for the southeast tip of the Florida peninsula and had run the slot through the Straits of Florida without incident.

At seven knots the roughly 150 mile trip took about twenty hours. The captain stayed in the wheelhouse the whole trip. He ate a lunch of cold roasted goat, black bread, and cheese that he had brought in an empty lard pail. He drank warm beer. There was no head in the wheelhouse so he pissed in a bucket. The boat was crammed from stem to stern with humanity. The hold, designed to contain tons of mackerel or tuna, was instead jammed with sweating, stinking human beings. The decks were crowded with people. Even the lifeboats, swaying steadily on their pulleys at the ends of the hydraulic carriers, were filled. There were two heads to accommodate the entire throng and these, of course, were not nearly enough. So the people pissed and shit on the decks.

The captain winced as he looked out of the wheelhouse through the huge curved window, high above the decks. Yes, he would stay up here until they reached their destination. He wanted nothing to do with this unwanted mass of humanity, desperate and smelly. Besides, among these people were the thieves and worse. Fidel had emptied his prisons of the scum of Cuba. Even the murderers. Yes, they would kill him for a song or less. Even him, the captain. No matter that he was the only one who could pilot the ship. The members of the societies would not balk at this small inconvenience. More than one captain had disappeared off his own boat while crossing the Straits.

So the captain was relieved when he passed the northern tip of Key Largo, then Old Rhodes Key, and finally Elliot Key, and then brought the ship around to a due west heading, steaming at last into the bay. They were boarded by the Coast Guard when still two miles out and then escorted into the docks.

Gabriel Flores' first home in the States was a makeshift camp at Homestead Air Base near Florida City, about twenty-five miles south along the coast from Miami. The camp housed 2,600 people, was fenced in by chain link topped by barbed wire, and was guarded by Air Police and U.S. Border Patrol officers. It was one of many scattered about south Florida and elsewhere. In all, some 125,000 souls had arrived in the U.S. from Cuba, far more than could quickly be processed, identified, interviewed, and assimilated into the country under the 1966 Cuban Refugee Act, which granted Cuban nationals special "political refugee" status under federal law.

The initial hardships of the camp were inconsequential to Gabriel. They were nothing compared to what he had routinely endured in Cuba, whether in the military or in prison. He bided his time, waiting. Weeks, and finally months, passed in the camp. An American military doctor had found the image of a dagger tattooed on his penis. He refused to discuss it with the translator who seemed agitated in his presence anyway and couldn't wait to complete the interview and leave. Gabriel had laughed at the small man as he sweated. The simpering idiot refused to look him in the eye. They took his fingerprints and they photographed him. They even took a picture of his penis, a close up showing the dagger. When they did that Gabriel laughed. He laughed until his stomach ached and tears filled his eyes. He waggled his cock at the little man, who let out a sharp yelp and ran out of the office. Gabriel laughed again. They returned him through the gate. He continued to wait.

In the evening he would stand along the north fence, gazing

into the blue distance, wondering what lay beyond the horizon. He was not well educated but he had attended school at the *bruja's* insistence and he could picture a map of the contiguous forty-eight United States in his mind. It was immense, almost beyond his capacity to comprehend, dozens of times larger than his native Cuba. While this state of Florida was similar to his birthplace he also knew that it was much colder in the north.

As he stood idly by the fence, beads of sweat dotting his face, he wondered what snow would be like. What would it be like to wear a coat in weather so cold you would freeze if you did not? It was a mystery to him, but a siren song nonetheless. He felt called by the cold, the imagined icy wind. Somehow his blood yearned for the coolness, the snow drifting down, piling up layer on layer, covering all the world with its whiteness. How exhilarating it would be to see black-red blood on the impossible whiteness of the snow! To see it coagulate as it cooled, steaming, releasing the wonderful iron-copper fragrance. He knew he was meant to go there, to the north. It must be a virgin world way up there—no witches. Witches arose from the fires of Hell, did they not? There would be no witches in the cold. He stood by the fence long into the subtropical nights, wondering about the snow.

But Gabriel was not a patient man. Not the *bruja*, nor the rites of *palo mayombe*, nor the military had bred patience into him. He was, after all, a *tata nkisi*, was he not?

One day a man, another *Marielito* who had been recently released, came back to the camp to visit a cousin, still interred, who was ill. The man, whose name was Rafael Quintana, had obtained employment as a clerk in a Cuban-owned grocery. His Quonset had been located adjacent to Gabriel's in the camp. They had become friends of sorts in the camp, though Gabriel had known him slightly from his earlier days in the military. They had attended RPG instruction at the shoulder-launched weapons range at the recruit training base together. Gabriel never, of course, had a true friendship. He did not find this necessary or desirable, drawing all of the emotional sustenance he needed from the ways of *palo mayombe*. As for his acquaintances, even those fellow students of *brujería*, they neither trusted nor liked him. They feared him mightily, however, perceiving his vast abilities as a *mayombero*, hence his boundless capacity for evil. Though his ill cousin was not aware of it, Rafael Quintana was a *mayombero* of minor stature.

Quintana felt Gabriel before he saw him. He felt the black eyes on him from someplace and the hackles rose on the back of his neck. *Palo mayombe* was a powerful force, he knew, being a practitioner himself, but Gabriel Flores possessed powers the likes of which Quintana had never dreamed. His black eyes, seemingly with no pupils, looked through you into your very heart. You guarded no confidences from him; you harbored no secret plans around him. He saw everything. He knew everything.

Quintana turned suddenly and looked across the beaten earth of the parade ground. It was near to high noon. Sunlight glinted off the white, hard-packed surface and heat waves danced upward in black, wavering lines. He saw nothing. When he turned back again Gabriel was there, standing five feet in front of him, the stygian eyes unblinking upon him. The closest cover was forty feet away. The hackles rose yet higher on Quintana's neck.

"Rafael, *¿Qué tal?* What's up?" said Gabriel. Or Gabriel's ghost.

Quintana swallowed. He tried to swallow again but found his mouth was too dry. "Gabriel, amigo," he said, forcing a smile. "I'm glad to see you."

"*Bienvenido*, Rafael." Welcome. Gabriel's eyes did not leave Quintana's face.

"I came to see my cousin," Quintana began. "She is sick with dysentery. She—" He ended lamely, fidgeting with one of his shirt buttons. He laughed nervously, continuing, "But, of course, my friend, you already know sufficient of these matters."

Gabriel nodded, silent.

"Well," said Quintana, sweating profusely now, loosening his tie and unbuttoning a couple more buttons on his white cotton shirt. "Can I help you, Gabriel?" He drew a sleeve across his brow. "I will do anything, of course. Anything you ask. I am always ready to serve you in any useful way." He couldn't look Gabriel in the eye and fixed instead on a small mole on the right side of his forehead.

Gabriel took him into his room. He gave him a styrofoam cup of cold water. Quintana sat on a stool.

"I must leave here soon," Gabriel said. "Within the week."

Quintana nodded. "It is hard, I know—"

"Within one week," repeated Gabriel, his voice lowering.

"Of course. Yes. Of course," stammered Quintana, his hands shaking. "What must I do?"

"You know what you must do."

"But Gabriel, you know that I have no influence with the authorities."

"No!" Gabriel held up his hand. The strength of the command was unearthly.

Quintana's tongue clove to the roof of his mouth. There was a sudden, tremendous pain in his chest. He felt as if a molten poker had been thrust into his abdomen. He gasped for air.

Gabriel studied him. Amusing. Quintana looked rather like a fish thrown onto a bank. "You know what to do," he said again, his voice returning to its melodious calm.

After a few seconds, gasping, eyes bulging, gasping more, Quintana found his voice and nodded affirmatively. Then, mercifully, the pain left him.

* * *

That night there was a waxing one-quarter moon, though it was hidden by clouds. Quintana left his hot room over the little grocery where he worked and walked into the humid evening. There was not even a breath of air to dry the sweat on his body. His clothes clung uncomfortably to him. It was four miles to the cemetery and he must walk because he had no car and he could not afford a taxi. How would he have explained his desire to stop at a cemetery out in the middle of nowhere at three o'clock in the morning anyway? He plodded deliberately along, carrying only a small, empty cloth sack.

At first he walked through the town, passing by darkened stores and bars. There were few vehicles on the road. The quiet was broken only twice, by barking dogs. In the heavy, still air the barking sounded lethargic and leaden; he jumped at the sounds and darted out of sight behind a utility pole once and a large green garbage dumpster the second time. No one saw him.

Soon he passed beyond the buildings of the town and emerged into the countryside, clocking patiently along the shoulder of a two-lane asphalt highway. He smelled the heavy perfume of honeysuckle drifting across the fields on the night air. When he had walked well over an hour he saw the high white face of the mausoleum emerge from behind the black hulk of a kapok tree: a ceiba, an *iggi-olorun*. The fortuitous appearance of the sacred tree made him both happy and afraid—happy because it was a good omen, afraid because it was almost too fortunate. Were the spirits aware of everything he did, watching him from the shadows and monuments? He shuddered when he remembered Gabriel's face. There were those who said that Gabriel was no ordinary *mayombero*, that he was a *tata nkisi*. Others said, "No, even the role of the black sorcerer cannot contain that one. He is a demon incarnate, perhaps a servant of Zarabanda himself." Quintana did not know the answer, but he knew that he was more frightened than ever before in his life.

He checked up and down the highway for the headlights of approaching vehicles, saw none, and then listened carefully for any sound coming from the silent graveyard. The dead rested quietly in their *nfinda kalunga*. He climbed the chain link fence and stopped halfway up, his heart in his mouth when the links rattled against the metal posts. In a few seconds he continued, quietly up and over.

He found a winding road, its bed of crushed white stone a luminous ribbon in the darkness. In only a few minutes he came upon what he was seeking, the high mound of a fresh-dug grave.

He headed to it, tripped on one of the large rocks lining the road, and fell onto his hands and knees, barking his shins and tearing his pants. He cursed under his breath, the fear nearly beyond endurance. He got up, steadied himself, listened once more, and went on.

At the grave he dropped to his knees and opened the sack. He was shaking so hard it took three attempts to find the drawstring. He mumbled a prayer for forgiveness to the spirit of the dead one beneath him and began to scoop handfuls of loose soil into the sack. When he judged he had enough he stood unsteadily and tramped quickly away, carrying the full sack in front of him like a pan of hot oil. He fell once more over an unseen object and stifled a scream; a whimpering, strangled sound emerged from his throat. His first thought was that the spirit of the dead-one, the *kiyumba*, had risen and caught him. He looked about wildly, his eyes white disks. Nothing. He dared to breathe. He went on.

An hour later he was home. He went immediately to his room and began to prepare the potion. Into an old iron pot he kept for this purpose went nine handfuls of the soil from the grave; then a handful of *azúfre*, or sulfur. Then a similar amount of *yerba bruja*. Next a few precious drops of *acéite de triunfo*. Finally, a splash of *amoníaco*, or ammonia. He set the kettle on the stove to heat.

He lit nine candles, four black and five green. They burned brightly on the little altar next to the other symbols of power and invocation: a dagger of steel, a pile of sea shells, a curious colored stone. In a short while the contents of the cauldron were heated through and sizzling. The steam was pungent and medicinal, the ammonia took his breath away. He grasped the pot with a rag-wrapped hand and placed it on a block of wood positioned in the center of the altar.

Lastly he retrieved a small white hen from its covered cage in a corner of the room. She had been sleeping and she cackled nervously and fretted when he opened the door of the cage and fetched her out. He returned to the altar and kneeled in front.

He held the hen in his right hand and with his left fingered the beads of the necklace he wore, seven brown beads alternating with three black, the necklace of Zarabanda. He began the incantation; slowly at first, hardly to be heard. Then steadily faster and louder. Over and over. He rocked to the tempo and his body quivered. Sweat ran in rivulets down the sides of his dusky cheeks and along his nose, dripping off his cracked lips. He bit the lower one and a trickle of blood mingled with the shiny perspiration on his quaking chin.

When he deemed the moment was ripe he grasped the hen above the wings with his left hand and its head with his right. With a twist and snap he ripped the head from the body. He rose quickly, flung the head aside and held the carcass over the cauldron, the wings still flapping violently. Red blood fountained out, spraying his face and clothing, spurting into the hot, boiling kettle. He held the slowly quieting body of the hen over the pot until the last drop had fallen. When he was done he laid the lifeless body gently before the altar.

Quintana slowly came back to his senses, the trance ended. His shallow breathing returned to normal. The sweat dried upon him. He surveyed the altar before him and carefully reviewed in his mind all of the things he had done this night. After a while a smile came to his face. Finally he laughed, feeling the power and joy of perceived success. He wasn't sure how he knew, but he knew. The gods had heard. They would act. Gabriel would be pleased. Indeed. *Aché!*

* * *

Three days later, on September 4, 1980, the long-delayed paperwork completed and indecision on the part of the authorities laid to rest, Gabriel Flores walked out of the camp at Homestead Air Force Base. He was free.

CHAPTER 9

    Magaly Rodríguez awoke with the lemon-clear October sun shining through the east window of her twelfth-floor room at the Pontchartrain Hotel. She lay for a moment luxuriating in the softness of the sheets. She stretched her legs and pushed the covers back, crossing her arms across her full, exposed breasts; she had slept unclothed since turning fifteen. She lay daydreaming for a moment, gazing out the window at the cloudless blue sky over the Detroit River and beyond to Windsor, Canada. She rubbed her eyes and absentmindedly brushed a wayward strand of black hair from her eyes. She didn't know what, but she expected something to happen today. Something good.
    She got up after a few minutes and took a good look out the window to the street below. Her room overlooked the downtown Detroit waterfront and East Jefferson Avenue. Her eyes lazily roamed from the street—almost bare of traffic at seven o'clock on a Saturday morning—and flicked across to Hart Plaza, the broad, brick-surfaced common that stretched upward from the river to the street. The water of the Dodge Fountain, the plaza's centerpiece, cascaded in silver ribbons and white spray, the cold grey water of the river running swiftly beyond. The green sward of Dieppe Park, in Windsor, rose up on the far bank like a band of tourmaline in the sun.
    It's beautiful, she thought. Not like the image she had acquired from reading about Detroit. She watched the sun ride higher in the sky and softly hummed an old Mexican folk tune under her breath—*Mambrú se fué a la guerra*. A Great Lakes freighter laden with its cargo of copper ore from the mines of

Michigan's Upper Peninsula plowed down the river, westward and southward with the current.

She showered and dressed, choosing a navy skirt and matching navy jacket. She selected a white blouse with a border of lace running down the front. Black flats would do. She might need to do a fair amount of walking today.

She left her room and stopped by the front desk in the main lobby, advising the clerk that she would be out for several hours and asking her to take any messages that came in during the morning. Then she went down to a continental breakfast at the hotel restaurant. She would have to scout around to find a more interesting place to eat but so far she hadn't had the time. It was her fifth day in Detroit.

As she munched on dry wheat toast with orange marmalade and sipped hot black coffee, she mentally reviewed her accomplishments to date. The first day, Tuesday, had been a waste. Tied up in traffic in New York, she had missed her afternoon flight. She hadn't been able to get another until the early evening. Tired out from completing last minute preparations for the trip, packing, a final meeting with her editor, and a number of phone calls, she had gone to bed fifteen minutes after checking into her room.

On Wednesday she talked to Gerry Talmadge at AP who took her to lunch at the Union Street Station on Woodward Avenue, near the Thirteenth Precinct Police Station. Tom Bacon of the Police Personnel Division was invited by Talmadge. Bacon proved an affable character who answered all of her questions diligently and without a hint of the usual Police Department b.s. When she described what she needed in the way of information for her article and asked for his assistance, he was eager to help. He immediately suggested she talk to Sergeant William Westonfield out at the Fourth Precinct in DelRay and told her about the get-together at Nancy Whiskey Thursday night. Payday, he said. She spent the rest of Wednesday with a department flack from the Public Information Unit who drove her around town and showed her the sights.

Thursday morning she went over to the police archives office and perused hundreds of old photographs and newspaper articles and stacks of memorabilia. After getting her ear filled with what she had discovered was the standard *ain't nothing wrong with this town* and *the Police Department has come a long way* schtick from the PR people, she was struck by the faces of the men, most long dead, whose eyes looked back at her from the cracked and dusty black and white photographs. They looked proud in their uniforms of blue serge, brass buttons shining, leather polished to a sheen. She recalled the more than two hundred names of policemen killed in the line of duty that had been pointed out to her, carved into the marble walls of police headquarters at 1300 Beaubien. If they were here to speak, what would these men have to say about the *new* Police Department? That was one of the things she wanted to find out.

She spent Thursday afternoon on a tour of the Communications Section at headquarters. And Thursday night had been the party at Nancy Whiskey. She could have set up a meeting with Westonfield through channels, but she had thought better of it. From Tom Bacon's description and anecdotes gleaned from other officers, she'd concluded that Westonfield was of a type she'd known before—not a cop-type at all. More like a professional soldier. A mercenary. She had done a piece on mercenary soldiers for *Harper's* two years before, virtually living in the field with a British mercenary who had been a member of Britain's elite commando group, Special Air Services (SAS). She smiled when she thought of Robert Shrewsbury. She wrote to him still.

In any case, that's what her instincts told her. She trusted her instincts. Even as a little girl her grandfather, a practitioner of *Santería*, told her that she had the sight, that she could divine things, see deeper into hearts than other people. It had proven true as she grew older and had revealed itself to be both a curse and a blessing. Bacon had shown her a recent photograph of

Westonfield. His eyes were like deep wells. Another thing her grandfather told her was that people who had the sight were usually aware of each other. Westonfield had it; he probably denied it, even to himself. She absently brushed her hair from her face again and nodded slowly, though she was alone at the table. There was a story here and she would have it, come hell or high water.

But Westonfield had turned her down. Flat. He was angry over the way she had approached him. Fair enough. But she knew that it had still been the best way. Had an "official" meeting been arranged, Westonfield would have wanted no part of it because he would have felt he was to be some sort of spokesman for the Police Department. He didn't want to do that, she knew, because he was unhappy with the Police Department and distrusted its administration. So she had decided to do it her way. He had refused, to be sure, but she still had hopes. This way it was one-on-one, just her and him: a writer (did he have a secret affinity for writers?) and a street cop. She thought of how Westonfield said "street cop," with an emphasis on the word *street*, as though it was an enormously important distinction.

On Friday morning she had tracked down Westonfield's partner John Rourke through Tom Bacon and bought him an early lunch at the Pegasus Restaurant in Greektown. Rourke, like Bacon, had proved talkative, friendly and willing to help. When they were through with lunch he took her to Holy Redeemer Church to meet Father Marko Lewendowski. What an unusual, interesting man! And Rourke was funny—both serious and funny, like so many of the Irish.

Rourke and Father Lewendowski talked about Westonfield with respect, but there was more than that: they unconsciously lowered their voices slightly when they referred to him. Strange. She pondered it for a moment while she sipped her coffee. She pursed her lips, and the clear, café-au-lait skin of her forehead wrinkled while she mulled it over. An image came to her of old people talking in the cool dark of a church in

Mexico, murmuring a prayer for the dying. That's it, she thought. Just like that.

The priest had said to her, "He'll protest and remonstrate, but in the end he will finally agree to cooperate with you on your article. I hope so, anyway. His story—you'll find it's a remarkable one—deserves to be heard. It's hard to explain, Miss Rodríguez, but in a way his story is *every* policeman's story. He's looked on that way, you see. At least by his peers and most of his subordinates." He chuckled. "Of course, the brass... well now, the brass doesn't seem quite so disposed to see him in the same light."

"Why is that?" she had asked. "Is it so simple? I can see how he and management would have different views, but it seems to me that no matter how intransigent the differences, the administration would at least respect Westonfield's dedication to duty. Look at his accomplishments. Officer Bacon showed me his record. My God! He's been through so much!"

The priest had smiled a little, an ironic flicker at the corners of his mouth. "Well, Miss, Bill's not a little outspoken, you see. The brass, the top dogs, they're politicians, really. Not policemen. Politicians of any stripe don't like outspoken people; they don't fit into their tidy schemes. Those glad-handing idiots that run downtown spend most of their time explaining how wonderful things are *already*, not working on ways to make things better. Just read the newspaper. Are things good already? But the fools play public relations games, working the worst instincts of the people, pushing all the right buttons—racism, brutality, occupying army—while the city literally burns. Bill Westonfield and those like him are easy targets for such cynicism." He paused. "But there's a special problem in Bill's case."

"Oh? What's that?" she'd asked, intrigued.

"They're afraid."

"Afraid?"

"Oh, yes," said the priest. "Petrified. Of... wolves in the fold. It has to do with what happens to men like Bill. We use them to clean up our shit because no one else will do it."

Magaly had been raised Catholic and the idea of a priest using such language in the off-hand manner employed by Father Lewendowski was enlightening, amusing, and a little unsettling. As the priest talked he reminded her of a raggedy old doll she used to have, its hair a curly mop like his, the spindly legs the same. She said, "Westonfield gets the shit-end of the stick."

"That's right," Lewendowski said. "These fellows go out and subject themselves to unspeakable indignities and emotional battery, not to mention physical danger, for weeks, months, and years on end. And all the while, they accommodate themselves to the peculiar twilight life they lead. They're caught in the *ether*, you see. Emotionally, they literally become detached from the real world. They become amoral, Miss Rodríguez, the unhappiest state of all—not a part of either world, the moral or the immoral. They live in their private Purgatory, until—" The priest's voice trailed off.

"Until what, Father?"

"Until the job is done. Or the managers, the bosses, know the job isn't *going* to be done."

"And then?"

"Then? Well, Miss Rodríguez, what does one do with such a creature, part of neither Heaven nor of the Earth, these wolves in the fold?"

"When Johnnie comes marching home?"

He smiled. "Precisely."

"At the risk of displaying a shocking lack of eloquence in contrast to yours," she said, "I would say integrate them back into the fold. Counseling. Time off. Desk work."

"That takes time, effort, and above all, Miss Rodríguez, money. Politicians don't like to even talk about money. Besides, it's far easier said than done. How do you really fit a square peg into a round hole?"

"So what do they do then? I mean what does the department do with these people if it doesn't actually take any of the actions that might help?"

"What politicians always do," the priest said. "Nothing... except whine about the fruits of their own creation."

"But that's irresponsible," Magaly protested. "Even crazy. You said the politicians are afraid."

The priest had leaned forward in his chair then and taken her by the hand. "As well they might be," he said. "But fear doesn't necessarily make for intelligent decision-making, does it? I think you can even make a good argument for the other way around. But let me tell you a little story, Magaly. May I call you Magaly?"

"Please."

"Good, then." He sighed. "There are other, better stories to be told. Perhaps you'll hear them another time. But I'll tell you this little anecdote because it has to do with the first time I was exposed to policemen like Bill. It was nine or ten years ago. I had been a priest here at Redeemer for about thirteen years, I guess, and had made friends with a lot of the coppers hereabouts. I was a new police chaplain then. I've been one ever since. One of the things a chaplain is supposed to do is to go out on the street with a scout car crew to get a feel for the job and the spiritual stresses attendant to it. I'd done this a few times before and found it rewarding and interesting." He'd laughed. "If you haven't noticed, I've developed quite an interest in police work.

"Anyway, I was scheduled to go out with a crew over at the old McGraw Station on the afternoon shift. The crew turned out to be Bill Westonfield and a fellow named Roger Maybury. Roger, poor fellow, he'd dead now... So we went out after four o'clock. Roger was very friendly and talkative. Bill was cordial, polite, but very quiet." He had patted her hand. "You'll get used to that about him.

"The day was more or less uneventful until near dark, when the radio suddenly came alive with the sound of other policemen calling for help; some kind of fight with a man caught breaking into a grocery store. We responded as did almost everyone else. Wait till you see," he'd interjected. "An officer in trouble—nothing else quite like it. Raises the hair on your head.

"When we arrived—I was cringing in the back seat, I don't mind telling you, after the wild ride to get there—I saw two policemen, big fellows, mind you, wrestling on the front porch of a house with the burglary suspect. The man they were fighting was enormous. He must have been six-and-a-half feet tall and weighed 280 pounds, at least. They were really going at it on the porch, all of them floundering from one side to the other, crashing against the railings. It was a terrible melee. Roger and Bill got out of the car, Roger running up and Bill just sort of walking in this purposeful, steady gait of his. Roger joined in the fight and soon the thief was throwing all of them about. I couldn't imagine what they were going to do.

"That was the first time it occurred to me that the proposition of deadly force was not such an easy one. The man wasn't armed, but he was a felon. And he was hurting the policemen. Two of them were bleeding from the nose. They were all cut and bruised.

"Suddenly the big man caught sight of Westonfield standing on the sidewalk. His eyes went wide. Then he just stopped. The fight ended as suddenly as it had begun. The silence was palpable. I remember listening to the heavy breathing of the men on the porch, like race horses after a long race. But the giant just looked at Westonfield and nodded ever-so-slightly. He allowed himself to be handcuffed and taken to the back seat of a scout car." The priest had sighed, his pensive eyes turned inward.

"But why did the guy stop?" Magaly asked after a moment, her eyes wide.

Father Mark had merely shrugged his shoulders. "The fight was over when he saw Bill."

"But why, Father?"

"Later that night I asked the thief that very question. I went into the cell block and talked to him. He looked at me like I was a fool. 'Do I look crazy to you?' he said. 'I know when it's time to give up.'

"'When is it time to give up?' I asked him. He looked at me then as if I were the biggest dolt that had ever walked the earth. 'When people like Mister Westonfield is around,' he said matter-of-factly. 'That's when it's time.' *Mister* Westonfield, he said. He turned his back on me, and that was all he would say."

Magaly had asked the priest what he thought the man knew or felt, but he had been vague, saying only, "It's just something for you to think about, Magaly. There's more than meets the eye with Bill. It would be well for you to understand that."

She had ruminated quietly for a while. Then she'd responded, "That big man. He was afraid, wasn't he, Father?"

"Oh, yes. He was afraid."

"Like the politicians."

Exhibiting the countenance of a school teacher satisfied with the day's lesson, the Priest had chuckled and said, "Indeed. Like the politicians."

She had studied Father Lewendowski for a moment, silent. Her thoughts went back to the words she had written in her journal Thursday night. Then she'd said, "Women find him attractive, Father?"

The priest had looked surprised. "Women? Well, I suppose so." Then he said, "You might watch out for that, too, Magaly, now that you broach the subject. Fear and attraction. Isn't it interesting how they sometimes go hand-in-hand?"

"You think I might find him attractive?" Magaly asked. "That strikes me as odd and somewhat presumptuous advice for a man of the cloth to give to a thirty-three year old writer, especially one you barely know." She had felt her face grow red and hot.

Father Mark had merely shrugged noncommittally.

"And if that were to happen," Magaly forged ahead, "an *innocent* woman like me and one of your terrible wolves in the fold… What then?" She had smiled the faintest of smiles and looked wide-eyed around the room in mock feminine awe, and added with biting sarcasm, "Might it be something like a moth drawn to the flame of a candle?"

"You *do* see," the priest had said mildly, ignoring both her tone and her embarrassment.

But the point he had striven to make was clear to Magaly nonetheless. Indeed, it had been clear since she first met Westonfield. "You're not offering a big brother's advice to a vulnerable sister," she said. "You can't be warning me to avoid a dangerous *liaison*..."

"Anything could happen," Father Lewendowski had rejoined, grinning. "But no," he concluded, shaking his shaggy head. "I wasn't referring to that especially."

Magaly responded softly after a long silence, "I really do understand, Father. I already know. He's a witch."

Marko Lewandowski's eyes had widened in surprise.

* * *

Magaly finished her breakfast and walked into the sunshine. She walked along East Jefferson to the underground parking garage where her rented car was parked, enjoying the cool breeze off the river enormously. She drove to the police academy on Park Street in the old downtown theater district and parked in a metered spot on the street. She went in and met the inspector-in-charge, who was expecting her. She spent the next three hours watching recruit classes practice self-defense drill and listening to the inspector explain how today's Detroit police officer is better trained, better educated, and more honest than his predecessors. She pointedly declined the inspector's invitation to lunch.

She decided to stop by Nancy Whiskey for a sandwich and a drink. She thought she might get a better feel for the place in the daytime, by herself, the pressure to make a good impression on Westonfield absent. She went in and at first headed for a small table in the back as was her habit. But as she passed the bar, Mary, the old barmaid, glanced up at her and smiled, saying in her Irish brogue, "Well, how are you, Little Miss? Didn't think I'd be seein' you today."

Magaly changed her mind about sitting inconspicuously in the back and went to the bar, hoisting herself onto one of the worn old stools. "I'm surprised you remember me," she said.

"Oh, now, deary. How could I not remember a pretty girl like you? All them cops was just fightin' to get ary a dance with you." She laughed a happy laugh. "It was a good thing to see, it was." She winked. "Reminded me of my young days in Derry."

Mary must have been sixty-five, but her face was still pretty. Underneath the tired exterior there was the sparkle of a youthful spirit that belied the lines of age on her face.

"I bet you were fought over by the boys, Mary. You're a beautiful lady."

"Well, I'll thank you indeed, Miss," she said laughing again. "And what was your name again? I'm good at faces, I am, but names are harder."

"Magaly. Magaly Rodríguez."

"A lovely name. Spanish, is it?"

"Yes."

"From around these parts, are you?"

"No. I live in New York. I'm here on business."

"Ah, I didn't think you was from around here. Don't talk like it."

"Oh, they tell me all the time that I still have an accent. A Spanish accent, I mean. Don't some Mexican girls in Detroit have accents, too?"

"Yes. Yes, they do. But that's not what I meant. You talk different in another way. Not like Detroit." She absently wiped the bar. "Like New York, I guess."

"Well, I lived in Mexico until I was nine. I was born there. Most of my family are still there. My father is a diplomat in Washington, D.C."

"Oh, my," said Mary.

"But now I'm an American citizen. Naturalized. I live in New York and I write for a magazine."

"You don't say, lass?"

Magaly smiled. "Yes."

"What would ever bring such a smart and pretty girl to our neck of the woods, then?"

"I'm writing an article for my magazine. *Harper's*."

"Is that a big one?"

"Yes, it is," said Magaly, her smile broadening, deciding she liked Mary very much.

"And what would be ever so interesting here that a fancy New York magazine would send one such as you to write about?"

"What else, Mary?" Magaly said, chuckling. "Cops."

"My," said Mary again. "But ain't there no officers in New York to write about?"

"Yes. There are. Twenty-five thousand or so. But Detroit's got a reputation."

"Aye," tittered Mary. "That we do."

"They say it's a tough town. What do you say, Mary? You work in a neighborhood bar in the middle of the city. A cops' bar. Is this a tough town?"

Mary paused, again idly wiping the scarred surface of the bar with a damp cloth. "It's a rough old town, I reckon. But it's home to a lot of hard workin' folks. Good folks, mostly. It's the few that makes it bad for the many."

"It's always that way, isn't it, Mary?"

"Perhaps it is."

Magaly looked up and gestured, her arm sweeping across the room. "Why do the officers come here, Mary?"

"Oh, I don't rightly know. It's just a place for them to go, I expect."

"But there must be dozens of bars in the city."

"Aye."

"Then?"

"It just sort of starts, don't you know? One or two comes in. They decide they like it. Then two or three more comes in. Like that. Soon it's all of 'em a comin'."

"It wouldn't have anything to do with the barmaid, would it?" Magaly said teasingly.

"I wouldn't think so, Miss," Mary said. "Not likely. If that's the way of it, then them boys is randier than I was thinkin'." She laughed, adding with a wink, "Though there's one or two of the older ones as would be worth a throw."

"What are they like, Mary?" asked Magaly suddenly, her bantering tone replaced now by earnestness. She touched Mary on the elbow.

"What are *who* like, Miss?" asked Mary, noticing Magaly's change of mood, looking up from the bar.

"The cops."

"Well, Miss, the officers are like anyone else, I would say. There's old and young, fat and thin, funny and sad."

"But they come here together."

"Aye. Company."

"They talk..."

"Sure they talk. About their wives and their kids and their houses and their cars. Men talk, most of it."

"And about their jobs?"

"Sure enough. A lot about their work."

"What do you think about it?"

"Oh, I don't rightly know, Miss. They just talk like anyone else would about their jobs. After a while all of the stories blend together like: chasin' and arrestin' and shootin'. I don't pay much attention no more. Some of the stories is too sad. I turn off my listener mostly now. I just sort of nod and make a comment or two. They seem to need to talk sometimes. If there ain't no others in, then I'm usually the one as gets talked to."

"What do you think of Bill Westonfield?"

"Lawks!" Mary seemed to find the notion amusing.

"What?"

"I saw you dance with him last Thursday."

"He's a good dancer."

"I'll wager he is, that Bill. Good at most things he does."

Magaly looked at her closely. "But what?"

"Well, it don't rightly matter what I think about him. Bill's his own man, he is. It don't really matter what anyone thinks about Bill."

"That's an interesting way of saying that you like him. I think I like him, too."

"But you've only just met him?"

"I'm afraid so."

Mary then nodded in assent. "Okay, Miss—what was your name, now?"

"Magaly."

"Aye. Pretty."

"Well?"

"What would you like to know? And mind you, I won't talk out of school. Nothing as shouldn't be said."

"Well, I don't have a lot of time," Magaly said. "I'm afraid I've got to get back to my hotel. In fact, I'm hoping Sergeant Westonfield calls me today. Just to get me a little bit up to date, though, if you would: he's going through a divorce, I understand?"

"He is that," Mary said softly.

"His second?"

"Aye."

"Could you tell me about his second wife?"

"She's an officer like him. Works downtown."

"You know her?"

"Sure. A little."

"You like her?"

"Sure I like her. Beautiful girl." Mary's eyes roamed over Magaly, taking stock. "Different than you. Night and day. She's got blonde hair and light skin. A bit taller than you."

"I'm surprised Sergeant Westonfield would ever marry a policewoman."

"I can see how you'd think that," Mary said. "But life's a strange thing. A mystery, through and through. Where love is concerned what seems right or wrong, good or bad, fair or schemin', don't really count." She looked into Magaly's eyes.

"Ever been in love?"

Magaly blushed a little. "I thought I was, once."

Mary nodded. "Then you know what I'm sayin'. Aye. There's no way to tell."

"They had problems over her affirmative action promotion, I'll bet."

"Her gettin' promoted out of order, you mean? Sure they did. And other things. Kids. Money..."

"Sounds great," Magaly said, raising her eyebrows.

"Worse than many, better than some," replied Mary. She drew closer, leaning forward on the polished surface of the bar. "But I'll tell you for true. Susan was good for Bill, in her way. Bill is... *serious*. Too serious, sometimes, for his own good. He's a worrier."

"What does he worry about?"

"Everything," Mary said.

"That can't be healthy for anyone."

"No. It isn't. Bill knows that. In his heart of hearts he knows it. That's why he married Susan. She made him happy. She wheedled into that tired, worried part of him and reminded him of the other parts of life. The simpler things. The happier things. She had a beautiful smile."

"And then?" Magaly asked.

"Well, it couldn't last, now could it? The two of 'em was like light and dark, soft and hard. Sad."

"Do you think they still love each other?"

"As I've said, love's a funny thing," Mary answered. "I still love my Danny, and he's been dead all these thirty years."

Magaly ate a corned beef sandwich on rye and drank a Stout. Her taste did not usually run to such fare—she had once described dark Irish beer as a good brew ruined with a handful of garden soil—but somehow it seemed the thing she ought to do. She ate ravenously. It was delicious.

She returned to the Pontchartrain at two o'clock. She went to the desk and inquired about messages. The clerk she had addressed that morning sorted through a pigeonhole behind the desk and produced a note, handing it to Magaly with a smile. Magaly looked at it: "Mr. William Westonfield called at 11:00 A.M. Wants you to call him at home. His number is—"

She had been right. Something good was going to happen today.

CHAPTER 10

Gabriel needed money before he could make plans for his new life in America. His skills lay in the netherworlds of assassination and *palo mayombe*, so he went first to Miami where there was work in the flourishing drug trade for those with these talents. Through contacts in the local Cuban-American population he made acquaintance with the regional *jefes* of the Medellín, Colombia drug cartel. They had heard of him and his capabilities. They put him to work immediately.

Within four days of his arrival in Miami Gabriel killed two Mexican *mules*, or couriers, whom the *jefes* had accused of skimming off profits before reporting the totals. The *jefes* believed there was a possibility that the men were informants to the Metro-Dade police as well. After skinning them alive, Gabriel cut off their heads and mailed them parcel post to the Miami office of the Drug Enforcement Administration.

Gabriel made a lot of money very fast. The *jefes* were, of course, highly pleased with his abilities since instances of informing to the police and profit-skimming virtually disappeared. But eventually they became afraid. Gabriel could not be controlled. In nearly every man in the trade there was a hook, a weakness, which could be exploited to maintain control—cocaine addiction, women, threats to family—but Gabriel seemed utterly unaffected by the normal frailties of men. He used no drugs as far as the *jefes* could tell and he never had any kind of relationship with women. His family, if he had any, was still in Cuba. He claimed he had no family in any case. He kept to himself, apparently saving his money and biding his time. This is what worried the *jefes*: biding his time for what?

In nine months he saved ninety thousand dollars; this for the murder of eleven men and two women. He enjoyed the work well enough but the siren song of the north called to him still. The perfunctory instructions and orders, issued in the most disrespectful manner by the *jefes*, became ever more difficult to endure. His patience grew thin as the pile of drug money grew larger and the urge to move again became strong.

One day Andrés Nuñez, one of the *jefes*, spoke to him in a particularly demeaning tone. Gabriel studied him with his black eyes, seemingly with no pupils, and the man flinched as if jarred by a physical blow. He began to sweat.

"I don't think I like you," Gabriel said softly.

"What does it matter what you like?" said Nuñez, the tremble in his voice belying his bravado.

Gabriel made his decision on the spot. "It will matter a great deal to you one day, *Jefe*. I promise you that."

As soon as Gabriel left the room Nuñez picked up the telephone and ordered his murder.

Forty-eight hours later, Tito Mendoza and Blanco Rivera, the hit men ordered to kill Gabriel Flores, were found hanging from the branches of a kapok tree by three boys hunting bullfrogs on the fringes of the Everglades a few miles west of Miami. They were hanging upside down with their own intestines wrapped around their necks. Their skin had been repeatedly slashed while they were still living, according to later reports of the Dade County coroner, and then inexplicably sealed with black candle wax. They had been bled dry. Macabre as the crime was, the authorities paid it little heed. Narcotics trafficking had virtually taken over the life's blood of southern Florida. Hundreds died violently every year. It was all the police could do to keep an accurate tally of the bodies. But the boys who found the hanging bodies had nightmares for a long time.

Gabriel's first intention after the Miami episode was to go north to Baltimore or Washington, D.C. But he had a nagging doubt that the time was ripe. As yet the bulk of the *Marielitos* were concentrated in the southeast. He feared standing out too much among the Anglo population. He was black and to the *Yanquis* he would look like any other *Negro*, but he barely spoke English. His Spanish accent was atrocious. *Sí*, he said to himself. The time is not yet come. He stowed away his impatience into a compartment in the back of his mind.

In the end he decided to go to New Orleans. There was a sizable Haitian population there as well as Cuban. He would blend in well. Besides, he wanted to learn the truth about the practice of voodoo there that he had heard about. He knew next to nothing about it but was curious.

He ended up spending the next eight years in the City of the Saints. Soon after his arrival, as in Miami, he became an assassin-for-hire in the drug trade. In the early 80s, due to increasing enforcement efforts in the eastern Gulf on the part of the Coast Guard and even the Navy, New Orleans became a magnet for Colombian cocaine funneled through Mexico. Gabriel rose quickly in the ranks of the *jefes* and after a while controlled a sizable portion of the trade himself, though this was not his intent. Money and the trappings of wealth had no hold on him. He rose to power more through the weakness of the men around him than through any aspirations to take their place. The Colombians and the Mexicans feared him. He laughed at them in their own faces and they dared not look him in the eye.

Though he possessed wealth beyond his dreams as a boy in Cuba it soon bored him. Women adored him—at least they adored what he could offer them financially—but he took no notice of them. Once an assassin in his employ, after too much drink, suggested to him jokingly that maybe he was a *maricón*, a faggot. Gabriel cut out the man's heart while he was still living, working so fast and with a knife so sharp that he was able to show the man his own still-beating heart before he was quite dead. He did much of the enforcement work himself, not trusting his men in some cases, and wanting to keep his skills honed to razor sharpness anyway. For eight long years he lived this life of discontent.

As for voodoo, soon after arriving Gabriel struck up an acquaintanceship with a few of the local practitioners, even of Jean Paul Maury, the most famous of them all. Gabriel found voodoo to be boring and useless, a false religion. Most practitioners were charlatans, not real believers in their own cult, out only to make money. Others, like Jean Paul, were true believers, but the voodoo gods were weak.

Jean Paul demonstrated a few of the incantations and potions to Gabriel, but he was not impressed. When Gabriel reciprocated with one or two of the simpler rituals of *palo mayombe*, Jean Paul became afraid. This puzzled Gabriel because they were, indeed, unspectacular rituals: he sacrificed a chicken to Zarabanda and made an old girlfriend who had abandoned Jean Paul come back to him; he got an employee of Jean Paul out of jail when the attorneys said it could not be done. After these favors were done for him Jean Paul no longer visited Gabriel. Gabriel thought about killing him for his lack of gratitude but eventually decided against it. Jean Paul's fear was his only vice. He was weak, but his heart was good.

Gabriel decided to leave and go north at last. He was ready. Over the intervening years hundreds of *Marielitos* had migrated north to the Latin communities of the great cities—New York, Chicago, Philadelphia. Now was the time. One night in the autumn of 1990 he sat alone in his room and studied a map of the United States, his black eyes roving over the pastel-colored pages, pausing at the big cities. He placed his index finger on each of them, one at a time, and closed his eyes, feeling. He rejected one after another until at last he placed his finger on the large black dot and clutter of unfamiliar names that was Detroit. When he closed his eyes and relaxed his muscles, willing himself to sense the ambiance of that city, the energy flowed through him, warm, almost painful. His penis grew turgid. Far north. Next to Canada. It must be cold there in winter. Very cold. The white snow would be everywhere. This was the place. He felt it with the same intensity as when he stood by the barbed wire at Homestead ten years before, the siren song whispering. Detroit.

He simply walked away from most of his holdings and enterprises in New Orleans. He told no one of his plans. He put a hundred thousand dollars in cash, a fraction of his worth, in a duffel bag and boarded a direct flight to Detroit's Metropolitan Airport. He caught a taxi and told the driver in his much-improved English to take him to Detroit. When the driver inquired as to exactly where in Detroit the gentleman wished to go, Gabriel told him he would tell him when he got there. In truth, Gabriel didn't know where he would go. As was his practice, he would just get there and then decide by intuition where to go, who to see, and what to do.

Metro Airport is located in the city of Romulus, about fifteen miles west of the city. The taxi driver took Interstate 94 straight from the airport into the southwest side of the city. The moment the cab passed beneath the Wyoming Street overpass and entered the city limits of Detroit, Gabriel knew he was home. This was where he was meant to be. Following his usual pattern, he sought out members of the Latin community, in this case *Marielitos* already in the city. There were several dozen, almost all living on the southwest side and the majority involved in the drug trade. He quickly set up residence in a house on 31st Street, just south of Interstate 94.

Within weeks he was in business. He found that the traffic on the southwest side was controlled mainly by American blacks, with increasing influence being exerted by the Jamaicans. The blacks, and the Anglos and Mexicans that worked with them, were terrified of the Jamaicans who patrolled the streets in three-car caravans, Mercedes sedans followed by nondescript American cars. The Mercedes contained drugs or money—whatever the Jamaicans were conveying at the time—but the American cars were occupied by three or four compatriots armed with Uzi sub-machine guns and 9 mm pistols. They had muscled in on much of the southwest side's narcotics business through ruthlessness and murder. Moreover, and to the furtherance of their reputations for mystery and ferocity, the Jamaicans were practitioners of voodoo.

Gabriel decided to make his mark early. He drew on forces of Zarabanda in a ritual that lasted three hours. He sacrificed a hen and a goat he obtained from a local Puerto Rican meat supplier. Into the smoking cauldron he put the blood of the animals until it steamed. Next he added two of his favorite ingredients, and among the most favored of Zarabanda: *acéite de yo puedo y tú no* (oil of "I can and you cannot") and *Sal pa fuera* (a powder whose name means "salt to make someone go away"). He contemplated for a moment adding a few grains of *precipitado rojo*, but decided against it. This powder was enormously powerful and dangerous. He felt that the concoction was already powerful enough to deal with the likes of the Jamaicans. It wouldn't do to offend Zarabanda by drawing on his powers in disproportion to the task.

He slept for eighteen hours after the ritual ended. Zarabanda came to him in his dreams and spoke to him urgently, the yellow eyes holes into Hell, the lips dripping blood, the breath rank with the smell of death. When Gabriel awoke he had forgotten the dream, but a small worm deep in the recesses of his innermost being was gnawing at him, whispering. Never before in his life had he been cautious, but the whispers warned him to be careful. Careful of what? Detroit was his final home, was it not? He had been drawn here after all of the years of waiting. His heart told him that this was where he would discover his ultimate purpose and achieve his greatest accomplishments as a *tata nkisi*. But beyond the whispers of caution there was a faint whiff of something else, something 'til then unknown to him: a slight thrill of fear, like the feel of cold metal on warm skin.

A week later the body of the boss of the Jamaican narcotics trade in Detroit was found in the downriver Detroit suburb of Trenton, in a county recreation area known as Elizabeth Park. The man had been flayed alive and his body stuffed into an abandoned rowboat at the county marina by the Detroit River. Violent crime was almost unheard of in Trenton, so the discovery was extraordinary. But surprise turned to consternation when a week later the Trenton Police Department detectives got their first look at the medical examiner's autopsy report. The dead man had eaten, presumably by coercion, several pages of a book. The few scraps that were retrieved from his stomach contents were miraculously still readable. The pages appeared to have been torn from the same book that was found tossed into the bottom of the boat along with the corpse: *Voodoo and Hoodoo—The Craft as Revealed by Traditional Practitioners* by Jim Haskins. The Trenton police, and the Wayne County sheriff's detectives as well, didn't know what to make of it.

But word got out in southwest Detroit to steer clear of 31st Street. Gabriel was in business once again. He scouted the area and learned the ways of the people and of the trade. He learned the locations of the churches and the cemeteries and the *botánicas* from which he could obtain the ingredients needed to perform his rituals. He would be performing rituals often.

In his first year in Detroit he acquired two more houses. In February of 1991 he took over a house on South Solvay in Del Ray. In September of 1991 he obtained a house on Merritt Street and set up an altar. Twice in September, and twice again in early October, he went to Woodmere Cemetery to acquire human bones for his rites. Even as Magaly Rodríguez' plane landed at Metropolitan Airport on the evening of October 15, 1991, Gabriel burglarized St. Anne's Church and stole a gallon of Holy Water. Ever and anon the *bruja* whispered to him from afar. The moon was waxing.

CHAPTER 11

Magaly found La Fuente de Elena without difficulty. Westonfield's directions had been precise and simple; she spotted the red brick and wrought iron facade exactly as he'd described it. She pulled into the small parking lot at 7:55 P.M., five minutes early.

She had returned his call as soon as she arrived back in her room after lunch with Mary at Nancy Whiskey. Westonfield said he wanted to talk to her about the possibility of cooperating with her after all on the piece for *Harper's*. He said he had a few things to do during the rest of the afternoon and then would be working his usual seven-to-three shift. Would she consider meeting him for dinner at a local restaurant while he was working? It was all Magaly could do not to sound like a silly schoolgirl on the telephone.

In contrast to the delightful autumn weather during the early part of the day, low grey clouds had started to move in from the west during the late afternoon. By 5:30 it was drizzling a cold rain and the temperature had dropped fifteen degrees. Magaly had heard about the changeability of Detroit's weather and had discovered it for herself: if you like the weather, just wait a while. She got out of her car and made her way to the door, stepping gingerly in her three-inch heels around the growing puddles on the uneven surface of the asphalt pavement. There were only five other cars in the lot. She wondered absently why this would be on a Saturday night.

She went in and was met by the hostess, a plump, middle-aged Mexican woman dressed in a black skirt and white blouse. Magaly asked for a table for two in the rear and was escorted there at once. Only six of the twelve or fourteen tables in the moderate dining room were taken. Once more she wondered at the lack of a crowd, but she liked the place immediately. It was decorated tastefully and with understatement—neither ostentatious nor formal, and not overly done in Tex-Mex style as was typical of Mexican restaurants in the U.S. The waitress, a pretty girl of about seventeen, with coal-black hair down to her waist, hovered over her shoulder.

Magaly smiled. *"Buenas noches."*

"Buenas noches, señorita," the girl said, returning her smile, *"¿Cómo está usted?"*

"Bién, pero un poco húmeda." Fine, just a little damp.

"Sí. La lluvia a mí no me gusta tampoco." I don't like the rain either, the girl said, shaking her head mildly. *"¿Espera a alguien más?"* Are you waiting for someone else?

"Sí, espero a un otro." Magaly looked at her watch, *"...ahorita."*

The girl brought her a glass of water and asked if she wanted a cocktail while she waited. She ordered a Carta Blanca and had only taken a sip or two when the door swung open and Westonfield stepped in. He didn't simply walk in without paying attention. He stopped just inside the door and looked around, his eyes scanning the dimly lit interior. His eyes locked momentarily onto Magaly's and then flicked on over the rest of the dining room. Apparently satisfied, he entered. The hostess looked up, saw him, and grinned broadly, slipping quickly over to give him a kiss.

"Guillermo!" she said, taking his hand. *"¿Cómo estás? ¿Qué hay de nuevo? ¡Hace tres semanas que no te he visto! ¿Quisás tienes una novia para reponerme, no?"* What's new? I haven't seen you in three weeks! Maybe you've got a new girlfriend to replace me?

Westonfield kissed her cheek and whispered something in her ear, pointed conspiratorially in Magaly's direction. The hostess laughed and patted him on the butt, pushing him toward the table where Magaly sat.

"Well, Sergeant, it would seem you're not new here," Magaly said, smiling up at him.

"Never been in the place before."

"I see. Then all the ladies just naturally act that way."

"What way?"

Magaly grinned again.

Westonfield removed his fatigue jacket, exposing his holstered Smith, the satin finish reflecting the candlelight. He sat, draping the jacket over the back of one of the unused chairs at the table-for-four. He set his radio on the table. Before he could speak again the waitress arrived with a bottle of Dos Equis beer, plopping it in front of him. She set two menus on a corner of the table and returned to the front of the restaurant.

Magaly raised her eyebrows. "They're also clairvoyant, I see. Dos Equis without asking."

Westonfield looked at the bottle of Carta Blanca on the table. "No, but everyone knows that Dos Equis is the only Mexican beer worth drinking."

"Even on duty?"

"Especially on duty." He took a sip.

"So... Hi," Magaly said in the silence that followed.

"Hello."

"Thank you for calling me back."

"Thank you?" Westonfield said. "Hell, Rourke and the priest practically forced me into it."

"Did they?"

"Yes. Pains in the ass, both of them."

"I think they're charming," Magaly said. "And I'm grateful to them. And to you for accepting," she added.

"I haven't accepted anything yet." Westonfiled replied. "I said we'd have to come to terms."

"My, but you're an impatient fellow. Name your terms."

"All right. First things first. I want to read what you write. Everything. Before you send it to the publisher."

"Okay," Magaly said. "You can read it."

"If I don't like it, it doesn't go in."

This was too much. "Who do you think you're kidding, Sergeant?" Magaly asked, chiding him. "Nobody gets that kind of veto over this kind of piece. Nobody. No disrespect, but that kind of control leads to whitewashed pap, not insightful analysis. I'm sorry, but that would be absolutely impossible."

"Do you mean analysis, or exposé," Westonfield retorted.

"I write for *Harper's*, not *The National Enquirer*," Magaly said evenly.

"Why should I trust you?"

"Why should you not?"

"Haven't you read the shit they write about cops all the time? How do I know you're any different?"

"Apparently your friends think I might be."

"They'd sell their souls to the devil if he was wearing a skirt," Westonfield said.

Now Magaly was angry. "Father Mark is a priest."

"When he wants to be."

Magaly fought down her growing anger, suddenly afraid it would spoil everything. She took a long, cool pull on her glass of beer. Then she said, "Let's make it conditional then."

"How so?"

"I'll let you read every word I write for publication, but even if you don't like it, it goes in." Anticipating his reaction, she hurried on, "—but after that, if you really can't accept what I've written, you stop cooperating. The project's off. I go home."

He stared at her. He hadn't exactly expected that response.

The waitress returned to the table. "Are you ready to order?"

Magaly reached for a menu. "Well, I haven't had a chance—"

"I'll order," said Westonfield. He looked from the waitress to Magaly. *"¿Té gusta almendrado de puerco?"*

"Sí," she said, smiling. "I like it. And I like it when you speak Spanish."

"All the girls say that," Westonfield said, inclining his head, his eyes twinkling.

The waitress took the order and left.

Magaly said, "I've been wondering since the day before

yesterday: where did you learn Spanish? You speak it very well."

"School."

"What school? You talk like a native."

"The University of Michigan."

"Tom Bacon showed me your record. It said you held a degree from the U of M. Nothing about Spanish, though. That's why I didn't know. But Spanish—why does a Welshman, as you say, from Michigan study Spanish? Was it your major?"

"Yes, my degree's in Spanish," he said. "Why? Because I liked it, I suppose." He sipped his beer. "Is there a better reason for a person to do something?"

"No, but— "

"But what?"

"Well, I was just hoping we could talk more about it sometime."

"That's why we're here, isn't it?" he asked.

"Yes, I suppose it is," Magaly said. She dredged a tortilla chip through the bowl of hot red salsa in front of her. Westonfield had the most curious way of throwing her off balance. "Well then, are there other conditions you would like to discuss?"

"A very important one," he said. "When you're in the scout car, you do precisely what I tell you to do, when I tell you."

"But if I need to see something, talk to someone for the article..."

"Fuck your story," Westonfiled said. "I'm talking about your life. It may depend on your reacting instantly to my instructions. Things can go very wrong very fast on the street. All I need is to wonder where you're at, or if you're okay when I'm trying to wrestle some shithead to the ground." He saw the blood rush to her face. "And I won't apologize for saying 'fuck,'" he went on. "One thing I won't do is change my behavior to accommodate your sensibilities. It's my world out there, not yours." He smiled. "And if you think Rourke can go two minutes without uttering four or five obscenities, you've got a rude awakening coming."

"My God, you're a condescending prick," Magaly said, unsure whether she was infuriated or bemused at Westonfield's antiquated posture. He was positively Victorian. "And I'm not uncomfortable with your language, Sergeant," she added pointedly. "I'm just not used to being lectured as though I were a child. I assure you, however, that I'm used to strong language. I've lived with SAS paratroopers."

"Good, then," Westonfield said, completely unabashed. "You'll be in practice."

After a very good (and civil) dinner he said, "Some *flán?*"

"No, thank you. I couldn't eat another bite."

"Coffee?"

"Sure." Over strong coffee with plenty of cream she said, "I wanted to ask you, this is such a good place, why isn't it more crowded? It ought to be. It's kinda nice."

"The crowds are over that way two blocks," Westonfield said, nodding his head toward the window. "At the glitzy places on Bagley. Mexican Town, they call it." He chuckled. "It attracts suburbanites precisely because it's *not* like a Mexican town."

"It doesn't surprise me, Sergeant," Magaly said. "I'm the Real McCoy, remember? That attitude, that ignorance, always disappoints me a little. But I'm used to it."

He nodded, suddenly very sober. "The Real McCoy."

"Yes," Magaly said, simply. Then, "All right. I'll do exactly what you say when we're on patrol. As long as afterwards you agree to explain to me exactly what it was you did and why you did it."

"Agreed," Westonfield said. "One more thing I'd like to clear up, though. This is all approved by the department? I'm not the most admired man about town. Frankly, I can't believe the chief's staff would allow it. They don't usually like media people to see... the truth." He shrugged. "How did you accomplish it?"

"A lot of promises, a lot of bull. My editor is a persuasive man."

He nodded again, doubt in his eyes.

"Now I have two more things," Magaly said.
"Yes?"
"When do we begin?"
"Are you ready right now?"
"Now?"
"Yes."
"Well, I didn't think... My! Your friend Jack wasn't kidding when he said you were quick to act when you made up your mind, was he?"
"No. What's the other thing?"
"You call me Magaly. I call you Bill."
He grinned. "Done."

* * *

She followed him to the Fourth Precinct station. When they walked into the Power Shift squad room Rourke was playing darts. "Slugging it out on your paperwork, I see," said Westonfield.
"It's a dirty job, but somebody's got to do it." He threw a bullseye.
"You two have met, I understand," said Westonfield, nodding toward Magaly, who stood by the door taking in the room.
Rourke threw another dart and waved at her. "Yep. We're acquainted." He winked at her. "Can I get you a coffee, Miss Rodríguez?"
"No, thank you, Jack. We've just eaten."
"Well, come on in and sit down."
She looked around for a place. There were only two chairs in the room, beat up old swivel chairs, one each for Westonfield and Rourke. At the moment both were piled up with papers and files.
Westonfield picked up the pile from his own chair and offered the seat to Magaly. She brushed a scattering of doughnut crumbs from the cushion and sat down as Rourke threw yet

another dart.

"You're sure we're not disturbing you, Jack?" offered Westonfield.

"Hell, no. Not at all, Bill. As a matter of fact, I was just going to ask you the same thing." He withdrew his gaze from the dart board and looked at his partner. "I bet you don't even feel guilty about wining and dining a pretty woman on company time, do you?"

"Not in the least."

Rourke looked at Magaly. "It's like I told you, Miss. The man's incorrigible."

"What have we got going, Jack?" asked Westonfield, removing the stack of papers from Rourke's chair and sliding into it, propping his feet up on the desk.

Rourke threw two more darts in quick succession and sat on a corner of Westonfield's desk. "Boys are on the street. Pretty quiet for a Saturday night so far." He looked out the dirty window. "Could be the rain."

"As of today we'll have a new partner, Jack."

Rourke nodded. "I can't exactly say that I'm surprised, Bill." He turned to Magaly. "He ain't nearly as hard as he thinks he is, is he, Miss Rodríguez?"

"He drove a hard bargain."

"Did he now? Well, be that as it may, welcome aboard. Glad to have you." Rourke glanced at the clock. "Almost 10:00, Bill. Think we ought to get out there and see what's cookin'?" He looked doubtfully at Magaly's attire. "You aren't exactly dressed for the street."

"I didn't expect to start so soon."

Rourke looked narrowly at Westonfield. "I suppose not. Well, if this douche bag gives you too much trouble, Miss, you come to see me. I know what medicine's good for him."

Westonfield said nothing. They went down to the car. Rourke drove and Westonfield took the passenger, or jump, seat. Magaly sat in the back. They pulled slowly out of the muddy parking lot, splashing water out of deep puddles. "Been trying to get the city to blacktop this lot for fifteen years," said Rourke. "Still waiting."

Westonfield punched the sign-in code into the MODAT as they pulled away. After about thirty seconds the acknowledgment came back, glowing in pale green letters on the video display. They were now connected with CAD. In answer to her question, Westonfield explained the functioning of the system to Magaly.

"I think I'll go by them crack houses on Radcliffe, Bill," said Rourke. "That pissant Jimmy Jones has been hanging around there for two weeks. Remember him? I told him if I saw him up there one more time I'd bang him. He'll be there. He don't listen."

"I remember him. Go get him if you want."

"How could you forget him, eh, Bill? Remember the first time we ran across that little turd?"

Westonfield groaned. "I said I remember the man, Jack."

"Yeah, I know, but I thought maybe Miss Rodríguez —"

Magaly leaned forward in the seat. "Call me Magaly, Jack. Okay?"

"Sure. Magaly. Nice name. Unusual. Anyway, I thought maybe you'd like to hear this story. It's a weird one. Me and Bill were driving around one night up on Michigan Avenue. Must have been about two o'clock in the morning. We were working the whores up there for some information on a couple of murders. All of a sudden we hear this squeal. Not a scream, but a high-pitched squeal, like a pig being stuck. Awfulest sound you ever heard. Anyway, we turned a corner toward the sound. It seemed to be coming from between two junk cars in a vacant lot. We parked the car and went out looking on foot with our flashlights. Bill found Jimmy laying on the ground between the cars, buck naked. Seems Jimmy'd found himself an empty quart-size milk bottle and lubed up the rim. Stuck his peter in. But when his dick got hard the bottle got stuck. You wouldn't think it for a little man, but Jimmy's hung like a breeding bull."

"All right, Jack, that'll do," Westonfield said.

"No," Magaly said, laughing. "That's really funny, Jack. What did you do with him?"

Westonfield shook his head.

"We took him to Ford Hospital," Rourke said. "They had to cut the bottle off with a glass cutter. Jimmy was as high as a kite. He's a crack head. It didn't hurt him all that much."

Rourke grinned wolfishly and Magaly giggled.

Westonfield continued to shake his head.

When they approached Radcliffe Rourke doused the headlights. They parked just off Lonyo in the parking lot of a bar, facing east. They could see the crack houses from there. A group of four or five people was sitting on the front porch of one of the houses. Every few minutes a car would pull up in front and an occupant would alight and go to the porch. It was too dark to see well from that distance, but items were exchanged, presumably crack cocaine for money, and then the purchaser would return to the car and drive away. Sometimes pedestrians would emerge from the shadows farther up the street, make a buy, and then disappear again.

"See that one in back?" said Rourke. "That skinny little fucker with the short hair on the top step? That's Jimmy, ain't it?"

"Too hard to see," said Westonfield. "I think so."

After a moment of debate, they decided to drive up the street and grab Jimmy before he could melt away into the surrounding darkness. Rourke dropped the car into gear and they lurched forward and burnt rubber down the street, the unmarked scout car fishtailing off the loose gravel on the apron of the lot. By the time the group on the porch realized what was happening the scout car was almost in front of the house. They scattered like sparks in a gale. Westonfield and Rourke ignored everyone but Jimmy, who ran straight into the house. Big as he was Rourke moved fast. He jumped out of the car and raced across the yard, up the steps two at a time and into the house. Westonfield brought up the rear, taking a last glance along the now-deserted street to make sure nothing unexpected was afoot. Then he, too, disappeared into the house.

Magaly got out of the car and stood by the fender, watching. It had all happened so fast: one minute Rourke was talking silly talk, seemingly harmless, paying little attention to the object of their surveillance. The next minute they were off, racing down the street and running toward the house. Now she was alone in a dope-infested neighborhood at eleven o'clock at night. She wouldn't have admitted it to anyone, hated to acknowledge it even to herself, but she was pretty frightened.

To her relief, in no more than a couple of minutes Rourke emerged from the house, pushing the handcuffed Jimmy Jones in front of him. Westonfield came out soon after. They brought him to the car. Rourke was chortling. "You don't mind riding in the back seat with Jimmy here, do you, Magaly? He won't bother you, will you, Jimmy?" Rourke held up a small plastic sandwich bag containing seven or eight small 'rocks' of crack cocaine. They looked like pea gravels, only softer, their texture almost like soap. "Jimmy's been a bad boy. I told you, you little scumbag, to stay away from here, didn't I?"

The little man looked sullenly at the ground, saying nothing.

Magaly rode all the way back to the station scrunched up against the door on the front seat of the police car. She was glad, at least, that Rourke had only been joking about her riding in the back with Jones. Rourke sat next to him in the back, twisted in the seat so that he could keep an eye on him. But the man didn't act up. He sat with his head between his knees, breathing hard. He never once looked in Magaly's direction. She nevertheless tried to stay as far away from him as possible. He stank.

They arrived at the station and reported the arrest to the office-in-charge of the desk, Bill's friend, Lieutenant Runyon, to whom Magaly was introduced. They filled out a fingerprint card and stood by while the turnkey, known in Detroit as the doorman, searched the prisoner. Then they went upstairs to type their reports.

CHAPTER 12

When Westonfield and Rourke were well along with their reports, typing two-fingered at their old Royal manual typewriters—Magaly thought they looked like a couple of mischievous children—she said, "I promised I wouldn't interfere. I didn't. And I won't." She paused. "I know this Jimmy Jones is not a stand-up kind of guy... Well, you said you would explain things to me after they happened. That was your promise to me, so I'm asking: this arrest wasn't exactly legal, was it?"

Rourke stopped typing.

"Illegal as hell," Westonfield said smoothly. "We were too far out and it was too dark for us to actually see an illegal narcotics purchase take place. Therefore, we had no legal basis to pursue Jimmy into a private residence. We had no basis for a full search of Jimmy's person prior to the arrest, which was illegal anyway." He took a sip of his coffee. "You bothered already? Maybe this was a bad idea."

"No, it wasn't a bad idea," Magaly said. "And I'm not complaining. I just wasn't expecting what I saw. And if you—" she cast a glance at Rourke "—or Jack are in the least concerned that I'll be a problem, don't be. I mean it. You've let me into a private corner of your lives and I'm grateful for that. I would never betray that trust. But I'm going to be honest with you. If I see something that I don't understand, I'll ask about it. If I see something I don't approve of, I'll say so. But that will be the end of it. It will never go beyond me. As far as publication goes, I will never try to print something that would hurt you. Okay?"

Rourke nodded, satisfied. He continued typing.

Westonfield pushed the typewriter back and picked up his coffee. He looked at her. "One of the first things you find out when you graduate from the academy as a police officer and get out on the street is that it's impossible to play by the rules."

"Really," Magaly said dryly. "How so?"

"You discover that the law isn't there to give you the tools you need. It's there to protect the majority of citizens who don't break the law from you."

Magaly smiled. "Then a rookie learns first hand and early on a valuable lesson about the price of a free society."

"But he also learns, and this is the point—"

"What point, Bill?" Magaly interrupted. "Isn't freedom from government tyranny the whole point of the system?"

"By tyranny I presume you mean tyranny of the majority? Of the government? Of the police?" Westonfield said. "A reasonable fear. God knows history's full of it."

"So," Magaly said, inclining her head, "you make my case."

Westonfield raised his hand. "The only thing is, how do we reasonably protect the majority from the minority?"

"In the big scheme of things, that just doesn't matter as much," Magaly said.

"Maybe not in a college civics class," Westonfield said quietly.

"What does that mean?"

"It means that if you happen to be a member of the so-called majority who is about to get his balls chopped off by a member of the minority, the lessons of our country's protectiveness of individual rights might seem a little less important."

"That sounds like something a skinhead would say," Magaly retorted. "It's simplistic. It's a way to scare people into giving up the freedoms they've got. Generations of Americans have fought and paid for those freedoms with pain and sweat. Benjamin Franklin said those who would give up freedom to gain security deserve neither freedom nor security. The argument doesn't become you."

"And I'm tempted to say you sound like a Girl Scout—until the day, if only once in her life, she really needs help."

Magaly's face reddened and she opened her mouth to make a choleric response, but Westonfield held up his hand again. Rourke stopped typing a second time. He climbed out of his chair and excused himself, shaking his head and muttering about having to take a leak.

"Wait a minute," Westonfield said. "No one has greater respect for our legal system than I do. But the problem is this: the notion of minority-versus-majority rights rests squarely on the premise that *all* members of society function within recognized norms of behavior."

"Of course."

"But what if that's wrong?"

"What if what's wrong?"

"What if the premise is wrong?" Westonfield said. "What if there is a segment of society that marches to a different drummer?"

"Go on."

"Maybe two hundred years ago, when they wrote the Constitution," Westonfield said, "they were right about all of us being inherently part of the whole, all of us being on the same fundamental page. But what if something strange and terrible has happened since then to change things? What if the actual character of the culture has changed?"

"What are you getting at? I still don't see—"

"What if we're *not* all the same anymore?" Westonfield interjected. "What if there are people who don't look at life the same way most people do, share the same basic values and principles? I don't mean the nuances of morality, Magaly, like race relations or abortion rights, I mean people to whom simple Judeo-Christian concepts like *Thou shalt not kill* are irrelevant inconveniences." He studied her for a moment. "There are people like that, you know."

"There have always been the few, the mentally ill, political assassins…"

"But it's different now," Westonfield insisted. "There are more. I don't know why, but there are."

"But there's still the law, isn't there?" Magaly said. "You can't get around that. You can break it, but you can't get around it. It's there for everybody and for all time. It's not perfect. But for my money, it's still the government that we need to fear most." She watched him, tapping a pencil against her teeth. "We've come full circle in the conversation, it seems. Where do we go from here?"

"Not full circle," said Westonfield. "Not quite. Let me tell you a story from the days before we had anti-stalking laws." He folded his arms and exhaled, closed his eyes, opened them, focused on the dingy ceiling, and began...

"One day a young woman was grocery shopping in the city. A middle-aged man approached her in the market. He was a little unkempt, but otherwise normal. The woman had never seen the man before. The man walked right up to her and started talking." Westonfield leaned forward, reached out and grabbed Magaly by the arms, pulling her to him, their noses almost touching, and looked into her eyes. His voice was suddenly fierce, yet quiet, cold as death. "*'I'm going to fuck you,'* the man said. *'I'm going to fuck you good. Not here. Not now. But soon, very soon. I'll follow you everywhere. Whenever you look out your window, I'll be there watching. I'm going to enjoy it.'*"

Magaly pulled away, startled. There were odd lights in Westonfield's eyes. His face was a mask. She shivered, looked down.

Westonfield released her. "Emma Brodecker was scared, too, Magaly. For a little while. Until the man killed her."

"How?" Magaly said. "Didn't she go to the police?" She sought Westonfield's eyes again.

"She went to the police," Westonfield answered. "I wasn't involved, but I know the cops who were. There was nothing they could do."

"What?"

"There was nothing the police could do. Under the law."

Magaly was indignant. "He approached her without her consent. He threatened her. He described exactly what he was going to do."

"Oscar Paris was crazy, Magaly. But he wasn't stupid. He made good on his promise to follow her. He finally raped and killed her. Emma Brodecker called the police seven or eight times. We responded each time and investigated Paris each time."

"And?"

"Oscar hadn't broken any laws."

"Anti-stalking law or not, Bill. Some of that behavior must be off limits."

"What had he done? Tell me."

Magaly merely looked at him. The priest's words of warning skittered through her mind like a shameful secret.

"What had he done?" repeated Westonfield. "He approached her in a public place—no law against that. He had as much right to be there as she did. He had no weapons. At least none that were ever in view. He was quiet, almost polite. He used no obscene language which could be heard by anyone but Emma Brodecker. He didn't shout, wave his arms, or in any way disrupt the market. He simply said what he had to say and then he left."

"He threatened her."

"He had no weapon. The threat was sexual. He never touched her. He made no attempt at the time to carry it out. He even told her in plain English that he specifically did *not* intend to carry it out at that moment. He wasn't drunk. He wasn't disorderly. He wasn't trespassing."

"But later. He followed her, harassed her?"

"My buddies told me that Emma called 911 one time at three o'clock in the morning and reported that Paris was standing outside her window trying to talk to her. She was petrified. They got out there and, sure enough, Paris was still there, standing quietly on the public sidewalk. They shook him down. He wasn't carrying any weapons. He was very quiet, polite, and respectful to the officers, claiming that he was out for a walk. They asked him why he'd chosen that exact spot to stop and he replied that it just suited him. He was comfortable there, he said. They talked to Emma and then they left."

"They left?"

"Exactly."

"How could they do that?"

"The question, Magaly, is not how *could* they, but how could they *not*."

"Loitering—"

"There's a ton of case law all across the country that voids loitering, in and of itself, as a crime," Westonfield said. "Merely standing in a public place while committing no other crime is not against the law. In Michigan and Detroit you can't stand in a public place and impede pedestrian traffic, but if you choose to stand quietly on a public sidewalk at three o'clock in the morning, you're committing no crime. New laws give you new tools, but the police still have to be careful."

"So they left," Magaly said, her voice soft, empty.

"They left," Westonfield said, nodding his head. "Then Paris broke into her house, sodomized her, raped her, and killed her."

Magaly shuddered once more. "That's a horrible story."

Westonfield's grey eyes, haunted eyes, studied the palms of his hands.

Magaly's intuition told her that it wasn't just *this* story that animated Westonfield, but many such stories in aggregate. How many horrific stories must there be in more than twenty years of big city police work? After a full minute of silence, she said, "I'm sorry."

"For what?" Westonfield looked up.

"For making you tell me that story."

"You didn't make me."

"Yes, I did," Magaly said. "I was a bore. In a way I guess you're right. I'm talking on one level, and you're talking on another. My level doesn't carry the emotional baggage, does it?

I'm here to learn, and I'm going to try very hard. I've upset you. I know I've upset you, and I'm sorry."

Westonfield shrugged. "I wanted to make a point. Out here, Magaly, we policemen have to make choices. The choices lead us down a slippery slope. Every rookie becomes aware of it sooner or later. He can obey the letter of the law, as he is solemnly sworn to do. Or he can improvise."

"Improvise?"

"What would you do, legally, about people like Oscar Paris?" Westonfield asked. "Sure, we've got the anti-stalking law now. But would you really want to have laws that make it illegal to approach other people in public places to talk? The Jehovah's Witnesses would be in trouble, wouldn't they? Would you want a law that would make it unlawful to stand on a public sidewalk on a quiet summer's night, taking in the air—a sidewalk in your own town, paid for with your own taxes?"

"What's your answer then?"

"There isn't any, Magaly. That's the point. There isn't an answer. It's a Catch 22."

She was silent, trying to absorb everything. It was so new to her, this line of reasoning. But that was Westonfield's way, wasn't it? No sugar coating for him. Why did he disdain the subtleties of things so much? She supposed he would say they were merely contrivances put in place to keep from finding the hard truths.

"So, what does he do then, the cop?" Westonfield went on.

"Tell me," Magaly said.

"I've already told you. He improvises."

"What you mean is—he lies."

"That's right. He breaks his oath."

"But that makes him no better than the crook," Magaly said. "He's sworn to uphold the law. Then he breaks the law. That can't be right."

"It isn't," Westonfield said. "But letting the Oscar Parises of the world have their way isn't right either."

"But if the letter of the law isn't the guideline a police

officer uses, what is?"

"He uses his own judgment."

"You use your own judgment?"

"More or less."

"But then who decides when to lie or not to lie, Bill?"

"Each man decides for himself."

"But isn't that another reason we have laws?" Magaly asked. "To make actions of agents of the state—cops—dependent on a common morality codified by the law?"

"Yes."

"But it just doesn't work in practice, you say."

"Ask Emma Brodecker," Westonfield said.

"But what if your own judgment fails? What if the direction your heart takes you as a cop is wrong? People are frail, aren't they? Cops have so much power... ought that much power be trusted to the vagaries of the heart?"

"No," Westonfield said simply. "Catch 22."

Magaly sat for a moment in thought, a little confused, sad.

"We're in the middle, us cops," Westonfield finally said. "The moral contradictions and paradoxes you and I have been talking about are part of our everyday life. The choices are real. Every day that goes by, every month that passes, the answers to the questions get harder to divine. After a while it becomes them and you—the good guys and the bad guys. The rules don't matter any more. The only thing that matters is the fact that you're a good guy because you say you are and the bad guys are bad because you say they are. Once you dance with the devil you can never go back." There was regret in Westonfield's voice, but no recrimination. "If you want to understand street cops—if you want to understand *me*—then that's the first thing you need to learn. I'm on one side, they're on another. And sometimes the line between us is as fine as the strand of a spider's web."

Magaly was almost too fearful to ask, but she felt compelled. "What would you have done with Oscar Paris had it been your call, Bill?"

"I don't know," Westonfield said softly. "I really don't, Maggie. Only—"

"Only?"

"I can tell you this: Oscar Paris wouldn't have killed Emma Brodecker that night."

Looking into Westonfield's grey, glittering eyes Magaly thought she might say, "No, I'd wager my life on that." But instead she said, "You called me Maggie. I like that." Then an image of herself leaning forward and kissing him on the lips rose unbidden in her mind. The notion surprised her and flustered her so badly that she didn't hear Jack Rourke come back into the office.

Rourke found them staring at each other, silent.

PART II—THE LIVING AND THE DEAD

"There is a passion for hunting something deeply implanted in the human breast."

Charles Dickens

"El que bién te quiere te hará llorar."
{Whoever really loves you will make you cry.}

Spanish Proverb

CHAPTER 13

As Magaly stepped from the shower and reached for a towel the telephone rang. It was nearly noon: she had slept well after the long day yesterday. Had it actually all happened in a day? There had been the morning observing physical training at the police academy, lunch at Nancy Whiskey, dinner with Westonfield at La Fuente de Elena, and then the rest of the night patrolling the southwest side with Bill and Jack, including the memorable arrest of one Jimmy Jones.

She wrapped the white cotton towel around her dripping body and pattered barefoot across the carpet of the Pontchartrain suite to the desk phone on a table by the balcony. She flicked a black tapestry of wet hair away from her face and picked up the receiver. "Yes?"

"Good afternoon." The voice was Westonfield's. "You awake?"

"Just barely," she said. "Actually, I was taking a shower. How do you guys get used to this schedule? I'm usually an early riser, so these late hours could get to be a real killer for me."

"You get used to it," Westonfield said. "But listen, I was just wondering if you'd like to come out with us again this evening. Jack didn't have any problem with last night. I didn't, either." He paused. "Would that be all right? You didn't say if you had plans."

Magaly suppressed her surprise. She had been worrying that Westonfield would be put off after their heated discussion of the night before. *Why am I so pleased?* she thought for an instant. But she stammered, "I don't have plans. Tonight would be fine.

Any particular reason so soon?"

"As a matter of fact, there might be something interesting happening," Westonfield replied. "I'm not sure, but we're going to check it out. Besides, like I said, I had an okay time."

"I didn't interfere then?" Magaly asked. "With the way you work, I mean? I was afraid you might be angry with me over— Well, I warned you! I'm blunt. Is that all right? That I'm blunt, I mean?"

"If it wasn't okay," Westonfield said, "would I be calling you? It's fine. It's even fair to say that I sometimes need someone to rein me in."

Magaly laughed. "What about Jack Rourke? He certainly seems to keep you in check."

"Yeah, he does," Westonfield said. "But he's not a girl."

"Oh," said Magaly, not knowing what else to say.

* * *

Magaly arrived half an hour early so she could observe roll call and get a look at what Westonfield and Rourke did to prepare for the eight hours of the working shift. When she walked into the office Rourke was sipping coffee and reading a report. He looked up, his eyes taking her in. "Now that's more like it," he said. "Now you're dressed for the street. Damned if you don't look like a regular lady copper. In fact, I hear they're hiring. You interested? I'll put in a word for you."

"I don't think so," Magaly said, laughing. But she did feel more comfortable. She was wearing blue jeans, a blue denim blouse, and jogging shoes. The front of her hair was held back by a headband, the rest of it swept back, spreading darkly over her shoulders. She sat in the old chair at Westonfield's desk. "Where's Bill?"

Rourke pointed down the hallway. "First door on the left. In the locker room. Go ahead, he ain't naked. Least I don't think so. Just give it a yell before you go in. Want a coffee first?"

"No, thanks, Jack. I just drank plenty. Maybe in a while."

She went down the hallway, pausing at the doorway Rourke had indicated. "Hello!" she called. "Anybody there?"

"Nobody important," came the reply. "Come on in."

Westonfield was alone, standing before an open locker, bare-chested and shoeless, clad only in faded blue jeans. He watched her enter and said, "I'm glad you could come."

He was one of a handful of men in Magaly's experience whose eyes revealed the nuances of their emotions more than their tone of voice, or whether they smiled or frowned. Westonfield's voice was measured, his mouth neutral. But his eyes said he was happy to see her.

Magaly was embarrassed to have caught him only partly dressed. The sight of his chest, its brown hair tinged with silver-grey, was unexpected and oddly disconcerting. She turned quickly and went for the door. "I'll come back in a minute."

"No, wait," Westonfield said. "It's all right. I'm just finishing up." He pulled a flannel shirt out of the locker and hurriedly thrust his arms into the sleeves.

Before Westonfield closed the shirt Magaly caught a glimpse of a silver religious medal dangling from a chain around his neck, and well below, nearly hidden in the thatch over his belly, a white, quarter-sized scar to the left of the navel. "You sure?" she asked.

"Yes. Stay." Westonfield pointed to the wooden bench that ran the length of the row of lockers. Magaly sat down facing him, straddling the bench.

Westonfield tucked in his shirt and pulled a pair of military jump boots from the floor of his locker. He slipped them on and sat down next to Magaly, deliberately lacing the boots. He could smell her perfume: ethereal, with the mingled scents of coconut and cloves. Caribbean. He remembered the way she had looked at him last night, just before going home.

"I'm glad you called," Magaly said. "There weren't any hitches last night that I could see. I feel good about it. We'll be fine. Maybe we can learn from each other."

"Maybe."

As Westonfield tied his laces, his leg came into contact with Magaly's. She could feel his warmth in the chilly room. One of the old frame windows was opened a crack and cool air streamed in. She knew he was attracted to her. Did he know that despite her many misgivings, she was attracted to him? She had little doubt that he did, recalling her own words: *He knows everything.* She pointed to his stomach. "Does that bother you? Does it ever hurt?"

He looked at her blankly for a moment. "Oh, you saw the scar. No. It doesn't hurt. Sometimes the waistband of my pants rubs against the scar tissue a little."

"Mmmm..." She watched him put on his holstered gun and speed clips and slip his handcuffs over his belt in the back, one cuff dangling down, the other beneath his waistband. The motions were compact and mechanical, accomplished without thought. He took his revolver out of its holster, careful to point it away from her, and checked the cylinder for a full load of cartridges. He spun it silently and closed it gently with his left hand until he heard the oiled metallic click of the latch. He returned it to the holster. "Almost ready."

She watched him take a bottle of Old Spice from the locker, shake a few drops onto his hand, and splash it on the back of his neck. He grinned his barely noticeable grin. "My kids. They get me a bottle every Father's Day."

"Actually I like it," Magaly said. "It reminds me of the Bay Rum my dad used to wear. I think he still wears it."

"A man of distinction."

Magaly raised her eyebrows. "Indeed. But I wanted to ask you— Watching you get dressed made me think of it. Why don't you wear a bulletproof vest? The department supplies them now, doesn't it? They're not mandatory?"

"They're not required. If you agree to accept one, then you have to wear it all the time; but if you decline it, then that's your own business."

"Why don't you wear one? Does Jack?"

"Neither of us do."

"Why?"

"I never thought about it, to tell you the truth," Westonfield said. "I suppose I just don't think it's necessary. I'm as careful as I know how to be."

"Doesn't every little bit help?"

"I'm still alive. So is Jack. Maybe we're too old to change. Maybe we can't change."

Magaly looked at him cryptically. "Can't? Why?"

Westonfield thought for a moment. "When it comes down to it, when it's your time to go, it's just your time to go. Wearing a vest isn't going to change anything. It might even make you careless. They can still shoot you in the head, or in the balls." He grinned. "Or through the openings at the sides. It happens every once in a while—through the side openings, that is…"

Magaly stood and shook her head with a mixture of amusement and incredulity.

Westonfield smiled with his eyes and ushered her back to the squad room.

In a few minutes the patrolmen began to drift in, casting curious glances in Magaly's direction. Westonfield held up his hand in response to their questions, saying, "Wait until everybody's here. I'll let you know in good time."

By 6:45 everyone was there, standing along the walls, perched on the desks, and leaning on file cabinets. Westonfield finally said, "In answer to your questions, gentlemen—and your admiring glances—I'd like to introduce Magaly Rodríguez. She'll be working with us for a while."

"Did you say *Miss* or *Ms.*, Sarge?" Arena asked, his eyes openly wandering over Magaly's curves. "You DEA, marshals or what, baby?"

Magaly looked pointedly at the young officer and said in Spanish, "I'm a writer, little billy goat. And if your dick was as big as your eyes, you might have something to offer me."

Westonfield had just taken a sip of coffee and he spit it halfway across the room. This is the girl whose sensibilities about obscene language he was concerned about? When he stopped laughing he translated for the rest of the group. There was a general chorus of delight and much ribald commentary at Arena's expense.

Arena hung his head in embarrassment. Magaly went to him and ruffled his hair. In English she said, "Don't worry, kiddo. It isn't over 'til it's over, right?"

Arena looked up and grinned. The rest hooted again.

"All right," Westonfield said, trying unsuccessfully to get the smile off his face. "That's enough horsing around. We've got a lot to cover, so let's get down to it." He scanned the group. "*Miss* Rodríguez is not a police officer. She is, in fact, a writer for *Harper's Magazine*. Any of you illiterates ever heard of it?"

Two or three nodded or waved their hands.

"Well, anyway, she's going to be spending some time with us. She'll be asking questions, looking at reports, observing roll call, and generally hanging out. She'll be hitting the street on occasion with either Sergeant Rourke or myself. Generally, answer any questions she has. If it gets sticky, as in a question about an informant or whatever, get back with me or Sergeant Rourke and we'll let you know. Any questions?"

In his thick southern drawl, Rupert Johnson said, "What all's she gonna write about, Sarge?"

"Why *us*, Rupe," Westonfield said. "Us."

Rourke interjected, "Any of you cowboys don't treat Miss Rodríguez here with respect, you better hope I don't hear about it. She ain't no narcotics cop. It'd be best to remember that."

Now it was Magaly's turn. She looked around the room at the young, expectant faces. "I appreciate Sergeant Rourke's concern, of course. But nothing could make me happier than you fellows just being yourselves. I'm the stranger here, not you. I'm intruding onto your turf, and I know that. You guys have one of the toughest jobs in the world. While it may seem to you sometimes that no one knows that, or even cares, I do. That's why I'm here." She looked at Westonfield. "I think your sergeant will tell you that you can trust me to be fair. The bottom line is that I want to write about what you really do every day, not what some bureaucrat downtown says. I believe that you deserve the recognition and I think the people have a right and a legitimate need to understand what their police officers actually do." She shrugged. "That's all I have to say. Please be yourselves and just forget that I'm even here. I promise I'll try not to get in your way."

She was not only pretty and smart, she was a tough customer, too, thought Westonfield. For a few seconds he found it hard to take his eyes off her. He pulled them away. "What I want to do tonight," he said, "is to set up a couple of surveillances, one over in Woodmere Cemetery and another on Merritt Street. As you know, Woodmere has been vandalized at least three times recently. Some dirt bag broke into four separate vaults and stole the bones of the deceased. Well, part of their bones, anyway—" He picked up a file report. "It says here they took the skulls, the ribs, the tibias, the fingers, and the toes."

Magaly's sudden, almost violent intake of breath was audible everywhere in the room. It was so noticeable it cut Westonfield off.

He looked up at her curiously. "Are you all right?"

Magaly nodded that she was, but she didn't say anything. Westonfield understood that something he had just said had caused the response, incongruous though it seemed to him, so he intuitively covered for her. "Something went down the wrong pipe?"

Magaly grimaced and looked at the floor. When she looked back up she said, "Yeah. I'll just get a sip of water. Sorry." As she stepped out of the room toward the hall drinking fountain she looked at Westonfield. Her eyes said *later*.

Westonfield went ahead, outlined the details of the plan and set the surveillance teams in motion, having provided, in addition to the file on the cemetery vandalism, the information gleaned from Katy Marroquín on the Merritt location. "If dispatch gives you any shit about signing on the MODATs, let me know. In the meantime, I'll call it in. You're covered." The crews went downstairs to draw their equipment and were soon on the street. Rourke went with them.

Magaly came right back, and when they were alone, Westonfield asked, "What was that all about? You look like you've seen a ghost." He went up to her and put the backs of the fingers of his right hand against her cheek. "You're as white as a sheet. Are you sure you're all right? You need to lie down?"

"No, I'm fine," she said. "But I was taken by surprise. I haven't seen a ghost, but I think I may have just heard about one."

Westonfield was nonplussed. "Riddles…"

"I'm sorry," Magaly said. "I don't mean to be difficult." She touched his hand.

Westonfield merely looked at her.

"Let me explain," Magaly said. "I grew up in Mexico. I lived there until I was nine. We lived in the city of Mérida in the Yucatán. Do you know it?"

"Yes."

"My father's family were prosperous business people there. Banking, real estate. They made a lot of money in the past ten years from the development of the so-called Gold Coast, down by Cancún."

Westonfield nodded his familiarity again.

"But my mother's people were poor. Mostly farmers. They grew sugar cane, sweet potatoes, and melons. My grandfather, my mother's father, was of Mayan blood. He farmed a plot of land he carved from the jungle nearly in the shadow of Chichén Itzá." Her eyes glowed when she thought of her grandfather. "I loved him very much. But the old man was a *Santero*. Are you familiar with this term?"

"A little," Westonfield said. "We run into it more and more now. We find the altars once in a while. Strange. I didn't think Mexicans went in for it, though—at least not back when your grandfather was farming the lands 'round Chichén Itzá."

"More practice it than you think," Magaly said. "You would be surprised to learn who practices the rites."

"Okay," Westonfield said. "But what about your grandfather?"

"He taught me a little about *Santería*, some of the ceremonies, the language, the history..."

"So this cemetery business sounds like *Santería* to you?" Westonfield asked. He thought for a moment. "All right, then. We can certainly use the help. Any knowledge you can share would be great. But why the reaction, Maggie? Look at you. You're still shaking." He touched her face again. "Vandalizing a grave is a stupid stunt. If we catch the bastard, I'll roast him. But I don't see the cause—"

"But a plain *Santero* wouldn't have stolen the bones you described," Magaly said. "He probably wouldn't even have taken the bones at all. Most of *Santería* is harmless really, and practiced for good ends. It's rarely used to hurt someone."

"It sounds almost like you believe in it yourself," Westonfield said.

"I told you I was close to my grandfather," Magaly replied, a little embarrassed. "I learned from him. He always said I had the *sight*."

"The sight?"

"He could see the future sometimes. Premonitions, you'd call them. He could read other peoples' feelings better than anyone I've ever known. He knew things that may seem—strange, did you say?"

Westonfield shrugged. "You can convert me later. What's your point?"

Magaly shook her head, sat in silence a moment. To even talk about it filled her with dread. Why this? Why now? She felt as if she were being pulled along, a path laid out before her, though she didn't know the way. It seemed to her that she had by some improbable twist of fate become part of a story already told. She was aware of forces building—powerful, frightening, and dangerous. It was as if she, Westonfield, Rourke and—someone, *something* else—were all bound together in some horrible tableau. Her eyes found Westonfield's momentarily, then flicked away. "Have you heard of *palo mayombe*?" Her voice was small and almost childlike.

"No. What is it?"

"You know *palo*?"

"Of course. Branch."

"*Mayombe* is an African word. Bantu. It means black. The color black."

"The Black Branch," Westonfield said. "What is it?"

"It's evil. It's sorcery, black magic, practiced by the Congos, the Bantus in Cuba." Magaly sighed, still pale. "I've heard that it's gaining influence, spreading... Do you believe in *evil*, Bill? Evil as a real, tangible thing?"

Westonfield looked at her with unwavering eyes. His eyes said both yes and no. In a moment he said, "What makes you think the cemetery thefts have anything to do with this Cuban cult? We don't even have that many Cubans here in Detroit. I wouldn't take it very seriously in any case. The people on Merritt are probably Cuban dope men, and that's bad news. It worries me. A lot of those guys are military-trained, real hard cases."

Magaly continued urgently. "The bones that were taken, Bill. That's how I know. Those exact bones are used in a rite the m*ayomberos* call 'the making of the *nganga*.'"

"The *nganga*?" Westonfield still found it hard to take Magaly seriously, despite her passionate reaction to the whole thing.

"It's a concoction they use to do bad things, to make spells to kill or destroy. I don't know very much about it. Mostly dark hints and anecdotes from my grandfather years ago. I remember one more thing, though: the moon. It's very important to them. All of their activities are tied to the phases of the moon. Spells can be cast only during the waxing phases. They can do little when the moon is waning. I don't think I can tell you much more."

"I can't see how a primitive cult can be much of a threat," Westonfield said. "I don't buy into any of it. It's all malarkey, Maggie. Merritt Street isn't the Borgo Pass, and Lon Chaney's dead." He was trying to lighten her mood with a little humor.

"But *they* believe it, Bill. That's what counts. The man who's doing this will go to any lengths to have his way. He'll do anything. Goodness is not known to these people, only evil. I hope I'm wrong. But I know I'm not."

"The sight again?"

Magaly nodded, still feeling the dread as her eyes were drawn again to Westonfield's. "What I just said about the moon—"

Westonfield smiled a bemused smile. "There's more?"

Magaly's eyes flicked to the calendar on the wall. "Today's the 20th day of October. Have you seen the moon? It's nearly full." She rose and walked over to the calendar, her finger tracing along the date boxes where the phases of the moon were printed in red. "In three days, on the 23rd, the moon will be at the full. That's the last day. After that the moon begins to wane again."

"And?"

"My heart tells me that before this is over, Bill Westonfield, you will know more of these things than Magaly." She wanted to tell him to be careful, but with Westonfield the admonition seemed peculiarly lame. He would resent it.

But Westonfield continued to stare silently at the calendar.

* * *

They collected Rourke and were out on the street by nine o'clock, Magaly in her usual spot in the back seat of the unmarked car. Westonfield was driving.

As they headed down Fort Street Magaly murmured a line of poetry under her breath, the prospect of *mayomberos* nearby heavy on her mind. In an almost inaudible voice she recited *"¿Qué es la vida? Un frenesí..."*

"What's that?" said Rourke.

"Oh, nothing. Just a snatch of rhyme."

"Well, let's hear it."

"It's in Spanish, Jack."
"That's all right. Go ahead. I'd like to hear it anyway."
"All right, then—
¿Qué es la vida?
Un frenesí.
¿Qué es la vida?
Una ilusión.
Una sombra, una ficción.
Y el mayor bién es pequeño,
Que toda la vida es sueño.
Y los sueños, sueños son."
Magaly watched Westonfield silently mouth the words. She had suspected he would know it. It was the famous last stanza of Pedro Calderón de la Barca's *La Vida es Sueño*.
"That was very nice," said Rourke. "I know a bit of poetry, too. Would you like to hear it?"
"Sure," said Magaly, intrigued.
Westonfield rolled his eyes.
Rourke screwed his face into his best imitation of a thoughtful and tortured James Dean in *Rebel Without a Cause*. To Westonfield he looked more like Oliver Hardy with bad constipation. "This is short, but powerful," Rourke said, then recited, "There we spied a nigger, with a trigger that was bigger, than an elephant's proboscis, or the whanger of a whale..."
Magaly laughed out loud. "Jack, it was beautiful."
"Damn right, it was. John Steinbeck wrote those words. It was in *The Grapes of Wrath*. Great book."
"Yes, it is a great book. But I don't remember that passage."
"Only because when you read the poem you didn't recognize it for its understated beauty," Rourke replied. "Go look it up. It's there."
Westonfield intervened. "It's there, Maggie. Don't bother. Jack recites it two or three times a week. He's very proud of it. The black guys on the shift especially like it, don't they, Jack?"
"Hell, yes, they like it," Rourke retorted. "Why wouldn't they? It's got a nice rhythm to it. It's earthy, and it's not prissy

like a lot of poetry. Besides that, it's a testament to the natural endowment of the black man." Rourke held his hands up about ten inches apart. "It's a matter of ethnic pride. And Steinbeck won the Nobel Prize for literature, too. He ain't no slouch."

"He's dead, Jack," put in Westonfield.

"Well, he wouldn't be a slouch if he was living, then."

Magaly reached forward and patted Rourke on the head. "I liked it, Jack. It was inspiring," she said.

Twenty minutes after they left the station Rourke retrieved a micro-cassette recorder from one of his large flapped jacket pockets and rubber-banded it to the sun visor in front of him. He pressed a button on the tiny silver box and at once the strains of *When Will I be Loved* by the Everly Brothers filled the car. Rourke began to caterwaul, "I've been cheated... been mistreated... when will I be loved?"

They listened to an eclectic selection of music from the 50s and 60s for the next four hours. As they patrolled through Del Ray, the music played and Rourke and Westonfield sang, sometimes separately, sometimes duets. They made light of it, a joke, but Magaly was delighted to discover that they actually sang quite well—both of them had good tenor voices, and they harmonized perfectly. She caught Westonfield looking at her a couple of times out of the rear view mirror. She was having fun. She knew they had accepted her.

"I think you're a good omen for us, Maggie," Rourke said. "Bill hasn't been this much fun in a year. Lately he's been mean as a snake." Rourke told funny stories about things he and Bill had done or seen, making Magaly laugh until her stomach hurt. "—then there was the time we got drunk with the firemen at the Riverside Park Station, by the river," he was saying. "They closed the building down a long time ago. Budget cuts. But they were a fine bunch of guys, those firemen. We used to play cards with 'em on the midnight shift. Anyway, one night in the summer we all took the fireboat out for a ride. We missed two police runs and almost swamped a big Bayliner off the tip of Belle Isle. Some shitbird at Harbormaster on the island saw us and turned us in. We lost three days on suspension." Rourke looked at Westonfield. "But it was fun, wasn't it? Worth every minute of the time off. Nobody does shit like that anymore."

None of them was hungry (which for Rourke was a landmark) so they didn't stop to eat a meal. But they went for coffee at Yum Yum's. The girl with the bad complexion was there and Rourke entertained her for half an hour. They responded to three radio runs, all family trouble, but there wasn't much to them. The radio was quiet: Sunday.

At one o'clock the dispatcher called them. "4-78? Radio 4-78?"

Rourke grabbed the mike. "4-78 by, radio."

"4-78, switch to channel five. Talk to 4-30." 4-30 was the call sign of the surveillance crew sitting on the Merritt house.

"Okay on 4-78."

Rourke reached down to the radio console, twirled a knob and watched the lighted dial change from the numeral 1, the normal Fourth Precinct radio district, to the numeral 5, the open channel for car-to-car communications. He picked up the mike again. "4-78 to 4-30, you copy?"

"4-30 here, 4-78," came the reply. The car was manned by Roberto Arena and a black officer named Benny Adams. "We just made a guy going into the house on Merritt. Looks like he's got a car full of boxes or something that he's carrying in. He's in the house now but he left the car door open, so I think he'll be coming back out pretty quick. Do you want us to talk to him?"

Westonfield looked at Rourke and said, "Tell 'em to hold on a minute, Jack. See if 4-31's on district five. Ask them if there's anything going on at the cemetery."

"Stand-by, 4-30," said Rourke into the mike. "4-31? You monitoring five?"

"Affirmative, 4-78," came the reply. "4-31 here."

"Anything going on at the ole graveyard, boys?"

"It looks quiet right now. We can't see all of the perimeter. This place is huge. But the main gate and all of the administrative buildings are secure. We've been driving all through the place, lights out. We haven't seen a thing."

"What do you think?" Rourke asked Westonfield.

"Tell 4-30 to wait a minute on their boy. Let's head down there, Jack. Have 4-31 stay put." They were on Michigan Avenue near Wyoming, about three miles from Merritt Street.

Rourke returned to the mike. "Stand-by, 4-30. We're heading that way."

A minute later the radio came alive again. "4-78? 4-30 here. Our man's back outside."

"Describe him, 4-30," said Rourke into the mike.

"Black, short, thin... hard to tell more from our eyeball position."

The information struck a discordant note in Westonfield. There was something about the situation that made him uneasy. "Tell them to be careful, partner. I don't like this."

"Use caution, 4-30. Are you sure you haven't been made?"

"Don't think so," came the reply. "I have a feeling this guy's Cuban, 4-78, like we talked about."

* * *

Gabriel had been watching the police car for ten minutes. He was hidden in the gloom of a clump of stunted trees next to a rusty fence, about eighty yards behind the police car. They were funny, these policemen. Did they really think they would catch him? They hadn't been here three seconds before he felt their presence.

The policemen were watching Tomás. Good thing there was nothing important in the boxes—a few empty cages, a live-trap, various packages of powders and oils—nothing that would link the house to him. The policemen were sure to arrest Tomás; that is, if he was intelligent enough to allow himself to be arrested. It would be better, really, if he did not. Tomás did not know Gabriel's true identity, but you could never tell. The police had their methods. How did they find this place so quickly?

Gabriel considered immediately shooting the policemen as

they sat in their car. He looked down at the AR-15 assault rifle in his latex-gloved hands. From this distance he could shoot them both through the head in about a second-and-a-half. No, it wasn't time for that. Soon, but not yet. The *bruja* whispered to him that this city was, indeed, the place where he was to accomplish his greatest feats, but the time was not yet come. Everything must be perfect. Then Zarabanda would come forth and walk among the world of men. The weather was getting colder already. Winter would come. The white snow would fall. No, killing the policemen now would only complicate matters. Soon.

* * *

They came rocketing south on Junction from Michigan Avenue, the big Chevy engine roaring, wind whistling through the cracks of the windows. From the back seat Magaly could see the red needle of the speedometer fluctuating near sixty. Junction was a residential street posted at twenty-five miles per hour. She held her breath. But the closer they got, the more overpowering Westonfield's sense of something gone awry drew him on, a fury of haste oppressing him.

Startling both Magaly and Rourke, Westonfield suddenly hit the brakes. Not hard enough to cause a skid, but hard enough to slam his companions forward violently in their seats. He came to a stop in the middle of the street three blocks north of Merritt.

"What the fuck are you doing?" shouted Rourke. "Trying to make me sick at my stomach? I feel like I'm on a goddamn rolly coaster. What did you stop here for? I thought we were in a hurry."

"It feels wrong, Jack. Can't say why yet." Westonfield's voice was very calm in contrast to Rourke's. His eyes scanned the darkness around the car as if they could pierce the shadows. "Listen. I'm getting out right here. I'm going to walk the last couple of blocks."

Rourke shook his head in exasperation but said nothing. When his partner got these peculiar notions in his head there was no dissuading him. Without further comment Westonfield got out of the car and Rourke slid over behind the wheel.

"Get back on channel five, Jack," said Westonfield, leaning in through the open door, "and tell Arena and Adams you'll be there in thirty seconds, and that when you get there you're going to grab the Cuban. Okay?" He looked across the back seat at Magaly and then back again. "Take her with you. Collar the asshole, shake him, and I'll be along in five minutes. I want to see what it looks like from the street up this way. And Jack—" he looked into the back of the police car.

Rourke nodded.

Magaly watched quietly.

* * *

Westonfield stalked deliberately southward, almost invisible in the deep shadows next to an abandoned warehouse, his jump boots nearly silent on the pavement. He watched the Chevy's taillights recede down Junction as Rourke drove toward Merritt. He continued walking until he came to the end of the warehouse. Past it there was a vacant field strewn with old tires, broken bottles, and an odd assortment of urban flotsam. About halfway between the end of the warehouse and Merritt Street, the field was bisected by a rusted chain-link fence. The fence itself was nearly obscured by a hedge of hawthorne and alder. Westonfield paused at the corner of the building, resting his shoulder against its faded brick, watching, listening. The sound of his own breathing was loud in his ears.

* * *

Rourke screeched west onto Merritt. Arena and Adams pulled out of their hiding place at the southern half of the field behind a mound of sand and roared out onto Merritt, bouncing over the high curb. Both police cars came to a halt some thirty yards from the Cuban, Rourke to the east and the other car to the west. The Cuban stood transfixed in their headlights, stock-still like a shined deer, a cardboard box in his arms. White dust billowed over him, kicked into the air and over the street by the furiously spinning tires of the police cars.

* * *

Westonfield heard the sharp *Pop!* of small-caliber pistol fire echoing the 150 yards across the field. He could see the cars and people on the street and sidewalk. Some were standing, some running, but the light was too dim and the distance too great to see who was shooting, or why. His instinct was to break for the sound of gunfire, but he remembered why he was here in the first place. He could feel a presence now, malignant and cold. He had to find it and deal with it before something even worse happened. Jack Rourke would have to take care of himself.

Even as Westonfield moved forward from the edge of the building into the field, his eyes picked out a patch of greater blackness imposed on the dark along the hedge. The shadow moved... moved again. For an instant the figure was silhouetted against the light between two trees. Whoever it was carried a rifle in his hands. Then the figure disappeared. The hair rose on the back of Westonfield's neck.

* * *

Magaly watched as Rourke hauled his large frame out of the scout car and began to walk toward the man holding the box. Arena and Adams came up on the other side, widely separated, revolvers in their hands. Rourke drew his own pistol, carried it pointed straight down. Then the man threw the box away and dived toward the car. He landed on his belly, his torso hidden behind the door, his legs sticking out. He reappeared almost instantly with a gun in his hand, crouching behind the car door.

Pop! Pop! Pop! Bright muzzle flashes flamed outward like Roman candles into the night, reaching for Rourke. Magaly's heart froze. Rourke must have been hit. He was so close!

Magaly's gut told her to dive for cover but she watched through the windshield, transfixed by the scene before her as the Cuban had been a moment earlier. She expected Rourke to scramble for cover as the Cuban had done, or *Please, God... No!* to fall. But if Rourke flinched or wavered, Magaly didn't see it. He brought his black pistol up in a two-handed grip and began to shoot. *Crack! Crack! Crack!* The report of his weapon was deeper and louder than that of the Cuban's gun. Rourke moved fast for a man so large. As he fired, the gun barely moved in his tight grip, though Magaly had seen men shoot before and knew that a large caliber handgun would buck upwards visibly with each shot.

The Cuban screamed an oath in Spanish, the agonized shout rending the air like a lost soul. Magaly saw the man writhing on the ground beneath the car door, the gun still in his hand, pointed at Rourke. After a pause of no more than a second, Rourke reacquired his target and fired again. *Crack! Crack! Crack! Crack! Crack! Crack!* Magaly could see dime-size holes appear in the open car door. The window glass exploded into a shower of glittering shards, catching the light from the street lights and flowering into the air like sparklers on the Fourth of July. Bits of metal ripped from the side-view mirror and ricocheted into the darkness, making whistling sounds.

Then the man lay still. From the Cuban's first shot until Rourke's last, perhaps five seconds had elapsed. Neither Arena nor Adams had fired a shot. There hadn't been time.

* * *

Westonfield was only thirty yards away when Gabriel saw him. It was only by chance that he did. A porch light came on at a house on Junction in response to Rourke's gunfire. When Gabriel turned momentarily in response, his eyes fell on the policeman. The pure shock nearly turned him to stone. His throat erupted in a primal scream of rage—was it fear? Never before in his life had he felt the humiliation of that emotion! He tossed the rifle away and ran.

Even as he coursed along the fence row, his legs pumping furiously, his mind raced desperately. How had this happened? The whole time he'd been chortling in self-satisfaction over finding the two policemen in the car and had snuck up behind them so easily, this other policeman had come upon *him*, found him in the dark. Why, by the blood of Zarabanda, hadn't he felt him approach? He forced the bad thoughts aside as he pelted toward Junction. His heart told him that he would need every ounce of his wits to escape from his unexpected predicament.

Westonfield saw the man throw the rifle and bolt. The fence enclosed the western end of the field so he doubted the man would head that way: a man might climb a fence when he came to it, but it would slow him down. Westonfield sensed that the man would head toward Junction. He was right. As he lurched into stride and paced after the Cuban he heard more shots reverberate from the direction of Merritt. No matter now. Nothing he could do. The chase was on.

Gabriel emerged from the field and ran onto Junction. He crossed the street and continued eastward on Merritt, skirting another warehouse on that side of the street. Westonfield was only twenty paces behind. But Westonfield wasn't young anymore. At forty-three his wind was no good. Gabriel began to pull ahead.

Westonfield was still only thirty paces behind when Gabriel reached the far corner of the warehouse and turned left. In the time it took to take two breaths Westonfield reached the corner behind him. If his ragged breathing had allowed it, he would have grinned with satisfaction. He knew this building and he knew that the man had fled into a blind alley—there was no outlet, the high walls of the storage buildings rose on all sides. The alley ended in an impenetrable wall of cement. The Cuban was trapped.

When Westonfield paused at the corner of the building for the barest fraction of a second, he eased his head past the brick façade just far enough to peer with one eye down the alley. He was stunned. The cul-de-sac was deserted. The man was gone. He thought at first that his eye was deceiving him. He looked again, his whole head emerging from behind the wall. Nothing. He stepped quickly out and walked warily down the alley, his .357 magnum at the ready. Had some workman left a door ajar, permitting the man to escape into a building? What rotten luck! But no, as he remembered, there were no doors, just the walls of the buildings... and the roofs were twenty feet in the air.

Westonfield walked all the way to the end of the alley, his eyes searching every corner and crevice. There were no parked cars. There were no trash dumpsters. There were no stacks of crates. The alley stood as clean and empty as an airplane hangar. There could be no mistake: the Cuban had simply vanished.

Westonfield holstered his revolver and stood for a moment in the darkness of the alley, the silence filling him. The cold, the sense of malignancy, was gone. But a trace of something intangible lingered in the air; a faint smell, so ethereal that he wasn't sure it was really there. He sought it, tried to identify it, finally lost it. He let the quiet and the silence fill him completely. After a while he smiled.

CHAPTER 14

The black eyes stared at her, through her. They had no pupils. The lids did not blink. The lips smiled a reptilian smile over yellow teeth. She was caught by the eyes, forced down, helpless. The eyes probed her mind, her soul, searching out her secrets. She resisted, twisting her head this way and that, like a little girl pinned to the ground by a bully, the bully's dirty hands crushing her wrists against the hard ground, his knees squeezing her ribs as he sat astride her, forcing the air from her lungs, suffocating her.

The urgent chanting filled her ears, the same alien words over and over, guttural and fierce: *Aguanilleo Zarabanda aribo, aguanilleo Zarabanda aribo...* She tried to understand, the words flirting with her consciousness, but each time the words began to form images in her seething mind the putrid breath of the bully distracted her, or the blackness of the depthless eyes seared her, and the images faded away into nothingness, their meaning lost. *Aguanilleo Zarabanda aribo.* In the dream she screamed.

Much later Magaly awoke to blue sky, and lemon-yellow autumn sunlight sifting into her room through the huge window. She stared out into the infinite pastel heavens for a moment, trying to remember where she was. The sun felt warm and caressing on her upturned face. Then she remembered.

She stretched her tea-brown legs over the sheets, her hands gently sliding over her breasts, across the flat of her belly, over the soft mound of her vulva and on to her legs. There was no reason to turn back the bedding, she had thrown it completely off the bed during her dream. The dream. What did the words say? Sadly, or mercifully, the chanted words were already fading from memory, like so many leaves in the wind, scattering and skittering away, teasing her mind until they were gone.

Last night. My God, last night! She raised her head to look at the clock. One o'clock. She dropped her head back down. She suddenly had a cracking headache, the whole top of her head felt as if it was going to come off. She lay still and let the sweat dry on her naked body, watched it glisten on her brown nipples, pool in the shallow well of flesh surrounding her navel. She lay safe and quiet in the softness of the sheets for another hour, drifting into sleep again. When she awoke it was after two o'clock. Her nipples were erect and there was warmth and wetness between her legs. This time she had been dreaming of Bill Westonfield. She swore an oath, castigated herself on her weakness, and stumbled into the shower.

It was three o'clock when she called Westonfield's number. No answer. She hung up, called Rourke's number.

"Yeah." Westonfield's voice.

"Bill, this is Magaly. Uhhh... What's going on?" The words rushed out breathlessly.

"Drinkin'."

"What?"

"Drinkin'."

"Drinking?"

"Getting drunk."

"Oh—" Pause. "But it's three o'clock. Oh—"

"Can't drink at three?"

"Well, I suppose you can."

"Drinkin'. Gettin' drunk," Westonfield repeated laconically.

"Just the two of you?" Magaly asked.

"Yep."

"From the sound of it, it seems like you started a while ago."

"Yep."

"Can I come over?"

"Don't think so."

"I'd like to."

"Don't think so," Westonfield repeated.

"Need company, maybe?"
"Got company. Me and Jack."
"Is Jack drunk?"
"Believe so."
"You?"
"Believe so."
"I'm coming over," Magaly said.

* * *

Rourke lived by himself in a rundown brick bungalow on the east side, near City Airport. In reality, he lived by himself only on his work days. He usually strung together his days off in groups three or four at a time, so that he could visit his wife and kids in their real home—Brown City, in Michigan's *thumb*. Like hundreds of other white cops, Rourke played the semi-legitimate "dual residency" game so as to comply technically with the department's Detroit-only residency policy.

Magaly waited on Rourke's front porch for five minutes after repeatedly ringing the bell and banging on the window. She was afraid neither of them would come to the door and let her in, either too drunk or too willful to do it. Finally she heard some stirring and the sound of footsteps approaching from inside. The door was opened by Westonfield. He looked at her, said nothing, but stepped aside and let her in.

She walked into the living room. Rourke was ensconced on a worn sofa which had seen better days, its stippled texture worn away, its original beige faded to a dirty brown. He looked up at her and smiled. "Hi, Mags. How're ya doin'?" he asked, quite drunk. He was wearing a tee shirt with the words *I'm Rowdy Roddy Piper, And You Are Not* printed in black letters across the front. A caricature of the irreverent wrestler was emblazoned below the words.

Westonfield followed her in, jerking his thumb at a stuffed chair which was the match of the sofa Rourke was draped across. He sat unceremoniously on the floor with his back against a bookshelf a few feet across the room so that he could see both Magaly and Rourke. Magaly sat down in her designated chair.

"Want a beer?" Rourke asked.

"Sure," Magaly said.

Rourke nodded up and down once, but he made no attempt to get up to retrieve the beer.

Westonfield pointed toward the kitchen door. "'Fridge is in there."

Magaly went into the kitchen, helped herself to a Stroh's Light, and returned to the living room, taking a gulp before she sat down. Cold. Good. She noticed the music for the first time. Enya. The music flowed from a battered cassette player in the corner. Soft. Beautiful. Magical. Magaly wondered sometimes whether the Irish people sprang from the music, or whether the music sprang from them.

The three sat in silence for a long moment. "See-no-evil, Hear-no-evil, and Speak-no-evil," Magaly finally said. "Here we are. Is this a wake?"

Silence.

Rourke held a bottle of Irish whiskey in his right hand. It rested comfortably, steadied between his fat legs. He was wearing a pair of worn cotton chinos and his red-grey chest hair poked over the top of the stretched neck of the tee shirt. He shrugged, remained silent.

Magaly turned to Westonfield. "Well?"

"Jack's gonna be off for a few days," he said. "Administrative leave: fatal shooting. Prosecutor's review. We're just keeping each other company." He looked at Rourke who seemed oblivious of them, taking long pulls on the bottle, listening to the music. "Company," Westonfield repeated. He smiled the smile that brothers smile to each other in secret. He returned his glassy eyes to Magaly. "Back to work for *me* tomorrow."

Magaly said nothing. Enya sang. The three friends drank. Jack finished the bottle, a half-smile on his bearded face, his head cocked down and to the side. He was asleep, breathing softly. Enya played.

"So what happens tomorrow then?" Magaly asked Westonfield. "Are you and me still out and about?" After five beers, she was feeling a little woozy.

"Suppose so," Westonfield said. "Deal, right?"

"Deal," she answered.

Westonfield looked at her searchingly. Even when he'd been drinking he was hyper-aware, Magaly understood. "Gotta stay here tonight, though," he said cryptically.

"Oh?"

"Uh-huh. Gotta stay."

"Jack?"

"Yep."

* * *

Magaly's mind drifted back to the previous night, just after the shooting, when Westonfield had come walking out of the darkness into the circle of light. It had been one of the most remarkable couple of hours of her life. Everything had slowed down to almost surreal slow motion. Everyone talked softly, slowly, deliberately. Everyone walked as if they were on eggshells. In contrast with the shooting itself, which had taken place in a moment and seemed to take mere split seconds, it was almost comical, like a skit from *Saturday Night Live.*

For one thing, she had expected Bill to run up to Jack, frantic with worry, to see if he was all right. *Hardly.* Westonfield had this silly grin on his face which, oddly, seemed to have nothing to do with the horrible bloody scene on Merritt Street. He had simply materialized from the dark like an apparition, glanced at Rourke, glanced at all the rest of the officers, glanced at her, taken in the scene, and then turned back to stare into the night out of which he had come. He didn't say a word.

Rourke himself poked around by the Cuban's body, idly kicking at bits of glass and metal with the toe of his shoe, talking quietly with Arena and Johnson and the others. Sirens were coming from everywhere, but they all ignored them. Only when a lieutenant and an inspector arrived, took charge of the homicide scene, made notifications, and started asking questions, did Westonfield break out of his reverie and start talking to her.

"Where have you been?" Magaly asked.

"Chasing someone," Westonfield said. "Chasing our man. It was him. I know it. But he's gone. Got away. Disappeared."

It was impossible for Magaly to gauge his mood. She finally said, "Well, it's dark. It'd be easy. I guess it happens, huh?"

"No, I mean he *disappeared*," Westonfield said. "He vanished. He ran down a deadend alley. I had him. I really had him. He was cornered. Then he was…gone."

"Well, he couldn't just—"

"But he did." Westonfield turned again and looked into the night. "He did, Maggie."

Not for the first time did a thrill of fear run up Magaly's spine. She shivered violently, her heart turned suddenly cold. "It's him, then. As you say, Bill."

Westonfield quietly nodded.

Before the arrival of the homicide team, the lieutenant, with the consent of the inspector, took initial steps to preserve evidence and organize the scene. First, Westonfield ordered a car to go back up to the vacant lot where he had discovered the man hiding and to secure the area. The scout car crew found the rifle the suspect had thrown away, nestled among some weeds. They let the weapon lie where they found it, and waited impatiently for it to be photographed, measured, and ultimately retrieved and tagged by responding evidence technicians.

Next the lieutenant requested a K-9 unit to come out to the scene to attempt a track of the suspect. The dog handlers arrived within a few minutes and were directed to the waiting officers along the fence line in the vacant lot. The dog, a big German shepherd, immediately picked up a scent from the ground, as well as from the rifle. He pulled eagerly at his leader and struggled against the leash, pulling his handler along at a trot. "Find him, Rocky," urged the handler, a young cop whom, to Magaly, looked like Andy Garcia. "Find him, boy!"

Within the next twenty minutes the homicide team arrived and ordered Rourke, as the shooter, and all of the witnesses downtown. Standard procedure. As a witness, Magaly would have to go as well. She asked for, and was granted, permission to await Westonfield's return before going. Fifteen minutes later, three police cars pulled away, heading up Junction toward Michigan Avenue. Magaly stood on the sidewalk in front of the house, watching the goings on. Rourke peered out at her from the semi-darkness of the back seat of the police car. He winked, smiled, and gave her a thumbs up.

The homicide team began a canvass of the neighborhood. They secured the scene. They called a judge for an emergency warrant to search the Merritt house.

Westonfield and the dog handler arrived back at the scene about the same time the search warrant arrived. Magaly took notes, and Westonfield stood quietly to the side. The handler reported that the dog had followed a strong scent all along the route Westonfield had taken in pursuit of the man, all the way into the deadend alley and down to its end. The dog had sniffed nervously along the blank wall for a moment and then sat on its haunches, staring straight ahead: it was trained to do that after locating the person it was looking for. It was doing its job. *"There,"* the dog was saying. *"There he is—in the wall."* Andy Garcia didn't know what to make of it.

Then they searched the house.

It was a two-story frame home typical of the neighborhood: vintage 1930s; faded paint; gutters askew; roofed porch across the entire front; no more than five feet of space between each house on the row. The shaded windows frowned down on them mournfully.

Westonfield asked Magaly to stay outside until an initial search was conducted—for two reasons. First, to make sure there was no danger; and second, to make sure no evidence was disturbed. Magaly assented without protest. She had terrible feelings about the place. It simply reeked of evil. She gladly remained outside with a uniformed patrolman while Westonfield, the homicide team, and two evidence technicians went up the steps and approached the front door.

There was no need to force entry. The weathered door stood ajar just as the Cuban had left it. Two homicide detective sergeants went first, followed by Westonfield and then the evidence techs. As Magaly watched with a mixture of concern for the officers and intense anticipation of what they might find, the men disappeared into the gloom within. For a moment the flickering light of their flashlights illuminated the interior with a pale glow, visible through the dingy windows. The house looked to Magaly like a giant, tortured Hallowe'en jack o'lantern, the upper windows the eyes, the transom the nose, and the door the mouth. She closed her eyes and suppressed a shiver. Then someone turned the lights on inside and the illusion vanished.

Less than ten minutes later Westonfield emerged through the door and onto the porch. His eyes found her in the darkness and he motioned for her to come up. Magaly grimaced, thrust her notepad and pen into the pocket of her jacket, and timidly ascended the rickety wooden steps to the porch.

"Nobody's left inside," Westonfield said, taking her by the arm. "But you need to see what else is in here."

They entered into the shabby foyer. Dread immediately fell on Magaly. She was almost crushed. "This is a bad place," she said softly, as if to herself. "Things have been done here. Things have happened here that have left their mark." She clutched his arm, her fingernails digging into his wrist.

Westonfield made no response other than to guide her across the nearly empty living room to a staircase that led to the second floor. When they were halfway up he said, "It's up here. In one of the bedrooms."

Then they were inside the bedroom and before them was the altar. An old credenza stood against the wall opposite the door, its walnut veneer scarred and stained by years of hard use. On its surface was an array of candles, black and green, some melted low, others yet unlit. In the center was a black iron cauldron. An assortment of dried animal skins, shards of stone, feathers, and colored powders took up the rest of the space.

Magaly blanched and wouldn't go near. Westonfield was anxious for her to see the material and didn't immediately understand the depth of her loathing, the paralysis of alarm that transfixed her. He pulled her by the arm like a little boy dragging his mother to see Santa.

Magaly suddenly screamed. She tried to suppress it, thought she had, then failed in one miserable moment. She felt the shriek rise in her throat involuntarily and issue forth with a life of its own.

Westonfield dropped her arm and gaped at her. The other cops came running to the room.

Magaly averted her eyes from the altar, smothered an overwhelming urge to flee, caught her breath, and managed to get out, "Oh, jeez, I'm sorry. Damn it! I'm so sorry..."

Westonfield motioned for the others to go back about their business. They left with *what the hell is this dizzy broad doing here?* looks on their faces. Magaly's embarrassment and humiliation were profound. She looked at Westonfield, shame in her eyes, her face flushed red. "Sorry," she mumbled again. She searched his eyes for what she assumed would be there: contempt and rejection. She was surprised to find both of them absent. There was confusion, but beneath there was only concern.

Retaking her arm, Westonfield ushered her to a chair in a far corner of the room. He intentionally positioned his body so as to block her view of the altar. He raised his eyebrows and the grey eyes asked, *Well?*

Magaly ran her hands over her face. "It's him," she said finally. "This is the center." The words came out slowly, measured, as she struggled to control her speech lest the words tumble out and the near hysteria return. She fought the bitter taste of bile in her mouth, swallowed, swallowed again. "But it *is* him," she said. "Here, in this place. There's *power* here... forces... bad forces. Terrible things have been done here, or the will to do terrible things lives here, in this room and within these walls. He's not alone now, Bill. He's... he's done something awful.

Something unholy. Do you understand? I don't know how to say it, let alone help you feel how *I* feel—"

Magaly reflexively glanced toward the window, hoping to catch a glimpse of the outside world. She found only the shuttered window. She looked back at Westonfield. "He's called forth help from his world. The *other* world. I feel it. I hear it buzzing in my ears." She sought the words carefully. "Like a change in air pressure, almost. You know how when you change altitude in a plane, or even when you're in a car and you climb a hill? Like that. Only—" She paused when she saw that it was too much for Westonfield to accept—too far out, too primitive, too obscure. The fact that his amusement appeared to be couched in genuine concern spared her little. "You wanted to know, so I'm telling you," she ended lamely.

Westonfield forced the amusement he did, indeed, feel off his face the best he could. But Maggie's intuition about one thing was right: he *was* concerned. "Go ahead, Magaly," he said. "Please." He unconsciously reached out and brushed away a strand of hair that had fallen across her forehead. The fact that he did this precisely as she often did herself somehow didn't surprise Magaly.

"That's all," Magaly said, forcing a weak smile. "I told you I'm not any kind of expert." Then, glumly, "I'm sorry I embarrassed you. I don't suppose the show I put on helped my standing around here."

"They'll get over it," Westonfield said. "It's not a big thing."

"I hope they'll get over it," Magaly said. "But I'm not sure I will. I've let you down. I promised you I'd stay out of the way, not attract attention, let you do your work, let everyone do their work. Before this day's over, I'll be known as 'the girl who screamed on Merritt Street.'"

Westonfield cast a final thoughtful glance at the unsettling altar and then led Magaly back down the stairs. They had seen enough, done enough, for one day. He'd let the techs do their job. They'd catalogue everything, measure everything, photograph everything, print everything, and bag everything. Tomorrow would be a new day.

* * *

Magaly's mind drifted back to the present. Rourke's house. The next day. "So you're staying here tonight?"

Westonfield looked at Rourke, who by then had fallen asleep on the floor, propped up against the sofa. He had slid down in stages as Magaly and Bill talked, in and out of sleep, first slouching against a pillow, then lying down. He found it was too difficult to take pulls on the bottle when prone, so he finally slid off the sofa altogether and sat on the floor, leaning back against the cushions. Then he went to sleep with the bottle wedged between his legs, his head lolled over onto his shoulder, his mouth open, snoring softly.

"He's all right now," Westonfield said. "Help me get him to bed." He bent over his partner and ran his fingers through his hair, combing through it gently with his fingertips. It was unkempt from all the tossing and turning on the sofa. Seeing Bill do that reminded Magaly of the way her father used to do it with her little brothers. The old man would faithfully tuck them in at night, and then he would smooth their wayward hair with his fingers. She was struck by Westonfield's act of familiar affection, performed so casually. It was an odd counterpoint to Westonfield's natural masculinity: it was an almost feminine act.

Westonfield shook Jack by the shoulder until his eyes popped open. The Irishman looked at them with bleary eyes. "Hummm. What?"

"Bedtime, Jack," Westonfield said.

"What time is it?" asked Rourke.

"Bedtime."

Magaly and Westonfield each took an arm, hoisted Rourke to his feet and ushered him into his bedroom. He didn't protest further.

Back in the living room Magaly asked, "Will he be okay now?"

Westonfield was standing by the open front door. He either didn't hear her, or he chose to ignore her, because he opened the screen door and went out onto the porch without an answer.

Magaly followed. "Bill?"

He was looking upward, watching a small commuter plane make its approach toward the airport. It was almost six o'clock in the evening and the sun was westering. The plane was coming in from the east, into the red sun. A few clouds drifted overhead, grey-tinged and tattered, like the ragged sails of a pirate ship. "What?"

"I asked you if Jack was okay."

Westonfield sat down on one of the two folding chairs Rourke kept on his front porch. Magaly sat next to him. "You think this shit bothers him?" he asked after a little while, still looking at the sky.

"Well, he's drunk," Magaly said. "He's drinking for a reason. I guess it does bother him. How couldn't it? I didn't do anything but watch and I'm still shaking."

Westonfield looked at her. "Jack doesn't give a shit about that dead Cuban fuck," he said. He returned his gaze to the heavens.

They sat in silence for a while and watched the daylight die in the east and the twilight spread its fingers westward across the purple sky.

Ten minutes later Magaly said, "Jack did what he had to do. I know that."

"The Cuban was a piece of shit. Now he's a *dead* piece of shit," Westonfield said.

Magaly shrugged, not knowing what else to say.

After another long while Westonfield said, "Go home now, Maggie. Thanks, but you can go home now."

"All right, Bill," Magaly answered quietly. "Jack's asleep. We can go now. I've had less to drink than either of you. Let me drive you home. Or I'll follow you home?"

"I told you I'm staying," Westonfield said.

"But—"

Westonfield cut her off. "Thanks for caring as much as you do, Maggie. I know now you're not just here for the story. You're here for me and Jack, too. I know that. But I'm going to stay. I've *gotta* stay."

Magaly touched his face. "Won't you tell me why?"

Pause. "Can't."

"Tell me."

Silence.

"Bill?"

Silence.

"I've earned it, haven't I?" Magaly asked, her frustration showing, her emotions raw after all of the events of the last twenty-four hours. She was tired, she couldn't get Westonfield to talk, and a man she'd grown fond of was lying drunk in bed, having shot a man to death the night before.

Silence.

"I thought we had a deal," Magaly went on. "I'm here to learn the truth. I'm here to learn the story." Her voice began to crack. Her eyes flooded. "Then I'm going to go back and *tell* the story. I'm going to tell the whole goddamned country about the shit you and Jack put up with every day." Her eyes brimmed over and tears ran down her cheeks. She flicked them away. "But you won't help me! You won't even talk to me. I don't...*know*, Bill. I'm not a cop. I can't will myself to have experiences I've never had. I need you to teach me. I need for you to shake me and say, *See, Magaly, this is the way it fucking is!* But I can't do it without you. I can't tell the story without you."

Westonfield looked at her and smiled, the hard, painful knot within him letting go for the first time in a long time. He said nothing, but his eyes said she was right, that it would be different now.

Magaly let the anger and frustration slowly drain away. She swallowed. Then she returned his smile with a wan one of her own. "You're the story, Sergeant Westonfield. I'm just the storyteller," she said.

"I'm gonna check on Jack," said Westonfield. He motioned for her to follow.

Jack was still sound asleep. He was flat on his back, his arms flung wide, snoring like a buffalo bull. They returned to the living room.

"This isn't about that Cuban, Magaly," Westonfield said, dropping onto the sofa. "This is about…something else. It's about—the *woman*."

"The woman," Magaly said, sitting next to him.

"Yeah. The woman. The lady at the edge of the bed."

"Who is she?"

"Who *was* she. We killed her."

Magaly's eyes widened. Mysteries within mysteries…

"We shot her a couple of years ago," Westonfield said. "Fifty-two-year-old woman. Mother. Grandmother. We shot her."

Magaly shook her head in confusion.

"She had a gun," Westonfield continued. "She was going to kill her grandkids. She shot her boyfriend right in front of us and then turned the gun on us. We couldn't do anything. We were too far away. We screamed at her to drop the gun. She wouldn't. We begged her over and over. But she just wouldn't drop it, Magaly." He lifted a glass from the end table next to him and took a sip of warm beer. "She haunts Jack now. She comes in the night. She comes and looks at him from the foot of the bed."

"Nightmares," Magaly said quietly. "That's so sad…poor Jack."

"Nightmares? No, she *comes*. Dead, bloody, and serene as a quiet lake she comes, Magaly." His voice was cold and flat, devoid of emotion.

"How long has this been going on?"

"Ever since we killed her," Westonfield intoned. "Ever since. But it's worse when something like this happens. It's not the Cuban—Jack would bury the scumbag himself. But this will remind him of it. It'll all come back now. Then she'll be there, watching."

"If it's that bad, why hasn't Jack tried to get help from the department?" Magaly asked. "Professional help."

Westonfield sighed. "What help? There's no help for that."

"Well, there's you—"

"Just me."

"So you're Jack's medicine for melancholy?" Magaly pondered everything for a moment. Westonfield always took care of everyone: Jack, his policemen, his own children. Father Lewendowski and Tom Bacon both told her that it was fundamental to Bill's nature, perhaps the most basic part of his character. He took care of people. The utter isolation of it must be overwhelming sometimes. Bill instinctively put himself in a place where no one else could go. And in the few days she had known him, she had never once seen anyone do anything for *him*. Not once. He was the sun in his own solar system, and the planets revolved around him, his gravity holding them on course. What must it be like to live in a universe entirely of one's own creation, apart, alone? Bill was strong, but was he strong enough? Didn't he have the right to have nightmares, if nightmares were what was supposed to come after something terrible happened? Didn't he have the right to be weak, to fail, to have a friend brush back *his* hair?

"So, you'll take the first watch," Magaly said to him at last.

"Yes."

"What about you, Bill Westonfield? Who watches over you?"

She might as well have asked him about the atomic number of lead.

"The rock?" she asked.

"What?"

"You. The Rock of Gibraltar."

"I don't know what you're talking about."

"Yes, you do."

"Let it be, why don't you, Magaly," Westonfield said uncomfortably.

"Why do you want me to let it be?" Magaly asked. "Because it hurts too much?"

"Let it be, I said."

"You need someone to watch over you, Bill."

"Bullshit."

"They use you, Bill, the people in your life. Every single one of them. I've seen it in the short time I've been here. They don't mean to, and they can't help it. But they do it."

"Well, you're wrong."

"It's your fault, you know," Magaly persisted.

"What?"

"Yes. You set yourself up for it and people who are weaker than you gobble you up."

"Fuck you."

"All of them need you—but not *you*; you don't need *them*."

"You're out of line."

"But you do need someone to watch over you, Bill. All of us do. You're wounding yourself like an animal caught in a trap. You invented the one-way street. Why don't you un-invent it?"

"You don't know what you're talking about."

"Answer me! I've asked you a simple question. Who watches over you, Bill?"

"Now? No one."

"What about before, then?"

"I don't know."

"Susan?"

"Maybe. A long time ago."

"Millie?"

"That was then, this is now." He looked away.

Magaly suddenly gave up, beginning to feel guilty. Who was she to tell him to be one way instead of another? He was a thoroughly remarkable man. His isolation and stolid confidence were two of the things that made him who he was. Better to let it be.

"Stubborn bastard," she said mildly.

They carried beer bottles into the kitchen and straightened up the best they could. This simple act seemed important to Bill—cleaning, ordering, straightening. In the end, despite his insistence, Magaly refused to go home. She took Jack's extra bedroom. Westonfield slept on the couch, passing the night in fitful sleep, watching, waiting impatiently for *the woman* to come: the lady at the edge of the bed.

CHAPTER 15

"It's Tuesday morning!" shouted Herman Vickers, Magaly's editor at *Harper's*, over the telephone. "It's fucking Tuesday morning! What the hell are you up to? You're in that hole of a town a goddamn week—" he looked at the calendar on the wall of his office and absently wiped the spit off his chin "—a week today, as a matter of fact, and you've already nearly got your ass shot off. What the hell's going on? You're supposed to be interviewing cops and their families and researching the archives and looking at training classes, Magaly, not getting in goddamn shootouts in the ghetto." He was livid, had to stop to catch his breath. "And why haven't you been calling the office like you're supposed to? Every day, remember? Every *goddamn* day! Not twice a week, not every other day. Every fucking day!" He paused again, retrieved a handkerchief from the pocket of his suit jacket and wiped his chin. He had a tremendous overbite and when he got excited he sprayed saliva on everything within five feet, including people, if there were any unfortunate enough to find themselves within spitting distance.

"Herman, calm down," Magaly soothed. "I'm all right. I'm fine. I wasn't even scratched. I know you want to know what's going on, so if you'll calm down a minute I'll try to get you up to speed." She liked and respected Vickers, a veteran newspaperman about sixty years of age, but he was old-fashioned, paternalistic, and very protective. Magaly knew that if she were a man, Vickers would have been pleased as punch that she'd been so close to the action. She went on patiently, "I've been busy, to say the least, boss. I've gone nocturnal. I feel like I'm a fucking bat. I've been out on the street with these guys a couple of times—

7:00 o'clock at night 'til three in the morning, you know? I sleep in in the morning after that, and I've been going non-stop every day since I've been here with meetings, interviews, and presentations. I'm tired."

"You're tired," retorted Vickers. "You're too tired to make a simple goddamn phone call? Don't do this to me, Magaly. You hear me? Don't play that shit with me. I don't know how I can make this any clearer: you are to call every day! What about that don't you understand?"

"I do understand."

"What did you say?"

"I said I understand, Herman. I'll try to do better."

"You'll try?"

"Gimme a break, will you, Herman? I *will* do better. Okay?"

"All right then. Now tell me all about it. Everything."

She told him.

* * *

It was eleven o'clock in the morning on the twenty-second of October. It was raining torrents outside Magaly's window at the Pontch. The telephone call she'd made to Westonfield an hour earlier was still unanswered. She'd slept fitfully at Rourke's home the night before and had awakened sore and cranky. To her surprise, at 7:00 A.M. both Rourke and Westonfield were up, eating a huge breakfast of eggs, potatoes, bacon, and toast: it was the smell of the food that woke her up. They'd let her sleep. She took a quick look into Rourke's bathroom mirror. She was a mess. Her hair was a tangle, her mascara was smeared and her eyes were bloodshot. Her clothes were wrinkled. All in all, she felt like shit. Oh, well! She joined them at the table after first drinking a cup of strong black coffee. She ate like a pig.

After breakfast, Rourke said he was going to pack up and leave for a couple of days to visit his family in the Brown City. Westonfield said he'd take the day off, too, and spend some time with his kids after school. First he had to go home to cut his grass and do some laundry. Magaly was free to go down to the station and see what was up or to do whatever she wanted, he said.

She said she'd think about it. What she really wanted was a hot shower. Nothing was said about the shooting. Nothing was said about the night before. Westonfield promised he would call her if anything came up. Then she'd left.

Magaly emerged from the shower a new woman. She'd tried Bill at about ten o'clock, had left a message on his machine. Still no return call. He could still be at Jack's. He could be anywhere. She flipped idly through some television channels for half an hour and then turned the TV off and went to the big window and watched the rain. It swept in curtains across the river and obscured the Canadian shore. Hart Plaza was deserted. A few pre-noon-hour pedestrians struggled against the wind, trying to get to their offices or to lunch without getting entirely soaked. Buses, taxis, and cars inched along East Jefferson, their windshield wipers beating against the downpour.

After a while, Magaly made a long distance phone call to her brother Aurelio in the hospital in New York City. He was an AIDS patient there, in the terminal stages. Her throat caught when she heard his voice on the telephone. He had been so strong and vital before he got sick. He was a stock broker on Wall Street and lived in a beautiful apartment in Manhattan overlooking Central Park. He was dark and handsome, with thick black hair and a perfect smile. He would have been a lady killer had that interested him. Not much interested him anymore.

"Hi, big brother," Magaly said.

"Hey!" Aurelio responded happily. He was always delighted to hear from his sister. He adored her. He even loved the sound of her voice. "How's things among the great unwashed, Sis? You all right?" He spoke deliberately and his voice was soft, almost a whisper.

"You wouldn't believe, *'mano mio!*" Magaly said, and she told him some of what had happened to her, leaving out details of the shooting and the information about the *mayombero*. Aurelio didn't need to hear about that.

Aurelio suspected she wasn't telling him everything there was to tell but he didn't bother asking her about anything. If she wanted him to know, she would tell him. She was willful that way, and in any case he was too tired. "I miss you, Magaly," he said.

"Miss you, too."

"Have you talked to *Papá*?" he asked.

"Before I left for Detroit," Magaly said. "You?"

"He called day before yesterday. He's doin' okay. Misses Mexico. The old places."

"Well, he's not a Mexican anymore."

"Sure he's a Mexican, Magaly. He'll always be a Mexican."

"Oh, I know it, 'Relio. I know. But he's got money. He can do anything he wants."

"He wants to be in Mexico," Aurelio said.

"I guess that apartment in Mérida isn't exactly his cup of tea, eh?"

"No."

"I think I'll call again," Magaly said. "Soon. I want to talk to him about some things. Remember the magic he used to talk about?"

"Well, it was you who were his father-in-law's star pupil. But, sure, I remember."

Magaly hesitated. "Do you believe in ghosts, Aurelio?"

"Haven't seen one lately, Magaly. But you're the *Santera*. Why ask me?"

"Just being silly, brother. Aren't I always silly?"

"One of the reasons I love you."

"So how are you, Aurelio?" Magaly asked, changing the subject. "Getting stronger?" He sounded weaker.

"About the same. I haven't been outside in days. It's just too goddamn hard. I got no wind."

Magaly could, indeed, hear her brother struggle for breath as he talked. "Well, I just wanted to hear your voice, 'Relio, and see how you were. I don't want to tire you out."

"That's all right. I miss hearing your voice. You have such a pretty voice. Do you still sing sometimes?"

"Sometimes." She was afraid he would ask her to sing.

He smiled, remembering, said nothing for a long moment.

"Aurelio?"

"Yeah, I'm here."

"Are the doctors and nurses treating you well? They better be!"

"Sure they are, Magaly," he said, chuckling. "They see a lot of cases like mine. You know that. They're great. They really are."

"Is there anything I can do, 'Relio? Anything at all?" She felt helpless, desperate to help him in some way, any way.

"Just what you're doin', Sis. Talk to me."

"But I don't want to tire you."

"You don't tire me. If there's one thing I miss most, it's talking to you."

"Me too, 'Relio. Ohhh...me too!"

"I've been reading a lot lately," he said. "Not much else to do. Can't stand the goddamn TV."

"Me neither. What are you reading?"

"Just bits and pieces of things. I don't seem to be able to concentrate enough to read anything very long. I was reading this article in *National Geographic* yesterday. It was about railroads."

"Railroads?"

"Well, not really railroads. It was actually about flowers," Aurelio said.

"What do railroads have to do with flowers?" Magaly asked.

"That's the thing," he said. "That's the most wonderful thing. See, the railroads have right-of-way across the open country. The railroad beds are sort of protected areas across the countryside. With all of the urban expansion and the loss of virgin prairie, the railroad beds are among the few remaining wildflower havens left in the Midwest. Did you know that?"

"I never thought about it," Magaly said. "I didn't know you were interested in flowers."

"Well, lying here in the quiet, doing this reading, I've been thinking about a lot of things I never thought about before," Aurelio replied.

"Yeah." Voice trembling, Magaly swallowed hard. "*Hermano*, I should come—"

Aurelio ignored her. "Remember those purple flowers on the long spikes that grew in the wet places by Aunt Juana's house in Maryland when we first moved to the States?"

"I remember."

"They're called loosestrife, purple loosestrife."

"Ohhh..."

"Yeah. Isn't that a great name? And those pretty daisy-flowers on the long stems, the purple ones with brown centers? Those are coneflowers. In Latin they're *Echinacea Purpurea*. That's what they get the herbal extract from."

"I remember them," Magaly said. "They were my favorites."

"We picked them for Juana all the time in August, remember? And the other ones that were sort of like them, only with yellow petals and a little shorter? Those are *Rudbeckia*. Gloriosa Daisies. Juana would put them in a big glass vase on the kitchen table. We were so proud." Pause. Breathing. "The Indians used to eat the purple ones. Every part of them: the roots, the stems, and the flowers."

"Want me to get some to cook for you?" Magaly teased.

"Not if you don't cook better than you once did!" Aurelio laughed a sleepy, gentle laugh.

"I'll have you know that I'm not half bad in my old age," Magaly responded, laughing in turn. "But, 'Relio, are you sure you're okay?" She had never heard her brother talk this way about a subject like flowers. Politics and economics had always been his *raison d'être*.

After a moment he said, "Sorry if I seem silly, Sis. Don't mean to. That's your department. It's just—it's just that things like flowers and prairies and railroads seem important to me now. People don't seem so important now."

"People?"

"It's like I've spent all my life striving for something I didn't have," he said. "Whether it was money, or cars, or a new relationship. It was always—I always measured myself against others, against what might be." He was quiet again for a moment, breathing. "But the flowers, the miles of grass along the railroads, are just *there*. They're what they *are*. They ask nothing, except maybe the right to be. When the deals, the hopes, the dreams of us humans are dead and gone, they're still there, doing what they've always done. Abiding. Do you understand?"

"I think I do," Magaly murmured. But she didn't.

"See, Sis, it's not about what *might* be. It's about what is. Just what is."

They talked for another few minutes and when Aurelio seemed utterly exhausted Magaly insisted on hanging up. "I'll call you again real soon," she said.

"Okay, Magaly. Soon." Then, "What you asked me before? About ghosts?"

"Yes?"

"Maybe I'll be able to answer that before too long," he said.

Magaly hung up and without coat or umbrella left her room, left the hotel, and went for a walk in the pounding rain. It cleansed her, washed her. She walked for an hour, all the way up Woodward Avenue to the Fox Theater, and back. When she entered the main lobby of the hotel drenched to the bone, her sweater plastered to her, rain dripping in streams off the rim of her skirt, water running in rivulets from her black hair, she ignored the curious looks of the bellman and the concierge as she waited for the elevator. She came back feeling a little better. It was raining. Policemen, *palo mayombe*, and editors be damned. It was raining.

There was a message from Bill Westonfield. He was home. She changed into some dry clothes and returned his call. It was after noon.

Bill answered on the first ring. "What's up?"

Magaly hadn't intended it to, but it came out. "My brother's dying."

"What?"

"My brother Aurelio. He's in the hospital in New York City.

He's dying of AIDS. I just talked to him on the phone. He's terribly sick. He's alone. He's weak and sad and he's dying. There's—there's not a fucking thing I can do about it. And it's raining."

"Yes, it is," Westonfield said, as if what she'd said made perfect sense. "It's a beautiful rain. My daughter Tracey says the rain is God's tears."

"I bet you don't even believe in God," Magaly said.

"God is just shorthand."

"What?"

"Shorthand for what is, Magaly."

"For what?"

"For what is. For everything. For everything that there is, or that there ever will be. For dying brothers. For the rain."

"Bill, I want to help him so bad!"

"I know you do. I know. I'll bet he's a good guy."

"He is. He's my mentor, my buddy, my soulmate."

"How is he dealing with it?"

"He just wanted to talk about flowers, Bill."

"Oh."

"Fucking flowers!"

"Why not, Magaly?"

"I just wanted to shake him, make him better, make him fight."

"I'll bet he fought for a long time."

"Yes."

"Maybe it's time for him to quit fighting now," Westonfield said.

"I don't want him to. I can't let him. I can't let him go..."

"I know."

She looked out the window. The rain was still coming down, cold and grey. "Fucking rain."

"Yeah," Westonfield said. "Fucking rain."

"What're you doing today?" Magaly asked after a while.

"Like I said, I'm seeing my kids tonight."

"How is Jack?"

"He's fine. We left at the same time. He should be home any time now."

"Good. Seeing them should help," Magaly said. "Seeing them always helps, doesn't it? Family, friends, *compañeros*, I mean."

"Yes."

"What's new on the case?" she asked. "Have you found out anything? Any results from the lab or anything on Merritt Street?"

"Got a pencil?"

"Yeah, sure," she set the phone down and retrieved a pen and a legal pad. "Shoot."

"The deceased's name is Tomás Mejías. He's a Cuban all right. A *Marielito*. Surprise, surprise. Came over in 1980, of course. Legal resident status."

"Okay."

"Held a part time job over at Hygrade's Meat Packing. One breaking & entering and one auto theft on his record," Westonfield said.

"Any connection to the house?"

"Yeah. It's rented to him by the owner." He paused, looking at his notes. "A Margaret Plawecki out in Taylor."

"Talk to her?"

"Oh, yeah. Homicide did. It's legit. The owner got a deposit. Rent's paid on time—two-fifty a month. She doesn't know anything. She checked on Mejías's work status, found out he was working and seemed reliable, so she let him have it."

"Anyone else?"

"Nope. That's it. He was alone when she talked to him. He said he would be living alone."

"You know he's not the one, Bill, don't you?"

"Yep."

"What about the one who got away? The one you chased?"

"Gone. Nothing."

"I know. I mean, is he the one?"

Silence. Then, "Don't know."

"Yes, you do."

"All right. He's the one."

"What else?" she asked.

"The bones found in the house, upstairs, around the altar? They're the ones taken from Woodmere Cemetery. Well, they're going to have them matched for DNA at the lab. They're sending them out to the FBI laboratory at Quantico. But they match up, part-for-part, with some of the bones missing from the bodies at the cemetery."

Aguanilleo Zarabanda aribo. Magaly shuddered. "I knew they would," she said.

"Me too."

"The guns?"

"Yeah. The pistol used by Mejías was a Walther PPK .380 semi-automatic. Nice gun. Stolen from a house in Melvindale a year ago. Mejías's prints are on it."

"Anyone else's?"

"No. Just his. And only his in the house. No other prints anywhere."

"Really? How about the rifle?"

"Now that's interesting," Westonfield said. "The AR-15 is stolen, too. But get this: it's part of a whole bunch of hardware taken in a B&E from a gun shop in Dayton, Ohio, three weeks ago. The bastards took five ARs, along with a couple of grenade launchers, a mortar, and all kinds of other shit."

"Any prints?"

"No. No prints at all. But you know those boxes? The ones the shithead was carrying out by the car? Most of them contained more of the powders and candles like the ones upstairs on the altar. They're all being sent out to the lab. Except there was one small package that contained a necklace."

"A necklace?"

"Yeah. Just a simple bead necklace. It had—wait a minute." Westonfield referred to his notes. "Okay, it had seven brown beads alternating with three black beads, all the way around. That mean anything to you?"

Aguanilleo Zarabanda aribo. Magaly closed her eyes, but the voice took her. Took her from within. She was instantly drowning in a clear lake, cold water filling her lungs with crystal death. The pain, the pleasure, were overwhelming. She almost wept with welcoming joy, the blood singing in her veins. *Aguanilleo Zarabanda aribo egun eko mare ho morire arere aguere aribo omo rire ogunde bamba aguanilleo Zarabanda aribo aguanilleo Zarabanda aribo egun eko mare ho morire egun ekomare ho morire arere he aribo llanya Zarabanda arere arereo he aribo llanya he aribo llanya Zarabanda arere arereo he aribo llanya aguanilleo arere arero aguanilleo oche oguña arere hoe hoe arigoñaña ache arere hoe arigoñaña ogunda...*

"Magaly?"

Nothing.

"Magaly?"

Nothing.

"Maggie!"

At last a voice, small and lost. "Yes?"

"You all right?" There was fear in his voice.

"Yes."

"What the hell's going on?" Westonfield demanded. "What the *hell's* going on?" There had been a flash, an ethereal vision, of black eyes without pupils, surrounded by yellow. Then it was gone.

"He knows, Bill."

"What?"

"He knows about us. He knows about me."

"What?"

"Like I told you before. He's not alone now."

"Mejías? No, we know that."

"No. Him. He's not alone. I hear him. He sings to me," Magaly said.

"He what?"

"He sings to me."

"Are you alone there?"

"I am now."

"Who's singing?"
"Him. Them."
"Who?"
"Them."
Jesus! "What do they sing?"
"I don't know."
"What language?"
"I don't know."
"Bantu?"
"I don't know, Bill."
"Magaly, do you want me to come over there?"
"No."
"I could."
"No. I'll be okay. It's over. He's gone."
"This is crazy," Westonfield said. "Don't you think we're letting ourselves get too spooked? This is just a theft case. True, they're not afraid to shoot cops, and they're robbing graves. But it's still just plain old crime." But the terrible vision haunted him. Should he tell her he'd seen it?
"I don't think it's that way," Magaly said.
"Well..."
Magaly suddenly didn't want to talk, was weary of talk. "Have a good time with your kids, Bill."
"I will, Maggie, but—"
Magaly interjected. "Can you arrange for me to patrol again tonight?"
"Sure."
"I'd like to do it without you and Jack, at least once. It looks like tonight is the perfect night. You've both got plans," she said a little wistfully.
"I'll take care of it," Westonfield said, not at all happy.
"Magaly?"
"Yeah?"
"*Cuídate.*"
At six o'clock she was on her way to the Fourth Precinct station.

CHAPTER 16

The rain had finally stopped but the overcast hung on. A fine mist mizzled down on a desultory breeze, coating the windshield of Magaly's Buick as she drove west on Fort Street, out of downtown. A Greyhound bus passed on the left, ran through a puddle, and threw a bucket of water onto her windshield. She felt for the wiper control and twisted it to a faster speed. Traffic was still brisk leaving the central city, but at 6:15 it was lighter than it had been. Inbound, the traffic was very slight: it was early evening in Detroit, and not many people ventured downtown after businesses closed. The daylight faded even as Magaly drove under the Ambassador Bridge. Dusk was settling in over the southwest side.

It took her only ten minutes to get from the Lodge Freeway to the intersection of Fort and Green and the police station. She pulled into the muddy parking lot and bounced through the potholes to an open space by the fence at the back. She guided the car in, climbed out, and picked her way across the mud to the open bay door of the precinct garage.

When Magaly entered the station proper through the heavy old door connecting the offices to the garage, a sudden gust sent a lapel flap of her jacket slapping across her face—the lobby door of the building was open and the interior air rushed out the back door to equalize the pressure. The air in the building was heavy and damp, like the air outside. As she walked down the hallway toward the stairway that led to the Power Shift office a feeling of loneliness settled on her. It felt strange being there without Bill or Jack waiting for her. Odd how new friends could come so quickly to feel like old ones.

When she stepped into the office she was greeted by a uniformed sergeant who introduced himself as Frank Meyers. He was about sixty years old with grey hair and a slight pot belly. His uniform pants hung loose in the seat. Magaly recalled a funny remark Rourke had made about "baggy-assed old men."

"Evening," said Meyers. "You've got to be... Mag... Magal... Sorry. How do you pronounce it? I talked to Sergeant Westonfield this afternoon and he told me to expect you, but I guess I didn't get your name down right."

"It's Magaly," she said. "Mah-gahl-ee. See, it's easy." She held out her hand. "I'm pleased to meet you, Frank."

"Me too," chimed Meyers, grinning. "Anyhow, Bill told me a little about what you're doing. I'm just filling in for tonight while him and Jack are both off. I'm on afternoons, the four-to-twelve, but somebody's got to handle the Power Shift roll call." He idly scratched the back of his right hand. He wasn't used to being around someone so pretty. "Can I get you a coffee?"

"Please."

Meyers went to the old coffee maker in the corner of the room and retrieved a steaming styrofoam cup of the strong brew for her. "I'll let you fix it how you like it," he said, motioning toward the sugar and dry creamer on the cabinet. "It's good and hot."

Magaly took the proffered cup. "I like it black," she said. "And hot," she added, smiling. "The fall is here already, eh? This'll do me good."

"It sure is, miss. Pretty cool," Meyers said. "Should I call you by your first name or your last name?" He pulled out a chair at Rourke's desk and asked her to sit.

"*Magaly*, please, Frank." She took the seat and leaned back, almost falling over backwards in the rickety thing.

"Watch yourself," Meyers cautioned. "As you can see, Ol' Jack Rourke's kind of hard on the furniture."

Magaly nodded. "So I see!"

"So how is Jack?" asked Meyers. "Have you talked to him

since the shooting? He's getting too old for that shit—excuse the language. Bill and him *and* me are too old, that is. All of us should get us a day job, something a little safer and a little drier." He pointed outside at the drizzle through the dirty window.

"Well, Frank, I don't know you very well," replied Magaly, "but I can't picture Jack and Bill shuffling paper in some bureau downtown, can you?"

"Guess not," Meyers said. "But it don't hurt to suggest it once in a while. They're not going to change anything out there, you know—no matter how hard they try."

"Can anybody change anything, Frank?" Magaly asked. "But, anyway, I have talked to Jack. He's up with his family now for a couple of days. He's all right. He doesn't seem to be overly upset about the whole thing."

"Good."

"Do you know him well?"

"Jack? No, not well, really. I came on about five or six years before those two. I'm over my time now. I can retire if I want. I've got twenty-nine years on. We've worked together here for quite a while, but I've always been on a different shift than them."

"Okay, then," Magaly said, "So, what's on the agenda tonight?"

"Nothing special," Meyers said. "I'll just do a quick roll call and get 'em out on the street." He looked down at a sheet of paper on the desk in front of him. "I've got the detail here. Let's see, we're running three two-man cars tonight." He handed the sheet to Magaly. "Have you met the troops yet? Anybody on that paper you'd like to go out with?"

Magaly scanned the detail. Roberto Arena and the lone black officer on the shift, Benny Adams, were assigned to 4-33. "How about these two?" she said, standing up, going over to Meyers, and running her finger under the names.

"Looks good to me," Meyers said. "Good guys."

She continued to chat with Meyers for another few minutes

until the patrolmen began to filter in. They all acknowledged her in a friendly manner, smiling and joking. They were mildly surprised that she was there without Westonfield or Rourke, and so soon after the Merritt shooting. When Meyers informed Arena and Adams that Magaly would be going out with them, she interjected, "Only if it's okay with you guys. If you'd rather not, I understand. Like I told you the first night, it's me that's the interloper here." They nodded a little self-consciously, but both of them said it would be fine if she wanted to accompany them.

Meyers was true to his word. He merely made sure everyone who was supposed to be there was there (they were), asked if anyone had anything to say (they didn't), and then sent them out to their waiting police cars. When the patrolmen had all left the office to draw their equipment and get their car keys, leaving Magaly and Meyers alone in the office, Meyers asked, "What do you think so far, Magaly? I mean, have you come to any conclusions about this operation yet? I've gotta say I can't figure out why the brass sent you way down here to us." He paused, musing. "You know what they call this area, down here in DelRay? Ever look at a map of Detroit? We're sort of in that little tail that runs down along the river between Melvindale and Dearborn on the west, and River Rouge and Ecorse on the east. Kind of like the business-end of a funnel. Some of the guys say this is the asshole of Detroit—pardon the talk—where all the crap comes out."

"But that's why I'm here," Magaly answered, amused yet again at how most of the older policemen were sensitive about bad language around her. "I want to learn about the crap. And you're right about downtown not wanting me here. But here is where I am, and here is where I'm going to stay, as long as you guys will have me. If this is the asshole of the city, then I want to be here to see what's coming out."

Meyers was a little surprised, but he nodded thoughtfully. Magaly shook his hand once more, thanked him for his patience and his time, and went downstairs to look for Bob Arena and

Benny Adams.

They were standing beside a black unmarked Chevy Caprice in the parking lot. The weather had continued to improve and there were a few breaks in the overcast. It was near dark now, and clear patches showed black against the lighter grey of the clouds. "We'll be set in a minute now," Arena said. "Go ahead and have a seat in the back if you want."

Magaly opened the door and slid in. The smell was familiar now: a musty mixture of wet cloth, fast food, stale blood, and urine. *I guess a girl can get used to anything*, she thought.

In five minutes Arena and Adams had finished loading their equipment, signed onto their MODAT, and driven out of the parking lot onto a dark Fort Street. The streetlights were out, a perennial problem in foul weather and rain.

"It's awfully dark for this early," Magaly offered.

"Yeah," said Adams, speaking for the first time. "Dark as hell. Glad you're driving, partner," he added, looking at Arena behind the wheel. "I hate to drive in the rain." He was a young man, no more than twenty-six, the youngest on the Power Shift. "Goddamn streetlights," he said.

They got a run almost immediately. "4-33," said the dispatcher. "You ready to roll?"

Adams picked up the mike. "4-33's ready to go."

"Okay, 33. Make Michigan and Wyoming. There's trouble at the Yum-Yum Doughnut Shop. They say an intoxicated customer doesn't want to pay." He repeated, "4-33, make Michigan and Wyoming... Yum-Yum's... the drunk won't pay."

"On the way," intoned Adams. He looked at Magaly and rolled his eyes.

"I've been there," Magaly said. "With Sergeant Westonfield and Sergeant Rourke."

"We all go up there for coffee," Adams said. "They're pretty good people. Treat you right. Java's free. I just hate the goddamn drunks. Stinky damn skanks. I hate to smell 'em. I hate to touch 'em."

Arena grinned. "You got that right. I just hope this one ain't too bad."

In five minutes they rolled into the parking lot of the Yum-Yum doughnut shop. The officers climbed out of the car and headed for the door, followed by Magaly. As soon as they entered, a fat waitress pointed to a corner. A smallish, dark-haired man of about forty-five was slouched in a booth. His lank hair was plastered to his unwashed scalp. His face sported five days' growth of scraggly beard. He was dressed in a tweed sport coat, chartreuse tee shirt, and stained black pants. Filth was caked underneath his fingernails. When they got close, Magaly could smell urine and cheap wine, and there were doughnut crumbs clinging to his lips.

He looked at them with bleary eyes. "How're you doin', officers?" he ventured drunkenly.

"What's the tab?" Arena asked, turning to the waitress, ignoring the bum.

"Buck-eighty," she said.

"Got a buck eighty, my man?" Adams asked.

"Yeah," the bum said. "Sure, I do." He fumbled for a long moment through the tattered pockets of his coat, pulling out bits of scrap paper, a package of saltines, a snotty napkin, and a packet of ketchup, while the officers watched impatiently.

"You don't have any money, do you?" Adams said.

The man looked guilty. "No—and I'm being perfectly honest with you, officer. I don't. Haven't got no money." He opened his arms in supplication and Magaly almost swooned from the stench of his unwashed body.

"Why the hell did you come in here and order a doughnut, then?" demanded Adams. "Did you think the *waitress* was gonna buy it?"

The drunk shrugged.

"Well, the boy ain't gonna pay, Frances," Arena said. "What do you want us to do?"

The waitress rolled her eyes and pointed to the door.

"Okay, bud," Adams said. "Time to leave."

The bum struggled to his feet. "Bless you, officers," he said.

"Bless you. Thank you for your help. I'm on my way. Yep, I'm on my way." He shuffled past the counter and out the door, nearly falling twice. Then he was gone in the dark.

The waitress came out with a soapy wet cloth and wiped the seat and table clean. "Thanks, guys," she said. "Want a coffee before you leave?" It seemed like she wished they did.

Adams and Arena looked at Magaly. She said, "Sure."

The awkwardness the cops felt gradually faded as they talked to Magaly, heard her views, saw her smile. After two leisurely cups of bitter coffee she asked, "Are you guys still out of service on this run?"

"Whoops—" chimed Adams.

"Time flies when you're havin' fun," Arena offered with a grin. He ran his hands through his black hair and looked at his watch. "Holy shit, you're right—we've been out on this for over forty minutes. It's a wonder dispatch hasn't been trying to get hold of us. Well, it's slow tonight." After a moment he said, "Fuck it. We could use a break after the last couple of days."

Adams picked up the portable radio from the table in front of him and called the unit back into service.

Magaly pulled her wallet from her purse but Adams touched her hand. "We'll get it," he said. He peeled a couple of bills from a money clip. Arena grabbed the money from his partner's hand and went to the counter. On reflection he added another two dollars. "This is for the jake's sugar pill," he said. "Have a good night, Frances."

"Thanks a lot, fellas," replied the waitress, a toothy smile on her red face. "You guys be real careful out there," she added as they walked toward the door. They returned her smile but said nothing.

"What's up now?" Magaly asked from the back seat.

"Well, since we're up here on Michigan Avenue anyway, let's go over to the house on Merritt and make sure everything's all right," Arena said. "It's on our special attention list. We gotta check it a few times and note it on our activity log. Might as well do it now."

"It's all locked up and cordoned off with tape," Magaly said, not anxious to see the house again. "What's the point?"

"It's just routine," Adams said. "The house is under police control now. Evidence. So we're just gonna make sure no vandals or kids or anything are hanging around."

Magaly grimaced.

Arena said, "Bad vibes, eh?"

"Yeah."

"First time you've seen something like that, I guess."

"Yes."

"Welcome to Detroit," Adams said. "One hell of a damned eye-opener! Bet you never thought you'd get something that wild to write about in your first couple of days. Just be glad no cops were hurt. Or you, either. Could have been different." He reflected for a moment. "It's not always like that. Sometimes it's real slow and boring. Only—"

"What?"

"Hard to say," Adams said. "Did you ever get a feeling?" He searched for the right words. "It's like... it's like in the *air*, you know? Like a change in the weather. I think something big is brewing with these Cubans. Since just before you came here. All this grave robbing. Then the shooting the other night. People are scared. I mean street people—gang bangers, informants. I can't figure it out."

Magaly could figure it out, but she said nothing. It was Westonfield's job to tell his people what they needed to know, not hers.

In a few minutes they pulled slowly into view of the house. It was completely dark. The whole street was dark: as on Fort Street, the streetlights were out. At first blush everything appeared to be in order. The front door still bore the padlock the police evidence unit had installed, and the yellow police-line ribbon was in place across the porch. No one was in sight. Everything was quiet. Preternaturally quiet, thought Magaly. But there was no sense of foreboding or terror. The house was old, dark, and melancholy, but no longer a place of stark horror.

Magaly was gratified at first, but then she wondered—why?

"Looks good," Arena said. "Quiet as church on a Monday." Then, as if in answer to her unspoken question, "He won't be back. The main man, I mean." He twisted in his seat and looked at Magaly before they drove slowly away. "Maybe he's not far, but he won't be back here again."

Magaly looked back at Arena silently. She caught a glimpse of the silver medal and chain he wore around his neck. When they got a few blocks away she asked, "That medal you're wearing—Saint Michael?"

"Yes. Saint Michael," Arena said.

"You're a good Catholic boy, I bet," Magaly said.

"'Course," Arena said. "Redeemer all the way. Class of '80."

"I notice that a lot of you fellows wear the medals."

"Uh-huh."

"How about you, Benny?" Magaly asked. "Are you Catholic?"

"Not hardly," Adams responded. "African Methodist. Least ways my family is. I don't go to church much."

"That's because it would burn down if you did," offered Arena.

"Could be," responded Adams.

"I've noticed Sergeant Westonfield wears one," Magaly said, remembering the glimpse she'd caught of it in the men's locker room a few days earlier. "But I don't think he's Catholic."

"He ain't Catholic," Adams said. "Or African Methodist, neither," he added, grinning.

"I wouldn't imagine so," Magaly said, liking the young officer's easy manner and infectious smile. "But he still wears the medal. How come?"

"Dunno," said Adams.

"'Berto?"

"He got it from a priest," Arena said.

"I bet I could put a name on him," Magaly said.

"Lewendowski."

"Nope. Good guess, but not him," Arena said. "They're good buddies, Sergeant Westonfield and Father Marko. But this was a different guy."

"All right. Who?"

"Father Neeson, over at Trinity."

"What did he give it to him for?"

"You better ask him that."

"Oh, come on—"

"Really," Arena said. "You better ask him. There's some things Sarge is funny about, and his personal business is one of them. You better ask him when you get a chance."

"Oh, all right," Magaly sighed in mock resignation.

"I'll tell you a story, though," Arena said. "Do you know the story of Saint Michael? How he came to be the patron saint of policemen? Are you Catholic? Magaly Rodríguez. Sure, you gotta be Catholic."

"Well, I'm Catholic," Magaly said. "But I still don't know the story."

"Okay, then," Arena said. "You know how there's a saint for everybody, I mean for every profession: teachers, lawyers, bricklayers, carpenters, farmers?"

"What about whores?" interjected Adams. "'Hoes got a right."

"Christ," Arena said. "No wonder they won't let your obnoxious black ass inside a church."

Adams said nothing more. Magaly chuckled.

"Well, in the beginning," Arena went on, "when God assigned a profession to every saint—including *'hoes*, I suppose—"

Adams looked innocently out the window.

"—he forgot to assign one to policemen. After a while he realized his oversight and asked for a volunteer among the saints. None of them came forward because they were busy with the ones they'd already been assigned. Then God said, *'Is there no one among you who will come forward to this task?*

Whom shall I set to protect the protectors?' Still none came forward. Then God said, *'It shall not be that there are none to succor those whose work it is to aid the rest.'* So he called upon Michael, the Archangel. Michael came forward as commanded. *'So,'* God said, *'from this day forth it shall be your duty, Michael, to watch over my policemen, for you are the purest of my angels; and who better to comfort them than thee? Take this, mine own sword, and permit not that Satan shall smite them, who are my right hand...'"* Arena stopped. "Well, that's the fable," he said. "The best I can remember it. Sergeant Westonfield told it to me like that."

Magaly cleared her throat and said softly, "That's quite a tale. A fine story, Bob. I—well, thank you for sharing it with me. Where did you get a memory like that? It's almost like you read it to me from something that was written down."

Arena seemed mildly distracted now that he was finished. "Yeah, it's kind of memorized," he said. He scratched his chin absently. "I don't think Sarge would mind me telling it to you. He got it from the priest, the one who gave him the medal. Neeson. The story came with the medal. But you can ask him if you want."

"I will," Magaly said. "I certainly will."

Arena drove quietly on, his restless eyes searching the darkness.

"Let me try this," Magaly said. "Benny, is Sergeant Westonfield a racist?"

"Damn!" Adams said. "You don't lack for being blunt, do you?"

"It's my trademark."

"I guess so!" He looked at her wonderingly. "Damn," he said again. "What kind of question is that?"

"It's the kind of question blunt people ask," Magaly said.

"Right."

"Well?"

"I don't even know what a racist is," Adams said. "What do you mean by racist?"

"I've heard the talk," Magaly said. "Talk around the department."

Arena guffawed.

Magaly turned to him. "All right. What about you then, Bob? What do you think?"

"I think it's the stupidest shit I ever heard."

"So, tell me," Magaly said.

"I'm a Mexican," Arena answered. "A Mexican cop. And here's a white sergeant, my boss, who, if he wanted, could spend his whole day fucking with me on account he doesn't like Mexicans. Well, as it turns out, he speaks better Spanish than I do. He knows more about my mother country than I do. He's got all these degrees and stuff from the U of M. And you know what? He's a gentleman. He's fair. He's decent. There isn't an anti-Hispanic bone in his body. He's more Mexican than I am, seems like." He thought for a moment. "Now, you know, Sergeant Westonfield is kind of hard. I mean, he's not patient. He's got no patience for laziness or dishonesty or cowardice. And he writes people up for it."

"He sure does," Adams said, laughing.

"Benny?" Magaly said.

"I don't know," replied the black cop. "Hell, I don't know. I mostly agree with Bob here. Sarge is a good boss. He's fair to me. I've never seen him act unfair to anybody else on account of their race."

"Do I hear an unspoken *but*?"

"No. No buts. What I said is true."

"What about the write-ups?" Magaly asked.

"Well, sometimes I think Sergeant Westonfield might be a little hard," Adams said.

"On account of race?" Magaly asked.

"That's not easy to answer," Adams said. "In the way you mean it, no. No way. See, about three-fourths of the newer officers are black now. Sergeant Westonfield writes 'em up a lot. I guess about three-fourths of his write-ups would be against black cops."

"That's what I've heard," Magaly said.

"Yeah, but like Bob says, Sarge is hard," Adams continued. "I think where the problem comes in is that he asks a lot. He asks a lot from all of us. But he asks even more from himself. In that way it's fair, see? He don't do anything on account of somebody being black, or somebody being white, he's just plain tough."

"I'm not sure I see your point," Magaly said.

"Sometimes I think Sarge is so worried about getting it right—know what I mean, getting it right?—that he forgets the rest of us are regular folks," Adams said. "These young black kids coming on the department now, they're coming up here with nothing. I mean nothing. They come from ghetto schools where they haven't even learned to read and write good, let alone be policemen. Understand? They don't have a clue about simple things like uniform appearance, coming to work on time, obeying orders, and all of that. It's the ultimate culture clash,'cause Sarge ain't even mortal. At least not like anybody else I've ever known." Adams paused again, collecting his thoughts. "So they fuck up, these kids, and Sarge writes the shit out of 'em. He don't give a rat's ass about their color, but maybe he can't see the other side sometimes." He looked at Arena. "What do you think?"

"Well, I see your point," Arena said. "I see what you're saying, Bennie. But listen, if Sergeant Westonfield don't try to weed out the bad apples, who will? Okay, maybe sometimes he's hard. Maybe too hard. But it's the people out here that matter, ain't it? What's more important, that some kid who needs a break gets it on this job, or that some poor slob who gets his house B&E'd gets the service his tax dollars are supposed to earn him? That's the question. Sarge is a cop, see? I mean he's a *cop*. He ain't a teacher or a social worker. He's a police supervisor. I suppose he figures that if you want to be a cop, then be a cop. If you can't or won't, then you should just quit."

"You're right, Bob. But I still think I'm right, too," Adams said. He turned to Magaly. "I guess there ain't no easy answer to your question," he said. "There's just this certain point of view you have when you're black, when you come from the black community. But then Sarge ain't an easy man, is he?"

"No. He's certainly not an easy man," Magaly said.

At ten o'clock they ate dinner at the Michigan Coney Island on Michigan Avenue. They shared a large plate of chili fries. The policemen each had a coke and Magaly had a root beer.

"So tell us about yourself," ventured Arena. "So far it's you with the questions. How about if it's our turn now?"

"Sure," Magaly said. "What would you like to know?"

"He'd like to start off with your telephone number," Adams said.

"True," Arena said deadpan. "But after I get that, how about—how old are you?"

"I'm thirty-three," Magaly said.

"Where are you from?"

"You mean where was I born and raised, or where do I live now?"

"Both."

"Mérida, Mexico; and New York City, in that order."

"How long and how long?" Arena asked.

"I moved to the States when I was nine," Magaly said. "My mother died when I was twelve. We lived in Maryland, Connecticut, and then New York."

"Brothers and sisters?"

"Three and two."

"Where are you in the pack?"

"In the middle. The fourth."

"School?"

"Georgetown."

"Ooooh," Adams said.

"Work?" Arena continued.

"The *New York Times, The New Yorker, Newsweek, Harper's...*"

"Ooooh," Adams said again.

"How long at *Harper's*?"

"Four years."
"First trip to *De-toilet*?"
Magaly laughed. "Yes."
"Do you like it?"
"Well, if you don't count being in a gun battle—"
"Boyfriend back home?"
"Now it comes," Adams said.
"No."
"Want one?" Arena asked.
"How about you?" Magaly said.
"Sure."
"I didn't embarrass you too much at our first encounter?" Magaly asked.
"Hell, no."
"You're sweet, 'Berto," she said. "But—"
"What?" Arena said.
"Well, I'm rather busy."
"Too busy even for love?"
"I'm afraid so."
"I think she's taken," Adams opined.
"Sarge?" Arena asked.
"Yeah," Adams said.
Magaly blushed. "No way. It's strictly professional."
"Look," Adams said. "We got her."
"Yeah, we got her," Arena said, chuckling. He stuffed four chili-drenched fries into his mouth. "We got her," he repeated, chewing.
When they left the restaurant and returned to the police car Adams said, "You think we should do some police work now, partner?"
"What do you have in mind?" Arena asked.
"Vernor Highway. The Cobras."
"Right on," Arena said. "Let's do it."

* * *

They went past Junction into the Third Precinct. They turned south on W. Grand Boulevard and took its meandering course to Vernor Highway. Then they turned back toward Clark Park. After a few minutes Adams spotted a teenage boy walking up Ferdinand toward Vernor. The officers got out of the car, talked to the boy, patted him down, and then told him to get into the back seat of the police car, next to Magaly.

"Hey, this is a humbug," the boy whined in the gangland vernacular used by all of his contemporaries. "You know that? This is a fuckin' humbug and a roust. I ain't did shit." He eyeballed Magaly. "Who's the bitch?"

"She's the rat catcher, *Chivato*," Arena said. "We just caught ourselves a rat."

"Oh, man! Where we goin'? I got shit to do. I got a lot of shit to do for my moms, you know?"

"You can shop all you want to where we're going, Rodolfo," Adams said.

"Fuck," the boy said.

"Miss Rodríguez, meet Rodolfo Carranza," Arena said. "He's the—what is it, 'Dolfo, the vice president?—of the Cobras."

The boy looked at her. "Who're you?"

"I told you, the rat catcher," Arena repeated.

"Shit," the boy said.

Magaly said nothing.

Arena pulled the police car into an alley south of Campbell off Vernor and turned off the headlights. He stopped next to a large green garbage dumpster. "Here's home," he said.

"Don't do this to me, officers," the boy begged. "Okay? I can't take this shit no more. That's some real stinky shit in there. I get sick in my stomach. I gotta be places, man. My moms is gonna worry. Let me go. I'll stay out of sight for a while, okay?"

"Yes, you will, 'Dolfo," Adams said. "Get out."

Magaly watched in uncomfortable silence from the back seat.

Adams took the boy by the left arm and pulled him from the car. Joined by Arena, who took hold of the boy, Adams opened the heavy lid of the dumpster and said, "You can climb in by yourself, or we can throw you in like we did last time."

"Aw, shit," whined the boy.

"You can't be serious," Magaly finally said. "You're actually going to put him in there?"

The policemen looked at each other. "No?" Arena said.

"You're asking me?" Magaly asked, incredulous. The circumstances were so ridiculous, and the boy's pleas so pitiful, that she didn't know whether to laugh or cry.

"Sarge said we could trust you," Adams said. "Do we or don't we put him in?"

"He's just a boy," Magaly said. "He really could get sick in there."

The cops shrugged.

"You can't put me in that position," Magaly said. "You go ahead and do what you're going to do. I'm an observer, not a participant." She looked at the boy, who was standing dejectedly in the darkness of the alley with Arena's hand on his coat sleeve.

Adams looked at the boy. "Well?"

"Shit," the boy said. Then he walked sulkily over to the dumpster, grabbed the top edge, found a toe hold on a side rail and climbed in. His head stuck above the edge despite the fact he was short. He was standing on three feet of garbage. The putrid smell wafted out to Magaly.

"Okay, sit down," Adams ordered.

The boy sat. "Aw, shit."

Adams carefully closed the lid. Then he and Arena walked a few yards into the darkness to a stack of cinder blocks. They each pulled a pair of gloves from their waistbands and put them on. For the next ten minutes, while Magaly's incredulity turned to astonishment, they piled three hundred pounds of blocks onto the dumpster lid. When their task was completed, Adams and Arena took their gloves off and brushed the grey dust from their uniform trousers. "That ought to do it," Adams said.

Then the three of them got into the police car. Before they pulled away, the boy shouted, his voice muffled by the heavy metal of the dumpster, "When you gonna let me out?"

"Oh, you'll get out," Arena said. "We're both off tomorrow and the day after, though," he added. "So it might be a couple of days."

"Aw, shit," the boy said for the last time.

"My God," Magaly said as they drove away. "That wasn't the first time you've done that?"

"Nope," Arena said.

"Would you care to explain it to me, if it's not too much trouble?" She was a little angry.

"He's a little puke," Adams said. "That talk about his mother? Hell, he'd knife her as soon as look at her. He's not wanted for anything right now. We checked before we left the station. So this is just a little chat-like. Just to remind him and his buddies that we're out here."

"Quite a reminder," Magaly said, shaking her head.

Adams smiled. "Now you're one of us," he said.

"Oh, no you don't," Magaly said. "You asked, and I said *do what you want*. That doesn't make me one of you."

"Let me see," Arena said. "You just witnessed us kidnapping and imprisoning a minor without a warrant—putting him in a nasty dumpster, as a matter of fact. Now that makes you a conspirator, doesn't it?"

Magaly opened her mouth to answer, closed it, opened it again, and then finally slumped into the back seat and sighed. She didn't have an answer to that. At least not one that was worth anything. Then she began to laugh. She laughed so hard her sides hurt and tears came to her eyes.

Adams and Arena looked at each other and grinned like Cheshire Cats.

CHAPTER 17

The house on Merritt Street discovered, its contents revealed; Tomás killed by the fat policeman; he himself almost caught—Gabriel Flores pondered the meaning. The house itself mattered little, since he had several. The authorities had found the altar and its artifacts, of course, and all of the accouterments for the rituals would be pawed over and defiled. Irritating, but unimportant. The weapons were clean. The house was clean. Nothing traceable to him. Tomás? He was a *gusano*. A detestable worm. Weak, feckless. In any case, he was dead, so he couldn't talk to the police, and there was nothing to connect him to his *mayombero*. But what of this new policeman? Here was something...dangerous. Gabriel savored the thought. *Peligroso.* He tasted it. He wasn't afraid—not quite. But here was something alien. He wasn't completely sure whether he hated it or loved it. The uncertainty made him shrink from it; the danger made him welcome it.

But how was it that at precisely the time he brought forth his Lord, Zarabanda, this strange, dangerous policeman should appear? He sought the answer from the *bruja* from afar, but no answer came. And the world around the policeman was dark, lost to him. He could smell him, feel him, but when Gabriel reached out to understand him, the image faded away like a mist. He tried several times, to no avail, and each time he grew more frustrated. But his heart told him that here was a foe worthy of him. At last he had found another witch.

But that wasn't all. There was another thing, an interesting thing. A woman. He could touch her better than the other. He tasted her. Enjoyed it. Why? He'd never been interested in women. She was very lovely. She was a *sister*, also. In two ways was she a sister: she was a *yaguo*, a practitioner of S*antería*, though a weak one; and she was Hispanic—Mexican, he thought. Yes. Lovely.

What to do? A game perhaps? Yes. A game. He could learn from the game. The game would buy him time. But where to play it, and with whom to play it? He gave it much thought. Eventually he decided to go out into the streets to seek more knowledge. There were subcurrents in the air, floating just beyond his grasp. Yes. He would go out and see what was to be seen. Then he would play the game. He would strike. Strike to the heart. Death was in his eyes and death was in his hand. All that remained was to decide upon whom it would fall, and when. The moon was waxing. Tonight it would be at the full.

* * *

Katy Marroquín kissed Danny Villanueva on the lips and held him close. They were in a back room at Danny's cousin's house on Army Street. The weather had turned cool and wet and the room was unheated. She snuggled close. "I love you," she said.

"I love you, too," Danny replied sleepily, meaning it. She was the best, Katy. "What time is it, baby?" It was dark in the room. Little light came in through the lone shaded window.

"It's almost eleven o'clock," Katy answered, caressing his flat belly with the palm of her hand. "I looked at the kitchen clock when I went to the bathroom a little while ago." She smiled at him, reached down and grabbed his flaccid penis. "Hijinio's gone. We're alone. Wanna make love again?" She stroked him gently.

He sighed, going with it, becoming hard very fast. When it was over she said, "Now that's the way to start the day."

"*Sí,*" he answered lazily, his hand cupping one of her breasts. "*Tu eres la mejor, niña.*" You're the best, little girl.

After a while she said, "They're looking for you."

"Who?"

"The cops. Sergeant Westonfield and that *gordo*, Sergeant Rourke. They talked to me in the park a few days ago, when you were out in Pontiac. I told them you were in Chicago."

"What did they say?"

"I think they believed me."

"Are you sure?"

"Yeah. I'm sure. You know, Sergeant Westonfield's sort of a nice guy."

"What?"

"He is. I almost hated to lie to him about you being in Chicago."

The gang leader raised up on one elbow. "You crazy? You wanna get me locked up?"

"No, Danny. You know I wouldn't do that. I didn't tell him. I wouldn't tell him. I just thought... I don't know. I just thought maybe we could trust him. Me and you both. Maybe we could go to him and explain. Explain how you got in that fight with Arranes, how it was self-defense and all. How he had a crow bar and everything. Maybe he could help us." She sighed. "I'm tired, Danny. I'm tired of all of this. Even the Counts, you know. Even the Counts. I'm scared about what's gonna happen to us. I'm sick of hiding and sleeping late and staying up late. Did you ever think about what it would be like having something to do everyday? I mean, having something important and good to do everyday? Getting up early in the morning, going about your business, and then going to bed at night knowing the day wasn't wasted?"

Danny looked at her strangely. "What the hell are you talking about? The Counts is all there is. You know that. What kind of life is there for the likes of me and you out in their world? None and none. And you know it." He touched her face. "This Westonfield. I know him. He's a straight shooter. He's all right. But he ain't gonna help us. He can't help us. It's gone way beyond us and it's way beyond him. We're who we are, sweetheart. Not who Westonfield, or you, want us to be. So he gets me out of this assault warrant business with Arranes—then what?"

Katy turned away.

He took her face in his hands and turned it back towards him. "No, Katy. Answer me. Then what?"

"I don't know," she said dejectedly. "I don't know, Danny." The day that had seemed so bright and promising just a few moments ago now seemed grey and sad.

* * *

Gabriel went out in the late afternoon, almost giddy with power. The moon would be at the full tonight. He felt as though he could do anything, see anything, hear anything. The doubts he felt earlier were dissipating with every hour. He was strong. He felt the hammer of Zarabanda with him. There was a necklace around his neck of glass beads, alternating, seven brown with three black. He was hunting. Catch a bird and make it sing!

This policeman. Who was he? He worked on the southwest side of the city, of course. He would be known to the local drug dealers and gang members. Even as Gabriel walked along the sidewalk on Vernor Highway near Springwells he could feel the man's presence, taste his taste, smell his smell. But he couldn't see him. ¡Hijo de puta! The immutable fact of it almost made him break the neck of the old woman who happened to be walking past him at the time the thought came to him. No! Wait— That was exactly the kind of thing that would ruin everything for him. But the anger continued to grow.

He spent an hour walking aimlessly along Vernor, up and down side streets, and along debris-strewn alleys. Then he spotted what he wanted. In reality, he sensed him before he saw him: a boy sitting by himself at a picnic table in Patton Park. The boy was idly carving gang epithets into the wood.

"*Hola, Chivato,*" said the table.

The boy flung himself backward so hard he fell off the bench onto the ground. He sprang up and looked wide-eyed at the table. Nothing. He scanned wildly around the park. Nothing at first, then the man was just... there.

"*¿Qué hay de nuevo, pendejo?*" asked Gabriel. What's new, shithead?

The seventeen-year-old boy, a member of the Latin Counts, said nothing, stared into the infernal black eyes without pupils.

"I say again, boy—what's new?"

"I'm just hangin'," the boy, whose name was Miguel Prado, stammered. "I ain't bothering nobody," he added. It occurred to him that he had somehow managed to offend the fearsome-looking man.

"Let's talk," the stranger said. Though the man's lips moved when he spoke, the voice seemed this time to come from the earth beneath his feet. The man walked forward and put his arm around the boy's shoulders. The arm was strong, but peculiarly cold. "I bet you're a real smart boy," the man said.

"Dunno," the boy said, fear showing in his brown eyes.

"You look like a smart boy to me," the man repeated.

"What do you want, mister?"

Gabriel laughed. "Everything, my young friend. In its time, *everything*. But now, not nearly so much. Now I merely seek information. Just a little knowledge. You'll help me with that, won't you?"

"What do you want to know?" The boy's concern grew. As they talked, the man guided him away from the picnic area toward a row of trees a hundred yards distant, where a small drainage ditch ran through the park.

Now that the time had come, Gabriel didn't know quite what question to ask. After a moment, still walking, he said, "You're not really a good boy, are you?"

"What?" the boy asked, becoming truly frightened.

"You've been in trouble with the police, haven't you?"

"Sure." Prado looked around for an avenue of escape, anyone else in the park. His heart sank. They were alone.

"Many times," Gabriel said.

"Yeah." The boy hung his head.

"You know some of them, do you? The policemen?"

"Yeah. I know some of them," Prado said. He looked around again, tentatively strained against Gabriel's iron grip to test its strength, found it irresistible, relented.

"Of course you do," Gabriel said, ignoring the boy's ridiculous attempt to free himself. "Tell me—who is the..." he sought the words, "...who is the *jefe*? Who is the one that tells the others what to do? The one who knows the most? The one who is the strongest?"

"I dunno," the boy said, near tears. "Where you taking me, mister?"

"Tell me, *chivato*, and I won't hurt you."

The boy looked at the *mayombero* and his heart said *liar*. "I know some of them," he said, starting to cry. "I know some. There's Officer Morgan. There's Officer Arena—"

Gabriel cut him off. "No, this one would be a lieutenant, maybe a sergeant. Not too young, not too old. Not afraid."

"Look, *señor*, I'm kind of new here. I'm from Chicago 'til six months ago." Prado stopped, sobbing now. They were in the trees by the ditch. No one could see them there. No one could help him there.

"You can do better, *pendejo*. Just a little more."

"There's Sergeant Rourke—"

The demon squeezed his shoulder, for he *was* a demon now.

"—and Sergeant Westonfield."

The demon squeezed his shoulder again so hard the boy shrieked in pain. At the sound of the name Gabriel's heart almost faltered. He was the one—this Westonfield. He was the one. "Only a little more, *Cabrón*," he said. "Only a very little more. Then it will all be over. No more pain for you! What about this Westonfield? He works near here? At the police station at Fort and Green?"

"*Sí,*" the boy wailed. He peed his pants.

"Yes?" Gabriel said, a sudden fury upon him.

"Please let me go, mister. Please!"

"Who knows him better, this Westonfield? Who knows

him?" Gabriel demanded.

The boy was silent except for the mewling animal sounds escaping from his drawn-open mouth. There was a sudden acid stench as he shit his pants.

Gabriel increased the pressure on the boy's shoulder yet again. There was a sickening sound of tearing ligaments, and finally of breaking bone.

"¡Ayúdame, Jesús!" the boy screamed.

"Tell me," the demon said gently in his ear, "and it will all be over."

"Katy," the boy finally whispered through clenched teeth. "Katy Marroquín and Danny—Danny Villanueva."

"Where are they now?"

The boy swooned.

"Where are they, I said? Just this little more!"

"Clark Park," gurgled the boy, so far gone now in terror and pain that he didn't care anymore.

The demon smiled a serene smile, the smell of death on his fetid breath. It was the boy's last observation on earth. With a quick twist, Gabriel broke his neck and rolled the body into the dirty water of the ditch.

* * *

Her grey sweatsuit soaked through, Magaly slid out of the car, stuck her head back in, and said, "Thanks, Jerry. But next time take it easy on the new kid, all right?"

Jerry Talmadge laughed. "Promise," he said. Tapping himself on the chest he added, "Not bad for an old man, eh?"

"No," Magaly replied. "Not bad for an old man." She shut the door of the Associated Press man's Chrysler and stepped back. She gave him a little wave, turned, and walked up the driveway to the lobby of the Pontch.

She had been hesitant to accept Jerry's invitation when he called in the morning. She had a couple of interviews scheduled, and she was feeling a little down. Now she was glad she'd acquiesced. The workout at Vic Tanny was like a tonic. Talmadge was very funny, and at fifty-six, he was an old-fashioned gentleman. He was from the South and had the air of a southern aristocrat. He worked-out twice a week at one of the suburban clubs where he had been a member since his AP assignment to Detroit in 1984.

Magaly walked into her room at five o'clock, wiping her still-red face. The telephone was ringing. It was Westonfield. "Hey, stranger," she said. "How was your visit with the kids?"

"Good," he said. "I miss them already, though. Every time I see them, when it's time to go, I miss them even more."

Magaly wondered what it would be like for a protective man like Westonfield to suddenly not be able to protect his own children, to lose them in a way. "Everything's all right?" she asked. "Nobody's sick?"

"No, they're fine," he answered.

"How about you? Is Jack okay?"

"Jack's fine, I guess," Westonfield said. "Haven't talked to him today. Me? I'm good for a man who's going through a divorce for the second time."

"Problems?"

"Nothing more than usual. Oh, hell... My kids' mom—Millie—she's getting married soon."

"Ahhh, just found out?" Magaly asked.

"I've known for a few days. Tracey told me last week," Westonfield said.

"Been thinking about it?"

"Yeah."

"Still hurts?"

"Two-time loser," Westonfield said.

"Do you think of it that way?"

"Hard not to."

"I don't know anything about your relationships," Magaly said. "I haven't even met your wives. But I don't think you're a loser." She could picture Bill's sad grey eyes.

Westonfield changed the subject. "So what have you been up

to?"

Magaly told him about going to Vic Tanny with Talmadge. "I'm whipped," she said. "But, God, I feel better! Physical activity always makes me feel better. Doesn't it you?"

"I don't have time," Westonfield said.

"Or the inclination?"

"Neither," he admitted.

"You could change," Magaly said.

"Me?"

"Yes. Even you."

"Not likely."

"Bill—"

"I called to see if you were coming out tonight," Westonfield interjected.

Magaly looked at her watch. "It's after five. I have to shower and grab a bite to eat."

Westonfield chuckled. "I appreciate the shower, but we can eat later. Together. At work."

"Whoa! He's laughing!" Magaly said. "A shower... Well, you're laughing." She brushed her hair back from her face, chiding herself for forgetting to take her headband to the club. "But anyway, I accept your invitation."

"Good. So, how were Adams and Arena last night?"

"Did you talk to them?"

"Yep."

"Lunatics," she said.

"Yep."

"Not like you, though," she said.

"Not at all."

"See you at six-thirty?"

"I'll be there," Westonfield said.

* * *

"Gets dark so early now," Danny Villanueva said. "It's barely six."

Katy nodded. She'd been quiet most of the day.

"Wonder where everybody's at?" he said.

Katy looked into the park, south across Vernor Highway. There was no sign of any of their fellow Latin Counts. It was a quiet fall evening, cool, but not cold. The sun was dipping behind the YWCA building on the west side of park. "Have you talked to any of them, Danny? Raúl? Ernesto?"

"No. I ain't seen 'em."

"Wonder where they are?"

They walked hand-in-hand across the street into the quiet north end of the park and then on into the middle, near where Rourke and Westonfield had talked to Katy several days before. They sat at a picnic table, their butts on the table, their feet on the bench.

Katy shivered. "It's cold," she said.

"It ain't that bad. Here—" He fished a joint out of his jacket pocket and handed it to her, followed with a Bic lighter.

She looked at it. "I don't want no dope now."

Danny studied her. "What's wrong? You been down all day." He sat silently for a moment, hugging her close to him, enjoying her body heat. He truly did want to please her. "Is it about the warrant thing?"

"I guess so. Yeah. It's... I just don't want to be sitting out here when I'm old, Danny."

He sighed. "I suppose it wouldn't hurt to talk to Sergeant Westonfield."

She looked at him in surprise.

"I just said *talk* to him, now."

Katy smiled broadly. "Thanks, Danny. You won't be sorry." She took him by the hand.

"Anything else on your mind?" he asked.

She shivered again. "Just a feeling."

"What kind of feeling?"

"I don't know. Cold."

"Me too."

After a moment she said, "Something's going on in the

neighborhood. Something spooky."

"What?"

"You heard about the Merritt thing, with the police?"

"Yeah."

"That was Sergeant Rourke and Sergeant Westonfield."

"I heard," Danny said.

"Tía Lúz—she told me about what was going on at that house." Katy related the story.

"Weird," Danny said.

"Yeah," Katy replied, shivering again. "Yeah." Without thinking, she lit up the joint and took a deep drag.

* * *

Since Rourke wasn't there, Magaly rode in the front seat. Three minutes after getting into the unmarked police car she said, "I'm hungry."

"That's what you said when I talked to you on the telephone," Westonfield said.

"Yeah, and that was two hours ago," Magaly replied.

He continued to drive up Fort Street, toward downtown, silent. When he showed no sign of heading for a restaurant, or even inquiring where she might like to eat, Magaly said, "I'm fucking hungry—"

"*Fucking* hungry?" Westonfield said.

Magaly studied him. "Right. Fucking hungry."

"In that case, where to?" Westonfield asked. Before she could answer, he said, out of the blue, "I'm glad you're here."

"I am, too," Magaly said, surprised.

In a moment Westonfield asked, "What do you feel like?"

"What?"

"To eat. What do you feel like?"

"Jeez, you have a way of switching gears!" Magaly retorted. "I was still working on the *I'm glad you're here* part."

The barest of smiles flickered at the corner of Westonfield's mouth. "Feel better?" he asked.

"Uh-huh."

"Good."

"*Almendrado,*" Magaly said suddenly.

"What?"

"La Fuente de Elena. It was great. The *almendrado* was great."

"Again?"

"Why not? It was wonderful."

"Okay," Westonfield said. As they headed in the direction of the restaurant he asked, "How's your brother?"

"Aurelio?"

"Is that his name?"

"Yes. Aurelio. He's dying, Bill."

"Nothing can be done?"

"No."

"Anything I can do?"

"No."

"Soon?"

"I think so."

"Then you'll have to go back."

"To New York? Yes."

"Will you come back here afterwards?"

Magaly looked at him, studied him closely as he drove. "You know that I will," she finally said. "I have another brother who's just like you."

"How's that?" Westonfield asked.

"Diego," she said. "Well, he's not really like you in most ways, but he is in the way I'm thinking about now."

Westonfield looked at her quizzically. "How?"

"About women. I mean about the women in his life. He thinks about them all the time."

Westonfield squinted at her with that funny squint of his. "You think I do that?"

"Uh-huh."

"What makes you think that?"

"My own observations. Things that you've said to me.

Things others have said to me."

Westonfield grimaced. "It's a tough time for me," he said defensively.

"Want to talk about it?" Magaly asked.

"Now?"

"Uh-huh."

"Some other time," Westonfield said.

They went to the restaurant, enjoying each other's company.

* * *

Gabriel was exhausted. The girl, the strange little blonde girl, had been surprisingly difficult. He had what he wanted in the end, of course. How could he not? But the girl made it more interesting than it might otherwise have been. He idly wiped blood from his arms with a dirty pillow case. He was nearly done. He carefully went through the house on Chamberlain one more time, room by room. Everything was in order. Nothing to associate him with the house. No fingerprints. No traceable weapons. No witnesses. The house, like the one on Merritt, rented by Tomás. Poor dead Tomás. Gabriel laughed.

He put the bloody pillow case into the big black trash bag, along with all of the tools he had used. He looked down at the bodies. He loved them. He would have liked to spend a little more time with them. But haste was upon him. He wasn't sure why, but he felt a need to hurry along. He glanced wistfully once more around the rooms and then went out again into the cool night. He laughed again. The breeze felt marvelous on his sweat-coated skin. Soon it would snow.

* * *

As was her custom, Mary Lempke was drunk by ten o'clock. She sat in front of the television set in the little shack on Chamberlain, a bottle of Jack Daniels beside her on the table, a half-full glass in her scabby hand. She was trying to watch one of the shopping channels on cable but couldn't seem to get it right. Then she heard the sound. Just barely. Her little house, which she rented for a hundred-fifty a month from that bastard Wally Lomax, was not really a house as much as it was a garage, or maybe a large chicken coop. It stood at the back of a large lot where there once had stood a house. The house was gone. Torn down. But the shack still stood, almost as an afterthought. She had electricity, water, and even cable, but you wouldn't have noticed the house unless it was pointed out to you. It stood only thirty feet from Gabriel's house. Even he hadn't noticed it.

Mary started hearing the sounds about nine, and they continued for over an hour. Strange, whining sounds, almost like the keening of a dog. A gut-shot dog, thought Mary, recalling her considerable experience with gut-shot dogs when she was a girl in Floyd County, Kentucky. Goddammit! How's a body to watch the TV with all that racket? There was even a high-pitched shriek or two thrown in, just for effect, she thought. Goddamned kids! Little Spic and nigger boys, raising hell all the time.

By eleven o'clock she had enough. After one last drawn-out moan she reached for the telephone. She almost spilled a whole glass of whiskey in her haste, which would have heaped enormous insult upon the already grievous injury she felt. Fortunately, she was able to save it. She punched in the numbers.

"911?" Mary said. When the faceless operator responded with the standard *Emergency center—where is the problem?* she retorted, "Well, if you'll hold on a minute, I'll tell you where the goddamn problem is!"

* * *

The run came out at 11:20 p.m. Arena and Johnson got it. "4-33?" said the dispatcher. "4-33, you available?"

Johnson grabbed the mike. "4-33's ready to go."

"Okay, '33, you're all I've got..." Normally a marked unit would get this kind of call, but the uniforms were all busy on other runs. "Make 6235 Chamberlain—stand by..." Momentary silence, then, "Make the house *next to* 6235 Chamberlain. The brown house with green trim, on the west side. They say there's people screaming and moaning and making a racket over there." He repeated the information.

"On the way, 4-33," Johnson said drolly into the mike.

* * *

"4-78? Radio 4-78?"
Westonfield retrieved the microphone. "4-78. Go."
"4-78, go to channel five for 4-33." The private channel.
"Okay on the info. 4-78's switching."
"4-78 to 4-33."
"4-33 here, Sarge. We're at 6241 Chamberlain." Pause. "You better get over here, boss." It was Arena. He sounded shaky.
"All right, 4-33. I'm on the way. What do you have?"
"Bad one, Sarge. Homicide. Looks like a double. Better get over here."
"You make your notifications?"
"Not yet, boss. Wanted to let you know first."
That was strange. Not like Bob. He would know that you always notified dispatch of the situation first, then placed phone calls to Homicide and the Control Section. Only then might you call for your immediate supervisor.
"Okay, '33. Make your calls. I'm on the way," Westonfield said.

CHAPTER 18

Magaly Rodríguez was puking her guts out. *Almendrado.* First it was projectile vomiting onto the left rear tire of the police car. But that was a few moments ago. Now she was on her knees in the grass by the curb, wheezing and hacking like the sick coyote she'd once seen at the Bronx Zoo—a sort of strangled, gagging sound, combined with whooping cough. All the food she had eaten at La Fuente was gone. Now there was just yellow bile and mucous, a little clinging to her lower lip. But she couldn't stop puking. And she couldn't stop the tears. She puked and cried at the same time.

When they arrived at the house on Chamberlain to meet 4-33 Magaly immediately knew something was very wrong, that this wasn't going to be a routine homicide. Johnson was at the side of the front porch, vomiting. Did cops ever puke over gore? Then they were out of the car and Arena, his normally brown Latin face a sickly yellow, said to Westonfield, "It's bad, Bill. It's—I think it's Danny and Katy." He wiped his moist eyes with the palm of his hand, his chin quivering slightly. "It's Danny Villanueva and Katy Marroquín. It's real fucking bad." *Arena called him "Bill,"* Magaly thought.

Then Westonfield was walking swiftly to the house, up the steps two-at-a-time, entering through the front door. Magaly trotted behind him, intent upon his reaction, oblivious to Arena coming up beside her, taking her by the arm and repeating over and over, "Magaly, don't go in there." She ignored him, pulled away. He shouted at her, pulling at her arm, "Please, you don't want to go in there." But she jerked free and went on, her attention riveted on Westonfield. They passed within two feet of

Johnson. He ignored them, continued puking.

Then she entered upon the most horrible scene of animal brutality she was ever to witness. Staggered as she was, though, by the sheer scale of the bloodletting and torture—clearly, it had been torture—the shock was subordinated by the look on Westonfield's face. It held her in rapt attention, turned her to stone. Something alive in him died, even as she watched. The look in his eyes was the look of a father observing the death of his own daughter. He was standing stock still, his head cocked at an odd angle. His eyes were wet, where no tears ever found a home. The sad, grey orbs drifted from sight to terrible sight, taking them in, absorbing the blood like a sponge. He nodded his head ever so slightly. Magaly could almost hear him speak, though he was as quiet as a tomb. She could hear him say the words: *"It's all right, baby. It's all right now. I'm here. I won't let him hurt you anymore."*

Westonfield stood that way for what seemed like an eternity to Magaly. Then Arena was beside her again, telling her, "Come on now, Magaly. Let's go now. You've seen enough."

She finally heard him, understood him, tore her eyes from Westonfield, looked at Arena. "Okay," she said. "Okay." Then, turning toward Westonfield, she said to Arena, "Bill—we have to get Bill."

Arena pulled her away. "No, let the sarge be. Let him be. He's going to want to stay for a while. He don't need us now. Let him be."

Finally the smell, the overwhelming stench of blood and excrement and vomit overcame her and she consented to be led away. The dead eyes in Danny Villanueva's severed head looked at her in surprise. Then she was sick.

* * *

Homicide Sergeant Gene Beck thought he'd seen it all until he got to Chamberlain Street. His first impression was that Hollywood couldn't have staged a better setting. From the moment he and his partner Morton Bickerstaff pulled onto Chamberlain off Woodmere in their unmarked car he felt as if he were inside a movie. The sky had cleared and a huge full moon rode high over the eastern horizon, pouring its silver light over the dark street. Several marked and unmarked police cars were parked haphazardly along the curb in front of a rundown old frame house. Uniformed and plainclothes police officers milled around in front of the house and on the front porch. *Goddamm uniforms,* he thought, *probably fucking up the scene.*

He and Bickerstaff had barely stepped out of the car when they were accosted by an old woman with a highball glass in her hand and whiskey on her breath. "You guys gotta be the Homicide detectives, I bet—aren't you? My name's Mary Lempke. It's me that called."

"Have you made a statement, ma'am?" Beck asked, rolling his eyes at Bickerstaff. "We'll need a statement from you. Look, talk to this officer right here." He motioned for one of the uniforms to come over.

"It's me that called, officer," said Mary drunkenly, ignoring Beck. She stepped off the curb, stumbling, sloshing her drink over the side of the glass. "I called it in. The goddamm kids—the little bastards have did it now, ain't they? Goddamn 'em to hell! I'm lucky it ain't me in there all butchered, I tell you. Goddamn Mex bastards!" She looked around her. "And the niggers, too, goddamn 'em. I don't never get no peace around here. Not never."

"We'll take care of it for you—Mary, did you say your name was? Now you talk to this young policeman here." Beck looked at the rookie who was standing by. "Take a statement from this nice lady, would you, officer?"

Beck nodded to Bickerstaff and they walked together toward the house. Then the smell hit him. Jesus! He noticed Arena, whom he was acquainted with, standing near the porch. "What you got, Bob? Jesus motherfucking Christ! It smells like a goddamm barf-a-rama out here. We're near waist-deep in puke." He studied Arena. "You ain't sick, are you?"

"No, I'm not sick, Sergeant Beck."

"Well, I'm glad we got one of you who can talk anyway." He looked around at Johnson and Magaly, who were by now done vomiting, but were in no shape to talk. "Whatcha got?" he repeated.

"Double, boss. Real bad. Blood every fucking place. They're cut up like chickens."

"Shit."

"Yeah." Arena wiped his eyes again.

"What's wrong, Bob? You know these people or something?" Beck asked.

"Local kids, Sarge. A couple of local kids. Gang bangers—"

"Hell, that ain't no loss," Bickerstaff put in lamely.

Arena looked at the Homicide detective. "Maybe. Maybe not." He looked at the ground for a moment and then looked up. "But I wouldn't say anything like that in there if I was you, Sergeant Bickerstaff. Sergeant Westonfield would... well, he might—"

"Bill's in there?" Beck asked. He knew him well. They had worked together at the old Tactical Mobile Unit years before.

Arena nodded. "He's in there. Been in there for forty minutes."

"He knows the victims?"

"He knows 'em."

"All right." Beck looked at Bickerstaff, then back to Arena. "Don't mind Morty. He ate some bad chicken salad earlier today. Didn't you, Morty?"

"Yeah," grumbled Bickerstaff. "Stomach." He looked at Magaly. "Who's the lady?"

"She's a writer from *Harper's Magazine*," Arena said. "She's been riding around with the Power Shift the last few days. She's out with Sergeant Westonfield tonight."

Beck looked at Magaly, looked at the piles of vomit scattered around, looked at the open door of the murder house. "She picked a good night," he said.

* * *

"Aw, shit," Beck said when they stepped through the door and he got a good look at the scene.

Westonfield turned to see who it was, recognized his old friend. He said nothing.

Well, he never was much for talking, thought Beck. "Goddamn, Bill. I hear you know these people."

Westonfield nodded.

"You all right?"

Westonfield breathed deeply. "Sure, Gene. I'm all right."

"Ready for us to take over?"

"It's all yours," Westonfield said. He looked at Bickerstaff, who'd come up behind. He didn't like him. Bickerstaff was a career bureau man, not much street time, something of a ghoul. "Hi, Morty," he said.

Bickerstaff blinked in answer. He didn't much care for Westonfield, either.

As Westonfield turned to leave, Beck said, "See you downtown for statements? We'll want to find out as much as we can about these folks."

"Yeah."

"Okay." He shrugged. "Sorry about this, Billy." Then, "What a night, Bill. This isn't the only one, you know. Not twenty minutes ago we got another one over in Patton Park. Kid with a broken neck, looks like. Gang banger."

Westonfield looked at him. "Oh?"

"Squad Seven's on the way over there now. Busy night. By the way, I got something else for you, too." He reached into the inside pocket of his jacket and pulled out a piece of crumpled paper. "I was going to give this to you anyway; was gonna give you a call. That shooting over on Merritt? Rourke's? We finally got around to going through that car—what's his name... that Cuban Mejías's car—and we found a newspaper clipping mixed up in some papers over the visor. It was on a killing they had down there in Trenton a while back. Remember? A

Jamaican something-or-other murdered and left in a boat at the county marina. Maybe there's a connection between them—you think? Maybe rivals, or whatever. 'Course, it could be just hero worship, too," he added, chuckling. "Hell, I don't know. I don't work dope. I'm just the assistant morgue manager, right?"

Westonfield was lost in thought for a moment. "Who's got the information on it, Gene? I'd like to get involved in this if I can. Can I follow up on it?"

"Give Buck a call. You know Buck, don't you?"

"Yeah."

"Okay, give him a call and he'll let you know what we've got. You want to work it, work it. Lord knows we could use the help."

"Thanks, Gene," Westonfield said. "Listen—would you mind if I went by the Patton Park scene to see what I can see before I go downtown? I think all this just may be connected in some way. I'd like to get a jump on finding out how."

Beck nodded. "Sure. Why not?"

Westonfield looked at Bickerstaff, who was already poking around the bodies. "Don't enjoy it too much, Morty," he said.

Bickerstaff ignored the remark.

Beck was glad. All he needed was for Bill Westonfield to beat the living shit out of his partner while they were on duty working a homicide case.

Then Westonfield did a strange thing. He went to where the little blonde girl lay on the bed—what was left of her: her naked body had been eviscerated, the intestines lying in a stinking pile on the floor beside her. The skin had been removed, one would say peeled, from her lower legs. The medical examiner would later report that this had been done while she was still living. There was an object of some kind—a black nightstick?—protruding from her vagina. A mucous-like material, perhaps semen, was smeared on her face. Her heart had been cut out of her chest; Bickerstaff was looking at it in the black kettle on the table by the wall.

"Liar," Westonfield said softly, pressing the fingers of his right hand gently against Katy's cheek. "Little liar. Danny wasn't in Chicago."

Beck looked quickly at Bickerstaff again, praying that his partner wouldn't admonish Westonfield for disturbing "the evidence." His intuition told him that that would be the most foolish thing Morty ever did in his whole foolish life. He sighed with relief. Morty was preoccupied with the girl's heart.

* * *

When Westonfield emerged from the house he completely ignored Magaly and everyone else. He hesitated for just a second on the porch, surveying the scene. Then he walked out to the sidewalk, peering in both directions into the darkness down Chamberlain Street. He stood stock still, breathing, sensing. He then walked all the way around the house, looking at the windows, looking at the walls.

Magaly began to walk toward him to join him. Arena took her by the arm once again. "I wouldn't do that yet, Magaly," he said. "You'll be wanting to ask him questions. He won't be in the mood to answer questions. Let him do what he's going to do. Give him a little time."

Magaly started to protest, but she knew Arena was right. She dabbed at her mouth and chin with a wadded Kleenex. "Guess I look pretty foolish…"

"Yes," Arena said. "You do." He glanced toward his unmarked police car and Rupert Johnson. "But no more than him," he said. Johnson looked back sheepishly out of the semi-darkness.

"What's he going to do?" Magaly asked.

"Sergeant Westonfield?"

"Yeah," Magaly said.

"Dunno," Arena replied. "I'd hate like hell to be around to see it, though."

When Westonfield returned to the front of the house, he summarily interrupted the uniformed policeman who stood with pen poised over notepad, interviewing Mary Lempke. "Did you ever see who lived in this house?" he demanded.

Mary looked up at Westonfield in surprise. She started to reply, but when she looked into his eyes something she saw in them stopped her.

"Did-you-ever-see-who-lived-in-this-house?" Westonfield repeated. His voice was calm, dead calm, but there was an air of imminent danger in it that frightened Mary. She was so scared, in fact, that she forgot she was holding a glass of whiskey, and dropped it. It shattered on the cement. The rookie jumped back.

"No, sir," she said, sobering quickly. "I always figgered it was kids. You know, them damn kids. Them gangs."

"Did you ever see a man?" Westonfield insisted. "A big black man? By himself—maybe with another black man?"

"No, sir, I didn't," Mary said.

Westonfield's eyes studied her. She flinched as if from a physical blow. Then he turned on his heel and walked away in dismissal. The patrolman took up his pad again.

There were always lights in Westonfield's eyes, twinkling amidst a field of grey. As he approached Magaly, she saw fire in them, a silver fire, reflecting the light of the moon. Cold as the grave. She went to him. She took his arm and held it. She thought he might push her away, but he looked at her and the faintest of smiles returned. Then his eyes went to the full moon and he held it in his gaze for a long time. At first, Magaly thought she felt him tremble. Then she heard the sound—a high, ethereal keening, just at the edge of hearing. It came from all around her, from the earth under her feet, from the sky above her, from the silver moon. Never before had she heard this sound. She looked around to see if others could hear it, but they seemed oblivious. The sound increased in intensity—slowly, steadily. The trembling continued, too. The sound and the trembling were in the texture of the air, in the atoms that made up the world, in the very fabric of space. Magaly's eyes found Westonfield's again. They were wells of molten mercury. There was death in them: death to whoever had perpetrated the deeds on Chamberlain Street. Then she understood. By chance, or bad luck, or twist of fate, she had been drawn into a great game—a preternatural game that would be played outside the normal rules; and the players were far beyond her.

Aguanilleo Zarabanda aribo. Space screamed. The earth screamed. The moon turned yellow for an instant. Magaly's heart froze. But she looked at Westonfield again, and he stood beside her. He was smiling that curious smile of his, and the moon turned silver again, and the trembling stopped. The singing stopped. The moment passed.

"It was him," Westonfield said.

Magaly nodded. "I know."

"He killed that little girl. He did all of those things."

"I know."

"I let him do it," Westonfield said.

"But you couldn't have known, Bill. You couldn't have prevented this."

"Her name was Katy," he said.

"I know," Magaly said, starting to cry again. "Bob Arena told me."

"I could have stopped him."

"No."

"I could have gotten her out of here."

"No."

"She was—" He held out his arms in supplication.

"I know who she was," Magaly sobbed. "I know."

"I'm going to kill him," Westonfield said.

"I know."

"I'm going to kill him," he repeated.

Magaly clung to his arm, wiped her tears, and looked into his eyes again. The silver fire was gone. Absolute singularity of purpose had replaced it. And the familiar lights were back, twinkling amidst the grey; but the death in them remained.

Magaly heard a shout coming from the house and turned to see Beck trotting toward them. "Bill," he said breathlessly.

"Glad I caught you before you left. I gotta tell you something. Something we found." He pulled a soiled hanky from his jacket pocket and wiped his face. "Jesus, what a scene! Never, in all my years on this fucking job, have I ever seen such a thing."

Westonfield looked at him patiently.

Beck went on. "On that girl's back, up by her shoulders, there's some letters carved into the skin." He glanced at Magaly, his face flushed.

"She's working," Westonfield said, too impatient to take the time to explain Magaly's presence.

"Of course, you can't be sure what the hell it means," Beck said. "Hard to say. But I know you've been working with the gangs down here. Then there's Rourke's shooting, and now that dead kid over in Patton Park, so—"

"What is it, Gene?"

"Well, it looks like it might be initials," Beck said, swallowing. "*W. W.* —William Westonfield, maybe?"

* * *

It turned out Westonfield knew the officer in charge of the Patton Park scene as well. His name was Paul Randazzo, a short, heavy-set veteran of thirty years. He talked like an old-time professional fighter. When the Homicide man saw Westonfield emerge out of the darkness and step into the circle of light cast by the generator-powered floodlights, he said, "Christ, Bill, why don't you get yourself a real job? You still fucking around out here in Beantown? You'd think a fella would learn."

"Yeah, but you know me," Westonfield replied. "I love my wetbacks. Speaking of which—" he gestured for Magaly to come forward—"this is Magaly Rodríguez."

"Now that there's a fine-looking wetback," Randazzo remarked. He grinned, taking her hand. "Your new partner?"

"She's a reporter."

"Well, get her the hell outta here, Bill!" Randazzo shouted, instantly angry. "You know we can't have reporters traipsing around a fresh scene. Have you completely lost your mind?"

"She's USDA-approved, Pauly," Westonfield said. "On assignment with me. Downtown knows about it. Don't have a heart attack or anything."

"All right, all right," Randazzo said, calming a little, peering suspiciously at Magaly. "I'm busy here, in case you can't tell. What do you want?"

"You know about the Chamberlain beef?"

"Yeah. Beck's on it."

"Right. Well, we were just over there. It's a bad one. I think these two might be connected."

"How come? I know Chamberlain's close by, but—"

"So let's quit wasting time," Westonfield interjected. "Show me what you got."

Randazzo led them a few feet through some trees to the ditch. "Watch your step, Miss," Randazzo said, "It's kind of slippery by the bank here." He pointed down into the defile. Miguel Prado's body lay on the muddy bank of the creek. His open eyes stared lifelessly into the sky, his head bent at an odd angle. "Broken neck, looks like," Randazzo said. "Maybe the left shoulder, too. Looks kind of cockeyed, don't you think? We'll have to wait for the medical examiner's report, of course." He looked at Westonfield. "Know 'em?"

Westonfield stared at the boy. "Yeah."

"Name?"

"Miguel Prado."

Randazzo wrote it down carefully in his notebook. "What else?"

"Not much. He's kind of new. Came in from Chicago a few months back." Westonfield thought for a moment. "Maybe this spring. He's a Count. A Latin Count."

Randazzo wrote it all down. "Anything else?"

"Not too much."

"Address?"

"We probably have it at the station."

"Okay," Randazzo said. "When you get back in, can you call me with it?"

"Sure."

"See anything that might tie this one in with the other one?" Randazzo asked.

"The kid looks scared to death," Westonfield said.

"More like he was neck-broke to death," Randazzo quipped.

"Yeah, I know," Westonfield said, ignoring the remark. "But look at his face."

Randazzo dispassionately studied Prado's face for a moment. "Yeah, I see what you mean."

"This kid knew what was coming," Westonfield said firmly. "That's why he looks like that, Paul."

"Sherlock fucking Holmes," Randazzo said, amused. "I guess you're the one that oughta be the Homicide dick, and I ought to be chasing gangsters in the company of pretty reporters out in Del Ray."

Westonfield ignored him. "They're related," he said. "The killings are related, Paul."

Randazzo shrugged.

"I think the autopsy will show that this one died a little while before the victims over on Chamberlain."

"Now how the hell would you know that?" Randazzo asked, incredulous.

They walked back into the open away from the ditch.

"He was looking for me," Westonfield said.

"What the hell are you talking about?"

"The guy who did this," Westonfield said, pointing toward the ditch, "and the guy who did the other one are one in the same. He's the shithead I chased over on Merritt and Junction, the one whose buddy Tomás—I don't know why, Pauly, but since then he's been looking for me."

The veteran detective scratched his head. "You think so?"

"Yeah," Westonfield said. "I'm sure."

"Okay, so how do these two murders tonight tie in?"

Westonfield looked back into the dark beneath the trees, and Miguel Prado's lifeless body. "He figured out how to find me," he said.

* * *

As they drove to the Homicide Section to make their statements, Magaly said, "I won't ask you now, but one day—one day, will you tell me about Katy?"

"She was sixteen," Westonfield said. "I let her die. Will that hold you for a while?"

"You're hurting," Magaly said. "Another time."

Westonfield felt suddenly guilty. Magaly had been patient through everything. She had instinctively acted to protect him when everyone else was merely afraid of him. "No," he said after a while. "It's me who should be sorry."

"Accepted," Magaly said.

"Good," Westonfield said. "You sure as hell walked into it, didn't you?"

"Yeah."

"You should quit," he said. "None of us bargained for this. It's not safe now, Magaly. I can't be responsible for you. Anything could happen. Look what he's done. Just look at what he's done—" There was a helplessness in his tone that Magaly had never heard before.

"I *should* quit," Magaly said. "If my editor knew everything, he'd make me quit. But I won't."

"Why?" Westonfield asked, a little surprised.

"Don't ask me that," Magaly replied. "You already know the answer."

"Yeah," Westonfield said. "Because you're stubborn like me."

"Something like that."

"You're worse," Westonfield said. But he was secretly glad she would stay, that she *wanted* to stay. If she left he would miss her. His second divorce was still pending, and it scared him to think how much he would miss her if she left forever.

"What are you going to do now?" Magaly asked.

"I told you."

"I guess you did," she said. *Kill him*, he'd said. *I'm going to kill him.* She thought about the dead blonde girl, Katy. Had she been pretty? What would the suburbanites think when they read the stories in the morning paper—when they read about her murder from the safety of their kitchens? Would they pause over their corn flakes? Would they dig out a map of the city to see where Chamberlain Street was? Would they wonder where she lived, if she had brothers and sisters, if she went to school? Who cared? As far as she could see, the sum total of those to whom Katy Marroquín's life mattered a tinker's damn was a handful of sad-faced cops. The loneliness of it, the unspeakable horror of it, the utter pointlessness of it, overwhelmed Magaly. She began to cry again.

Westonfield left her alone, let her weep. Sometimes tears were the only medicine that would make the pain go away. But not for him—never for him. He drove in silent self-loathing, the image of his initials cut into Katy Marroquín's back burning a hole into his brain. The simple truth as he saw it was that she had not died in *spite* of him, she had died on *account* of him. And the moonlight glowed down upon him, painting the whole city nickel-white, for the rest of the long night.

CHAPTER 19

Rourke was surprised to hear Magaly's voice on the telephone. "Decided you couldn't live without me?" he asked.

"I left my teddy bear in New York," Magaly said. "You're the only teddy bear I've seen since I came to Detroit."

"I'm a happily married man," Rourke said. "Shame on you." He was highly amused, having been called many things in his life, but never a teddy bear. "Bill give you my number?"

"Yes," Magaly said. "Is it all right that I called?"

"Sure. How's Bill doing?"

She told him all about the day before.

"I should have known things were too quiet up here," Rourke said. "I guess I'll pack up and come back. Sounds like a real shit storm. Bill don't feel completely satisfied without a maniac or two trying to kill him. Gives him something to do. Revenge and undying hates—grist for the Westonfield mill. I better get down there before he wipes out half the crooks in town, or else they kill him first."

"Don't you have a couple more days off coming?" Magaly asked.

"Well, yeah, but—"

She said all in a rush, "Would you mind... do you think... could I come up there for a visit? I don't want to be responsible for making you come back to all of this, Jack. Your friend can take care of himself for a while. You, of all people, know that. But I'd like to talk to you about what happened, hear your feelings on a few things. Would that be all right?"

Rourke thought about it. Carol would probably like to meet her. He could call Bill and find out what the hell was going on, and then come back to Detroit after the weekend. "You sure you want to drive all the way up here?" he asked.

"Yes, I'm sure," Magaly answered. "Your wife won't mind?"

Rourke decided then and there that the girl was clairvoyant. "No," he answered, "she won't mind." He gave her directions.

* * *

Jack and Carol Rourke lived in a small bungalow on an acre of grass between a small apple orchard and a field of sugar beets. As Magaly drove up the dirt road toward the house she saw that there were a few late apples hanging from the trees in the orchard, though most were already picked or had fallen to the ground. The day was warm and her window was cracked a little. The pleasant, sweet smell of rotting apples drifted in. When she pulled into the white-graveled driveway, Rourke was raking leaves beneath the limbs of a huge maple tree. He had already filled a couple of garbage pails, but several big piles of leaves dotted the lawn. He turned at the sound of the car crunching up the driveway.

"Keeping busy, I see," Magaly said as she got out of her car and walked up to him. "You have a beautiful place. Where's your help?"

"Carol ran out to the store for a few things," Rourke said. "Company coming."

There was something endearing about the big grin on his unshaven face, his thinning hair a mess atop his head, his belly pressing out the flannel shirt over his belt. When he held out his hand Magaly took it, but she stepped close and hugged him, resting her head on his chest. He was caught by surprise, standing silently for a moment, the rake cradled in the crook of one arm, the other arm encircled her shoulders.

"It was awful," Magaly said. "I never want to see anything like that again. Not ever."

The way she said it, the way she hugged him, somehow

reminded Rourke of his daughter. "I know," he said. "I know."

When she pulled back, she said, "I'm scared! I'm scared for Bill. I'm scared for Bob and Rupe and Benny and all the rest of the guys. What's going to happen now, Jack?"

Rourke set the rake down and methodically pulled the gloves off his hands. "Let's go in the house and get us some coffee or something, all right? Carol's baked an apple pie and some hellacious pumpkin cookies, though I suspect she'd kill me for spoiling your appetite if you were to eat any—she's got a dinner planned for us. She's anxious to meet you. Excited, more like it. Carol don't get to meet many new people way out here."

* * *

Magaly sipped her tea in a sunny spot at the oak table by the bay window in the kitchen. It was good to be with Jack again, to talk to him. "I can see why you live here," she said. "It reminds me of my aunt's house in Maryland. It's so quiet and peaceful." She was looking out the window at the wild asters growing along the banks of a creek that flowed out of the orchard and across a corner of the Rourke property, the flowers' mustard-yellow centers bright against the purple petals. They made her think of her brother Aurelio. "It's so beautiful! You must be very happy here."

"Like pigs in shit," Rourke said.

"That much?" Magaly said, laughing. "I'm glad, Jack. I am. This is so different from the city—your own private piece of the 'good life,' safe and hidden." She put more honey in her tea. "Do your kids like it, way out here away from the hustle and bustle? I'm thinking kids might like the social life more than the wildlife sometimes."

"It was an adjustment for them at first," Rourke said. "But they got used to it pretty quick. They like their school. They both get good grades and they've never been in any kind of trouble. Sheila's in the Girl Scouts and Steve's in a couple of clubs at school. There's kids their age nearby to hang out with. All in all, it's been good. Only problem is that I miss them all like hell when I'm back down in the city working."

"I wish it was different for you," Magaly said. "I wish you didn't have to live that way. It must be hard."

Rourke nodded. "It is. How's the tea?"

"Wonderful. And the cookie, too. I promise I won't tell Carol a word."

"Deal," he said. Then, "You saw the whole thing—with Danny and Katy?"

"Yes. I saw it."

"Hard."

"Yes."

"How was Bill?"

"How is he ever?"

"I mean, how was he with Katy? For some reason she was special to him. I don't know why."

"Tell me about her, Jack."

"I don't really know much," Rourke said. "She was sixteen or so. She went with Danny for quite a while. She ate, breathed, and slept the Latin Counts. She ran Vernor Highway with her friends. I think she came from a big family. I remember her saying something about having a lot of brothers and sisters. I always thought it was kind of funny, her being blonde and having blue eyes and all, her being Mexican."

"It's not so strange," Magaly said absently. She was remembering Westonfield's reaction to the scene of horror inside the house. "Bill was very quiet," she said. "But he was bleeding on the inside. I could see it. I could feel it in him. It made me want to die, he was so sad. He blames himself. He says he should have been there, should have done something."

"Bill would feel that way," Rourke said. "It's his way to feel like that. If he didn't, he wouldn't be Bill." Rourke took a big bite of a cookie, slurped his coffee. "He's probably home painting his garage."

"What?"

"He's most likely cut his grass a time or two by now, washed his car, changed the oil, done a lot of laundry, filed his taxes, and then moved on to the painting." Rourke looked pensive. "If I remember right, the siding on his garage was peeled. I bet it needed a good scraping. Bill will like that; there'll be enough to keep him busy for a while."

Magaly looked at him. "Jack, what the hell are you talking about?"

"You ought to ask one of his wives that, Maggie. They could tell you better. They suffered longer and with more regularity than me."

"Neither one of them will talk to me," Magaly said. "I've asked. They both turned me down for interviews."

"Well, I'm not surprised," Rourke said.

"Me, either. But what are you talking about?" she repeated.

"Bill likes to be in control."

"Of what?"

"Now that's a good question," Rourke said, finishing the cookie, sipping his coffee. "Of everything, I guess. Everything that he can."

"Why?"

"I'll tell you a story—" He looked at his watch. "Carol will be home soon, so I'll make it a short one. One day a friend of Bill's on the job, fella by the name of Short Johnny Peters—I won't tell you how he came by that name—was on a traffic stop on the Lodge Freeway. This was about three years ago. Anyway, Short John was out of his scout car, talking to the guy he'd pulled over. He was scrinched up as close as he could get to the guy's car, but it just wasn't John's day. A kid came flying along in a Z-28 and creamed him. I mean this kid must have been doing eighty. He caught John with his right bumper and launched him into orbit. Knocked him completely out of his shoes. I swear to God," Rourke said, crossing himself, "his shoes were laid out on the shoulder like they were put there by his mom before he went to school."

Magaly looked at Rourke in silent astonishment.

"So," he went on, "John came back to earth about a hundred yards down the freeway, right in the center lane. A Kenworth tractor and trailer hauling live pigs over to the Eastern Market hit him then. He got caught up in the under carriage of the truck and then spit out the rear. Then three or four cars came along and hit him. They bounced him along another few hundred yards or so. Then the Kenworth jack-knifed and turned over. The trailer opened up and the pigs started running all over the highway. One or two of them got hit, too."

Magaly stared at him. "This is true..."

"Gospel," Rourke said.

"That's terrible, Jack."

"If Shorty hadn't been in eleven pieces scattered along the pavement, he would probably have felt the same," Rourke said. "But the point is, me and Bill heard the call and went on down there. Hell, there was nothing we could do. It looked like a demolition derby crossed with a 4H Club meeting. We got the state police on the scene and we helped them block traffic and all. We had to be careful ourselves, though. We were in an unmarked unit. So, what does Bill do? He gets out of the car, finds out it's Short John, and starts walking up and down the freeway, picking up pieces of John and carrying them back to the police car. He laid them out on the shoulder in more or less the proper order, like a puzzle. Now, you have to understand, when Bill starts doing something like that, there's no stopping him. So I just stood there and watched him collecting John and putting him in order. Hell, I liked John, too. A hell of a euchre player, as I recall. But if he wasn't dead and beyond repair, then I don't know who was. But it was real important to Bill, absolutely critical, I mean, that John be put back together."

"Bill did that?" Magaly asked.

"Oh, that's not all," Rourke said. "He got god-awful frustrated when he couldn't find Short John's left leg. He looked all over hell for it and just absolutely could not find it. He came over to me after a while and asked me to help him look for it. I refused, of course. I told him it might have got hung up under a Toyota and carried to Chicago. He got pissed at me and called me a few motherfuckers, but he kept on looking for the leg. Fortunately, a couple of EMS guys found it sticking out of a bush and brought it over. Bill would probably still be out there looking for the goddamn thing if they hadn't."

"Why did he do that?" Magaly asked. "What was the point? I guess somebody would eventually have had to do it, but—God! This man was his friend."

"Yes, he was," Rourke said. "And you know, I've given Bill's peculiar behavior a lot of thought over the years. I think I've figured this one out. See, all of these things, all these horrible things that you see out there on the job—well, you can't do anything about them. Squat. Not a goddamn thing. So Bill has this hangup about little things. You can control them. Understand? You can't stop Shorty from being dead, but you *can* arrange him. You can't stop any of the terrible things that happen in life. Bill knows that. So he controls what he can. You know: do the dishes, wipe your feet, remember to turn the lights off when you leave the room. That stuff. It's his way of coping, of putting his stamp on things. Safe, predictable, orderly."

"I think I understand," Magaly said. "Maybe you're right, Jack. But what about you? How do you deal with it?" The absurd image of Westonfield carrying body parts on the freeway lingered in her mind. When he was doing that, did he have the same look on his face as he did when he was looking at Katy Marroquín's mutilated corpse?

"It ain't easy," Rourke said. "We each have our way." He looked around the kitchen. "I have this. But that's not really the answer to your question. The truth is that Bill just cares too much. It's got in his head somehow that he has to care about everything. He just cannot let it go. Everything matters. And what's more, it's *his* job to make everything right."

"I told him that once," Magaly said. "I told him that he was hurting himself, like a wounded animal in a trap."

"Do you think I haven't?" Rourke rejoined. "How would you like to be married to him, Maggie? Millie—that's his first wife—she told me one time that she got up late at night once to take a leak, and when she came back, the bed was made." Rourke laughed. "Now, that's a joke, but I know Bill's behavior took its toll."

"I suppose it did," Magaly said.

"Damn straight," Rourke replied.

"Was it his fault, then? The divorce?"

Rourke looked at her. "I never said that."

"Whose was it then?"

"I think Millie still loves him," Rourke said. "So it couldn't have been that bad, I guess."

"She's getting married to another man in a couple of months," Magaly said, "and she still loves Bill?"

"Ain't it funny?" Rourke said with a half-grin. "It's all part of the traveling Westonfield sideshow."

They heard the sound of the back door banging shut and footsteps clocking across the linoleum floor of the utility room. Rourke's wife emerged through the doorway into the kitchen hoisting two bags of groceries. "Hello, guys," she said brightly, carrying the bags to the counter. She walked over to the table and held out her hand to Magaly. "I'm Carol," she said. "I hope I haven't kept you waiting too long. Jack wasn't clear on what time you'd be, and I needed a few things, so—"

Magaly took her hand, liking her immediately. In great contrast to Jack, Carol Rourke was smallish, almost delicate. She had short hair, done in a flip, and an unpretentious, pretty face. "Magaly Rodríguez," Magaly said. "And no, you haven't kept me waiting too long. Jack and I were just making small talk. He's been an excellent host."

"I can see," Carol said with mock gravity, carefully examining her husband's face. She reached out and brushed cookie crumbs from his lips. "You promised," she said.

"Well, I know I did," Jack mumbled guiltily. "I even told Maggie."

"That's true," Magaly said, jumping in to save him. "He said we shouldn't eat them."

Carol smiled and held up her hand. "Now don't be starting our friendship with prevarication, Miss Rodríguez," she declared, unabashedly stepping closer and squinting at Magaly's lips. "Evidence is gone in your case," she said, stepping back, "but don't think I'm fooled. Just because you're more fastidious than Jack—which doesn't take much effort, mind you—doesn't mean you haven't been into my pumpkin cookies. I'm not the only one around here with an investigator's eye. I've got fifteen years of experience with my kids, and eighteen years with Mr. Rourke. Larceny in their hearts, all of them."

"I confess!" Magaly said immediately. "The cookies were wonderful."

Jack looked at her. "Some accomplice," he said.

In a little while the Rourke children, Steve and Sheila, came in from school. Introductions were made and Sheila helped her mother and Magaly set the table and finish up supper preparations. Jack went out into the yard with Steve to finish the raking. In an hour they ate a delicious dinner at the kitchen table. It was a merry time, with much joking and teasing. When it was over, the kids went out to visit friends and Magaly helped Carol with the dishes. Jack disappeared out into the yard somewhere again.

"I'm glad you came," Carol said. "We don't get a lot of company up here. Especially not people with interesting jobs like yours. Have you really done all of those exciting things, and been to all of those places? I can hardly imagine what it would be like. Sometimes it seems like life has just passed me by."

Magaly looked at her soberly. "I'll trade you," she said. "Every adventure and every hotel room. For a house like this. For children who loved me. For a husband like Jack. I'll trade you in a New York minute."

Carol smiled. She already liked her immensely. Though ten years her junior, Magaly knew exactly what to say. "A New York minute," Carol said. "Well, I guess that's a minute you'd have available to trade! But we *are* happy here. Life at the house down by the airport was getting to be impossible. Did Jack tell you about some of the things that happened down there?"

"No, he didn't," Magaly said.

"Well, it got so bad with the shootings and break-ins that the kids were scared to death, and so were we. All of our old neighbors moved out and new ones moved in, all of them bad. When they found out Jack was a police officer, they started harassing the kids. We didn't know how bad it had gotten until one night I was asleep and a noise woke me up. Jack was at work. I couldn't tell what the noise was at first, but I thought I saw something moving out in the hallway, past my bedroom door. Then I looked and I could see that it was Stevie. He was crawling on his hands and knees from his bedroom to the bathroom. I got up and asked him what he was up to. I thought he might be sleepwalking or something, but he was wide awake. He said he had to go to the bathroom, but he was afraid to walk past the window because the boy next door said that he would shoot him when he got the chance. So he was crawling below the window so he couldn't be seen." Carol sighed deeply. "To make a long story short, I told Jack about it the next day, and within a week we were moved in with his mother in Brown City. A month after that we found this house and moved out here."

Magaly looked at Carol with new eyes. "What an evil thing!" she said. "It must have broken your heart."

"Almost," Carol said. "But we're past that now. The kids are fine. Me and Jack are fine. We're out here in the clean country, and we're going to stay."

"Good for you," Magaly said.

After a minute Carol said, "Jack told me a little bit about what happened yesterday."

"Ahhh."

"Some things he tells me, some things he doesn't," she went on. "I can never make up my mind whether I want him to or not.

One way, I'm spared the hurt. The other, I feel like I'm missing out on an important part of his life. I'm not sure which is better."

Magaly looked her in the eye, trying to judge her mettle. "Maybe yesterday was one of the times Jack should have left well enough alone," she said softly. "It was terrible, Carol. I hope God spares me from ever having to see anything like that again."

"You're stronger than me," Carol said. "I'd have died of fright right then and there." In a minute she said, "Jack says you're close to Bill Westonfield."

"Close?"

"Forgive me!" Carol exclaimed, instantly embarrassed. "I didn't mean it that way. I just meant—he says, Jack says you're sort of two peas in a pod. Maybe it's the Spanish connection..."

Magaly put her arm around Carol's shoulder. "Don't be sorry," she said. "I know what you mean, or what Jack meant. He's right. I don't entirely understand it, but it's almost like I'm here for a reason. Does that make sense?"

"I think so," Carol said. She wiped the last dish dry and set it in the cupboard. "Join me for a cup of coffee?"

Over steaming cups of hazelnut coffee Carol continued. "Aren't you afraid?"

"I'm scared to death," Magaly said.

"What about those awful initials?" Carol asked. " How much does the killer know? What else is he going to do? I'm afraid for Bill. I'm afraid for you. I'm afraid for Jack. He's going back to work on Monday—if I can keep him here even that long. It makes me so scared and nervous I just want to cry sometimes." There were, indeed, tears in her eyes.

"Jack is strong," Magaly said. "And *you're* strong. It'll all work out in the end."

"Do you think so? How can you be sure?"

Magaly pondered that for a moment. Then she said, "Because of Bill."

"Ah, Bill..."

"Do you like him?" Magaly asked.

"Oh, I like him," Carol said slowly. "I like him a lot. But he's so different from Jack. Hard, sometimes. There's a look he's got—a look in his eyes. Have you seen it? Not cruel, really. Just hard. Like there's a sense of purpose, or something. Like God put him here for a reason, and Bill knows exactly what the reason is. It's almost as if he knows the answer to the question before it's asked."

"Maybe he does," Magaly said.

"What?" Carol said, confused.

"Maybe Bill actually does know the answer to the question."

"But that's blasphemous," Carol said. "Only God can know things like that. Only God has the certainty to be that *right* about something."

"Maybe that's the tragedy of Bill Westonfield," Magaly said softly. "Knowledge is power; and knowledge is hell." She told Carol about the night after the Merritt Street shooting, and about how Westonfield had told her of Jack's struggle with bad dreams.

"Of all the things Jack has been involved in over the years, that's the one thing that's got the better of him," Carol said. "It's the one thing that he can't come to grips with. That woman. The nightmares. He doesn't have them often, but they come; sometimes when you'd least expect them. It's all so strange. This shooting that you saw doesn't seem to bother him all that much. But in some way, part of it—going down to headquarters and that sort of thing—it brings it all back to him. And then the dreams start."

"I'm sorry," Magaly said. "Jack is a fine man. He doesn't deserve to go through something like that."

"No, he doesn't," Carol replied. "But there doesn't seem to be a damn thing I can do about it."

"Maybe that's part of why Bill takes care of Jack," Magaly said.

"I know Bill takes good care of my husband," Carol said.

"Jack worships him."

"Then cherish him," Magaly said. "He'll keep Jack alive—maybe under circumstances where no one else could. Look at Jack, so big and strong. He takes care of you. He takes care of the kids. He takes care of his policemen. Who but Bill could take care of him?"

Carol had no answer for that. She said simply, "Bill must be lonely."

Magaly said nothing.

Jack came in sweating. "Damn leaves," he said. "Any more coffee, Carol? Or did you two birds drink it all up?"

She poured him a mugful. "Pie?" she asked.

"Yep. Big piece."

"We were just talking about Bill," Magaly said.

"Oh?"

She told him about her night with Adams and Arena.

"Those jack-offs," Rourke said. "They'll get in trouble with that trick one day and get suspended. They're just not as creative as we used to be. We used to catch shitheads breaking into boxcars up on the railroad tracks. Instead of taking them in, we'd lock them in an empty car and send them to Cleveland. Cold ride in the winter."

Magaly laughed and Carol grimaced.

Then Magaly explained what Arena had said about the Saint Michael's medal. "Please tell me about how he got it!" she pleaded.

"He got it from Father Neeson, like Bob said," Jack replied. "A guy named Felix Davenport shot Bill's partner during a raid at Porter and Ste. Anne. The cop's name was Tom Bacon. I believe you've had the pleasure," he said with a grin.

Magaly was shocked. "You're kidding."

"No, I'm not kidding. See, just when you reporters think you know everything."

Carol poked him in the arm. "John Rourke, behave yourself!"

"All right," he said. "Anyway, Bacon, such as he is,

obviously survived. But he was in a world of hurt for a long time. Hospitalized for three months. We launched one of the biggest manhunts in the department's history for Felix but weeks passed and we couldn't get so much as a smell. Then, lo and behold, Father Neeson shows up at police headquarters one day with Davenport and Davenport's attorney, and turns him in. Bill just about went nuts."

"I can imagine," Magaly said.

"Right," Rourke said. "Well, a week or so later Bill happens to be driving by Trinity and there's Neeson watering flowers out front. He spots Bill and flags him over. It's all Bill can do to keep his composure. *I wanted to talk to you about Officer Bacon,* says Neeson. *I wanted to explain.* Of course Bill says there's nothing to explain; that he, Neeson, had harbored a fugitive, and a vicious cop-killing son of a bitch, to boot. Father Neeson says to him, *Well, you'd have killed him if you'd had the chance.* Bill says he deserved to die. Father says, *Some that die deserve to live. Can you give that to them?* So this went on, back and forth, for about ten minutes, with Bill saying Neeson was a law breaker and no better than Felix, and the Father saying that everybody, even Felix, needed someone to watch over them."

Magaly shifted uncomfortably in her chair, recalling that what the priest had told Westonfield years ago was precisely what she herself had said to him just a few nights ago at Jack's place by the airport. *Way to go, Magaly!*

Rourke went on. "Of course, then Bill declared that he didn't need anyone to watch over him, especially not the likes of self-important Catholic priests, that he could take care of himself. Then Neeson asked him if he was Catholic. Bill says no, he's not. Neeson says, *Do you know about Saint Michael?* Bill says no. Then the Father tells him the story that Bob Arena told you. Then he reaches around his own neck and pulls off this Saint Michael's medal and hands it to Bill. *Here,* he says, *this is for you. Saint Michael will protect you.* Bill was so damned surprised he didn't know whether to shit or go blind.

Before Bill could think about giving it back, Neeson just walked away."

"That's quite a story," Magaly said.

"Bill has worn that thing every day of his life since that hour," Jack said. "I think he showers with it." He took a bite of apple pie. "Him and the old boy became great friends after that. They disagreed with each other on just about everything you could imagine. Fought like cats and dogs. But they were friends for a long time—until Father Neeson was killed in a car wreck a while back," Jack added, chewing thoughtfully.

"Father Neeson is dead?"

"As a doornail," Jack said.

"So much death," Magaly said.

Jack shrugged.

"Bill told me he was going to kill the man who did those things yesterday," Magaly said quietly.

"I expect that he will," Jack said.

"What's going to happen now?"

"With these new threats there's a whole new ball game," Rourke said. "The department will go nuts. A third of the brass will want to do something to protect Bill, another third will keep their fingers crossed that maybe this is a golden opportunity to get rid of their problem, and the other third won't have any idea whatsoever what to do."

"Enough of this stuff," Carol said suddenly, brightly, standing and carrying empty cups to the kitchen sink. "Let's put our jackets on and walk Magaly around the property. Evening's going to be coming on and I won't have this pretty day wasted with talk about only bad things."

In a short while the three of them found themselves strolling through the orchard near the little creek. "There's still a few late apples," Jack said, looking upward through the branches of one of the trees. "Cortlands—they're my favorites." He stretched up and grabbed a high branch, pulling it down until he could reach the few apples dangling there. He held the limb with one hand and deftly plucked off three apples with the other, handing them to Carol. Then he released the branch, watching it spring away in a flutter of green-brown leaves and the smell of winesap. "Here," he said with a flourish, "a present for each of you."

Magaly was going to say she couldn't eat another bite, but somehow she wanted the apple, wanted to taste its tart taste, smell its fragrant smell. She wasn't sorry. When she bit into the crisp apple, it almost exploded with juice. The flesh was firm and fine-textured, the juice cool and sweet. "God, that's good!" she exclaimed. "These are Cortlands, you say, Jack?"

"Right. Best there is."

"Best there is," Magaly affirmed, her face radiant.

Carol went to the creek bank and picked a handful of perfect asters. She came back to Magaly and with her fingers brushed back her hair on the left side. She carefully placed the stems behind Magaly's ear. The flowers looked almost tropical against the black mane of Magaly's hair. "There," Carol said. "Now there's something from me."

Magaly found no words to say.

"I'm going to tinker with Stevie's four-wheeler for a bit," Jack said. "I'll leave you two girls alone again, if that's all right."

They both assented, and Jack ambled away to the garage.

"Let me show you my vegetable garden," Carol said enthusiastically, taking Magaly by the arm. "There's not much left now; it's mostly gone by. But we'll be getting parsnips all through the fall, until the ground freezes."

As they walked Carol asked, "Do you have a big family, Magaly? Brothers and sisters?"

"I'm one of six," Magaly said. "Three brothers and two sisters."

"Are they all in this country?"

"Yes, we're all here, including my father. But he never really liked it here."

"Why not?"

"Oh, I don't know," Magaly said. "Too big, too fast-paced, too everything. He's got a warm-weather heart, I think. Mexico

225

is home."

"I understand," Carol said. "Home is everything. Where's home to you, Magaly?"

"New York City."

"You said that," Carol said. "I mean, you told me before that you live in New York—but is it home?"

"I suppose it is," Magaly replied thoughtfully. "It's where I work. I've been there a long time."

"I bet there aren't any places like this in New York City," Carol said.

"No, there aren't," Magaly said.

"After a while simple peace becomes dear to you."

"I believe that," Magaly said. "Not long ago I might have taken exception, but not now."

"Have you ever been married?" Carol asked.

"No," Magaly said. "I'm afraid I'm an old maid."

"How old did you say you were?" Carol asked, laughing. "Thirty-three? Hardly an old maid!"

Magaly unconsciously put her arm around Carol's waist as they walked along. "Remember what you said a while ago, about life passing you by? I suppose that's how I feel when it comes to marriage." She kicked her feet along contentedly through the grass, the flowers bright in her hair. "It seems like I'm so busy all the time. I've had boyfriends, of course. I guess none of them ever struck me as the one I wanted to spend the rest of my life with..."

"It's good to be cautious," Carol said, responding in kind, slipping her arm around Magaly. "Life's too short to waste with someone you don't love, or with someone who doesn't love you."

When they got to the garden Carol proudly pointed out the neat rows and where this or that had been. "We canned a lot this year," she said. "Beans and beets, mostly. We froze a lot of corn and carrots. Then we've got potatoes, onions, and squash in the fruit cellar. Would you like to take a few things back with you?"

"I'd love to," Magaly said. "But I'm afraid there'd be

nowhere to keep it, or to cook it. I'm staying at the hotel."

"That's right," Carol said. "I'm getting foolish in my old age."

"Not at all," Magaly said. "Thanks anyway!"

As they talked, daylight gradually faded from the sky. The scattered trees began to cast long shadows across the property. A cool evening was coming on. They walked arm-in-arm back to the house. Now that the time had come to leave, Magaly was loathe to go. Carol sensed this and asked, "Is there something you wanted to talk about, Magaly? Something we haven't gotten to?"

Magaly was amazed once more at how quickly she had come to trust Carol. Without hesitation she said, "I guess there is. You know, one of the cardinal rules of journalism is that you never, *never* get personal with the people you're working with in the field. It's a good rule. It keeps you on the straight and narrow and helps you avoid nasty pitfalls, personally and professionally. For one thing, how can a writer portray her subject objectively when she's involved with him? She simply can't. That's the only right answer. I know that, and know it well. For eleven years it's never been a problem. But now—"

"There's Bill Westonfield," Carol said.

"That's right," Magaly said. "Now there's Bill."

"How do you feel about him?"

"To be perfectly frank," Magaly said, "I don't have the vaguest notion how to describe my feelings for him—but I know they're not what they ought to be."

Carol laughed. "Silly girl! Bill has a way with women, doesn't he? And do you know what the funniest part about it is? He doesn't have a clue." They went into the house through the back door. "I wouldn't worry about it just now," she said, as they walked into the warm kitchen. "These things have a way of working themselves out. You're a very smart lady. You'll know the right thing to do when the time comes. So will Bill."

CHAPTER 20

Even as Magaly pulled into Jack Rourke's driveway a hundred miles away, Ruth Dillworth's eyes flicked away from Westonfield with an air of dismissal. She looked at Milton Lucas, the deputy chief of the Major Crimes Division—and one of the few ranking blacks in the current Police Department administration whom Westonfield respected—and said, "Chief, I would ask you to reconsider. This whole thing has gone too far, and we dare not let it slip away even farther. The potential consequences are so disastrous that I'll speak frankly, and not be overly concerned with sparing Sergeant Westonfield's feelings." The Fourth Precinct commander shot a glance at Westonfield, who sat impassively across from her at the conference table on the third floor of police headquarters. "It's no secret," she continued, "that I think the sergeant has been a loose cannon. Have you had an opportunity to review the write-up on the Deacon Street barricaded gunman, Chief?"

"Yeah, Ruth, I've looked through it," Lucas said noncommittally.

"Then you can see my point," Dillworth said. "The press is circling like sharks outside my office right now. They're going to want answers. They're going to want to know what we're doing about the killings, who's handling the investigation, if we have suspects, if this is a serial killer. CNN has a man in town on the story already. That Talmadge guy from the Associated Press has been hounding me all morning." She took a deep breath. "Now, I think we've been generous enough with this Rodríguez woman from *Harper's*. You know better than I that this is going to be a difficult investigation. It's going to require a lot of time and resources unless we're very, very lucky. We have to cooperate with the press, of course, but we don't need a reporter on the inside, ready to screw up the investigation at every stage with leaks. I think we should call her editor and pull the plug." She looked at Westonfield again. "Especially in light of Sergeant Westonfield's...unorthodox methods. You know about his hostility toward some of the department's most important programs. And what about these threats? I'm persuaded that Miss Rodríguez might be in danger as well."

Lucas looked at Westonfield. "Well?"

"With all due respect, Chief, what are you afraid of?"

Lucas frowned. "I know your reputation for being blunt, Westonfield," he said, "but I can tell you that you're pushing the envelope."

Dillworth could barely hide a grin of satisfaction. Westonfield might just be crazy enough to hang himself.

"Why is Magaly Rodríguez here, you want to know?" Westonfield said evenly. "She's here to tell a story. She's here to observe what happens on the street and then write about it. For the first time ever, boss, I believe a reporter might actually tell it straight. Does it make sense, any sense at all, that just because we find ourselves in the middle of a tough investigation we cut her off and lose this golden opportunity? Flat out, Chief, are you afraid of what she might have to say?"

"That's not the point," Lucas replied evenly.

"What is the point, Chief?"

"Commander Dillworth has raised a couple of legitimate issues," Lucas said. "One, how do we keep control of unauthorized leaks on the part of Miss Rodríguez; and, two, what about her physical safety? I won't have a well-known New York writer seriously hurt, or maybe even killed, on my watch." A slight smile came to his face. "Now, you may not like politics, Sergeant Westonfield, and you may have little patience for it, but that's the reality of life in the Big Store. That's the football I play with every fucking day." He looked at Dillworth. "Sorry for the language, Ruth."

"That's precisely what I'm saying," Dillworth said. "It's not for a precinct sergeant to decide these matters. It's *your* job. And mine. That's my precinct out there. It's simply too volatile. John Rourke, Sergeant Westonfield's partner, was involved in a fatal shooting just a few days ago. Apparently, this was related in some way to the Prado, Villanueva, and Marroquín murders. We're going to need a steady hand. This is a classic Homicide case, from beginning to end. Let's just handle it at that level. And let's put the brakes on this *Harper's Magazine* situation."

"I understand your concerns, Commander," Lucas said. "And I agree with them in the main." He turned toward Westonfield to emphasize the point. "But you need to understand that I made a personal commitment to this reporter's boss that we would go forward. In light of the latest circumstances, I took the liberty of talking to Mr. Vickers on the telephone just this morning. Despite some concerns he has about his employee's safety—" he looked at Westonfield again and raised his eyebrows "—and despite his ire over what he regards as her less-than-efficient communication with him on the recent events in our bailiwick, he wants to continue."

"Well, he would, Chief!" Dillworth exclaimed in frustration.

Lucas held up his hand. "He has further assured me that she will not report on any matter that is currently part of any criminal investigation within the Detroit Police Department, or share such information with any other media source, until given the go-ahead by proper departmental authority."

"You can't trust these media people," Dillworth argued. "You know that, Chief. And it's still too goddamn dangerous!" she added loudly, whacking the table, forgetting herself in her rising frustration at the turn of events.

Lucas carefully shuffled the jumble of papers in front of him into a neat pile and eyed the unrepentant object of Ruth Dillworth's frustration. "I have two pieces of news for you, Sergeant Westonfield," he said. "First, as of right now, you are Magaly Rodríguez' personal bodyguard. Second—" he leaned back in his chair and let out a long, slow breath— "second, welcome to the Homicide Section of the Major Crimes Division, *Detective*."

Dillworth almost fainted. Partly to mollify her, partly to address his own lingering concerns, Lucas added, "Don't make me regret this decision, Sergeant."

When Westonfield offered perfunctory assurances, Lucas bit off his words, "Don't be casual with me, Westonfield. I mean it. You know the rules. You know your responsibilities. If you embarrass me, or the department, for any reason whatsoever, I will have your ass in a hand basket. That is not a threat. That is a promise."

* * *

An hour later Westonfield sat at a desk at the Homicide Section on the fifth floor of police headquarters. "Your desks are as delapidated as the ones at Fort & Green," he said to Buck Fry as he pulled open the drawers one at a time, peered inside, and slammed them shut again. "Whose desk was this? Redd Foxx's?"

"Yeah," Fry replied laconically. "Redd retired last week." He leaned over and glanced with mock gravity into the trash can next to his own desk. "Oh, yeah. There's still some of his empty wine bottles in there, and some Vaseline he used to jack off with."

"You're disgusting," Westonfield said mildly.

"I know it," Fry said. "My wife takes the liberty of reminding me of that everyday."

"How is Judy?"

"Her usual pleasant self," Fry said. "What makes you think she'd be any different just because you haven't seen her in a couple of years?" He leaned back in his decrepit swivel chair and put his feet on his desk. He was wearing scuffed brown wingtips with a grey suit. "So, what's the scoop?" he asked drolly. "The suspense is fucking killing me."

"Gene says you have some information on Jack's shooting,"

Westonfield said.

"Which one?" Fry asked, grinning.

"The most recent one, Buck."

"Well, Bill, the fucker's wasted so many shitheads it's hard for me to keep track," Fry replied. "I wasn't too good at math."

"There were supposed to be some newspaper clippings from one of the Downriver papers about a drug killing in Elizabeth Park," Westonfield went on, ignoring him. "You brain surgeons came across them after only a day or two. Good work."

"We're awfully overworked down here," Fry said.

Westonfield opened his arms beseechingly. "Well?"

Fry slowly took his feet off his desk and rolled out a heavy file drawer from the cabinet next to him. He fished out a manila envelope and tossed it to Westonfield, the attached red evidence tag fluttering in the air. "It's in there," he said. "Gene told me you'd be by for it."

Westonfield opened the envelope and pulled out the contents: newspaper clippings from the *News-Herald* about the discovery of a mutilated body in a boat at the Elizabeth Park marina. He quickly read the piece. It didn't say much, just that the body of a black man with dreadlocks was found in a boat by some fishermen. Police wouldn't reveal details of their investigation, but did indicate that there was reason to believe that it might have been a narcotics-related killing. There were vague comments by the police to the effect that other materials were found at the scene which, in combination with the deceased's probable Caribbean background, suggested some kind of black magic or perhaps voodoo aspect to the case.

"Jesus, Mary, and Joseph," whispered Westonfield. Then louder to Fry, "Anybody talk to Trenton about this?"

Fry said, "Nope. Not yet. Take the ball and run with it, my man."

"I will," Westonfield said. "First update me on Chamberlain."

Fry pulled another file from his desk drawer and opened it. He grabbed a pair of bifocals from the desktop and put them on, sliding them down low on the bridge of his nose. He read silently for a minute or two while Westonfield shifted uncomfortably in his chair. Fry reminded Westonfield of a distracted Willy Loman from *Death of a Salesman*. Fry looked up. "All right. Here's the skinny up 'til now. We're waiting for lab results, of course. That'll take a couple of weeks, as you know. But we got some tentatives. Surprise, surprise! The house on Chamberlain was rented by one...Tomás Mejías."

Westonfield got excited and Fry held up his hand. "Rented from some old broad, Bill, like the house on Merritt. Just Tomás, nobody else listed as a renter." He went back to his place in the file, searching along the text with a finger. "Also like Merritt, no prints. I mean *no* prints. Weird, eh? We're looking for hairs, fibers, and all of that, but I'll wager we don't come up with anything. Preliminary blood tests indicate all the blood at the scene belongs to the victims." He looked up from the file again. "Besides being one sick fuck, this jack-off is a real ghost. Just thinking about how he slipped away on you when you chased him makes my hair stand on end." The Homicide veteran shifted his bespectacled eyes back to the report. "On the good side, the powders appear to match the stuff on Merritt. Lab tests will let us know for sure, but I think we can bet our balls that they'll match. It's strange how, on the one hand, this guy leaves a trail an elephant could follow, and on the other, he's slipperier than a coon climbing a greased pole. Anyway, that's really all there is that could help you get started. Wait—here's one more thing. The white material on the girl's face? Again, surprise, surprise! It was cum. Bona fide, certified gism. Prelims indicate—get this, Bill—it wasn't the bad guy's load. It says here that it supposedly matches the other stiff's blood type. Villanueva. Lab thinks it's probably his. They can't be sure until the DNA comes back." He looked at Westonfield in amazement. "Looks like this freak made the stiffs get it on before he went to work on them."

In three minutes Westonfield was on the telephone to the Trenton detectives. In fifteen minutes more he was in his unmarked car, southbound on the I-75. He picked up his cell phone from the seat next to him and tried Magaly's hotel room again. Still no answer. Still no message. Shit. Well, he'd catch up with her later.

It was 2:30 in the afternoon when he walked into the detective bureau on the second floor of the Trenton police station on West Jefferson, only two blocks from Elizabeth Park. The sane environment he usually encountered when he visited suburban detective divisions never ceased to amaze him, and Trenton didn't disappoint. The space was clean and bright, the walls lined with new file cabinets, the desks covered with modern office equipment. Except for the occasional ring of a telephone, clatter of an old typewriter, or the shuffle of paper, it was quiet and businesslike—more like an insurance office than a police station to Westonfield's way of thinking.

Dale Ward was thirty-six years old, but today he felt like fifty-six. His right arm hurt like a son-of-a-bitch. That crazy bitch Michelle had finally gone over the edge and turned violent. All he wanted to do was talk to her about getting back a few things he'd forgotten at her place when he moved out a few days before. He was as polite as can be, but Michelle wouldn't have it. When he showed up at her place at ten o'clock last night and asked for a set of engraved pens he had last seen in her bedroom, she lost it. Sure, he'd had a beer or two, but it wasn't like he was drunk or anything. He didn't know exactly how it happened, but he hadn't been there five minutes, standing at her door just trying to talk to her, when she started yelling and screaming.

He was afraid the neighbors would start coming out to take a look-see so he took a quick step inside her door and tried to calm her down. That really set her off. She started whacking him in the back with her fists. *Well, what the hell?* he figured. *I'm in now. I might as well get my pens and a thing or two.* She followed him around everywhere he went, ranting and raving, until he had all of his things gathered up. When he had it all together and was walking through the kitchen toward the door, she suddenly opened up her refrigerator-freezer and yanked out a five-pound package of frozen rabbit and threw it at him with all her might. He was an avid hunter and had killed the rabbit the first day of hunting season, dressed it, and left it in Michelle's freezer. His mistake. He didn't see it coming in time and the package, hard as a rock, hit him in the right shoulder. "Here, take your murdered bunny, you no good son-of-a-bitch," she shrieked, "and get the fuck out of my house." He'd picked up the rabbit and taken it too. But she'd caught him just right. She must have bruised a bone or something.

As Westonfield approached, the detective rose from behind his desk to greet him. "Dale Ward," he said, shaking Westonfield's hand and pointing to a chair in front of his desk. "Find the place all right?" When they shook hands Westonfield noted that the man winced a little and seemed to favor his right arm.

"No problem," Westonfield said. "I think there might be two turns between here and Downtown."

"That would be about right," Ward said, grinning. "Coffee?"

"Thanks, Sarge, but I think I'm coffee'd out."

"All right, then. But call me Dale. You're Bill, right?"

"That'll do."

Ward picked up his own mug of coffee and took a long sip from it, taking stock of Westonfield. He quickly decided the Detroit officer had the hungry look you saw in city cops sometimes. But Westonfield was impeccable in his blue blazer and grey trousers, his tie obviously expensive, in contrast to many Detroit policemen, who Ward felt tended to the slovenly. "From your phone call it sounds like Detroit's got a hell of a mess," he said. "I don't know anything about it except what I read in this morning's *Free Press*, but if they got half their facts right—which would be a miracle, I know—it was a goddamn slaughterhouse on Chamberlain."

"It was," Westonfield said. He opened the evidence envelope he'd brought with him and pulled out the clippings. "Last Sunday my partner John Rourke shot a drug dealer by the name of Tomás Mejías. Do you know the neighborhood where it happened? Merritt Street?"

"That's not far from Holy Redeemer Church, isn't it?"

"Not too far," Westonfield said. "These clippings, from the *News-Herald*, were found in his possession. Actually, they were in his car, up over the visor, but he had them." He handed the clippings to Ward. "Don't worry, they've been processed. You can handle them all you want."

The Trenton detective looked at them. "Yeah, I've seen them. They're from the Wednesday edition of the *News-Herald*, all right." He got up and rummaged through a stack of newspapers atop a nearby file cabinet. "Yeah. Here it is." He handed Westonfield the whole newspaper.

Westonfield read the headline, scanned through the copy, and said, "Can I see the file on this case?"

"You think it's related then?" Ward asked.

"I'm pretty sure," Westonfield replied. "Have you identified the victim? What have you got in the file?"

"I'll show it to you," Ward said. "But what do you guys have that would bring you all the way down here? I know you're too busy to come down without a good reason."

"All right," Westonfield said. "Here's what we have as of right now. Number one: we have reason to believe that the Merritt Street shooting involving Mejías is related to the Chamberlain murders—Mejías rented both homes, for one thing, plus articles that apparently were used in certain black magic rituals by this crew, and which were seized at both scenes, match up." He raised two fingers. "Two: I chased a guy on foot at the Merritt Street shooting scene. I lost him. I think our appearance at the scene and the fact that I almost collared the guy pissed him off big time. He carved my initials into one of the Chamberlain victims' backs. The girl. Katy Marroquín was her name." Westonfield anticipated Ward's next question, saw it coming in his eyes. "*W. W.*—for William Westonfield. And I know it was a message for me, just because I know."

Ward nodded. This was cop shorthand for a sure hunch and he knew what it meant.

Westonfield held up a third finger. "Number three: we found

these clippings in Mejías's car. Your murder, from just the bullshit in this article, appears to have black magic aspects, like our cases in the city." He paused, looked at the suburban detective. "Adds up pretty good, huh?"

"Seems like it to me," Ward said. Westonfield's analysis was undoubtedly accurate. He was sure, though, that there was more to the story than Westonfield was telling him. He pondered it all for a moment. "What did this guy do to those people on Chamberlain?" he asked.

Westonfield told him the details.

Ward listened attentively, his impassive face betraying little of the excitement and—was it apprehension?—he felt. He might be a suburban detective without the experience to match Westonfield's, but he knew a great case when he saw one. Westonfield was right. It added up. He walked over to a file cabinet marked *Category I* and pulled open the top drawer. He retrieved a heavy brown portfolio and walked back to his desk, placing the file carefully in front of Westonfield. "It's all in here," he said. "We've identified the victim—Joseph Allen, late of Jamaica and Detroit." He sat back in his chair and took another sip of coffee. As Westonfield unwound the string from the fastener on the accordion file and reached inside, Ward said casually, "It would appear the nice gentleman you're looking for paid a midnight visit to this little burg before he got busy in the big city. I think we're looking for the same man."

Westonfield looked up at Ward and smiled.

An hour later they were standing on the gravel of the Elizabeth Park marina, looking at an open spot where the rowboat had once stood which contained the flayed body of Joseph Allen. "That's where it was," Ward said. "Not much to see now. The boat's in the DPW garage behind a locked fence. It's been processed already. Hell, we can't do that kind of work ourselves, of course. We farmed it out to the state police. Same results you got. No prints, no nothing."

Westonfield nodded. "I'm not surprised," he said. Then he reached out and touched the right sleeve of Ward's suit jacket.

"Hurt your arm?"

Ward grinned self-consciously and told him the tale.

"Rabbit, eh?"

"Hit me like a fucking bowling ball," Ward said.

"Women," Westonfield said.

"Women," Ward agreed.

"Maybe we could go small game hunting some time," Westonfield said, a little wistfully. "When this is all over. I used to go. Haven't for a long time."

"We could do that," Ward answered. "Lots of good places to go down this way."

"We'll just keep the rabbits away from the girls," Westonfield said conspiratorially. "It'll be safer that way."

"You married?" Ward asked.

"Going through my second divorce," Westonfield said.

"Yeah?"

"Yeah."

Ward smiled. "Nice girl, huh?"

"Hell of a nice girl," Westonfield said, smiling back. "Just can't live with her."

Westonfield went over the ground carefully, but found nothing useful. He didn't expect to. The state police were pretty good. He was following his habit of getting a feel for the setting, trying to look at the scene through the eyes of the killer. In a moment he said, "You're right about there not being anything to work on here." As he talked, his restless eyes roamed the perimeter of the fenced facility, the docked boats still in the water this late in the year, the handful of fishermen at the river's edge, and came back to rest on the place where the rowboat had stood. "He was here, all right, Dale. I can feel him. Can you?"

"Well, they say that an evil act has a way of making its mark, of leaving a trace of itself in the place where it happened," Ward said. "I've heard that anyway. I never thought about it much, one way or the other. I don't go in for the occult. I just work the cases as they come."

"Then you're already a mile ahead of a lot of investigators

I know," Westonfield said. "But I'm not talking hocus-pocus. I'm talking hunches. Know what I mean? Sometimes the *feel* of a case can turn it for you, Dale. But I'll tell you something. This is no normal case. It would be well for us to study up a little on witchcraft as we move forward." He cast another searching glance around the marina, breathing the air, then looked at Ward with his piercing grey eyes. "Getting information like that is likely to prove as useful as anything else we can do." He suddenly stooped, picked up a small pebble, and tossed it a few feet into the air. He caught it deftly in his left hand and closed his fist around it. Then he held his clenched fist up to Ward and opened his hand, palm up. The stone was gone. "See?" Westonfield said, winking. "Things are not always as they seem."

When they returned to Ward's unmarked car and headed back to the Trenton police station, Westonfield told him the details of the Mejías shooting, and all about Magaly Rodríguez. "Sounds like you have a built-in tutor on witchcraft already," Ward said.

"Guess so," Westonfield answered. "—that is, if I can find her. She hasn't returned my calls today. I hope she hasn't gotten herself into trouble. She's my responsibility now. Like I needed more."

"Women," Ward said again.

"Women," Westonfield repeated.

On the short drive back the thought occurred to Westonfield that it might be a good idea to recruit Ward to work directly on the Detroit case. He could use the help. And while Ward didn't know it until today, he had already spent a lot of time looking for the same killer. It might be interesting to work with someone with a different perspective. Ward seemed like a pretty sharp guy, dedicated to his case, and he was easy to get along with. Westonfield made his decision immediately. He turned to Ward. "So, what are you gonna do to get your department to let you work with me on this?" he asked.

"Whatever it takes," Ward said instantly, beaming like a little boy. "Whatever it fucking takes." It was funny how a day could turn around. One minute your loony girlfriend is trying to brain you with your own friggin' rabbit, the next you're working on a big time homicide beef with the Detroit PD. Weird, but it sure as hell made life interesting.

In the next hour, Westonfield met and talked to Ward's boss, Lieutenant Pat Banks, and arranged a conference call between himself, Banks, Ward, and Deputy Chief Lucas. Lucas was pleased with the progress Westonfield had already made on the investigation, and Banks was glad to get one of his people involved in a major media case. The arrangement was easy. Detective Sergeant Dale Ward now belonged to Westonfield.

When they were alone, Westonfield grinned, held out his hand, and said, "Welcome to the wonderful world of homicide."

Now that the moment had come, Ward's gut lurched uncomfortably. For the second time in twenty-four hours he asked himself what the hell he had gotten himself into.

Westonfield looked at his watch—four-thirty. "I have to get out of here," he said. "Here's what we'll do. Photocopy your file and bring it with you tomorrow to headquarters. Can you be there at seven-thirty?"

"I can be there."

"Good," Westonfield said. "I'll have a copy made of our file and have it ready for you. We'll go over the whole thing from scratch with a fine-toothed comb. Sound all right?"

"I'll be there," Ward said again. "With bells on."

"Don't be *too* excited," Westonfield said. "This is a real ballbreaker. I want this guy."

"So do I," Ward said. "We'll get him."

"Oh, we'll get him, Dale," Westonfield said quietly, looking out the window. "We'll get him. But at what cost?"

* * *

It was seven o'clock in the evening when Westonfield's telephone rang at home. It was Magaly. "Where the hell have you been?" he asked with considerable irritation.

"Apple picking," she said.

"Apple picking?"

"Yes. Cortlands."

"Cortlands," Westonfield said blankly.

"The fellow I was with says they're the best," Magaly said.

"Really?"

"Yes."

"Did you bring any for me?" Westonfield asked, bemused now.

"No," Magaly said, laughing. "Jack said you don't deserve any."

"You were at Jack's..."

"Uh-huh."

"How the hell did that come about?"

"I thought you needed some time to yourself. I knew you'd be busy." She was serious now.

"I did and I was. Thank you," Westonfield said.

"It was as simple as pie," Magaly said. "I called Jack up and he said sure, so there I went. I just got back in."

"I was worried," Westonfield said. He liked the sound of her voice. He wondered if she could get angry enough to throw a frozen rabbit at him. The notion amused him so much he almost laughed out loud.

"Sorry," Magaly said. "I didn't mean to scare you. I had a wonderful time. The kids are delightful. Carol is great. We became friends instantly."

"I'm not surprised," Westonfield said. "Carol's good people."

"Yes."

"So how's Jack?"

"He seemed fine," Magaly said. "Like always. He's worried about you."

"Is he now?"

"Uh-huh."

"When is he coming back to Detroit?" Westonfield asked.

"Well, he wanted to come back right away when I told him about, you know—"

"And?"

"Carol talked him into staying until Sunday night or Monday morning," Magaly said.

"Good."

"I thought so." She sighed. "It's so beautiful up there, Bill!"

"I know," Westonfield said. "It's nice to get away from the shit, isn't it?"

"It's marvelous," she said. "You can close your eyes and make the rest of the world disappear."

"I've got some news," Westonfield said. He told her about all that had transpired during the day.

"So you're assigned to the Homicide Section?" Magaly asked.

"Yes."

"Where does that leave Jack?"

"He'll have to stay at the Fourth Precinct," Westonfield said. "It won't make a hell of a lot of difference, though. That's where I'll be spending all of my time."

"What about this Trenton officer, Ward?"

"I think he'll be fine," Westonfield said.

"And you're to be my bodyguard," Magaly said. "Exactly what does that mean?"

"We'll have work that out," Westonfield said. "But you can't be alone now. It's too dangerous."

"The moon is waning," Magaly said hopefully. "Danny and Katy were killed on the day of the full moon. He won't be able to act for two more weeks."

"We'll see about all of that," Westonfield said. "So far, it looks like you've been dead right, but—"

"Dead right," Magaly interrupted. "You said it. So why the 'but'?"

"Well, hell," Westonfield retorted, "we can't exactly base our responses on Cuban magic, now, can we?"

"Why not?" Magaly asked. "*He* will."

She had him there, and Westonfield knew it. Even if the magic wasn't real, the murderer probably thought it was. It made sense that he would act according to the dictates of his own religion, or whatever he called it. "We need to bring in an expert to help us anticipate this guy's moves," he said. "Maybe you can help with that?"

"I'll try."

"I know you will," Westonfield said.

As was her habit, Magaly changed subjects abruptly. "So Herman Vickers signed off on my staying here on the assignment?"

"That's what Lucas said."

"And Lucas said you were to be my bodyguard?" she asked.

"Yes."

"And Vickers signed off on that, too?"

"Yeah," Westonfield said. "But not before he told Lucas that he was highly pissed off that you hadn't seen fit—his words—to keep him up to date on what was happening here."

"I'll call him now," Magaly said. She dreaded that!

"That's probably a good idea," Westonfield said.

Magaly switched gears again. "I had a thought during the drive back to Detroit from Jack's. An idea about something that happened to Katy."

"Yes?"

"The nightstick," she said. "The black club he stuck inside her."

"Yeah."

"Remember what it looked like, Bill? How it protruded out of her, with that—I don't know—handle or something sticking out to one side?"

"Yes," Westonfield said. "The hand grip."

"He was trying to send you another warning," Magaly said. "I'm convinced leaving your initials in her back was one of *two* messages."

"Go on." His throat suddenly constricted.

"Think about what it looked like," she said.

Westonfield reluctantly summoned back the image of the nightstick protruding from Katy's vagina. No matter how hard he tried, he could make nothing of it. To him it signified nothing but horror. In a moment he said, "It was just another indignity he subjected her to."

"I don't believe so," Magaly said. "Think! It was a stick of black wood, and the handle protruded above Katy's body like a branch. He left us another message, Bill: 'This is *palo mayombe*,' he was saying. 'The black branch.'"

* * *

When she finished her conversation with Westonfield, Magaly called her editor. Vickers was in a far better mood than she had anticipated. "I thought you were going to jump down my throat," she said. "Thanks for not doing it."

"You owe me for that—and more, kid," Vickers said. "I should kick your butt all the way back here to New York and then assign you to cover Beautification Week in Hackensack."

"I know it, Herman," she said.

"But I won't," he said, his voice softening. "I guess it's been a rough week for you, huh?"

"Yeah, boss. It's been a little rough."

"All right, then," Vickers said. "Let's start fresh. Just remember what I said—keep in touch. Let me know what's going on."

"I will," Magaly said. "This time, I will. I promise."

"Good. Now, I've got an understanding with the Police Department about a few things. This is important, so listen carefully. We have to play this right or I won't have to recall you to Hackensack—they'll do it for me."

"Okay."

"The department wants unequivocal assurances from us that no information about their pending investigation on this screwball gets published prematurely. That's understandable. Now I explained to Deputy Chief Lucas that, first of all, you are not even there as a police beat reporter. You're there as a *feature* writer, which means you're taking the long view on a human interest piece, not the short term view of spot reporting. So I assured him that that was the way it would be—*Harper's* is not going to publish anything except as part of an in-depth piece later on. I further assured him that neither you, nor I, nor anyone else at our magazine, would share information with any other news source. Fair enough?"

"Of course," Magaly said. "Who else would I give privileged information to?"

"No one, Magaly," Vickers agreed. "I'm just letting you know what transpired between me and Lucas. You know, you need to appreciate just how fortuitous this serial killer thing is—"

Magaly was apalled. "Fortuitous! The despicable crimes committed by this monster are fortuitous, Herman?"

"Hold onto your britches, little miss," Vickers said. "I simply mean that it happened. Whether we were there to cover it or not, it happened. As it turns out, we were there. So that gives us a whole new dimension to this story, a whole 'nother way to approach it when the time comes. That's all I mean. There's going to be national interest in Detroit when all of this hits the fan, so our follow-up story is going to attract a hell of a lot of readership."

"They don't care, Herman."

"What? Who doesn't care?"

"The readers. Anybody. They don't care."

"What the hell are you talking about?" Vickers said.

"Katy Marroquín. Nobody cares about her."

Vickers didn't understand Magaly's point, and what he didn't understand, he didn't like. "Are you all right," he asked.

"I'm fine."

"Then what the hell are you talking about?"

"Shit, Herman. I'm talking about *shit*," she said, letting go a floodgate of pent-up emotion. "These cops out there—they eat, breathe, and sleep it twenty-four hours a day. Great, heaping piles of it. Katy Marroquín ate, breathed, and slept it, too. Now she's dead. And no one knows and no one cares. Not about her life. Do you know what the people really want to watch while they're sipping Budweiser in front of their Magnavoxes? Do you know what our readership really wants to see in *Harper's*? They want to know about her death. They want to know all the goddamn dirty details. They want to know about the torture. Do you know what that maniac son-of-a-bitch did to that baby?" Her voice broke.

"Maggie—"

"Don't you *Maggie* me, Herman Vickers!" Magaly said, the tears starting, her pain and suppressed anger finally breaking loose, flowing out with the tears. "He skinned her leg. Can you understand that? In the darkest recesses of your mind, can you imagine it? He flayed that girl's leg while she was still alive. He smeared semen on her pretty face. Then he took a fucking nightstick and shoved it up inside of her."

"I'm sorry," Vickers said. "I—"

"No! I don't want to hear you're sorry. I am sick and tired of hearing how everybody's sorry. I'm tired to death of platitudes and horseshit. You know what I want, Herman? I want to hear you say her name."

"Oh, Magaly," Vickers said. "What have you gotten yourself into? You can't let yourself look at things this way. It's not always so bad. Our readers—"

"Bullshit!"

"Magaly, I—"

"Say her name, Herman."

"This is absolutely not nec—"

"Herman, I-want-you-to-just-say-her-name." There was a quality to Magaly's voice that Vickers had never before heard. A deep and abiding pain came through the tears.

Vickers was silent for a long moment. Then he said softly, "All right, Maggie. Her name was Katy. Her name was Katy Marroquín."

"That's right, Mr. Vickers," Magaly said. "That was her

name. And don't you forget it for as long as I work for you."

For all his bombast and vitriol, Herman Vickers was a decent man. "All right, Magaly," he said. "That's fair. Let's make it my promise to you. I won't forget that poor girl's name. But you know what? That's *your* job. It's your job to see that people know about these things, that people understand them, that people remember them. You're the writer, I'm just the editor. Go after this assignment! Listen. Learn. Then come back to New York and tell the whole country why they *ought* to care about the Katys of this world. Win the Pulitzer Prize, Magaly. Earn it for *Harper's*. Earn it for the cops. Earn it for Katy Marroquín."

PART III—KNOCKING ON HEAVEN'S DOOR

"The joy of love is too short, and the sorrow thereof, and what cometh thereof, dureth over long."

Sir Thomas Malory

"I shall tell you a great secret, my friend. Do not wait for the last judgement. It takes place every day."

Albert Camus

CHAPTER 21

In the night Magaly dreamed that her brother Aurelio was dead. When she awoke in her Detroit hotel room the next morning, he was. "'Galy," said her brother Diego on the telephone, "Aurelio's gone. Come home." It was eight o'clock in the morning on Friday, October the twenty-fifth.

Telephone calls to Westonfield, Rourke, Talmadge, and Vickers. The flight on Northwest from Metro to La Guardia. Her apartment. Home.

"Is there anything I can do, Maggie?" Westonfield had asked.

"No, Bill. There's nothing you can do."

"But you'll be alone."

"Yes."

"Everything's up in the air with this guy. We don't know if you'll be safe."

"He's in Detroit, not New York City. I'll be leaving danger, not heading into it. Besides—the moon is waning."

"I know."

"Be careful, Bill."

"Cuídate también."

That made her smile. She had cried enough anyway. She wept so much for Katy Marroquín that there were no tears left. Not even for Aurelio. She wept silently for him for months as he wasted away and she would weep for him silently still.

Her apartment. Why did it feel so strange? She had been away for longer periods many times before, but had never returned with the feeling that she was somehow a stranger in her own home. The furnishings, the mementoes collected over the years, and the framed photographs were familiar, but it was as if they belonged to someone else, were part of someone else's life. She prowled around the quiet rooms as a burglar would. She idly ran a finger across a bookshelf, looked at the week's worth of dust on her fingertip. She looked at the books on the shelf: *The Collected Poems of W. B. Yeats; Cien Años de Soledad; Sophie's Choice...*

She went into her bedroom, lay down on the flowered comforter, stared upward at the ceiling. She tossed her shoes onto the floor, ran her stockinged feet over the softness of the bedspread. She swept her fingers through the tangle of her black hair, pulled it away from her face. She nibbled delicately at the cuticle of one of her fingers. She absently scratched a nonexistent itch on her cheek.

She restlessly rose again, wandered more, through the bathroom, through the kitchen. She opened the refrigerator door. A quart of milk. She retrieved it and opened the cardboard flap. Held it up to her nose. Sour... She took it to the sink and poured it, gurgling, down the drain. She turned on the tap and watched the swirling water wash away the white of the milk. She clicked on the garbage disposal, listened to its guttural hum, turned it off; flicked on the fan in the hood over the range, turned it off.

She went back to her bedroom, stripped off all of her clothes, and flopped onto the bed, naked. She ran her hands over the smooth sheets. She ran her hands over her smooth belly. Her mind wandered, too. Fields of wildflowers in the Maryland countryside in July. The surf off Cozumel, impossible turquoise fish flitting along the Palancar Reef below. Cold nights on Salisbury Plain with the British SAS. She thought of her brother Aurelio. She thought of the *mayombero*, his black eyes without pupils. *Aguanilleo Zarabanda aribo*. She shuddered, but it passed immediately: he was far away, and he didn't know where she was. She thought of Emma Brodecker. What kind of person was she? Strong? Frail? Happy? Melancholy? She thought of Bill Westonfield, the sadness in his eyes as he gazed upon the pitiful, rent corpse of Katy Marroquín. Grey eyes, the color of sea-foam. She smiled the faintest of smiles to herself, and passed slowly, in stages, into sleep.

* * *

"I love you, Magaly," Diego said, holding his sister close, his dark face buried in her hair. "Missed you. Glad you're home." He stepped back. "You getting skinny? Don't they feed you in Detroit?"

"They feed me fine, Diego," she said, grinning at him. "You just want me to be fat and ugly."

"Of course I do," he said. "Every brother wants his favorite sister to be fat and ugly. Then he doesn't have to worry about her so much." He laughed. Then his laughter died as he remembered why they were together. "Poor Aurelio," he said.

"Yes, poor Aurelio," Magaly said. "Where is *Papá*?"

"He didn't want to come to the restaurant." Diego paused. "I think he's angry at himself. Angry for not being here to spend more time with 'Relio, angry about—you know—about Aurelio's *preferences*."

"I know." There was a hint of bitterness in her voice.

"It was hard on the old man," Diego said, looking at her unhappily.

"It was hard on Aurelio," she said.

Diego said nothing.

Magaly shook her head resignedly. "All right, Diego," she said. "I will talk to *Papá*. Good sister Magaly will fix it."

Diego smiled, still silent.

"Well, I think you look great," put in Ignacio Madero, Diego's oldest friend and business partner, to break the awkward quiet. He had been a friend of the family for years now, and was thoroughly in love with Magaly.

"Thank you, Iggie," Magaly said. "At least one of you has the good manners to compliment a lady who has been away."

Ignacio grinned at her like an idiot.

"Where are Federico and the girls?" Magaly asked, referring to her remaining brother and her two sisters.

"They should be here any time," Diego replied. "Fred is supposed to pick up Rosa and Margarita at Rosa's place and drive them over."

"Good."

"Yes, it's good to have us all together again," Diego said. "If only the circumstances were different."

Magaly took a sip of her margarita. "Yes, if only things were different."

"When everyone is here we can talk about the final arrangements," Diego said. "Freddie and I went with *Papá*. You were out of town, of course, and the other girls said to just go ahead. I hope that's okay with you, Magaly."

"I'm sure you selected a fine one, *mi hermano*."

"I don't know. It's a casket," Diego said. "There is no good box to put your brother in so that you can bury him in the ground."

"No."

"But all of that can wait," Diego said. "When the rest get here we will go into the details. We won't have an opportunity to hear your gossip then. I could use some conversation about anything except funerals and burials right now, I'll tell you."

"You want to hear my gossip, silly brother?" Magaly said, glad for the opportunity to talk casually with Diego for a while before the gathering became big, noisy, and contentious, as she knew it inevitably would. "Ask me any question you are confident will not invite an answer you'll regret hearing." She chuckled mischievously.

Not one to miss an opportunity to learn details of Magaly's personal life, Ignacio immediately chimed in, "So tell us about Detroit then. Having a good trip so far?"

"Good, but very busy, Iggie," she said. "It's different from what I expected."

"Is it as dangerous as they say?" He was chronically

worried about her, and unhappy with what he considered her overly adventurous lifestyle.

"Both yes and no," Magaly said. "It's really quite beautiful. My hotel room—I'm staying at the Pontchartrain—overlooks a big plaza and the Detroit River. You can see Canada from there. It's less than a mile across. I've met many wonderful people who take great pride in their city. There is crime, of course, and far too much. But that is only part of the story."

"I'm sure you'll tell the whole story, Magaly," Ignacio said. "That is your way." He looked at her with longing eyes. "Have you made close friends there? You make friends so easily, I know. Among both women and men."

"Children, too," Magaly added wryly. "And I feel complimented, Ignacio. But you are referring to my professional associations, of course," she added pointedly.

"Of course," Ignacio said, embarrassed to have been so obvious. Normally an artful conversationalist, his affection for Magaly perennially clouded his judgment and rendered him inept and tactless. "Your private relationships are naturally none of your readers' business," he ended lamely, taking a drink of his whiskey highball. "Or mine."

Magaly smiled, satisfied. Ignacio wouldn't try prying again. At least not for a while. "I'm flattered that you think of me so much," she said, patting him on the arm.

She turned to Diego then. "Speaking of relationships," she said. "I wonder if you can give me some insight. I met this man in Detroit. An interesting man. One of the police officers. He's going through a divorce. His second. There is this curious thing about him. You would think that he would be angry, or bitter, or jealous, or hateful in his attitudes about these women. That is usual, isn't it? But, instead, he is just—I don't know—he still loves them." She smiled. "Forgive me, Diego, but I can't help remembering that you felt much the same about your friend Sarah. In fact, I told this policeman that I have a brother who reminded me of him in this way. How is it that after so much hurt a man still loves a woman?"

Ignacio put in, "They say that women live in the future and men live in the past."

"Is that true, Diego? Do men live in the past?" Magaly asked.

Diego shrugged. "Perhaps. But what of women? Is Ignacio correct? Do women only have time for the future?"

Magaly thought for a moment then said, "Maybe it is that women feel themselves more vulnerable. They need to nurture themselves and their children at all costs. For women there may be no time to waste on what is done and over. We look to what the future can bring us."

"When the mine peters out, the gold-digger moves on," intoned Ignacio.

"That is *not* what I meant," Magaly said, frowning.

Ignacio blanched.

"Well, do you still love Sarah?" Magaly asked, turning to her brother.

Diego didn't hesitate. "I still love her. Yes."

"And it makes me want to shake him!" Ignacio exclaimed.

"Why?" Magaly asked.

"Because if your love-struck brother has no pride, at least he has friends who bleed for him." Ignacio looked at Diego and gave a little slap to his own forehead with the palm of his hand, as Latins often do when frustrated. *"Madre de Diós,"* he said.

"Why do you still love her, *'mano mio*?" Magaly asked, ignoring Ignacio, searching her brother's eyes.

"The poets say love is forever," Diego said.

"The less poetic would say that this is true for some, and not for others," Magaly said. "And Sarah is one of the others?"

"Yes," Diego said softly. "Sarah is one of the others."

"She was a pig," Ignacio declared flatly. His friend Diego's attitude about his old girlfriend was a sore point for him. He truly loved his friend and his frustration at his obduracy was commensurate with his affection. "Her house was a sty—dishes piled in the sink for days; crumbs and junk all over the floors; dirty diapers lying around in stinking piles. You had to fight your way to the bathroom to take a leak. I'm surprised there were no *cucarachas*. I never saw any of them, at least."

"We shared our lives for a year-and-a-half," Diego said.

"You shared your pocketbook," Ignacio went on. "You paid for that woman's divorce. You bought her clothes. You bought her jewelry. You bought her kids clothes. You gave them a Christmas when their own father would not. You fixed up her house. You made house payments. You got her car fixed."

"It wasn't about all of that," Diego said mildly.

"Oh, of course not, Diego. I forgot. She slept with you."

"It wasn't about that, either," he said.

"Pobrecito," Ignacio said, shaking his head in pity. "Magaly, her children were out of control. One of the boys, poor little fellow—she had two boys and a little girl, beautiful children—he was so neglected he pissed down the heat vents in his bedroom just to get attention. He shit in his own clothes closet. He started stealing from stores."

"I know all of those things," Diego protested. "But it's not that simple, 'Nacio. I keep telling you that sometimes a man can see faults and yet still have hope that things will get better, that love and patience are enough to bring change. Besides, I myself was not perfect in the relationship."

"Of course you were not perfect, Diego," Ignacio said. "No one can be perfect in a relationship with anyone. Even his own mother. What do you do, search your memory for every inconsiderate thing you ever said to her, review in your brain every time you showed impatience or anger at her outrageous behavior? Crazy! You gave her everything. You talked to her endlessly. As far as I can see, you never had a decent conversation with that horrible woman. How can you work on a relationship when only one side talks? She drank beer, made a fool of herself in public, lied to you, broke every promise she made, neglected her children, and dreamed about a rich man coming to take her away. She was too lazy, jealous, and selfish to ever do the hard work of relationships." Ignacio turned to Magaly. "Look at your crazy brother. Here is a prince of fools."

"Diego is no fool, Iggie," Magaly said. "Why does it offend you so much that he loves this woman? Is there so much love in the world that it can't use a little more—even if it's given to persons who may not deserve it in your eyes?"

"I care only for your brother's humiliation, Magaly," he said.

"Sometimes a person must suffer a little to gain a little," Magaly said. "A thing worth having is worth fighting for, is it not?"

"Now you are talking nonsense," Ignacio said. "Is that what the poets say, too?"

"Perhaps." Magaly quickly looked at Diego, then glared at Ignacio. "I am sorry for even bringing this up, Diego. We were going to have some innocent talk to brighten our gloom over the death of our brother and now we are arguing about love and women. I forgot how—frank—your friend likes to be."

Ignacio hung his head. He was crushed that he would be accused of creating pain among friends who were already suffering. He meant only to get Diego to stand up for himself.

"No, it's all right," Diego said, touching his friend's hand. "Ignacio meant no harm. I would answer you like this, Magaly. When I look at all of the days we spent together, one by one, and compare them to what those days might have been like had we never been together—then I think I was happy. Understand?" He took a long drink from his glass of Carta Blanca. "After that, I don't think the rest matters. She had this smile—"

"Devils can smile," Ignacio said petulantly, not ready to give up.

"She was not a devil, Iggie," Diego said. "She was just Sarah Miller. My love for her was a part of me. You can't take my love for her away any more than you can take my arm away, or my leg. And I loved her children. I miss them. Do you want me to forget them? How can I do that? Sometimes things come to an end. Then you move on. But you don't forget. You shouldn't forget. Aren't human beings worth enough that they are worth remembering? Aren't weeks and months of your own life worth respecting?" He looked at his friend. He looked at Magaly. "I loved Sarah Miller, *hermana*. I will always love Sarah Miller." He drained his beer. "Maybe this friend of yours, this policeman in Detroit, is the same."

"I'm becoming ill at my friend's ridiculous sentimentality," Ignacio said. "I think I will go visit the bathroom before I become truly sick." He shook his head, threw up his hands, stood up, and walked stiffly toward the restrooms at the back of the restaurant.

Magaly was embarrassed for her brother, but Diego seemed not to be embarrassed at all. He had made peace with that part of his life long before and seemed philosophical about it, if not entirely content. "It must have hurt you very much," she said.

"I was hurt," he said. "But do you know what? It's not the thing I choose to remember." He looked off into the dim interior, his thoughts far away. After a moment he said, "I cherish the autumn. On a clear day the sky is high and blue, and the sun, it has the color of the flesh of lemons. Do you remember the lemons in Mérida?

"I remember them," Magaly said. There was a bittersweet melancholy in Diego's voice that tore at her heart. Had he felt anger, it would have been easier for her to forgive Sarah Miller.

Diego's eyes came to rest on the window at the front of the restaurant. They lingered on the evening sunlight streaming in, split by the prism of the glass into a rippling saffron fan, a cipher in the smokey air. "Do you know what I remember about her when the weather turns like this?" he said.

"Tell me."

"We would wake up together in the mornings with the sun shining through her windows just like that. She would rest her head on my chest and look into my eyes, neither smiling nor frowning. Like a child, she would take her hand and stroke my face with her fingertips, and all the while she would study me with serious eyes. I know that she loved me then, *mi hermana*— even if the time came when she loved me no more." He squeezed Magaly's arm. "That is what I remember."

Within ten minutes the rest of the Rodríguez siblings arrived. There were congratulations and teasing, reminiscing, and complaining. And there were many tears. They spent nearly three hours in the restaurant, planning their dead brother's funeral.

* * *

Magaly picked up her father at Diego's house at noon the next day, Saturday, and took him to lunch.

"I want no lunch," the old man said. "I don't like these New York restaurants. They remind me of brothels and medical clinics."

"Then we will have to find a good place for you, *Papá*," Magaly said. "Will you please be patient with me? The restaurant will give us a chance to talk."

"We can talk at Diego's house."

"I want to talk to you alone."

"Why? You have secrets?"

Magaly laughed. "Do you think your daughter has been a bad girl, *Papá*?"

His gruff banter was a sham, his way of handling his middle daughter, cultivated by years of dealing with her jealous sisters. She was his favorite. Any request from Magaly, no matter how trivial, was inevitably granted. "You are always a bad girl, Magaly," he said. "That is why I worry more about you than Rosa and Margarita. You are your mother's daughter." He looked out the car window at the city streets flowing by like a Monet painting. "Now is when I need your mother."

"I know, *Papá*," Magaly said.

The old man studied her. "The older you get the more you favor her, *mija*."

"Do you think so?"

"You have the look of the Maya, except you are taller than your mother's people. That you get from my side."

Magaly patted his knee as she drove. "How do you feel?"

"Old and tired," he muttered. He was seventy-five. It galled him terribly that, though fifteen years his junior, his wife had died long ago—twenty-one years this winter. He had loved his wife too completely to ever remarry.

"You are not so old," Magaly said soothingly. "You look as handsome as ever to me."

"You flatter me as ever, daughter. You know the key to your old man, don't you?"

"Of course," Magaly said. "I get that from *Mamá*, too. The sorcerer's side."

They went to a small Mexican restaurant Magaly knew in lower Manhattan called Ixtapa. It was quiet and intimate. The food was excellent. Despite his earlier feigned irascibility, Carlos Rodríguez was content. "Good," he said, over a mouthful of milanesa, the pounded, seasoned, and fried steak he loved so well. "Not like home, but good."

"I'm glad you enjoy it," Magaly said. "Tell me now, how are you really?"

"I suppose you mean about Aurelio," her father said drily.

"*Sí.*"

"Poor," he said. "I have dreams."

"I know he forgave you, *Papá*."

"But I didn't forgive my son," the old man said. "Not while he was alive. And now he is dead."

"But he knew," Magaly said urgently. "That is what matters."

"No," her father said resignedly. "In my selfish, foolish pride I failed him." The old diplomat wiped his eyes. "He was her favorite, you know—your mother's favorite of the boys, the way you were my favorite of the girls."

"*Sí.*"

"If *Mamá* was here, she would not forgive me for what I did to her son."

"Oh, *Papá*," Magaly said. "You are talking like a silly old fool. Do you think for a single minute that *Mamá* would condemn you for being yourself? She lived with you for all those years. She gave you six children. She worshiped you, the handsome Spanish man from Mérida! Now you think that she would turn from you when you need her most? Never. She is with you now, *Papá*. I feel her. In the night last night I saw her face, clear as if she was truly in my room with me. Aurelio is with her now. They are together."

"It is nice to think of that," the old man confessed.

"Yes, it is," Magaly said.

"But I should have tried harder to understand," the old man said sullenly. "It is hard for me! These new ideas...When I was young, 'Relio's—his *ways*—were not discussed. There were men like that, but it was a quiet thing that no one talked about. And this terrible disease, this AIDS. This was not a thing we knew about. I told your brother that it was God's way of punishing him for his bad behavior. I was wrong to do that. Am I God to know such a thing, to decide how and why and when He exacts his vengeance? Now I must pray to God to forgive me for this terrible and arrogant blasphemy."

Magaly said softly, "We all need forgiveness, *padre mío*. Tonight we will pray together—for Aurelio's soul, and our own."

"I would like that, daughter. I would like for us to do that very much. Are you still a good Catholic?"

"I try."

"But not too hard." The old man managed a grin.

"*Papá!*"

"You can't fool this old man," he said. "I am not the fine *Santero* your mother's father was, God rest his soul, but I am given to know certain things."

"You have been talking to Diego, *Papá*! I know you have. We had a long talk last night. There's nothing of *Santería* here. He promised me he would say nothing about Detroit."

The old man laughed and waved his arms. "Don't fault your brother, *mija*. He loves you very much. We boys just like to gossip."

"Yes," Magaly retorted. "Worse than old women."

"Tell me about this new man," he said.

"There is no new man," Magaly answered firmly. "And there is not much to tell. I mention to Diego that I am fascinated by this policeman's behavior, and now you have me mixed up in some affair. You are a nasty man! Diego, too."

"Tell me about him, *mija*," the old man repeated, undeterred.

Magaly frowned. "He is forty-five. He is twice divorced. I bet that whets your appetite for the details of your favorite daughter's life, nosey father. That is another thing that you did not talk about in the old days, no? Divorce?"

"I accept some things more readily than others," he said slowly.

"I'm sorry, *Papá*. I shouldn't have said that."

"Nonsense," he said. "Now I turn the tables on you. Do not apologize for being my wonderful, direct daughter."

Magaly smiled. "Okay."

"So?"

"He is a witch, *Papá*.

"What do you say?" the old man asked, shocked.

"*Es un hechicero*," she said. "He sees things. He understands things. He has power. He denies all of this. But he knows."

"You are always looking for danger, aren't you, daughter?" he said, shaking his head. "Might I assume that you have found it once again?"

"Of course."

"Naturally, you will tell me nothing about what is really happening in that distant God-forsaken city."

"I cannot, *Papá*. I cannot. I have an agreement with my boss, Herman Vickers—you remember him. You met him once at Diego's house, at my birthday party a few years ago."

"Yes."

"Well, then," Magaly said, "about our business here..."

* * *

Another thing accomplished, another matter put to rest. Magaly was tired. It always fell on her to mediate, to explain, to cajole, to apologize. Margarita was older, but responsibility rolled off her like water off a duck's back. Despite her wandering habits, it was Magaly who was the tie that bound the family together. Maybe it was the fact that she looked so much like her mother that naturally placed her in that role. Whatever it was, it was hers to play, for better or worse.

Three hours after finishing lunch with her father she walked into the offices of *Harper's Magazine*. On the telephone earlier in the morning, Vickers said he would be in the office Saturday afternoon catching up on some paperwork and would like to see her. She breezed into his walnut and dark leather suite and plopped down onto the love seat across from his desk before he had an opportunity to even rise and greet her. As was its wont, a swatch of hair fell in front of her face. She didn't bother to move it. She peered through it like a one-eyed sheep dog.

Vickers smiled despite himself. "Aren't you a sight," he said. Magaly's natural beauty never ceased to surprise him when he saw her, no matter how often it was. He walked around the desk, bent down and gave her a peck on the cheek. "I'm terribly sorry about you brother," he said. "If there is anything *Harper's* can do, or anything I can do personally—"

"Thank you, Herman," she said. "No, there's nothing you can do. Unless you can raise the dead." Her direct way of speaking was another thing that never ceased to surprise Vickers.

"I can do many things, Magaly," he said. "Unfortunately, raising the dead is not among them. Write the funeral home address down for me if you would, though. I would like to send flowers, if that's all right."

"Father and the rest of the family would appreciate it," she said. "Me, too. I'm sorry. I don't mean to be insolent. I've been through a lot this week."

"Yes, you have," Vickers said. "Too much." He pulled up a Louis XIV chair from its place next to his desk and turned it to face her. He dropped down onto its rose-colored upholstery with the air of a worried father. "I should pull you off this assignment," he said.

"Herman, don't you dare!"

"I'm unhappy about the whole thing," he said. "It's getting out of hand. You're burning the candle at both ends, Magaly. Now there's the death of your brother. You'll need time with your family."

"I'll spend time with my family," she said. "Then I'll go back and do my job—do what you pay me a lot of money to do."

"This has nothing to do with money," Vickers said. "It has to do with your health, emotional and physical."

"I'm fine," Magaly insisted.

"Are you?"

"Yes."

Vickers sighed. "Can I get you some coffee? Tea?"

"Tea, please."

He went to the door, opened it, and said to his secretary, "Tea, Gena. Lemon and cream." Instead of returning immediately to his chair, he walked across the office to the huge window that overlooked Central Park. He gazed down onto the treetops through a fine rain that had come up in the last hour. "The summer just flew by," he said. "Here it is the autumn. Hallowe'en's around the corner, and I still haven't found the time to buy the new bathing suit my wife wanted."

"Time does that as you get ever older, doesn't it?" Magaly said. "The days go by in a blur."

"Just wait till you're my age," Vickers said with a smile. "Then they positively race by. Actually, I just read an explanation for it. In *Psychology Today*, I think. They say it has to do with the fact that, subconsciously, the yardstick we use to measure the passage of time is our own life's experience. The older you are, the more months you have lived—the more months you have lived, the shorter any given number of months seems, because that number is a progressively smaller part of your total experience. Makes sense, I suppose." In a moment he said, "How is your father?"

"He's doing as well as he might," Magaly said. She told him about the old man's difficulties with accepting her brother's sexual orientation.

"Life never gets easier, does it?" Vickers said. "But they're strong people, your father and Diego and the rest. They'll work all of these things out and move on. Maybe your father will go back to Mexico to be among his friends. All of the others are busy. Life has a way of grabbing you and pulling you forward."

"Just don't pull the plug on me, Herman. Please don't do that."

Gena knocked and came in with a tea service on a lacquered tray. She put it on the credenza against the wall and slipped back out.

Vickers walked over and fixed two cups of strong tea. Oolong. He knew how Magaly liked hers. He handed her a porcelain cup and saucer, an ornate silver spoon delicately balanced alongside. He sat down again on the Louis XIV chair and said, "There is a fine line that editors must walk, Magaly. There are many things to consider, each important in its own way. There is loyalty to the writer. There is loyalty to the company and to its editorial integrity and artistic standards. There is timing. There is loyalty to the subject of the piece. All of these things play against each other and vie for the starring role. In this case, I worry about your emotional objectivity, as well as having some very real concerns for your physical safety."

"When have you ever found me lacking in objectivity?" she asked.

"Never," Vickers said. "Never once."

"Why now, then?"

"Your brother's death can't help but affect you," he said. "These shootings in Detroit. Bullets whizzing by. Those horrible murders."

"You want to protect me?"

"Yes. Of course."

"Then let me do my job, Herman. With all due respect, I'm not your daughter. I'm an employee of this magazine. A fine one, you say. Then let me do my job. It's what I do. It's who I am. I have never failed you. I won't fail you now."

"I have a feeling, Magaly."

"What feeling, Herman?"

"I don't quite know," Vickers replied. "See what I mean? Now you've got me talking like you—in metaphysical gibberish. I don't need to tell you that you are merely an observer, not a participant—on this story and on every story. You can't cross the line and become an actor in the play. Then you lose objectivity. You lose credibility. Something tells me that maybe you're flirting with that line."

"It can't be because I insisted you say the murder victim's name—" Magaly said.

"Absolutely not," Vickers said. "I had that one coming." He got up again and walked to the corkboard on the wall next to his desk, pulling a couple of pushpins out. He held up a strip of paper so Magaly could see it. **KATY MARROQUIN** was written in bold black letters across it. "See? A promise is a promise. I look at that board every day and the name is there."

Magaly smiled. "Thank you, Herman. I'll not doubt you again," she said. "But what are you getting at?"

"I'm talking about loyalty to my writer, Magaly—my *employee* as you want it. The buck stops here, in this office. As senior editor, I have to act in the best interests of all of the parties. That includes you."

"I want to be their voice, Herman. The cops'. Like we talked about."

"Their *objective* voice?" Vickers asked.

"Of course," Magaly said, nervously sipping her Oolong.

"All right, then," he said. "Tell me about it. All of it. Leave out nothing. Tell me about this Sergeant Westonfield and his merry band."

An hour and three cups of tea later, Magaly said good-bye to Herman Vickers, leaving with hard-won assurances that she could continue her work in Detroit.

When the door closed, Vickers stared at its dark walnut sheen for a long time. Then he hit the intercom button on his telephone. "Gena," he said, "would you come in here for a moment?" He handed her the slip of paper upon which Magaly had written the address of the funeral home. "Send some flowers right away to this address, would you? Put them on the company account. And one more thing—do you still have the telephone number handy to Chief Lucas at the Detroit Police Department?"

"Yes, sir. It's right on my desk," Gena said.

"Good," Vickers said. "Try to get hold of him, would you? I know it's Saturday. Maybe you can get someone in his office to help you if he isn't immediately available. I want to find out where another funeral is going to take place—in Detroit. I'll be sending out two arrangements. The second will be for a young lady named Katy Marroquín." He leaned back in his leather chair and stretched. "Put the Detroit order on my personal account," he said. "Mrs. Vickers and I would both very much like to pay our respects."

* * *

Aurelio's funeral was arranged for Monday, the twenty-eighth. When Magaly emerged from the meeting it was not quite five o'clock on Saturday afternoon. Despite the rain she decided to go for a walk in the park. She had already begun to dread the evening, the first night at the funeral home. She hated those places, where they displayed people's loved ones like slabs of meat at the grocery.

She balanced her umbrella over her head and wandered along the paths beneath the red-gold canopy of maple leaves. She loved the sweet smell of the leaves borne on the rain. The park was deserted except for a passing policeman on foot patrol and a few adventurous spirits taking late afternoon jogs. Vickers' warning about avoiding personal entanglements haunted her. Was he so completely wrong? And the words of Father Lewendowski floated back to consciousness: men like Bill Westonfield were wolves in the fold, he'd said. She recalled her own intuition about Westonfield's nature the very first night they met at Nancy Whiskey—*You're playing with fire*, she'd thought.

Katy Marroquín was dead; and the Prado boy; and Danny Villanueva; and the Jamaican at the marina. The improbable *mayombero* was still at large after issuing a psychotic personal challenge to Bill. What was to come of it? From what she knew of Westonfield's nature, he was likely to become almost a rogue cop. He told her that he would find and kill the murderer. It had all seemed so right then. The evil sorcerer *should* die for what he'd done, shouldn't he?

Vickers had talked about editorial lines. As a journalist, where did she draw that line? If, in that role, she saw Bill do something illegal—terribly illegal—where did that put her morally, emotionally, and under the law? She knew well that she had already crossed the Rubicon, traipsed too nonchalantly over the unseen boundary of journalistic ethics. She'd sat in a police car and watched two police officers essentially kidnap a boy and seal him into a trash bin. While troubling, it had seemed strangely liberating at the time, even funny. But she sensed that what was coming was going to be very different in both substance and degree. They had all been right—Jack, the priest, and the others. They'd given fair warning of the consequences of meddling in the affairs of men like Westonfield. The storm was gathering, and now she must reap the whirlwind. She pulled the collar of her raincoat close around her neck and shivered with a sudden chill. There could be no doubt. The storm was coming.

* * *

Magaly spent all day Sunday with her best friend, Erica James. Like Magaly, Erica was a journalist, an op-ed page editor with the *New York Times*. At forty-two Erica was almost a decade older than Magaly, but they were soulmates. They met when Magaly went to work for the *Times* as a fluff writer ten years earlier, her first real job in journalism, and had been close ever since.

"What do I do?" Magaly asked over a mug of hot chocolate. She was sharing the sofa with Erica in the den in her home on Staten Island. Magaly held the cup to her nose and savored the magical smell of Mexican chocolate and cinnamon. "I don't mind telling you I'm scared," she said.

"Scared about journalistic ethics, scared about being stalked by a bloodthirsty psychopath, or scared about getting silly-in-love with a Detroit cop?" Erica asked.

"All of the above," Magaly said. "I'm terrified of them all, Ricky."

"If that creep gets you," Erica said, "I'll write your epitaph: 'Here lies Maggie Rodríguez. She was many things, but she definitely was NOT boring.'"

With her Maine accent, Magaly thought Erica sounded like Katherine Hepburn. She could spend hours just listening to her speak. It was nice to be with her again, safe and warm. Her sweet, sometimes bawdy, humor never failed to draw Magaly out.

"What I'm trying to tell you," Magaly said, "is that I realize how little my stamina has been tested until now. If he does ever get to me, I promise I'll haunt you forever."

Erica set her cup down and put her arm around her friend. "Golly-my-'Galy," she said, "What am I gonna do with you?"

"Put me away safe in a box until this is all over?" Magaly said plaintively.

"See," Erica said, "you say that, but you don't really mean it. You love what you're doing, don't you?"

"To death," Magaly said, fully appreciating the ambiguity.

"I wouldn't trade my life—danger and craziness and all—for another one; not for an office with a window overlooking Central Park, not for love nor money. Maybe some other time, in another decade. But not now."

"See," Erica said.

"See what?"

"You want it both ways, Maggie. You like the danger… just not too much."

"Maybe," Magaly said musingly, tilting her head.

"Don't you 'maybe' me, girlfriend," Erica retorted. "Wake up and smell the roses. Everything comes with a price." She withdrew her arm. "You want a piece of my mind?"

"Mmmm."

"Well," Erica said flatly, "here it is, whether you want it or not. Number one, as far as the legal shenanigans go, don't sweat it. Look at it this way: reporters go to war, right? Remember that famous picture of the South Vietnamese officer shooting that handcuffed prisoner in the head during the war? It was before your time, but I know you must have seen it."

"Yes."

"It doesn't get more extreme than that, does it? But no one said anything about the journalist's participating in an atrocity. Get it? You stay detached. You let the actors act. You avoid any pretense of involvement. You note, you observe, and eventually you report. That's it." She thought for a minute. "You know, it's funny. Most people think there are laws that require witnesses to report crimes, or even to help the victim. Not so. Unconstitutional. Period."

"I know that," Magaly said. "But what about civic and moral responsibility?"

"Civic?" Erica said. "Maybe. But there's a tradition of free press in this country, and it's not just platitudes. It may sound cliché, but it's true. Journalists need access to the unvarnished truth. People understand that. They really do. As to your moral responsibility—Magaly, that's your call. Only you can decide when you've had enough. Personally, if it was me, I'd stand back and watch your policeman squash that piece of shit's brains out like he was a potato bug."

"He's not my policeman," Magaly said.

"Ahhh, so we come to it," Erica said. "Do you want him to be?"

"To be mine?"

"Uh-huh."

"I've only known him a week, you fruit cake," Magaly said. "He's still married. I've never met his children. I've never been to his house. I guess you could say I barely know him."

"So what *do* you know about him?" Erica asked.

"Only a little."

"Like—"

"He's smart," Magaly said. "He's funny. He's self-deprecating. He's brave. His subordinates worship him. He speaks Spanish like a native."

"My God, he's a Boy Scout!" Erica said, laughing.

"He excites me," Magaly said.

"I didn't notice," Erica said.

"But he worries me."

"Well, you have some sense left," Erica observed. "Not much, but some. Listen. All men are dangerous. All men make you worry. Hey, we're the ones with the holes, they're the ones with the pegs, right?"

"Jesus, Erica."

"I could have asked you if he had a big thing, Maggie, so give me credit! But think about it. That's the way it is. Men are bigger and stronger than us. We women can only choose from a variety of dangers. If we choose well, it works. If we choose poorly, we're screwed. End of story."

"You make me want to run out and buy a wedding dress," Magaly said. "You should go into marriage counseling."

"I would," Erica said, "but there's no percentage in it. Anyway, you got me way off track. I did the best I could on your journalistic conundrum. On to the second of your fears: getting killed. Now that's Mr. Darwin all the way. Pure evolution. Fight or flight. Do you believe this policeman can protect you?"

"Better than anyone else. That's all I can say," Magaly answered.

"Then go for it," Erica said. "Maniac medieval torturers notwithstanding, go for it. If you let that Cuban puke kill you, I'll never forgive myself for having told you this, but—yeah, go for it."

"You're quite the cheerleader, Ms. James," Magaly said. "*Hey, fuckin' go for it!*" She lowered her voice in imitation of Rocky Balboa.

"At last we come to fear number three," Erica said. "Your Sergeant Westonfield. Actually, I've known one or two like him."

"Really."

"They're a peculiar lot, these guys. They're the purest, most honorable men in the world. They're plain decent, with a capital 'D'. But their trouble starts with their peculiar sense of purpose. Really, it's their compulsion. They're on a mission. They're driven by guilt, or anger, or some deep—something. They burn white hot. If you get too close, Magaly, they burn *you*."

"A priest I met in Detroit warned me about that once," Magaly said. "I asked him if he was talking about Bill and me when he described what happens to moths when they fly too close to the flame of a candle."

"Well," Erica said, "it sounds like you ran into an amazing cast of characters in that town. But let me show you something." She popped off the sofa and went to one of the bookshelves that lined the walls. "There's an intriguing account about a man very much like your Bill in a book I have, a history of the Indian wars." Her eyes ranged over the rows of books, searching for the title. "Here we are," she said, hoisting a heavy volume. She thumbed through the pages, looking for the right chapter. "Here. It's about Major Hart Greene, United States Cavalry, and his presence at the massacre of Chief Little Crow's Northern Cheyennes near Sweetwater, Wyoming, in 1872." She dropped back down onto the sofa. "Greene was a West Pointer, a career officer who had dedicated his life to the army. He served with General Hooker at Missionary Ridge in the Civil War. It was attested that he was as loyal an officer as ever was, absolutely dedicated to the integrity of command and the necessity of discipline under fire."

"I'm sure it's a wonderful story," Magaly said mildly, "but what does any of this have to do with Bill Westonfield?"

"I'm coming to it," Erica said. "Listen. Sweetwater was no battle, Magaly. It was a slaughter of old men, women, and children. Greene was in command of a regiment directed to attack one end of the village. He and his men were arrayed on a ridge overlooking the fighting. Greene sat on his horse on that blistering day and refused orders to attack—while troops under his command were engaged right in front of him. Understand, there were some Cheyenne warriors who found weapons and attempted to defend the village, so there was danger to the soldiers. But Greene still refused to attack. Several witnesses later reported that a sergeant repeatedly begged him to give the order to advance. Greene wouldn't even look at the sergeant, they said, but watched the slaughter with tears on his face." Erica cleared her throat. "Sometimes I can almost see his tears," she said, "sliding down through the dust on his cheeks. 'At ease,' he said each time the sergeant came to him. I guess those two words were all he could say."

Magaly looked mutely at Erica.

"Afterwards, Greene was charged with dereliction under fire. He was eventually acquitted of the charges when the truth came out, but by then he was a broken man. Here's a picture of him." She handed the book to Magaly.

Magaly took the book. It was an old black and white photograph like one of Matthew Brady's from the Civil War. Greene seemed both proud and stern in his uniform, and his chiseled face had a haunted look to it. His eyes looked back at her with eery pathos across an ocean of time. Erica was right. It was the look Magaly often saw on the face of Bill Westonfield.

"Greene was a great man," Erica said.

"Yes."

"But he was *dangerous*," Erica said. "That's why they tried to crucify him after the massacre. How could his superiors justify their own actions without condemning his?"

"I don't suppose they could," Magaly said.

"I think Bill Westonfield is probably dangerous like that," Erica said.

Magaly said nothing. She was thinking about the other story Lewendowski told her, the one about the crazy on the porch who gave up as soon as he saw Bill.

"Problem number three rears its ugly head again," Erica said. "Dangerous is sexy, no?"

"What?"

"I simply mean that your cop's dangerous—and you like that about him."

Magaly shrugged. "Maybe."

"'Maybe' my big fat ass," Erica said. She held up her empty cup and asked if Magaly wanted more.

"Please," she said, a little uncomfortable that Erica found it so easy to pin her down.

When Erica came back, Magaly was perusing the book.

"Understand what I'm saying?" Erica asked.

"I think so. Yes."

"Sleeping and dying," Erica said. "They're like danger and sex. Two sides of the same sheet of paper—mirror images of each other. Hemingway called sleep 'the little death'."

"What the hell are you talking about, Ricky?"

"I'm talking about killing and fucking, Magaly. Quit being so willfully obtuse. They're both sex. All anyone has to do is go to the movies to find that out. It's in our genes." Erica smiled and touched Magaly's face. "Fight your dragons, 'Galy. Climb your mountains. But this Westonfield character will break your heart in the end. He'll break it because he still loves those other women, or he'll break it because he'll be killed by that madman, or he'll break it on account of something else. But he'll certainly break it. He won't mean to. But he will."

* * *

On Monday at nine o'clock in the morning Magaly attended the long Catholic services for her brother. Mr. and Mrs. Vickers were there. Many friends from *Harper's* were there. Erica was there. Westonfield called the night before, as had Carol Rourke, Tom Bacon, and Jerry Talmadge.

Aurelio looked pale, shrunken, and old as he lay cold in his silk-lined coffin. *Papá*, Diego, Federico, Margarita, and Rosa were each lost in their own memories. But Magaly stood alone at the head of the open casket before the priest began the service and looked down upon the powdered face of her eldest brother. *We all have our sins*, she thought. *We all have our guilt. I was afraid he would ask me to sing the last time we talked on the telephone.* After a moment, through the tears, with halting voice, she began to sing an old Spanish tune that Aurelio had been fond of. As she sang, her heart lightened, and her soul soared not only with that of her brother, but with the souls of all of the murdered ones—Katy, Danny, and Emma. "It's all right," the words said. "He can't hurt you anymore."

CHAPTER 22

Professor Hector Saldívar parked his black Volvo in the parking structure at Monroe and St. Antoine and walked out into the overcast afternoon. Detroit police headquarters was just down the block. He felt more than a passing curiosity as to why a policeman—a homicide detective, no less—would have need of a professor of religious studies from Wayne State University. Whatever he wanted, it was a matter of urgency. "Can you meet with us tomorrow?" the sergeant had said. "Saturday afternoon at headquarters?" He had been vague about the purpose of the meeting, revealing only that the police were looking at certain unusual circumstances surrounding a murder investigation. Saldívar normally set Saturday afternoons aside for meetings with his graduate students, but he had agreed to meet with the authorities. He arrived in less than two minutes, gave the revolving door at fabled 1300 Beaubien a shove, and stepped gingerly inside. Six hundred miles away, Magaly Rodríguez was eating lunch with her father in New York City.

Westonfield was keeping a watchful eye out for his guest consultant. He easily picked him out through the desultory Saturday activity at the Homicide Section. At fifty-seven years of age, sporting a salt-and-pepper goatee and wire-rimmed glasses, Hector looked neither like a cop nor a witness. He poked his head tentatively around the open door. Westonfield approached him with his hand outstretched. "Professor Saldívar?"

"Yes, I am Saldívar," the academic said. "You must be the gentleman I talked to on the telephone last night." His words were carefully enunciated in that curious way of lifelong teachers.

"That's right, professor. I'm Bill Westonfield. Thank you

for coming down this afternoon."

"Not at all, sir," Saldívar said with a smile. "The pleasure is mine. It isn't every day that a teacher is called upon to help the police in the resolution of a criminal case. I can assure you that my Saturday afternoon is likely to be more interesting than it might otherwise have been."

Westonfield grinned back, immediately liking the man's natural dignity and charm. "Come this way, professor." He led him through the maze of office cubicles to the conference room where the others waited. Inside, he made the introductions. "Professor Hector Saldívar, meet Sergeants Paul Randazzo, Buck Fry, Gene Beck, and Morton Bickerstaff of the Detroit PD; and Sergeant Dale Ward of the Trenton police department. Gentlemen, Professor Saldívar." Over the nodding heads and *glad-to-meet-yous*, Westonfield asked, "Can I get you a coffee, professor?"

"That would be wonderful," Saldívar said. "Black, please."

When everyone had a fresh cup of coffee, Westonfield said, "I think what I'll do first is recap the case. That way the professor will have an understanding of the facts, and it may even give the rest of us a sense of perspective on the whole thing. So far, we've been finding out things piecemeal, putting them together like a puzzle."

"That's because we're a bunch of ace detectives," Buck Fry offered, moving his legs and feet—which he had firmly planted on the conference table—just enough to allow himself easy access to his genitals. He scratched them contentedly. "We're just like Dick fuckin' Tracy."

Westonfield looked sheepishly at the professor and was a little surprised to see that Saldívar appeared not to be offended. "So I'll go through the main points in order to convey the flow of events," he said, scowling at Fry. He cleared his throat. "Over the last several months, there have been a number of grave robberies out at Woodmere Cemetery in the Fourth Precinct. The doors to several crypts have been forced open, the locks broken, and body parts—bones—removed."

Westonfield referred to a notepad. "The skulls, ribs, tibias, fingers, and toes."

Saldívar's eyes widened with interest. He took a sheet of paper from his jacket pocket and scribbled on it.

"We're not sure if it's related," Westonfield continued, "but Saint Anne's Church in the Third Precinct made a report of some Holy Water being stolen in a B & E on the fifteenth of this month. A whole gallon of Holy Water, mind you."

The veins in Saldívar's temples worked and he hurriedly scribbled more notes onto the paper.

"I'm getting ahead of myself," Westonfield said. "A week before that, on the ninth, the body of one Joseph Allen, later identified as a dope dealer from Jamaica, was discovered stuffed into a boat at the county marina in Elizabeth Park down in Trenton. That's why Sergeant Ward's here, by the way. Two big points: Allen had been flayed, much of his skin stripped off, and he had been forced to eat some pages from a book found with his body. The book was a volume on the subject of Voodoo—"

Saldívar interrupted excitedly. "You say this person, this... Mr. Allen, was forced to eat some pages from this book? You have the name of this book?"

Ward opened a file. "*Voodoo & Hoodoo* by Jim Haskins," he said.

Saldívar's eyes widened even further. "I see," he said, scribbling more notes. "Please, continue, Mr. Westonfield."

"Word has been out on the street for the last few weeks that Cubans are moving into the neighborhood. Dope men. *Marielitos*."

"Cubans," the professor said, still writing.

"Yes," Westonfield said.

"What more do you know about them?"

"Not much. Rumors going around concerning animal sacrifices."

"Sacrifices!" Saldívar exclaimed. He made no attempt to conceal his agitation now. "What sort of sacrifices?"

"We're coming to that," Westonfield said.

"Of course," Saldívar replied apologetically. "I am used to dealing with students at the university, I'm afraid. I forget myself. Sorry."

"That's quite all right, *Señor Profesor*," Westonfield said. "We are only glad you were kind enough to come."

"There is much here that interests me," Saldívar said.

"Now we come to Sunday, October the twentieth. Acting on information from informants about these unusual activities—the involvement of Cubans, animal sacrifices, possible connections to the cemetery thefts—we staked out a house on Merritt Street off Junction. When confronted during the course of the evening's surveillance, a Tomás Mejías, a green-carded Cuban national, a *Marielito*, fired upon my partner John Rourke. Rourke returned fire and killed the man. Meantime, I myself observed another individual hiding in some shrubbery in a vacant lot nearby. He was armed with an AR-15 which was later determined to have been stolen in a burglary of a gun shop in Dayton, Ohio. I lost this guy after a foot chase." Westonfield went on, telling how the tracking dog followed the scent to the wall in the dead-end alley. "He just disappeared," he said. "I have no earthly explanation how."

A rivulet of sweat ran down Saldívar's temple and across his cheek. He could scarcely conceal his agitation now. With great effort, he maintained his silence.

"With Mejías dead, warrant in hand, we searched the house," Westonfield said. "We found a lot of interesting stuff, which I'll get to in a minute, but for now understand that we didn't find anything to help us identify the shithead I chased. No prints, nothing. The house had been rented to Mejías by a woman from Taylor. She knows nothing about any of this business. That has been thoroughly checked out."

Westonfield looked again at his notes. "On Wednesday, October the twenty-third, we had two more homicides in the Fourth Precinct." He gave cursory descriptions of the scenes on Chamberlain Street and in Patton Park. "Again, the house was rented to our man-about-town, Mejías. Same deal. Place was clean. As on Merritt, we recovered an assortment of interesting material. Later on, we discovered that at the time of his death, the unfortunate *Señor* Mejías had in his possession some newspaper clippings from the *News-Herald* on the murder of Joseph Allen. As Sergeant Fry has cogently pointed out, being the Dick Traceys that we are, we figured there might be a connection." Westonfield sipped his coffee and looked at the professor, who was on the edge of his seat in rapt attention.

"Please," Saldívar said.

"Those are most of the essential facts of the case so far," Westonfield said. "But before we bring out our evidence for the professor's inspection, let me throw out just a little more information for you to chew on. A few of you may know some of it. I don't believe any of you know all of it. As to the Chamberlain scene, while we don't have physical evidence linking what happened there to the man I chased, think—it sure as hell wasn't Mejías. Thanks to Jack Rourke, he's with us no more. And there's another interesting feature of the case: Magaly Rodríguez." He explained Maggie's background and the nature of her assignment. "Miss Rodríguez's grandfather was a *Santero*. That is, he was a practitioner of a Latin religion called *Santería*, which employs animal sacrifice, incantations, and paraphernalia like candles, powders, and colored beads."

Saldívar nodded enthusiastically.

"Miss Rodríguez has become close to the investigation," Westonfield said. "She has been to many of the scenes, and she is privy to all of the information. While not a *Santera* herself, she learned a lot about the religion from her grandfather. She informs us that there is another cult, more dangerous than *Santería*, called *palo mayombe*, which she is convinced is involved here. In any case, since coming here, she has offered some useful information. Interestingly, she has also experienced a couple of trance-like episodes, in which an apparition appeared to her."

There were a few twitters among the assembled cops.

Westonfield looked slowly around the table at each of them. "It's nothing to laugh at when you've been there," he said stonily. "Anybody see anything funny about any of this? No? Good, then." He referred again to his notes. "Now, accompanying this vision is an incantation."

Saldívar stopped all pretense of scribbling and stared openly at Westonfield.

"Pardon my pronunciation," Westonfield said. "I'll do the best I can. I'm not fluent in either Yoruba or Bantu, unfortunately. All right, here we go... *Aguanilleo Zarabanda aribo.*"

The professor gasped and crossed himself. *"Madre de Diós,"* he murmured.

"There's more, Professor Saldívar."

The academic took a handkerchief from his pocket and wiped the sweat from his face.

Westonfield continued: "In addition to the dreams, and also consistent with *palo mayombe*, are the following: One, there was a full moon on the night of the Prado and Marroquín - Villanueva murders, and it was in its waxing phase at the time of the Mejías shooting. Two, the bones stolen from the cemetery are the very bones needed to perform cult rituals. Three, some of the items like powders and candles seized at the scenes appear to be consistent with the cult. Four, other evidence particular to Chamberlain Street supports the hypothesis. My initials—W.W.—were carved into Katy Marroquín's back, and a black nightstick with a branching handgrip was forced into her vagina, i.e., a black branch. In Spanish and Bantu, gentlemen, 'black' and 'branch' translate as *palo mayombe.*"

This was more than Bickerstaff could bear. "I saw the initials, Sergeant," he said laconically, emphasizing the word "sergeant" to remind everyone that Westonfield did not outrank him. "There's no doubt that a connection exists between Mejías and Allen, and maybe you're right about the bones and powders. But you're reaching way too far with these other things. This dream stuff seems like a whole lot of hooey. These weird visions your Rodríguez woman is having; maybe she's been reading too much of the crap in her own magazine."

Randazzo asked sarcastically, "Do you read *Harper's*, Morty?"

Bickerstaff went on, ignoring Randazzo. He was on a roll, not only agitated over Westonfield's discourse, but filled with lingering disgust at what he considered to be Magaly's girlish vomiting at the Chamberlain scene. He described it to the group. "Maybe she had indigestion," he said leeringly. "Maybe she's pregnant," he added, looking pointedly at Westonfield. "Whatever. And this 'black branch' nonsense. That's reaching, too. I was at the scene. In my opinion, there's no factual basis whatsoever to draw the conclusions you made."

Westonfield sat impassively as Bickerstaff spoke. To the ever-mild Beck's dismay this served only to embolden Bickerstaff. All the talk of cemeteries and lady journalists recalled to Bickerstaff's mind certain rumors going around the department a few years earlier to the effect that Westonfield had been seen screwing Susan Lawrence, whom he later married, in Woodmere Cemetery. "Maybe you have a thing for cemeteries, Bill. Ghosties and ghoulies, and all of that. Speaking of bones, I heard you did have a certain bone examined in the cemetery a while back. Maybe this new lady, your hot tamale reporter, has already examined a bone in the graveyard."

Buck Fry grinned. The meeting wasn't as boring as he had anticipated it would be. He couldn't wait for the classroom shit to be over so the fun could start.

Oblivious, Bickerstaff went on. "This woman is nothing more than a distraction to the case, in my estimation. Let's send her packing back to New York. Maybe then, Bill, you could pay more attention to the work at hand than to your handiwork." The fact that he didn't have much luck in his amorous advances toward policewomen when, reputedly, Westonfield had plenty, was galling to Bickerstaff.

Gene Beck looked at Westonfield, wondering how seriously he intended to hurt Morty. The idiot just didn't know when to keep his mouth shut. Morty deserved whatever retribution Westonfield decided to exact, but Beck felt he ought to make at least a half-hearted attempt to defuse the situation. Morty was his partner, after all. "With all of his usual tactfulness," Beck said, "Morty is pointing out some concerns we all have about at least a few of these things, Bill. You gotta admit, this is pretty strange stuff. I mean, really out of the ordinary. I've been busting my ass down here for umpteen years and I have never seen anything like it. Never. We've really got a bad one out there and we don't need to be going off half-cocked on wild goose chases, with all due respect."

"That's why Professor Saldívar is here," Westonfield said, not looking at Beck, but focusing on Bickerstaff instead. The look on his face was a combination of amusement and dismissal, the look a cat gives a mouse after playing with it for a while. He turned to Saldívar. "Your thoughts, professor?"

Saldívar coughed into his handkerchief. "My apologies, gentlemen," he said. "I understand completely the hesitance and caution with which you approach a subject so important as murder. But, frankly, even without having examined the materials—I very much look forward to having a close look at them—I suspect that Sergeant Westonfield is correct in his surmise. Believe me, I know perfectly well how difficult and controversial belief in the reality of these things can be. From just the brief description of these matters I have heard this afternoon, however, I would hazard that you do have a most unfortunate happenstance in this affair, even more complex and tragic than you are already aware. There are many questions I have. There are several things I can only guess at as yet." He turned to Westonfield. "Sergeant, would you be so kind as to get me another cup of your delicious coffee?"

Westonfield grinned. "Certainly." He left the room.

"Delicious?" Randazzo said. "Come now, professor!"

Saldívar chuckled. "It is my nature to be polite," he said.

When Westonfield completely disappeared around the corner, Beck looked bitingly at Bickerstaff and shook his head.

Bickerstaff shrugged, said nothing.
  The professor looked out the window uncomfortably. An interesting and no doubt talented group of men, he thought, but most unusual. Fry farted loudly, which brought another smile to Saldívar's face. "You have a problem with several bodily functions, I perceive," he said to Fry. "Chronic itching as well as flatulence. You should have them looked at. It doesn't pay to put health matters off too long."
  Fry raised his eyebrows and scratched his scrotum again through his pants. "Maybe I should do that, professor," he said, his face serious. "Itching and farting have ailed me most of my life."
  Saldívar nodded gravely. "I had an uncle with much the same problem," he said. "Unfortunate man."
  "My apologies for my colleagues, professor," Randazzo said. "I hope you will forgive their, should I say, *informal*, conduct." He eyed Bickerstaff. "Five to three Bill throws you out the window, Morty," he said.
  Bickerstaff swallowed.
  "I'll cover that," Fry said, reaching for his wallet.
  Ward sat listening to the entire exchange in disbelief. This was what it was like to be a detective in Detroit?
  The professor continued to smile. He liked these men.
  Westonfield came in carrying a steaming cup of coffee, handed it to Saldívar. "Well, sir," he said, "how about a look?" He went to a long folding table in a corner of the room. An old sheet was draped across it, concealing the shapes and sizes of a number of objects laid out on its surface. Westonfield pulled off the sheet. He motioned for Saldívar to approach. "Here's the goods, *Señor Profesor*."
  Saldívar's eyes took it all in. Yes, it was as he thought—no, *knew*—it would be. He reached out to touch the cauldron, looking to Westonfield for approval. Westonfield nodded his assent. The professor's fingers at first touched, then almost caressed the charred black surface of the pot. Never before had he seen so many genuine objects of *palo mayombe* gathered

together in one place, at one time. After a long moment he said quietly, "It is as Sergeant Westonfield says, I am sorry to tell you. You have a *mayombero* here. And more. Very much more. Be prepared to set aside your beliefs now, gentlemen. Steady yourselves for the phantasmagorical. For better or worse, you have come face to face with a being out of your normal reference—evil, calculating, capable of monstrous acts such as you are not likely to have seen before."

Saldívar's eyes continued to roam over the macabre items. "Indeed," he went on in a soft voice, thick with emotion, "whether you choose to believe or not will hardly matter. Because, you see, *he* believes. And as long as he believes in the magic, he will act according to its dictates." Saldívar drank hot coffee, wiped his face again with his handkerchief. "Here," he said, holding up a cup which contained a coarsely ground yellow powder. He held it closer to his nose, sniffed it tentatively—"*Azúfre*," he said. "Yes. Sulfur. Used in many incantations." He reached for a plastic baggie, held it up in the light. It contained some wilted leaves. "*Guao*," he said. "Poison ivy. For works of destruction." He held up other packages, one after the other, peering at them closely, smelling, gently touching. "*Amoníaco*: ammonia. *Yerba bruja*: witch's herb. *Precipitado rojo*: a red-colored precipitate used to harm an enemy. Very powerful. It goes on, my friends. Many more." He turned to Westonfield. "I will label them, if you like. Make a list."

"We would appreciate that very much, professor. When you can. What about these other objects?"

"Oh, yes, my sergeant. There is more. And more disturbing even." The professor turned back to the table, shaking his head worriedly. "Here is the *nganga*, the cauldron of the Congos. They use it for powerful spells, also called *ngangas* by them. The most powerful of these spells is the *ndoki*. I see here candles," the professor continued, sighing. "Green and black. I see a knife, and a hammer of iron. I see a necklace of brown and black beads, alternating seven brown with three black." He fixed his gaze on Westonfield. "These things—the hammer, the knife, the candles, the necklace—these are the possessions and symbols of the most evil and destructive of all of the gods of *palo mayombe*: Zarabanda. You recall the incantation, Sergeant Westonfield? The one you say was heard by Miss Rodríguez in her dream? *Zarabanda aguanilleo aribo.* That is the spell used by the *mayombero* to call this god to earth to assist him in his worldly evils."

Saldívar sat down heavily in the closest chair to the table and looked out the window for a moment. After a while he said, "No ordinary *mayombero* can do that, I am afraid. We have here a *tata nkisi*, a practitioner of the highest order. I have heard of such a thing by word of mouth in my travels. I have read of them in my research. But I always thought them matters of legend, part of the myth of the cult more than things of substance. Whether it is true or not, that is for you to decide. But the monster believes it, rest assured."

The professor surveyed the laden table as one in a dream, who has only to wake up and the terror will be over. But the objects were truly there. Wishing for their disappearance would not make it happen. "So there you have it," he said, looking at Westonfield questioningly. "This man. The one you face. The one who carved your initials into the girl's back. He talks directly to his god."

No one breathed. Not even Morton Bickerstaff. Buck Fry almost forgot he had herpes.

Westonfield opened a file folder and flipped through its contents. He found what he wanted: photos of the scene at Chamberlain. He carried it around the table to Saldívar. "I have some photographs here, professor. I'm afraid they are graphic. Would you mind looking at them? You can see for yourself what the altar looked like and then judge how much what happened there can be connected to *palo mayombe*." He paused. "If you would rather not, I understand."

"Not at all," Saldívar said. "I must help you in this. You already know it is serious, of course. People are dead. But I can not but try my utmost to impress upon you and your colleagues that this man whose name we do not know is a killer of an order of magnitude beyond our ordinary ken. You know your business, and I won't interfere, but let me tell you that, as a *Marielito*, he likely has military training in the Cuban armed forces. Like many, and particularly because we know him to be a *mayombero*, even a *tata tkisi*, he is probably a member of a society of assassins. If I must look at a terrible thing in order to help, then I will do so."

"Thank you, *Señor Profesor*," Westonfield said. He set the folder in front of Saldívar.

The professor had steeled himself for what he was about to see, but he could not possibly have imagined the twisted savagery with which Gabriel had gone about the business of the murders. He studied the photographs carefully. Despite his most Herculean efforts, tears filled his eyes. "This is terrible. The most horrible sight I ever hope to see. I am not used to things like this and I know you will forgive me for my display of emotion." He removed his glasses and wiped his eyes with his fingers, brushed them dry on his trousers.

Westonfield was again moved by the man's strength and dignity. "I understand, professor," he said. "We thank you for your help. I *personally* thank you for your help. Your insights may be the key to locating this man and...bringing an end to his activities."

Saldívar nodded his thanks. He had thought Westonfield was going to end his sentence with a platitude like "and bring him to justice," but noted with interest that he did not. He suspected he knew what the policeman actually meant by "ending his activities."

"You have a passion for this case, Sergeant," Saldívar said.

"Yes," Westonfield said. "We have passion in common, he and I. I wonder who will win?"

"I wonder also," the professor said. "I wonder, indeed." He flipped the file closed and looked around at all of the men in the room. "We have work to do. But come! I will help."

Everyone nodded.

"Miguel Prado is my case," Randazzo said, opening his file folder. "He seems to be the forgotten man here. We have precious little to go on. How does this kid's death tie in with all of the rest?" He rummaged through the folder, found a report. "The medical examiner places the time of his death at about five hours before the Chamberlain killings. We're still processing the evidence, but it looks clean like Chamberlain. The ground was soft around the ditch. I was hoping to maybe get shoe impressions, at least. Nothing. We're looking for prints on the kid's leather jacket. I doubt we'll find any. No weapons used. No witnesses. Looks like the kid's neck was snapped by a very strong person using only his hands."

"Prado was a Count, Paul," Westonfield said. "My guess is that he was simply in the wrong place at the wrong time. I believe our man was looking to identify me and figured this kid might know something. Prado probably gave him the information on the whereabouts of Katy and Danny."

Randazzo slowly nodded his head. "Makes sense, Bill. Especially after I've heard this other information from the professor and all." He turned to Saldívar. "What is this guy, professor? Some kind of goddamm spook or something? What about these dreams or visions or whatever Bill's reporter is having?"

"I am not a great believer in things supernatural," Saldívar replied hesitantly, searching for the right words. "But I think it most likely that Miss Rodríguez is truly experiencing some sort of communication with, or connection to, this man. Supernatural? No. Say rather *preternatural*. That is to say that what is happening is not inherently beyond our understanding, but, at present, remains part of an "undiscovered country." There may come a time when we can understand these matters, but we must wait a while yet for the answers. Is this man a 'spook,' you say? He thinks he is, as I have said. And that, really, is the basis upon which I urge you to proceed."

"For instance," Randazzo said.

"Well, for one thing," Saldívar said, "the moon is very

important, just as Miss Rodríguez has suggested. The *mayombero* acts when the moon is in its waxing phase. When the moon is waning, he waits, like a patient spider. He is at his most powerful on the actual day of the full moon." Saldívar took off his glasses again, wiped them with his dirty handkerchief, and held them up to the window. "But you must understand this," he said, looking at Westonfield. "This limit to his activities applies only to *himself*, his personal actions, his incantations, his evocation of Zarabanda, and so on. Remember—he is very canny and worldly, as we have seen. I would venture that he has other helpers besides this Mejías. What he may exhort *them* to do in the time of the waning moon is impossible to predict. If they are murderers, they will not hesitate to kill at his behest." Saldívar looked around the room for a calendar on the wall, found none. "Would one of you gentlemen have a calendar?"

Dale Ward pulled a business card-sized calendar from his shirt pocket, handed it to the professor. "This is 1991, Mr. Saldívar," he said. "1992's on the other side."

"Thank you," Saldívar said. "I need only to look at November. Next month." He slid his glasses low on his nose and peered at the small figures on the plastic card. "Yes," he said. "The next full moon is Friday, the 22nd of November." He slid the card back across the table to Ward with a nod and looked at each of the men in turn. "That is a date I would concentrate on," he said. "November 22nd."

Bickerstaff was looking at the material on the table. "One thing I would like to know," he said, "is why this guy is paying so much attention to Sergeant Westonfield. Why would he kill this Prado kid just to find one cop? Why would he kill Marroquín and Villanueva just to get revenge on this same cop? Why would he carve this one policeman's initials into one of the victims? I haven't heard anything that would explain that to me." He looked across the table at Westonfield. "Okay. You chased the asshole over on Merritt. Fine. You lost him. He got away. Why the big time revenge angle?"

Saldívar shrugged. "That would be difficult for me to specu—"

"He likes it," Westonfield interjected. "He likes it, Morty. It's a game. A challenge. He's daring me to find him."

The professor studied Westonfield, looked into his grey eyes, saw the lights in them. "Yes," he said. "This idea of the jokester is consistent with the personality of the *mayombero*. He probably came here to Detroit to sell drugs. The matter of Joseph Allen in Trenton would seem to bear that out. As Sergeant Ward has pointed out, Allen was probably a rival in the narcotics trade. Our mysterious Cuban killed him as a rival; for professional reasons, but certainly for personal reasons as well. As to the book on voodoo, I am sure he thought that making his rival eat the book was very humorous, indeed. 'You dare to trust in this silly voodoo,' he was saying. 'Then you may eat your own words.' For whatever reason, Sergeant Westonfield, I would agree that he has singled you out for this game of his. You will need to stop him as soon as you can."

Buck Fry stirred in his seat. "He probably focused on Westonfield because Bill's the only one of us that's nearly as crazy as he is," he said nonchalantly, scratching his privates again.

There was a general laugh.

Saldívar looked thoughtfully at the *nganga* on the table, the cauldron that had held the dying heart of a sixteen-year-old girl. But he was thinking of what he had seen in Westonfield's eyes. He mentally crossed himself. Life was truly strange. Only this morning he was preparing a lecture on the relationship between the Peronistas in Argentina and the Catholic Church. Now he was at Detroit police headquarters talking with policemen about *palo mayombe* and a deadly killer. Destiny had brought them all together at this juncture—himself, Westonfield, Miss Rodríguez. For what purpose, this meeting of these certain few personalities in this wrinkle of time? Only Heaven knew. Or Hell. Saldívar rubbed his chin in concentration.

Westonfield set a legal pad in front of him. "Your catalogue, professor," he said. "And when you are done, any further observations you may care to make on any aspect of this case."

Saldívar cleared a spot on the evidence table and began to write. The others went over every detail of every murder scene, seeking for any overlooked clues or new insights. Three hours later the professor had made a complete inventory of every item on the table, and had written a synopsis of his opinions about the evidence photographs, the physical evidence itself, and everything he had heard about the investigation. Westonfield thanked him profusely and told him that he would certainly be in contact with him as matters progressed. The professor shook each of the detectives' hands in turn, thanked them for their trust and confidence, and walked out into the hall with Westonfield.

When Westonfield returned, he observed that Morton Bickerstaff was leaning back in his chair, balancing on its two back legs, looking through a case file. Westonfield quietly walked behind him, took hold of the chair back, and pulled Bickerstaff backwards. He held the chair exactly balanced for a moment as Bickerstaff reached out to grab the table, a look of surprise and panic on his face. Too late. Westonfield pulled the chair back another few inches and let go. Bickerstaff went over backwards, his arms flailing in the air like an injured albatross. He went down hard with a crash, his legs draped ridiculously over the front of the chair, his shoulders still pressed against its back.

Gene Beck looked resignedly and calmly down at his errant partner, wondering if Westonfield felt that upending Morty would be sufficient—hoping that he did. He didn't move or say anything, waiting for the storm to pass.

Dale Ward looked from Bickerstaff to Westonfield, a look of wonderment on his face, his eyes nearly popped out of his head.

Buck Fry looked casually over the top of the file folder he held in his hands and frowned down at Bickerstaff. The unflappable old veteran was heartily disappointed. He had been quite sure that Westonfield would actually throw Morty out the window. When nothing more of interest seemed about to occur, he scratched his groin again and returned to the file.

CHAPTER 23

"It's not your weekend, Bill," said Millie on the telephone Sunday morning. "And I'm not sure it's a good idea for Tracey to go to a funeral anyway. I don't think she's ready for it."

"It's not a funeral," Westonfield said. "I just want to take her to the cemetery for a little while. And I believe she'll be able to understand. You know how smart she is."

"I didn't say she wasn't smart enough, Bill. I said she wasn't old enough," Millie said in exasperation. "There's a difference. I wish you could understand that. She's six years old. Not sixteen. You talk to her like she's an adult."

"Well, she's more intelligent than most adults," Westonfield said. "She reads at the eighth grade level and she's in the first grade." He sighed. "Look, Millie, let's not argue, okay? I would like both of the kids to come with me. It isn't all that much to ask."

"Billy's got a project due tomorrow in school," Millie said. "He plans to spend all day on it. He has to. There's several hours of work to do and today's the last day to do it."

"Does he need help?"

"He's got help."

"How quickly I forget."

"Yeah, Bill. How quickly you forget."

"Just another day at the 'Y', huh?"

"Bill, don't start your shit."

"All right, Millie. All right. I just want to see the kids today. It's important to me."

"Billy is going to work on his project. That's it, Bill."

"Okay, I understand," Westonfield said resignedly. "But I

would still like to have Morg."

"Why is it so important, this one day?" Millie asked.

"A lot of things have been happening on the job," Westonfield said. "I'd like the kids to see just one small, safe part of it."

"Murder and torture. I've been reading the newspaper."

"You find the time?" Westonfield scarcely concealed his sarcasm.

"I try hard," Millie said coldly. "Why in God's name would you want your children to have anything to do with something like that?"

"It's just a small ceremony at the cemetery, Mill," Westonfield said, tired of arguing.

"It's always a short little this, or an inconsequential that, isn't it, Bill? Haven't you learned any lessons from everything you've been through? It's all pain, suffering, and sorrow, and I'm sick to death of it. I won't have you bringing up our kids like that."

"Look," Westonfield said. "It's my job. It's my life. It's who I am."

"Then keep it and love it! Or hate it, or do whatever it is that you need to do with it! But keep my kids out of it."

"They're my kids, too."

"Then remember first that they *are* kids," Millie said.

"Sure," Westonfield said. "I even remember when they were *our* kids."

"Cut the b.s., Bill. As usual, we're talking in circles."

"I guess we are."

"Look, you can have the kids next weekend," Millie said. "Like you're supposed to."

"I want Morgan today," Westonfield repeated.

"Her name is Tracey, Bill. You know I don't like it when you call her Morgan."

"Morgan *is* her name. It's her middle name. It belongs to her just as much as Tracey does."

"I'm concerned it will confuse her," Millie said.

"How in the hell is addressing her by her middle name going

to confuse her?" Westonfield asked.

"I call her Tracey," Millie said. "Her friends call her Tracey. Her teachers call her Tracey. Her grandparents call her Tracey. Everyone calls her Tracey."

"Billy calls her Morgan sometimes," Westonfield said.

"Well, Billy. Because of you."

"Yeah, I'm a bad influence," Westonfield said. "You helped name her, for Christ's sake."

"I don't want to argue any more," Millie said. "I mean it. I'm all done with it."

"I'll pick her up in an hour," Westonfield said.

"I will *not* have my daughter infected with whatever disease it is that ruins people like you," Millie said, angry, frustrated, on the verge of tears. "I-will-not-let-that-happen, Bill! Do you understand that? It ruined us, and I'm not going to let it ruin my children."

"*Our* children," Westonfield said softly. "And I will never let anyone, or anything, hurt them."

"I've heard that before," Millie said. "It gets old after a while: Bill Westonfield against the world, the savior of the downtrodden! Save them yourself, why don't you? Just you and John Rourke and the rest of your buddies. Leave the kids out of it."

"It's just a short burial service at Woodmere, Millie. That's all it is."

"I'm afraid for them," Millie pleaded. "Can't you understand that?"

"I'm afraid too," Westonfield said.

"Damn you, Bill," Millie said simply. "Damn you."

"I know," Westonfield said.

"Quit, Bill," Millie urged plaintively. "Quit the police department while you can. Get out before you lose everything. Whatever you may think, I don't wish that on you."

"You know I can't do that."

"You could retire."

"But I won't."

After a long silence Millie said, "This is old business, Bill. I'm sorry. Please, I didn't mean what I said about you and Jack."

"I know."

"How is Jack?" Millie asked. "I read about what happened."

"He's all right," Westonfield said. "He's home with Carol. He's coming back to work tomorrow."

"Tell him I'm thinking about him," Millie said. "Give Carol my love."

"I will."

"While I'm thinking of it," Millie said, "a woman called me last week. A reporter, I think. She had a Spanish name—Ramírez or Rodríguez, or something. She said she wanted to talk to me about our life together. I don't know how she got my telephone number. I told her no."

"I know her," Westonfield said. "She's with *Harper's Magazine*. She's all right."

"I thought you didn't trust reporters, Bill. Is she good looking?"

"She's as ugly as a mud fence."

"Sure," Millie said. "Like Susan Lawrence."

"It's part of the job."

"It always is, isn't it?" Millie said. "It's always about the job. Have Tracey back by five o'clock. I mean it!"

"Five it is," Westonfield said. "I'll have her back no later than that. I'll see you in an hour."

"What should she wear?"

"I don't know," Westonfield said. "A dress."

"It's cool outside."

"Send a coat with her. I'll keep her warm. We'll have cars out there. There'll be people to help."

"Cops," Millie said.

"Yeah, cops," Westonfield said. "Who the hell else would go?"

* * *

On the way to pick up his daughter he thought about what Millie had said. Maybe he really was pushing the envelope. He was definitely marked for revenge by the Cuban. But he knew how to take care of himself, so he could certainly take care of Tracey. It had been quiet for several days, and the moon was waning. It was still hard to think in terms of horror movie methodology—he would have to work on that. But there was no feeling of immediate danger. He put enormous stock in his instinct for danger. Hell, what was he supposed to do? Crawl into a hole? He wasn't about to let anyone, even a killer, stop him from seeing his own children.

Tracey met him at the door wearing a midnight blue dress with white lace trim. A ribbon was in her blonde hair, which was pulled up in the back. "Hello, Daddy," she said, grinning, reaching to be picked up.

Westonfield swung her into his arms, giving her a kiss on the cheek. "Love you, Rosebud," he said.

"You too, Daddy," she said. "Billy can't come. He's been bad."

"Oh?"

"Yes, he's been bad."

"Well, your mommie says he has to do homework, and that's why he can't come," Westonfield said.

"But he's been bad, I bet," Tracey said, laughing. "I can't ever fool you, Daddy."

"That's because I'm too smart," he said.

"I know," Tracey said. "You're the smartest daddy ever." She hugged him tight. "I miss you." She kissed him full on the mustache and patted his cheek, studying him with serious eyes. "I love you more than anything, Daddy."

In the car Tracey said, "Where are we going? Mommie said we're going someplace special, so I had to wear a pretty dress. Do you like my dress?"

"It's beautiful, Morg. You're the prettiest girl I ever saw. Do you know that?"

"Yes, I know that," she said. "You tell me all the time."

"Do I, now?"

"Uh-huh."

"Only because it's true."

Tracey grinned. "Where are we going?"

"Do you know what a cemetery is?"

"Uh-huh," Tracey said. "My teacher Mrs. Carmichael told me. She's teaching us about Hallowe'en. She says it means 'All Hallow's Eve.' She says cemeteries are places where the dead ones sleep."

"That's right," Westonfield said. "I didn't think you'd know."

"I know lots of stuff," Tracey said.

"I'll bet you do."

"Billy isn't really bad, Daddy," she said suddenly.

"I know it. You were joking."

"I like to joke," she said.

"Good," Westonfield said. "It makes me very happy that you like to joke."

"Smiling makes my face feel good," Tracey said matter-of-factly. "My sad face hurts."

"Really?"

"Yep."

Westonfield impulsively decided to show Tracey the neighborhood where Katy Marroquín used to live. He engaged her in lively conversational all the way to Clark Park. When they pulled onto Clark Street he said, "This is a place where a girl I once knew used to play. Her name was Katy." He slowed down, pulled to the curb and stopped. "She talked to her friends in this park." He looked out into the trees and grass, pointing. The sun had come out and was shining brightly, though the temperature was only in the upper 40s.

Tracey sat up straight in the passenger seat. She could barely see over the sill of the window, especially with her seat belt on. Westonfield reached over and unsnapped it. She immediately swiveled around and got on her knees, peering through the glass. "It's pretty," she said.

"Yes, it is," Westonfield said. He had associated the park with Katy for so long that it was hard to imagine it without her. The idea that she would never be there again struck him right through. He thought how strange it was the way the mind inextricably associated people and events—songs with old lovers, the first snow of the season with the Christmas you got your favorite bike. Now he would forever associate a rundown city park with a murdered girl he once knew. He felt empty, depressed, and old.

His daughter sensed his mood. "What are you sad about, Daddy?"

"Katy won't be playing here anymore," he said. "That's why we're going to the cemetery, Morg. They're putting her with the sleepers today."

"Ohhh," Tracey said, looking at him knowingly. "Will you miss her? Mrs. Carmichael says the sleepers won't ever come back."

"She was right, Westonfield said. "The sleepers never come back. And I will miss Katy."

"Was she pretty like me?"

"Yes. Well, not quite as pretty as you!"

Tracey smiled. "Mommie says when people die you give them flowers."

"Sometimes," Westonfield said.

Before he could react, Tracey opened her door and jumped out. "Tracey!" he shouted, scrambling out the driver's door and running to the curb side of the car. His daughter was already running up a sidewalk toward a house. An elderly lady, dressed in a sweater, men's trousers, and house slippers was standing on the porch watching them.

Tracey looked up at the woman and stopped. "Hello!" she said gamely. Undeterred, she walked straight to the small flowerbed by the side of the house where a few white chrysanthemums lingered, snow-bright in the autumn sunshine. Tracey tried to pick one, but the stem was too thick for her little fingers to break.

Westonfield came trotting up. "Tracey, you can't just go into people's yards and start picking flowers!" He looked up at the old lady. "Sorry. She gets a little rambunctious. She didn't hurt anything."

The woman laughed a pleasant laugh. "Of course she didn't hurt anything," she said. She came down off the porch and walked over to them, peering down at Tracey, adjusting the glasses on the end of her nose. "Lord have mercy!" she exclaimed. "I do believe this is the most beautiful child I have ever seen." She spoke with the accent of a southern gentlewoman.

"I need some flowers," Tracey said. "I wasn't stealing."

"Of course you weren't, honey. A body can't steal a flower any more than they can steal the sunshine. Pretty things belong to everybody. Flowers are the Lord's gift for anyone with eyes to see them. How about if we pick some together? I'll even get a vase for you to keep them in."

"Don't go to any trouble, ma'am, please," Westonfield said. "We didn't mean to bother you." He looked down at Tracey and frowned. "Morgan is precocious."

"Is she now?" said the woman. She held out her hand. "I'm Nora Granger. And don't go apologizing for brightening an old lady's morning. Usually all I get to look at is bad kids selling drugs, and trash blowing around this here park. It ain't often I see little angels in my dooryard."

"I'm not an angel," Tracey said. "I'm still alive."

"Are you, now?" Nora Granger said, laughing again, patting Tracey on the head. "Well, I guess you are."

"Katy is an angel, though," Tracey said.

"Katy?"

"She's moving in with the sleepers today. My daddy used to play with her in the park. But he won't get to see her anymore 'cause now she's dead. So we need some flowers to give to her."

Nora's jaw dropped a couple of inches. "How old is this child?" she asked. "She don't look to be more than five or six."

Westonfield grinned. "Morgan marches to her own

drummer," he said.

"I'll bet you're right proud, mister," Nora said. "She's as pretty as a peach and smart as a whip, too. That's quite the young lady you have there. My own grandbabies are all in Memphis and Marietta. I don't see them nearly as much as I'd like to. Sometimes I think they've forgot me. Except I do get cards on the holidays and my birthday." She looked at Westonfield. "So you've lost a loved one, have you?"

"I work in this area," Westonfield said. "A girl I met a couple of years ago died last week. She died quite suddenly, actually. I was driving by to show Morgan where Katy used to spend her time." He looked at his watch. "We have to be at the cemetery in about half an hour for the service."

"I read in the paper about a girl from this neighborhood being—" Nora looked at Tracey. She seemed oblivious, still trying to pick the stubborn flowers. Nora lowered her voice. "I do believe her name was Katy. The story said she was killed over on Chamberlain. Your Katy and that one wouldn't be one and the same, would they? The paper said the poor girl was being buried at Woodmere today."

"One and the same," Westonfield replied, watching Tracey work on the flowers, his face expressionless.

"I'm mighty sorry for your loss," Nora said. "Were you close?"

"Close enough," Westonfield said.

"I knew that girl myself, mister," Nora said. "Leastways, I knew who she was. I talked to her once. I know it was her because they put a picture in the newspaper and I remembered seeing her here in the park so many times. I recollect one time some bully boys was giving me a hard time out front here and she made them stop. Not many of them youngsters will do that—go against their own to help somebody else. I always appreciated that so much. Lord knows what might have happened to me if she hadn't stepped in. She had blonde hair and the prettiest blue eyes. Come to think of it, she looked a lot like your daughter here."

"Uh-huh," Westonfield said.

"Growing up down here," Nora said sadly, "I would guess there won't be but a few at the cemetery. I sure do hate to think about what happened to her. Do you think the police will catch the one that did it?"

Westonfield pulled his eyes away from Tracey. "I can tell you that they're going to try very hard, Mrs. Granger."

Nora looked at him closely. "You wouldn't be a policeman, would you, Mr. Westonfield? I bet that's how you knew Katy."

"I worked at Fort and Green for a long time," Westonfield admitted. "Please...call me Bill."

"All right, Bill. I will if you'll call me Nora. Nobody calls me Mrs. Granger except the mailman. I bet I saw you out there in the park more than once. It's a small world, ain't it?"

"It is."

"Well, I've taken up enough of your time," Nora said. "I know you'll need to be going. Let me just run into the house for a minute and I'll get some pruning shears and a vase. Me and Tracey will make us up a nice bouquet." She turned and disappeared into the house.

"They're too hard for you, Morg," Westonfield said. "Wait till Mrs. Granger comes to help."

Tracey stood up puffing, her face red. "All right, Daddy," she said. "They are too damn tough."

Westonfield grinned and shook his head, glad that Millie wasn't there to lance him for teaching Tracey bad language.

Nora returned in a minute with a large vase and a pair of pruning shears. She took Tracey by the hand and they walked over to the flowerbed. Westonfield watched as the two chattered merrily, the old lady cutting the stems of the flowers, Tracey plopping them into the vase. It was as if the two had known each other forever. They were done in just a few minutes, and the vase was filled to brimming with beautiful mums.

"There you go," Nora said happily. "Now you won't be empty-handed when you get to the cemetery."

"I don't know how to repay you," Westonfield said. "You've

made Tracey's day. Thank you."

"No, Bill, I'm the one that owes the thanks to you. Morgan... did you just say Tracey?"

Westonfield chuckled. "Morgan is her middle name. I like to call her that."

"Tracey or Morgan," Nora said, beaming. "They are both comely names to go with a wonderful little girl. But, as I was saying, it's me that owes the debt. Now that you know where I live, Bill, you come by here any time. I'll set out a glass of cold milk and cake, or a piece of pie. I would appreciate the company. I get fearful lonely here by myself sometimes." She looked down at Tracey, who was studying an ant crawling along the lip of the vase. "Bring this one back, too. And, mind you, bring your handcuffs with you. I might be tempted to keep her here with me and you'll be needing to lock me to my bed post."

Westonfield thanked her again, gave her a little peck on the cheek, and walked Tracey back to the car. Nora followed, and before Westonfield strapped Tracey into the passenger seat with the seat belt, Nora leaned in and gave her a big kiss on the cheek. Then she looked up at Westonfield. "You get that bad man," she said. "I know you will. I seen it in your eyes."

As they pulled away from the curb, Westonfield looked into his rear view mirror. Nora Granger was standing on the sidewalk watching them, a thoughtful look on her face. Dressed as she was in the oversized men's clothing, brown and formless, she looked like the stump of an old tree standing watch at the edge of a field. She watched them go all the way up to Vernor Highway. Then Westonfield turned the corner, and she was gone from view.

"Look-it, Daddy," Tracey exclaimed proudly, holding up the heavy vase with both hands. "Isn't it pretty? Grandma Nora says Katy will have it when she's with the angels. She says Katy will be carrying the flowers in her arms when she knocks on heaven's door."

* * *

Delbert Denton was nervous. The idea of being in such close proximity to so many Latin Counts was unsettling, even if the place was crawling with cops. He was the leader of the Cobras, the Latin Counts' chief rival in Detroit's gang wars. He was twenty-one, and he felt that he would like to live to see twenty-two. Danny Villanueva had been twenty-two already. Now he was dead. Word on the street was that his head had been cut off when he was killed with Katy Marroquín.

The sun was shining through blue sky, but it was fairly cool. Delbert was wearing a thin jacket over a tee shirt. Not being completely foolish, he had elected to leave his leather jacket emblazoned with the Cobra colors at home. Woodmere was in the middle of Count territory and he would be attending a Count burial service. He was scared. If his fear of the new terror in the vicinity wasn't even greater than the uneasiness of being alone among a bunch of Counts, he wouldn't have come to the cemetery at all. He stood by himself near the front gate, watching the entrance for the arrival of Westonfield. He barely knew him, but he wanted to talk to him. He had no personal knowledge that Westonfield would even be there, but he had been told by a buddy who knew Westonfield that he would attend, no matter what.

In a little while Delbert spotted Westonfield driving into the cemetery in a blue Taurus. A little girl sat next to him in the front seat. The child's face was invisible, completely covered by a huge bouquet of flowers. The car wheeled past and followed the winding road into the grounds, disappearing behind a ridge covered with monuments. Delbert walked quickly along behind, anxious to take care of business and be gone.

Westonfield observed Denton standing half-obscured by a holly bush near the gate as soon as he drove in. He hoped it didn't mean trouble. Surely the Cobras weren't stupid enough to try something with a dozen cops present. When he pulled up to the parking area a hundred yards from the gravesite he was relieved to see Arena, Johnson, Adams, and several of the other patrolmen standing in small clusters in the vicinity. Monica Franklin, the fat black policewoman from his friend Lieutenant Runyon's shift, was there, as were a number of others from all three shifts at the precinct. Two uniformed officers in a marked scout car stood by in an open corner of the small lot.

All three local news outlets had reporters present, busily attempting to interview anyone who seemed willing to talk. Their news vans, remote satellite booms rising out of their roofs, stood side-by-side. Cameramen roamed about, taking videotape of monuments, the grounds, and Katy's grave itself.

Westonfield told Tracey to stay in the car. He stepped out and motioned for Arena to come over. He held out his hand. "'Berto," he said, "how are you?"

"Not bad, Sarge. Considering. Pretty good turn-out from the guys. A lot of Katy's family are here."

"Good," Westonfield said. "But I think we have a problem, Bob. I spotted Delbert Denton standing by the gate when I pulled in. You know anything about that?"

"No way, Sarge," Arena said, his eyes wide. "Shit! Did you see where he went after you drove past? I'll let the guys know."

"No, I don't know where he went," Westonfield said. "But I've got my daughter with me, and the last thing I need is trouble. Have those uniforms check it out and—"

Before he could finish his sentence, Denton ambled around the corner. He looked around, saw Westonfield standing with Arena, and immediately headed in their direction. Westonfield automatically stepped several paces away from his car so Tracey would be out of the line of fire, however unlikely a fight might be. Arena did the same. They studied the gangster as he approached. Nothing in his manner appeared immediately threatening. Denton observed their defensive posture and held out his hands. "No, man," he said, coming within a couple of yards. "This ain't about nothin' like that, officers. I just wanted to talk to you for a minute." He carefully lifted the hem of his jacket to show that there were no weapons hidden in his waistband. He turned slowly around while holding the jacket up so Westonfield and Arena could see that he truly was not armed. "See, I ain't got nothin'," he said.

Westonfield swivelled his head, his eyes flicking over the area, looking for other dangers. He saw nothing. The uniformed patrolmen spotted Denton, whose face was well known by every policeman at the Fourth Precinct. They got out of their car. Denton looked at them, then back at Westonfield. "I ain't carrying, Sarge. I really ain't. And I'm alone. There ain't another Cobra within a mile of here. I promise."

Arena quickly patted Denton down. "He's clean, boss," he said. "You're about a bold motherfucker, Delbert," Arena said. "You here to pick out a final resting place for yourself? We could accommodate you easy."

Westonfield motioned for the uniforms to return to their car, that everything was okay. They nodded and sauntered back to their vehicle, giving Denton baleful looks before they turned.

Denton suddenly focused his attention on something behind Westonfield. Westonfield turned his head to see what it was. Tracey was walking forward, past him, looking earnestly at Denton. "Would you hold these?" she asked, walking right up to him, thrusting the bouquet in front of her. "They're too heavy. I'll come and get them after a while. I want to go see that hole over there." She pointed to Katy's green-canopied grave. A mound of raw earth rose next to the perfect rectangle of the open grave, awaiting the arrival of the hearse that bore Katy Marroquín's body. Tracey smiled a radiant smile at the gang leader.

Before Westonfield could say anything, Denton reached out and gently took the vase from Tracey. "Okay," he said. "I'll hold it for you." He even returned her smile.

Monica Franklin, who had been watching and had come closer to help if necessary, came up and took Tracey by the hand. "I'll watch her, Sergeant Westonfield," she said. "You take care of business for as long as you need. Me and this little princess are going to take us a walk."

Tracey grinned. "Good morning, Monica," she said. "Are

you here to say good-bye to the sleepers, too?" They strolled quickly out of earshot.

Westonfield turned back to Denton. The young gang leader looked slightly ridiculous standing there holding a vase of chrysanthemums in his arms.

"Ain't he cute?" Arena said. "It looks almost like he's going on a date."

Denton looked around for a place to set the flowers. Westonfield took them and set them down on the asphalt next to his Taurus. "What do you want here, Denton?" he asked. "You show even less class than I thought you had showing up here. What are you trying to do, start a shoot-out? If Jack Rourke was here, he'd have shot you already and been done with it."

"Like I said, it ain't about that," Denton said, an edge of fear showing. Westonfield had a reputation for being volatile. He didn't want to be shot. "Look, man, I'm here to help."

"Yeah, help yourself to some territory, now that Danny's gone," Arena said. "But you know what, *chivato*? The bastard that got Danny cut his head off and stuck it on a spike. You want that to happen to you? The big boys have moved in. The barracuda. You little fish better get out of the way!"

"Aw, man, gimme a break. That's why I'm here. I want to help. These Cubans. You know, they play by their own rules. There ain't gonna be no kind of peace as long as they're around here doin' their thing."

"What kind of help?" Westonfield asked, openly skeptical.

"Well, you know, I got my sources," Denton said.

"Information?"

"That's right," Denton answered. "Information. What do I get if I give you good info about the Cubans?"

Westonfield studied him. "You might get dead."

"I know it, but what can I do? I feel like I need protection."

"What do you mean?"

"Protection from the Cubans."

"How so?"

"Come on, man," Denton protested. "They killed Danny,

didn't they? What's to say they don't decide to kill me? Danny was in charge of the Counts. I'm in charge of the Cobras. Maybe this Cuban has a jones for gang bangers or somethin'. Maybe he thinks we're in his way. Whatever. I just don't want to wake up some morning with my head on backwards like Miguel Prado."

"Smart kid," Arena said.

"What do you know?" asked Westonfield.

"Right now?" Delbert said. "Nothing. I wanted to talk with you first, see what you had to say. If we can work together, then I'll see what my peeps can come up with."

"Like I say, Delbert, there are two sides to this coin," Westonfield said. "Either side could carry your death warrant. Are you sure you want to get involved in this little game we're playing? You want to be one of the players? You got the balls for it?"

"The way I see it, I don't got a lot of choice," Denton said. "How do you see it, Sergeant Westonfield?"

"You're a pretty smart kid, Delbert," Westonfield said. "The sooner the cops get the Cubans off the street, the safer you're going to be, right?"

"Simple, huh?" Denton said.

Westonfield turned to Rupert Johnson, who'd come alongside him. "What do you think, Rupe?"

"Oh, I don't know, Sarge," he said in his soft Kentucky drawl. "I think we might be able to work with him a little. Ol' Delbert looked almost friendly with them flowers in his arms."

Denton smiled a rueful smile. What had he gotten himself into?

* * *

"Those were beautiful flowers you brought, Tracey," Monica said. "Where did you get them?"

"We got them from Grandma Granger. She lives by the park where Katy used to play." Tracey told Monica how her acquaintance with Nora Granger came about.

"It sounds like you have a new friend," Monica said. "That's good. People need a lot of friends. You remember that. Sometimes friends is all you got."

"I will," Tracey replied seriously. "I'm a good rememberer."

Monica laughed.

They walked over to the grave and Tracey peered into the aperture while Monica held her hand. "Is that where they're going to put Katy?" she asked.

"Yes, honey."

"Why do they put people in the ground, Monica, after they fall asleep?"

Monica considered her answer. "Well, I suppose it's to keep them safe from harm, little angel. It's a place where we know that our loved ones are going to rest. It's a place we can visit when we want to, to bring flowers, or just to talk to the one we lost."

"Can the sleepers hear you when you talk?"

"The sleepers," Monica said. "You call them sleepers? Lord, I haven't heard that term in a long, long time. My grandmother used to call the dead sleepers." She debated her answer again. "Some people say they can. I think they maybe can hear you."

Tracey nodded thoughtfully, still looking into the grave.

"Where is your big brother?" Monica asked, tugging Tracey gently away from the edge.

"He's home," Tracey said. "Mommie wouldn't let him come. He has schoolwork to do. And I think he's been bad." She looked at Monica out of the corner of her eye.

"You don't say," Monica said. "What did he do?"

"I don't know," Tracey said. "Sometimes he's just a very bad boy."

Monica grinned, looking up toward the parking area. She saw that the conversation between Denton and Westonfield had concluded. Still holding her young charge's hand, she strolled in that direction.

Tracey was slightly disappointed that no one ever believed her jokes.

* * *

"This is a very interesting young lady," Monica told Westonfield when they walked up. "She's just full of comments and questions. Sometimes I don't know who's teaching who."

"That's Tracey," Westonfield said with a smile. "Thanks for the help, Monica."

"The pleasure's all mine, Sarge," she said. "You bring her to me anytime. We'll go get us some ice cream and go to the movies."

Now Westonfield took Tracey by the hand and they went for a little walk of their own. "So, what do you think of this place, Morg?" he asked.

"It's pretty quiet," Tracey said. "Everybody's sleeping, don't you know."

"That's true," Westonfield said. "What else?"

"I was thinking I'm sad. I won't ever get to meet Katy, will I?"

Westonfield shook his head.

"She would be like a sister, I bet."

"Could be."

"I wish I had a sister. Brothers are no fun."

Westonfield felt a pang of remorse again. How would Tracey ever have a sister now?

"Katy's grave is deep, Daddy. How will she be able to get out to go to heaven?"

"I think her body will stay here," Westonfield said. "But her soul will go to heaven. Do you know what a soul is?"

"Uh-huh, Mrs. Carmichael explained it. It's the part of you that no one can see. It's the part of you that lives inside. When you die, it goes someplace else."

"That's right."

"Does your body get lonely when it doesn't have a soul anymore?"

"Maybe." Westonfield's mind went to his enemy, a man who

surely had no soul. Was he capable of loneliness? Of remorse, or guilt? Saldívar had suggested that he was not.

Then a black hearse came into view from around the ridge and pulled slowly up to the burial site. It was followed by an old black Lincoln. An equally old rusty blue Buick Electra brought up the rear. The cars came to a halt. Westonfield walked over and stopped a few yards from the vehicles, Tracey in tow. She watched curiously. The doors of the Buick and the Lincoln were thrown open. Six Latin men wearing dark suits emerged from the Buick. Three of the men were in their fifties or sixties, the remaining three were younger. Westonfield surmised the three younger men were Katy's brothers and the three older men uncles. They all looked ashen despite their dark complexions.

Then the occupants of the Lincoln emerged. Westonfield was happy to see that one of them was Father Lewandowski. The others consisted of two middle-aged women, an elderly woman, and two older men. Lewandowski saw Westonfield and came over at once, holding out his hand.

"Bill, good to see you," he said. He, too, looked grey. "Where's Jack?"

"Still home," Westonfield said. "He'll be back tomorrow. I talked to him on the phone this morning. I told him not to come. There's no point." He noticed red stains, probably salsa, on the priest's black shirt. Despite his mood, a smile flickered across his face.

"No, I don't suppose there is," Lewandowski agreed, glancing around. "Still, there's a better turnout than I expected." He motioned toward the parking area, where Delbert Denton continued to loiter like a fish out of water. "I certainly didn't expect to see that fellow."

"Life is full of surprises," Westonfield said, raising his eyebrows.

"Indeed it is," rejoined the priest, divining that here was another Westonfield connivance of which he would learn more in good time. He looked down at Tracey, who clung to her father's side. "And who is this?"

"I'm Morgan," Tracey said. "Are you a magician?"

Lewandowski chuckled. "Raising her Catholic, eh Bill? Hasn't this poor child ever seen a man of the cloth?"

"Not if I can help it," Westonfield said.

"Are you?" Tracey repeated.

"A magician?" Lewandowski asked.

"Uh-huh."

"Well, no, dear," Lewandowski said. "I'm afraid I'm not. Magic is your father's job. I'm a priest. Do you know what that is?"

"Yes. They teach people about God. They live in big houses called rec... rect—"

"Rectories," said the priest.

"Rectories," Tracey said. "Daddy says priests are unhappy because they can't have wives. Do you have a girlfriend?"

Lewandowski gave Westonfield a sidelong glance. "No, I'm afraid I don't, Morgan. But I have lots of other friends."

Tracey nodded enthusiastically. "Monica says people need a lot of friends."

The priest patted Tracey on the head. "Like father, like daughter," he said, glaring at Westonfield, crossing himself. Then he walked back to the others and returned with one of the middle-aged women, holding her by the arm. The other woman of about the same age followed close behind. The woman with Lewandowski was wearing a frayed black dress. Though obviously a Latina, her hair was a natural dishwater blonde. Her face was puffy, smeared with tears, her mascara smudged around her hazel eyes.

"This is Blanquita Marroquín," Lewandowski said. He stepped back a little so the other woman could come forward. "And this is Lúz. They are Katy's mother and aunt. Ladies, this is Sergeant Westonfield."

Blanquita Marroquín held out her hand. "I am very pleased to meet you, Mr. Westonfield. I'm so glad you are here. My Katy... she talked about you sometimes. She said that you helped her, that you treated her fairly. I thank you for that." When

Westonfield took her by the hand and stepped forward to hug her, she started to cry.

"I thank you, too, *Señor* Westonfield," Tía Lúz said. "More than you know. It was near my house on Merritt Street that this monster—" She, too, struggled with tears. "That this man's companion was killed by your officers. I thank you for doing what you have done to bring justice to us."

Tracey looked up at the blonde woman and said, "Are you Katy's mother?"

Blanquita looked down, really noticing her for the first time. She smiled through her tears. "Yes, I am," she said. "And who would you be, so pretty in your blue dress?"

"I would be Morgan," Tracey said. "But my real name is Tracey," she added.

"Ahhh," Blanquita said, studying her face. "Then shall I call you Morgan? Or shall I call you Tracey?"

"You can call me whatever you want," Tracey answered sincerely.

"Very well," Blanquita said. "Tracey, then. Did anyone tell you that you look like my Katy? Did you know her?"

"No, we played in different playgrounds," Tracey said. "Did Katy look like an angel?"

"Yes," Blanquita said. "She looked just like an angel."

"That's what my daddy says," Tracey said. She pulled loose from her father's hand and ran to his car where the flowers still stood on the pavement. She hoisted the vase up with both hands and carried them to Katy's mother. "These are for Katy," she said. "They're for when she goes to heaven."

Blanquita went to take them, but burst into tears again, suddenly wracked by shuddering sobs. She held onto the priest's arm with one hand and patted Tracey on the head with the other. She couldn't speak.

Lúz took the vase from Tracey. "We will put these flowers on my niece's grave," she said, starting to cry herself. "We will put them at the very front, where she can see them."

Westonfield saw the pain the women were going through,

and told himself again that it was because of his own negligence that the murdering son-of-a-bitch did what he did to Katy. The Cuban wanted to play a sick game with him, and had killed Katy Marroquín to begin the game. Westonfield leaned forward and kissed Blanquita on the wet cheek. "I failed you," he said softly. "I caused this. I'm sorry."

"No," Blanquita said, uncomprehending, through her tears. "You have done nothing but help. I know this is true." She looked down at Tracey again. "You keep your little one safe, Mr. Westonfield. That is all you can do now." She smiled bravely and let Lewendowski lead her away.

When all the mourners were gathered around the gravesite, even Delbert Denton, Father Lewandowski began his eulogy. Watching him, Westonfield knew his pain was genuine. He loved his congregation. He suffered with them. The assembled Latin Counts, bereft of two of their own, eyed Denton coldly, but they did nothing. They listened. They were not church-goers by nature, but there was something about the way Lewendowski talked that made them want to listen.

"I shall begin with the words of Robert Bly," the priest said. "*What shall the world do with its children? There are lives the executives know nothing of...*" He went on for ten minutes. He had a marvelous speaking voice, and the force of his emotion held everyone in sway—except for Tracey, who was watching a squirrel play on the branch of an oak tree above the priest's head. Lewendowski talked of hope, and love, and remembrance of things past. He talked of courage in the face of terrible odds. He talked of honor and trust. He spoke of patience and faith in God. Finally, he spoke of the lives of the children of the streets.

Tracey could sense that the priest was almost done by the tone of his voice and the change in the rhythm of his cadence. She looked at the faces of the people. They were crying—old and young, man and woman. Even Delbert Denton wiped his eyes with the sleeve of his borrowed jacket. Tracey looked up at her father. Yes, they were all crying, except for him.

"I began with Robert Bly about children," Lewandowski

said, "And I will end with William Blake. His words are simple, yet they speak in this hour, and in this place, more clearly and compellingly than any others that I know. So often it is that children are the victims of the world we elders have made, yet it is always the children to whom we go to find a moment of peace. Blake wrote:
When the voices of children are heard on the green
And laughing is heard on the hill,
My heart is at rest within my breast
And everything else is still."

Tracey continued to watch her father. His eyes had grown moist, and when the priest ended he wiped away a tear. Tracey had never before seen him do such a thing. It startled her. She had no idea what to do, except what her father might have done for her. She leaned close and put her head against his warm side. She patted him on the leg. "Don't worry, Daddy," she said. "I'll take care of you."

When the priest ended, the squirrel stopped playing and held still on the branch, watching. It cocked its head and looked at Tracey. It sensed that she was the only one who paid it any mind. Tracey looked into the squirrel's round brown eyes.

CHAPTER 24

Anonymous and safe in his house on 31st Street, Gabriel considered his situation. He hated the waning moon. It remained one of the disappointments of his life that on the very next day after the full moon—the height of his power—the moon went on the wane and his strength flowed out of him like blood from a wound. This bitter fact robbed him of his full measure of joy. He felt that it was no less than his right to savor the sweetness of his victories over his enemies in the fullness of his strength. Didn't his grace and authority, his faithful adherence to Zarabanda's commands, earn him a moment of reverie in which to fully appreciate the fruits of his labor? He was doomed to achieve his goals and then to fade away into obscurity, to await the next moon. In the times of the waning moon he paced the house like a caged black panther, his eyes yellow, his bloodlust raging.

But his jest on Chamberlain Street had gone well. He had taken more pleasure in the killing of the little people than he had in any other thing for a long time. True, they were unimportant players in the game, mere motes in his eye. Their deaths would normally have been no more than a few drops of pleasure, flakes of snow falling into a seething green-black ocean. No, it was the *man* that made it so sensual—this Westonfield. It pleased Gabriel that the *rubia*, the blonde girl, knew the man so well. It made her pain especially exquisite. Gabriel laughed when he thought of how she begged him for death. Of course, he had not given it to her—not until later. Much later.

What to do about this man? Gabriel had learned much from

the boy, and more still from the girl. Facts, names. places. These were useful, but he still couldn't really *feel* the man. The strange mist veiled him as much as ever. This continued to cause Gabriel great consternation. Also, something the girl had said gnawed at him. Occasionally someone who fell under his knife showed courage. This proved true of the girl. A little unusual, perhaps, but not remarkable. It took a great deal to impress Gabriel, and a flash of bravery from a girl under torture did not impress him much. He had even laughed at the time. But what she had uttered, between the screams, had come back to him unbidden several times since the night of her death, floating into his consciousness on a mist like the one that surrounded Westonfield.

This obscurity discomfited Gabriel mightily. All of his life, he had been the one to send messages on the ether. It was a measure of his authority, of power and control. It gave him much pleasure. Now he was the one *receiving* the message. It came on this strange mist. *He won't let you do this to me,* the girl had said. Gabriel had just stripped a long piece of skin from her calf. He held it up so she could see it, dripping blood onto her naked belly. When she was finished screaming, she looked at him with those blue eyes—he hated her blue eyes—and said in a very calm voice, "he knows you." Gabriel had stood transfixed. Never in all his years of torture had anyone said such a thing. Then she said, "You're already dead. Just like me." And that's when Gabriel laughed, continuing at his leisurely pace. The strange girl said nothing else. She only screamed.

Gabriel stood in the window, watching, and the words came back. He hated this waiting. The Latina reporter was in New York, having returned there on Friday. Unlike this Westonfield, her thoughts were laid open like a book. Porfirio and Gregorio had followed her to the airport and confirmed the information. Money could still buy information. Information on anything. The woman's *maricón* brother was dead, according to the intelligence. No matter. She would return—she had purchased round-trip tickets. But he knew it anyway. The woman would stay, at least for a while, until the matter was resolved.

The dead girl was buried in the cemetery on Woodmere Street on Sunday. It was the very place from which he had taken the bones for the making of his *nganga*. He had watched it on the six o'clock news. He was ambivalent about the attention. The fact that the reporters and the policemen were looking for him was not good for business. Already certain Colombian contacts had dried up. The *Indios* suspected he was at the bottom of the killings. The brutality of the slayings, and the presence of black magic, made it clear to them that the perpetrator was, indeed, Gabriel Flores. The recalcitrance of the South Americans was unfortunate, and it complicated his delivery schedule, but he was beyond that now. At one time the complications would have vexed him, but of late he was preoccupied with the matter of Westonfield. He was becoming bored with the trade anyway, and it seemed to him that he should end his stay in Detroit. Kill this strange, hidden policeman, this Westonfield—and be gone. Fate was pointing him in that direction, and he soon became obsessed with it.

But if there was one thing the *bruja* taught him it was patience. He must wait until the moment was perfect. There was plenty of time. He must certainly wait until the seventh of November, when the moon began to grow big in the autumn sky. At least he would have to wait personally. But he could send them a message in the interim, these policemen and their lapdog reporters. Porfirio and Gregorio were reliable. More so than Tomás. Yes. Perhaps Gregorio and Porfirio should have some fun. It wouldn't do to wait too long to act—then the policemen might think that he was finished. He couldn't have that now, could he?

He went into the living room and sat on a chair in front of the television. It was almost six o'clock. He turned on the evening news program. After a while the black anchorwoman, the one he thought he might kill one day because she was too pretty, began to talk about all the fires that Detroit had suffered over the years on so-called Devil's Night, the thirtieth day of

October. She talked about how the police and thousands of volunteers were mobilizing to prevent the arson that left parts of the city in flames every year. Devil's Night. Such a silly name. These people knew nothing of the devil. It was so arrogant of them to describe these childish acts, the burning of abandoned houses, as deeds of the devil. It would be amusing to give them a taste of the real devil on this night. It was a travesty that he, himself, could not go forth into the city, but much could still be done. Devil's Night! He would show them.

* * *

Carol Rourke watched her husband carefully place his underwear and socks into his suitcase. It was part of the routine they had become accustomed to over the last couple of years. Jack would bring his dirty laundry home after a week or two in the city, Carol would wash and iron everything, and then the suitcase would be packed for his return to the city—until next time.

But somehow this time was different. Carol didn't know why. Maybe it was the killer running loose in Detroit; maybe it was the visit from Magaly Rodríguez. Maybe it was both. They were the latest pieces of reality that had intruded on her family's idyllic rural life, insinuating themselves like tumors upon their efforts to escape the city. Sometimes she thought the effort was in vain. As long as Jack worked there it would follow them like some ancient curse.

"It's bad, isn't it, Jack," she said, coming from behind and reaching into the suitcase, rearranging the clothes. Rourke was not a competent packer of suitcases. "This murderer, I mean. He's different from all the others you've had to deal with."

Rourke nodded noncommittally, enjoying the smell of the just-washed clothes, admiring the way Carol could arrange them into the small space in two minutes better than he could if he'd taken all day. "Probably so," he said.

"What will you do?"

"Just go to work, Carol," he said. "Just go to work like every day for the last twenty-three years. We'll look for the guy, of course. Maybe he's done killing. Maybe he made his point and he'll move on. He's getting a lot of attention. Dope men—he's most likely a dope man, regardless of whatever kind of a witch doctor he may be—don't like attention, for obvious reasons."

Carol repacked the suitcase in silence. After a while she said, "You don't believe that, do you? You don't really believe he's just going to leave. He'll stay until he's won or lost, or you and Bill have won or lost, won't he?"

Rourke looked at her. "Probably."

"Then stay home, Jack. Take some sick time. Stay with Stevie and Sheila and me."

In all of their years together, Carol had never asked him to do such a thing. "You know I can't do that, Carol," he said. "Bill's being personally threatened by this guy. I have to be there to see it through."

"Bill's been transferred," she said. "He's at Homicide now."

"I know it," Rourke said. "But all the action is in the Fourth—my precinct. I expect the way we work together won't change much. Bill's gonna be around every night."

"I'm afraid for Bill," Carol said. "And I'm afraid *of* Bill."

"I know."

"What will he do now?"

"Go to work, Carol. Just like me."

"Don't be like that with me, Jack. What will Bill do?"

"He'll look for the killer," Rourke said. "I expect when he finds him he'll kill him."

"Unless he gets killed first."

Rourke frowned. "I suppose so."

"What if Bill gets you killed, Jack? He's not like you."

"What?"

"Bill's harder. There's a coldness about him. You're not like that."

"I thought you liked Bill Westonfield," Rourke said in

surprise. "Damn! He's been my partner ever since he came to the Fourth Precinct. He's been a guest in our home a dozen times. He's been a good friend to our children. He saved my life more than once."

"I know all of that, Jack. And I don't mean to make light of it. But, well, it's like Bill was meant for this awful business. It's almost as if he likes it."

"Carol!" Rourke exclaimed, "What that son-of-a-bitch did to that poor girl broke Bill's heart. How can you say something as godawful stupid as you think he likes it?"

"I don't mean it that way," Carol said. "I just mean to say that Bill was made for this. He's a lone wolf. In his way, he's not much different from this Cuban." Seeing the look in her husband's eye, she said, "Not evil, Jack, but in the way they think about the world: no grey areas, only black and white. It's a contest. Can't you see that? The killer is coming from one side of the moral spectrum, and Bill from the other, but it's still only a game. And the thing is, Jack— the thing is, when people like that get into fights everyone and everything around them is in danger. Weaker people get hurt, suffer, and die."

"You're not making any sense," Rourke said. "Bill is a cop, just like me."

"But you're not like him. Can't you see that?"

"No, Carol, I can't."

Rourke carried the heavy suitcase into the kitchen. He sat down at the kitchen table. Carol sat across from him.

"Well, it's late," Rourke said. "I guess I should go."

"What do you think of Magaly Rodríguez?" Carol asked suddenly.

"Maggie?" Rourke said. "She's great." He looked closely at his wife, wondering about her mood. "We already talked about that. You like her, don't you?"

"Yes, I like her," Carol said. "I like her a lot. I hated to hear about her brother. When is she coming back to Detroit?"

"Bill says today."

"Can he protect her?"

"Better than anybody else."

"I think she likes him."

"Well, they've been spending a lot of time together, honey. I guess she wouldn't be coming back and spending more time with him if she didn't like him."

"No, Jack. I think she's falling in love with him."

"Oh," was all Rourke could manage.

"I'm afraid for her," Carol said.

Rourke was getting frustrated. "Seems like it's your sovereign duty to be afraid for everyone this morning," he said.

"It's got to be somebody's duty," she snapped. "You aren't very good at it."

"Maybe not," Rourke said with resignation.

Carol gazed out the kitchen window at the orchard. A gust of wind tossed the branches of the trees, boiling off a flutter of brown leaves like a flight of partridge. "I want to tell you something before you go," she said. "I know... I know that, over the years, there have been other women." She stifled a sob with her hand. "A woman knows these things. I don't understand what it is that makes policemen do what they do, but I know that most of you do it." She studied the backs of her hands. "But I also know that you love me, and you love your kids. You've always come home to us. I just want you to know that I love you, too. More than life itself, Jack. And I forgive you. I just wanted you to hear me say that before you left this time. I didn't want this one, great secret to be left between us."

Rourke could only stare at her.

* * *

Westonfield picked up Magaly at the airport at dusk on Monday. It was gloomy and overcast. He found her exactly where she said she would be, standing in front of the Northwest Airlines terminal. She was silhouetted against the fluorescence of the terminal lobby, alone on the sidewalk in the light drizzle. She was partially protected from the rain by a glass overhang, but her hair hung limp and wet nevertheless. Like Herman Vickers a few days earlier, Westonfield was almost startled. The rain and humidity did nothing to detract from her beauty. If anything, the tangled black hair upon the shoulders of her trenchcoat enhanced it. You somehow forgot how striking she was when she was gone, and when she was back again you couldn't take your eyes off her. Magaly hugged him and kissed him—not on the cheek, but on the lips. Westonfield was surprised and didn't instantly respond. By the time he made up his mind to, her lips were gone. But he hugged her tightly. She smelled like fresh cloves.

"Hello, bodyguard," she said.

"Hey, you," he answered. His mind was so full of jumbled emotions that he didn't fully trust himself to say anything else.

Magaly seemed to understand and simply grinned. When they were on their way she said, "So, everybody's buried and gone. Where do we go from here?"

"My house," Westonfield said smoothly.

"Your house?"

"Right."

"What about my hotel?" Magaly said.

"You're checking out."

"What are you talking about?"

"I'm your bodyguard," Westonfield said. "How can I protect you at your hotel if I'm at my house? We're not going to be working every waking minute, you know."

"I know, Bill, but I didn't think—"

"Didn't think what? That we'd be staying together?"

"No," she said evenly. "I knew we'd be together. I just never got around to thinking about the specifics of the arrangements. You could stay in an adjoining room at the hotel."

"I've got a perfectly good house," Westonfield said. "Who would pay for the hotel room? The department? Ain't that a joke."

"But—"

"I've got three bedrooms, Magaly," he said. "You can take your pick."

"Oh, I see," she said. "Three. What if I pick yours?"

"Then it will be a more interesting arrangement than I thought."

"I said your bedroom, not you," Magaly said. "What if I pick your room? You said I can pick from three."

"My bedroom's a package deal," he said. "I go with it."

"Then I'll pick from the other two."

"Fine," Westonfield said, feigning disappointment. "But they don't have heat."

"All right, you win," Magaly said. "That is, I'll stay at your house. But take me to my hotel first. Let's take care of everything at once. I'll need to settle up with them and check out."

"That was easier than I figured it would be," Westonfield said. "I thought you'd object."

"I did," Magaly replied grimly. "You just didn't notice."

Westonfield laughed. Magaly punched him on the knee.

After a while Westonfield asked, "How's your family?"

"As good as the circumstances allow," Magaly said. "Family, you know. *Papá* was difficult. My brothers and sisters are good. Poor Diego—a girl broke his heart."

"The girls will do that," Westonfield said.

"Diego's friend says she's terrible."

"Did he love her?"

"Yes."

"Well," Westonfield said, "he probably loved her all the more for the fact that she was terrible."

Magaly groaned. "I said to you once that I had a brother like you."

"Indeed," Westonfield said.

"Wait a minute!" Magaly said, not quite ready to surrender the field. "Explain that to me. Do you guys have some kind of masochistic streak? Is that it?"

"I can't explain it," Westonfield said. "You just said we're crazy. Go with it." He grinned and turned on the radio. It was tuned to his ubiquitous oldies station.

Magaly sighed, defeated for the moment. She hated it when

he refused to be serious, particularly when it was important to her that he *be* serious. Of course, there were the times he insisted on being serious when she didn't care a whit if he was serious or not. "Motown," she muttered.

"Yep. What group?"

"The Four Tops," Magaly said, not caring if it was.

"Nope," Westonfield said. "The Temptations. *Ain't Too Proud to Beg.* David Ruffin. Another voice from the grave."

"He has a wonderful voice," Magaly admitted. "He's dead?"

"Uh-huh."

"When?"

"This year. In May."

"Really. How?"

"Cocaine overdose in Philadelphia. Some limo driver dropped him off at the emergency room. 'He's in bad shape,' he said. 'He was with The Temptations. His name is David Ruffin.' Then he drove away. Dave was already dead."

"*Dave.* You knew him?"

"I knew him," Westonfield said.

"Really? How?"

"Well, I had tickets to a couple of concerts—"

"Damn it, Bill!"

"I know, Maggie," Westonfield said. "I'm a royal pain in the ass." But he didn't answer her question.

They got Magaly checked out of the hotel in short order. Twenty minutes later they were standing in Westonfield's living room.

"Here's the cottage," Westonfield said. "My humble abode."

"The spider's lair," Magaly said.

"No, no spiders," Westonfield said.

"Just you," Magaly said. "A great big one." She looked around. "Where's my room?"

"In there." Westonfield showed her.

CHAPTER 25

Wednesday, October 30, 1991. Devil's Night. Ben Garvey hated it. As a lieutenant with Ladder Company 13 on the southwest side, it meant endless hours of hard work. It also meant unnecessary danger for his people. He thought of his firefighters that way: his people. For the last ten years Detroit had engaged in a frenzy of arson on one hellish night. The situation had become a media event and got nationwide news coverage. Senseless. Stupid. This year it would be even worse. A psychopath was running loose in the city, skinning people. It hadn't taken long for the news outlets to connect the two situations. It made no difference whether they were actually connected. It made great copy: would the killer strike on Devil's Night? Christ!

It was three o'clock in the afternoon. Garvey was poring over a wall map in the squad room. With him was his friend of seventeen years, Sergeant Kevin O'Brien. It was a pin map of the part of southwest Detroit covered by Ladder 13. Garvey stared at the map, his eyes glazed over. Before him was a kaleidoscope of colored pins, almost covering the surface of the grid. In places you could barely make out the outlines of the borders, or read the street names. The red pins were for nuisance fires—those started in dumpsters, trash fires in alleys, small brush fires. The yellow pins were for automobile arsons. The green pins were for abandoned residential buildings. The blue pins were for abandoned commercial buildings. The white pins were for occupied residences. The black pins were for occupied businesses.

"This is what we had last year," Garvey said dully. "Think this year will be any better?"

O'Brien looked at him. "I know you're kidding."

"A fella can always hope, can't he?"

"If wishes were horses, beggars would ride," O'Brien said. "Hell, Ben, look at the goddamn map. It's like a five-year-old went spastic with a box of pins for two hours. It'll be worse. The little bastards will try to outdo each other. They'll be handing out trophies, just like the academy awards: *Most Houses Burned in a Single Night; Best New Arsonist; Best Original Conflagration.*"

"Thanks," Garvey said. "I needed that."

"Any time, pal," O'Brien said. He checked his watch. "The fun begins in about three hours. Are we ready?"

"As ready as we'll ever be," Garvey said. "I hope to God nobody gets hurt this year."

"Have you seen Carter lately?" O'Brien asked. He was talking about Chuck Carter, a Ladder 13 veteran who had been seriously hurt when he fell through the roof of a burning pet shop last year. Chuck had gone up on the roof last Devil's Night to do what he could. He was an animal lover. But his effort was in vain. Eleven dogs, nineteen kittens, assorted guinea pigs, gerbils, and rats, hundreds of tropical fish, and four rare parrots had been cremated. And Chuck had broken his back. He would never walk again.

"Naw, I haven't seen him in a while," Garvey said. "It hurts to see him that way, you know? Confined to that wheelchair. He was such an outdoorsman. What a goddamn, dirty rotten shame. The little pukes who burned that store should be stood up against a wall and shot."

"I haven't been over, either," O'Brien said. "We should go over for a visit once in a while, Ben. Both of us should. I know it's hard. But we ought to. It could be us in that fucking chair."

"Yeah, I know," Garvey said. "You're right. How about me and you go over this weekend? At least we can drink a beer or two with Chuck. Seems like he's glad to see us when we go over."

O'Brien nodded.

* * *

Magaly scowled at Rourke over Westonfield's kitchen table. "Actually, I have a separate bedroom," she said. Rourke had just asked to see where they were doing it.

Dale Ward's prurient interests were as strong as anybody's. He looked at Westonfield for his reaction. He was somewhat disappointed. "You're disgusting, Rourke," Westonfield said mildly. He was facing the TV in the livingroom and, though it was thirty feet away, he was trying to watch CNN. The anchor was discussing Devil's Night. Westonfield didn't even bother to turn his head to issue his retort. "They're talking about us," he said.

"Your sleeping arrangements?" Rourke said.

"Our *boy*," Westonfield said, straining to hear the television. "They're talking about our killer and how it fits with Devil's Night."

"Damn," Rourke said. "I thought it was something interesting."

"It is interesting," Magaly said. "Don't you think so, Dale?"

"Guess so," Ward said. "What are we going to do about it?"

"What do you mean?" Westonfield asked.

"They're turning the whole thing into a circus," Ward said.

"It is a circus, Dale," Westonfield said, sipping his beer and looking at Rourke. "I don't mind. I don't think our Cuban friend will mind. Do you mind, Jack?"

"I don't mind," Rourke said. "It's just that I was hoping to hear about your sexual escapades on CNN. That would be interesting."

"See, Dale," Westonfield said. "No one cares."

Ward shook his head. All policemen were strange to some extent, whether they were from Trenton, Detroit, or Peoria, Illinois. But this crew carried idiosyncrasy to the level of an art form. Sometimes he felt as if he were living inside a cartoon. Sometimes Westonfield's level of concentration on the murder case was so intense it was frightening. At other times—sometimes just when Ward felt the circumstances justified intensity—Westonfield would slide into a ridiculous frame of mind. When that happened, almost nothing could break him out of it. Ward presumed this was one of those times.

"What time do we get going?" Magaly asked.

"Couple of hours," Westonfield said. He was still watching the news broadcast.

"Let's not get too serious too fast," Rourke said. "I just rolled in, you know. It takes a gentle soul like mine a while to get acclimated to the nitty-gritty."

"I forgot," Westonfield said in the same mild tone. "Sorry."

Magaly grinned.

"Speaking of just rolling in," Rourke said, noticing the smile. "I have a message from Mrs. Rourke to Magaly Rodríguez."

Magaly's smile widened. "Really? What?"

"She says that you've been a stone doomed to roll. She says for me to tell you that you'll always have a home with us in Brown City."

Magaly nodded. "Tell her I'll remember that," she said. "Tell her I said thank you."

"Done," Rourke said. He turned again to his partner. "I see you picked up a real gun," he said, pointing toward the Sig Sauer pistol in the shoulder rig slung around the back of an empty chair.

"I think I may soon need two pieces. What do you think?"

"I think you may," Rourke said. "I hate to say it, but those CNN assholes might be right. The arrogant son-of-a-bitch just might not be able to resist an opportunity to rub our noses in it tonight." He shifted his gaze to Ward. "How about you, Dale? Do Trenton coppers carry real guns?"

"Sig P226," Ward said. "You like the Sig?"

"Best goddamn gun in the world, kid. You got another gun? A pea shooter, maybe?"

"Well, I've got an old Colt .38 in the trunk of my car," Ward said.

"Good," Rourke said. "Get it, clean it, and load it with some good ammunition. Carry it along with the Sig. And carry two extra clips for the autoloader, too. You got 'em?"

"Sure, I got two extra clips," Ward said. "You take this pretty seriously, don't you Jack? I mean this Devil's Night stuff."

"Yep," Rourke said. "I do take it seriously. As should you. Isn't it only natural for the devil to come out on his own night?" He cocked his head and peered at Ward, but there was no smile on his face.

Magaly shuddered involuntarily.

Westonfield went on watching television. Ward noticed that a commercial had come on. Cartoon characters were capering all over the screen, singing about a new brand of peanut butter. Westonfield seemed fascinated. Magaly watched Ward watching Westonfield. The suburban policeman's reaction amused her. Hell, she had known Westonfield longer, had spent the last two nights in his home, and she still was caught up short. Rourke was the only one of them who seemed to truly understand him.

Magaly daydreamed. The last two nights: talks about *palo mayombe*, talks about kids, talks about police work. At least one minor mystery had been solved. She had learned about Westonfield's relationship with David Ruffin. As it turned out, his first patrol area had included Hitsville, the original W. Grand Boulevard location of the Motown recording studios of Berry Gordy. Bill had loved the music and eventually introduced himself to the staff and Gordy himself. Over the next few years he met many of the big stars—Marvin Gaye, Smokey Robinson, Martha Reeves, Diana Ross, Mary Wells—and had even struck up friendships with some. They permitted him to attend a few recording sessions.

Westonfield allowed Magaly to look through his scrapbook. In one clipping about David Ruffin's funeral there was a wide-angle shot of a group of mourners standing outside the New Bethel Baptist Church against a backdrop of hundreds of cars in the procession. Foremost in the photo was Martha Reeves, dressed in black, her face partially obscured by the wide-brimmed hat she was wearing. But on the far left, in the back, was Westonfield—clearly it was Westonfield—his white face standing out in a sea of black faces. He was wearing sunglasses, but Magaly could almost feel his eyes watching the pall bearers as they carried Ruffin's flower-bedecked casket through the door of the church to the waiting hearse.

New Bethel. Magaly had been astonished to discover that this was the church of the late Reverend C.L. Franklin, father of Motown great Aretha Franklin, and radical spokesman for black activism. In 1968 two Detroit policemen had been gunned down—one killed, and one seriously wounded—on the street near the church by members of the Republic of New Africa. The perpetrators had fled and taken refuge in the church. After a protracted standoff, and the controversial involvement of a black circuit judge at the scene, the matter finally came to an end. Several suspects had escaped in the confusion. Westonfield had attended the police academy with the dead officer and counted him a friend. Yet here was this photograph. Here was Bill Westonfield—the great racist, as some of his supervisors had it—attending the funeral of a black Motown singer, dead of a drug overdose twenty-three years after the famous shoot out, outside of the very same church. Magaly wondered what Westonfield's bosses would think of that.

* * *

As Gregorio Puente drove to the warehouse with Porfirio Pinzón, he hummed a little song. Porfirio's name amused him no end. It had a certain alliterative quality. Gregorio had never heard of alliteration, had never read a poem as far as he could remember, but he loved to play with the name nonetheless. He loved to joke. *Porfirio Pinzón.* What was that American play on words? *Peter Piper picked a peck of*—Porfirio Pinzón. Yes. That was very good. *Peter Piper picked a peck of Porfirio Pinzón. Pretty little puta pounded pud with his bone. Pretty soon a*

Porsche pulled up alongside, and when they saw the puta play, they laughed until they cried... He said it aloud twice. He felt that he was very clever.

Porfirio was not amused. He didn't like Puente much. He might even have killed him because of the song, except Gabriel would have been angry, perhaps angry enough to kill *him*. Porfirio Pinzón! One of the few things he was afraid of in life was dying at the hands of the *mayombero*. Still, it gave him some satisfaction to think about cutting Gregorio's throat. But he was more preoccupied now with the task at hand than with the song. They had to go to the warehouse and set up an ambush. It was a simple matter, easily done, but he was troubled by nagging doubts. He couldn't quite put his finger on it. He didn't like his weapon, for one thing. The AR-15. It was accurate and effective, but it lacked the familiar heft of the AK-47 upon which he had trained in the Cuban special services. He could shoot the eye out of a chicken's head at two hundred yards with the Kalashnikov. Another problem was that there was too much media attention to the situation. He certainly didn't lack audacity, but there was a fine line between audacity and foolishness. He felt at this moment that maybe he was flirting with this line. Oh, well. Too late now! The die was cast, the order given. He would do what he could. Maybe when it was done he would move on. Gabriel made him nervous.

It was just becoming dusk. They parked their car several blocks away, according to plan, removed their weapons from the trunk, and walked to the abandoned apartment building across from the warehouse. The rifles were wrapped in rags to disguise their appearance. There was almost no residential property in this area for anyone to notice them. They saw absolutely no one. They slipped inside the back way, and up the dilapidated stairway to the second floor, making their way to the street side of the building. They entered into the room they had chosen for the mission. Porfirio went quickly to the window, checking the street below. Clear. Dusk had deepened. Everything was quiet. He raised his eyes to the big building across the street. They had done well in picking this spot. He had a perfect view of the entire main entrance to the warehouse. It was a scant seventy-five meters across the street. There was a fire hydrant directly across the way. The firemen would be sitting ducks.

* * *

It was not quite full dark. In fifteen minutes the quick descent into full autumn night would be complete. As Garvey had predicted, all hell broke loose. First the small trash fires were started in the alleys and vacant lots. Then a few garages went. It was otherworldly. Like last year, like the year before that. The smell of smoke was in the air, subtle at first, then growing stronger with each passing minute, coming to Garvey's nostrils on gossamer wings. The firefighters called it dragon's breath. It was a good name. After a while, drifting clouds of denser smoke rolled in, blue-tinged against the gathering night. Garvey and O'Brien could see the scattered red-orange flares of the working conflagrations, dotting the skyline along the riverfront—The River Styx, the soul of the dragon, the gates to Hell. They were driving in a marked fire vehicle, traveling from one scene to another, organizing resources, trying to maintain a reasonable plan of action where there was no reason, bolstering morale, trying to prevent disasters like the one that had befallen Chuck Carter.

An hour after slap dark the dispatcher called them. Fire runs had been coming in non-stop for two hours, a virtually continuous stream of information and calls for service flowing from the radio. But this time there was a direct call to them as a supervisory response unit.

"2585? Radio 2585?"

O'Brien picked up the mike. "2585, radio."

"2585, we've got a report of a major fire at the Fillmore Paper Warehouse, on Federal off Junction. Can you check it and advise?"

"On the way," O'Brien said into the mike. He hung up the

microphone, looked at Garvey. "That son-of-a-bitch is huge, Ben. You know the place?"

"I know it," Garvey said.

"Christ, if they've torched that place we'll have a five-alarmer."

Ben Garvey nodded. He said nothing.

* * *

Magaly was once again in the back seat of an unmarked police car. As was his wont, Westonfield was driving. Dale Ward sat tensely in the front seat, overwhelmed by the enormous scale of the burning. Like anyone, he was aware of the annual arson. Media coverage was intense. But to see it, to smell it first-hand, was another thing altogether.

Typically, Westonfield was quiet, seemingly detached.

Magaly was awestruck. "I can't believe this is real," she said. "It's like a movie." Her eyes watered, stung by the acrid smoke that hovered like a thin fog over the whole southwest side. The smell of burning things assaulted her senses. "I've seen this on television. Hell, I read Ze'ev Chafets's book about Devil's Night, but none of it prepares you for this. Only Kafka could understand it." She looked at the back of Westonfield's head, caught a glimpse of his right eye as he turned momentarily toward her. *Or him*, Magaly thought. "I miss Jack," she said. She ruffled Ward's hair. "No offense, Dale."

"None taken," Ward said. At the moment he didn't care much whether Magaly missed Jack or not. He had other things to think about.

"He's around," Westonfield said for Magaly's information. "Jack's on 4-78, as usual."

"Can we see him?" Magaly asked.

"You just saw him at the house, Maggie." He looked at his watch. "About four hours ago."

"I know it," she said. "Can we?"

Westonfield shrugged. "One of your feelings?" He looked at

Ward. "Ask for 4-78's location, Dale."

Ward did.

They found Rourke sitting in his unmarked car at the scene of a downed power line. With him was Benny Adams. They were waiting for a patrol unit to respond to protect the scene until a Detroit Edison crew arrived to repair the line. A garage had been torched. The flames had burned through the 220-volt main line that was strung along the back alley.

"Hello, children," Rourke said through his open window when they drove up next to him. "Checking up on me, eh?"

"Ask her," Westonfield said, jerking his thumb toward Magaly.

Rourke squinted into the darkness of the other vehicle's back seat. "Can't live without me, eh, Mag?"

"Something is going to happen tonight," Magaly said. "I can feel him. Not strong, like other times. But the killer's out there watching. Remember what you told me Professor Saldívar said, Bill? The monster can get people to help him when the moon is waning. He's done that. I know he has. It's just come on me over the last few minutes. I wanted to tell you together, you and Jack, at the same time. You talked about it this afternoon, Jack. I think you were right."

Ward stared at her. "Goddamn, woman, I guess the fires and the smoke aren't creepy enough." The whole situation was beyond his experience. He unconsciously touched the stock of his belt-holstered Sig and reached up to feel his Colt snubby in the shoulder holster—he had taken Rourke's advice about carrying a backup. The cold steel of the weapons reassured him a little.

"Sorry," Magaly said. "I think I need to tell somebody when I have these feelings."

"I know it," Ward said dully. "I've just got a case of the willies is all."

Rourke looked at Westonfield. "So what are we going to do?"

"What we've been doing," Westonfield said. "Drive around,

check things out, monitor the radio and wait."

The severed power cable writhed on the ground in the darkness of the alley, hissing like a giant snake, its glowing end the serpent's mouth. Every few seconds the bare tip whipped through a puddle of water, causing a loud bang followed by a shower of silver sparks. The smell of ozone permeated the air, more powerful, even, than the stench of the fires.

Westonfield had fallen silent again, his face obscure. But his profile emerged, stark and blue-white in the intermittent flashes of the grounding power cable. From the side Magaly could see his pupils dilate as the brilliant arc of light struck his liquid grey eyes. The striking image seared itself in her brain. It was in that moment that she completely understood that this was Westonfield's element. He was home.

* * *

Porfirio and Gregorio peered cautiously both ways down Federal Street from the dark doorway of the apartment building. No one. It was quiet as the grave. Smoke was drifting everywhere, carried on a desultory breeze. The horizon glowed faint orange. Well, they would soon have their own little bonfire. They hurried across the street carrying the two-and-a-half gallon kerosene cans. In less than three minutes they jimmied the lock of a side entrance to the warehouse and entered the building, lugging the heavy cans inside.

"You got your lighter, Porfirio?" Puente asked.

"Sure, I got my lighter," Pinzón said, liking Gregorio no more than he had an hour earlier.

"Then take your can down this hallway to the stairway that goes down to the basement. Splash the gas around real good. Then leave a trail coming back up the stairs. I'll get the second floor."

Porfirio walked away muttering.

Gregorio went to the staircase on the opposite end of the hallway and ascended the stairs. He splashed gasoline all around the stacks and pallets of paper products there and then left a trail going back down the stairs. When he emerged onto the first floor Porfirio was just coming back down the hallway toward him. "Done?" he said.

Porfirio nodded.

"Good. Now you take that end," Puente said, pointing in the direction from which Porfirio had just come, "and I'll take the other end of this floor. Do the same thing. Splash everything real good, then come back here."

Twenty minutes later the work was done, the smell of gasoline heavy in the confined space of the building. They would need to be careful when they lit the fire. If the fumes were too dense, they would blow themselves to smithereens before they could get out. Gregorio smiled. *Smithereens.* It was a wonderful word. The Americans had such a way with words. It appealed to his sensibilities as a poet.

They exited the building through the same door they had entered. Gregorio pulled a notebook from his shirt pocket and ripped out a page. He lit a corner of the paper with the lighter Porfirio grudgingly handed him and tossed the flaming page onto the trail of gasoline. There was a burst of flame and a great *whoooosh*. In an instant the whole first floor was engulfed. Gregorio had been right—if there had been only a few additional minutes for the fumes to accumulate, they would have been cremated on the spot. In the event, it was a perfect arson. Within ten minutes the entire structure was involved. It was beautiful, Porfirio thought.

The companions returned to their second story perch in the building across the street, made themselves comfortable, examined their weapons for the tenth time, and waited. Porfirio enjoyed these moments of calm before the storm. He was able to take his mind off Gregorio's bullying. He caressed his rifle gently. He had a slight erection.

Gregorio noticed this and frowned. Porfirio was an animal. He had no subtlety.

* * *

Garvey and O'Brien could see the glow of the fire from a mile away. Their worst nightmare had come true: a huge warehouse fire at a time when resources were taxed to the limit. "Fuck!" O'Brien exclaimed. "Would you look at that corona." He meant the glowing halo around a large fire when viewed from a distance at night. "They must have fired the whole goddamn building." His eyes wonderingly took in the scale of the burning. Three minutes later, as they pulled onto Federal, in full view of the raging fire, he said, "This ain't kids, Ben. This is pros. Holy Mary, Mother of God, would you look at it!"

* * *

Ward was the first of them to see the mammoth glow off to the left. "Oh, Jesus," he said. "What the hell is that?"

Westonfield looked, and as soon as he saw it, he knew. It was *him*.

Magaly looked and knew it, too. She shrunk silently into the darkness of the back seat.

Westonfield said, "Go to channel five, Dale. Raise Jack and tell him to look off to the left."

Ward grunted and did as he was asked to do. He couldn't take his eyes off the red-yellow glow which grew progressively bigger as they moved toward it. What in God's name had he gotten himself into? His stomach contents turned to hot, churning liquid. His sphincter tightened.

"Yeah, I see it," Rourke said. "I'm heading that way."

Westonfield said, "Ask dispatch where the big fire's at, Dale. North of Vernor, east of Livernois."

Again Ward complied. After a short wait while the police dispatcher contacted the fire dispatcher, the voice on the radio said, "3475 Federal Street. The Fillmore Paper Warehouse. Federal between Junction and Livernois. Fire's just getting on the scene. They're calling it a three-alarm."

Westonfield reached across the dash and impatiently grabbed the microphone while he drove. He switched the radio frequency to channel five. "You hear that, Jack?"

"I heard it," Rourke said. "I'm coming. How do you want to approach it?"

"Pull to the end of the block," Westonfield said. "Let's take a look. I don't like it."

"Me neither," Rourke said.

Westonfield, Ward, and Magaly met Rourke and Adams at the corner of Junction and Federal. They could see the rotating white and red lights of Garvey's battalion chief's car in front of the building. Sirens were coming from up Junction. A big rig rolled by. A pumper. Then a ladder truck flew past, lights zigzagging frantically in the smoke, siren wailing.

"Apartment building across the street," Rourke said through the open window of his car. "I think it's vacant."

"It is," Westonfield said. "Feels like a set up."

Rourke nodded agreement. "What do we do about it?"

"The firemen are completely exposed," Westonfield said. "It'll be a turkey shoot." He thought furiously for a minute. "Get on the radio, Jack. Tell our dispatcher to have fire dispatch instruct those fire units to stay out of sight of the building across the street. It'll be slow. I guess you better go tell 'em yourself, buddy, after you try the radio. I don't think we have much time." He glanced at Ward, grinning. "Me and Dale here are gonna roll up the alley behind the apartments and take a look. We'll probably go in. Meantime, keep your fat ass out of the line of fire. It isn't going to do those firemen any good for you to get it shot off in front of them." He floored the gas pedal, fishtailing, burning rubber for twenty feet.

* * *

Gregorio was gratified to see the two firemen pull up in front of the building within just a few minutes of the setting of the fire. Perfect. They looked like big shots. He considered shooting them both immediately, but decided to wait until a few more trucks arrived. Then he could shoot several. Gabriel would like that very much. Gregorio put the fireman who had been driving in his sights just for fun, motioning for Porfirio to wait. Porfirio nodded. Like Gregorio, he amused himself by sighting on one of the firemen. Soon they heard the sirens of the approaching fire trucks. Only a minute or two now.

* * *

Garvey and O'Brien stepped out of their rig when they heard the approach of the first ladder truck. They did so at the exact moment their dispatcher tried to contact them with Rourke's desperate information. Neither man was equipped with a handheld radio, so neither heard the call. The roar of the big diesel engines and the incessant wail of the sirens made it impossible for any of the men in the responding units to hear it clearly, either. In another three minutes sixteen firemen were working in front of the Fillmore Paper Warehouse, hauling hoses, making hydrant connections, and extending radial ladders off the rig.

* * *

Westonfield doused his headlights and proceeded swiftly along the alley to the rear of the apartment building. He motioned for both Magaly and Ward to get out of the car along with him. He studied Magaly's body armor one more time. He had insisted that she wear it. She wore it like a flak jacket, over her outer clothing. It was heavy and awkward, but it reassured both of them. He would have preferred Magaly to wait in the car, but knew she would refuse. He shook his head grimly, figuring that at this stage of the game she was as much a part of the mess as he was.

When they got to the back door, Westonfield paused and listened carefully. He turned to Ward. "They'll be upstairs, Dale.

That's where they'll get the best shots. I don't think they're expecting to be caught, but be as quiet as you can. They're probably Cuban military. They'll be good. Magaly, you follow behind Dale. Several yards back. Do you understand? Several yards. Wait for Dale to be halfway up the stairs, then come on. You've got a radio." He touched her waist where the portable was hooked. "If you need to use it, you'll know what to do. Just give the dispatcher our radio code and location. Got it?"

Magaly shook her head once firmly up and down. She said nothing.

Westonfield walked rapidly across the junk-strewn backyard and up to the door, which stood ajar. He listened again. Nothing. He motioned Ward forward.

Ward was shaking so hard he was afraid the cartridges in his weapons would rattle and warn the people they were stalking. He unzipped his jacket and touched both guns. They were impossibly warm. The warmth almost startled him. Westonfield had already opened his jacket, positioned his Smith and his new Sig.

Magaly quietly, carefully, brought up the rear.

Westonfield arrived at the upper landing and paused once again, waiting for Ward to come up. He heard faint voices coming from somewhere down the dark hall. He cupped his ear and motioned in that direction, indicating to Ward that he should listen. Ward strained for a few seconds, finally heard the voices.

Magaly heard them, too.

Westonfield pulled both of his weapons from their holsters, the Sig Sauer in his left hand, the Smith & Wesson in his right. Ward slid his own Sig 9mm from its holster, held it in his right hand, ready in the port position.

Magaly held back, waiting.

Westonfield stopped every few feet to listen. Soon he stood poised like a coiled spring outside the closed door of the room from which the voices emanated. They were speaking in Spanish, and there were two of them. He placed himself exactly in front of the door, well back, holding both guns at port. He leaned backward to give himself as much momentum as possible, and raised his right leg to kick the door. He surged forward.

* * *

Rourke came barreling up Federal all the way to the warehouse. He came to a screeching halt partway behind the big pumper in order to give himself and Adams as much cover as possible. They threw their doors open and jumped out, spotting the two fire supervisors at the same time.

* * *

There were so many excellent targets to choose from that Gregorio almost didn't know which one to shoot first. He motioned for Porfirio to get ready. Suddenly he saw the brown car careen up and skid to a halt behind the fire truck. This perplexed him. The car did not appear to be a fire vehicle. Then he saw the two men leap from the car and run toward the firemen. They were wearing street clothes, but Gregorio knew policemen when he saw them. No matter. They were too late. He would kill them, too. He gave Porfirio the go-ahead signal and carefully sighted on his chosen target. He took a deep breath and slowly let it out. Then he squeezed the trigger.

* * *

Westonfield kicked the door hard. The frame gave way and the door flew open, crashing against the wall. He plunged in, side-stepping instantly to the left, allowing Ward to enter from behind. Westonfield's and Gregorio's shots were almost simultaneous. Westonfield centered his .357 magnum on his enemy's back and emptied the gun in three seconds, the reports deafening in the enclosed space.

Porfirio fired his rifle the same time Gregorio fired his. Ward intended to shoot him but was distracted by Westonfield's rapid-fire fusillade. Even as the Trenton detective leveled his weapon, Porfirio got off two more quick shots. Ward squeezed the trigger of his automatic and the Cuban's head vaporized in a red-grey mist of blood, brain and bone. But the sickening image didn't have time to register because Westonfield, with virtually no waste of motion, now turned his Sig on the man, pouring a sustained volley of 9mm bullets into him before the sound of Ward's shot had died away.

Gabriel's hapless assassins had managed to get off four rounds out the window. Now they lay dead on the floor, shot so many times that even in the dim light they looked like rag dolls attacked with an ice pick.

* * *

Rourke was running furiously, shouting at Garvey to get behind a truck, when he saw the fireman's head suddenly expand and then contract like a creature from cyberspace on one of his son's computer games. Then the whole back of his head disintegrated, a viscous red spray showering over both himself and Adams.

Adams screamed.

Rourke lurched past Garvey's falling body and tackled O'Brien, pinning him heavily to the ground. Then Rourke heard shooting from across the street. A lot of shooting. He heard the sound of bullets striking metal and the sound of men yelling. Then everything was eerily quiet. He lay heavily atop O'Brien, their faces close. The fireman didn't notice him, wasn't even aware that a 290 pound man had just tackled him. He was looking at the dead face of his friend of almost two decades. The left eye was gone. But the right eye looked at him in surprise.

Rourke yanked his gun and pointed it in the general direction of the apartment building's second floor. Westonfield concealed himself behind the window frame in case Jack was inclined to shoot. He shouted down that everything was all right, waving his arm back and forth across the window. When he looked again, Rourke had holstered his gun and was helping Kevin O'Brien to his feet. He looked up at Westonfield and waved. Westonfield watched for another minute. He wanted to know if more than one fireman had been hit. No—fortunately, the second Cuban's aim had not been as good as the first. He turned back to the room. It was filled with smoke, some from the fire across the street, some from the shooting. The air was acrid with cordite.

Magaly stood by the door, staring at the bodies of Gregorio and Porfirio.

Ward stood exactly where he had stood since firing his first and last shot. He looked at Westonfield, his eyes glazed over, a stunned look on his sweaty face. "I don't know if—"

"You got him, Dale," Westonfield said. "Your shot got him first. You can put your gun away now," he added mildly. "You did real good."

He pulled the Sig from its holster and calmly removed the empty magazine from its grip. If he was the least bit unnerved over what had just transpired, he didn't show it. Ward could see that he wasn't even breathing hard.

Then Westonfield retrieved a full magazine from his inner jacket pocket and slapped it into the gun. As Ward watched uncomprehendingly, he stood over the body of Gregorio Puente and fired seven more shots into his back. Bits of clothing twitched as the hollow points thundered home, ragged holes opening in the dead man's bloody shirt. Without a pause, Westonfield stepped over and fired seven more shots into the body of Porfirio Pinzón.

In a different era, and in a different setting, Westonfield would have cut off their heads and jammed them on a stake.

Magaly hadn't moved or spoken since she followed the policemen into the room. In the semi-darkness her eyes were black holes in her shadowy face. She tore her eyes from Westonfield and looked for a while at the ruined bodies of the Cubans. Choking back overwhelming emotion, she finally whispered fiercely, "That was for Katy Marroquín…that was for *me*." Then she turned and stumbled out of the apartment, looking for the way outside.

CHAPTER 26

When Magaly woke up on Hallowe'en morning, the image of Ben Garvey's dead face was in her mind. She knew that it would take a long time to fade from her consciousness, as would many of the memories of that strange Devil's Night. When she left the apartment building she'd walked straight across the street to where Jack Rourke held onto a dazed Kevin O'Brien. If Rourke had let him go he would have fallen on his face. The three of them stood staring at Garvey's corpse. A handful of the fireman's brains spilled out onto the grass. After a while Rourke got a rubber coat from one of the trucks and draped it over the body.

"Two of them are dead," Magaly said to Rourke, her eyes still on Garvey.

Rourke nodded. "Dale and Bill okay?"

Magaly smiled oddly. "Sure."

Rourke grunted. Then he turned and helped O'Brien to the police car. When asked, O'Brien told Rourke his name, and Rourke said, "Well, come on Kevin. Us micks gotta stick together. Let's get to the warm car. I think I can find us something Irish to drink."

Magaly came back to the present. She had slept in Bill Westonfield's bed, and her right hand was resting on his naked belly, rising and falling with his rhythmic breathing. He was still sound asleep. Magaly looked at the clock on the night stand. Eleven o'clock in the morning. God! She looked at Bill's sleeping face. Peaceful, calm, so unlike its watchful expression when awake. She lifted her hand from his body and gently ran a finger along the contour of his cheek. He murmured in his sleep but didn't move. Feeling suddenly warm, she pulled the sheet down to her waist. Looking at her chest she saw several salt-and-pepper hairs glued to her breasts. She smiled, picked them off one by one, fluffed them off her fingers onto the floor. She kicked the blankets farther down and moved a hand between her legs. Warm. Moist. Dry white flakes in her pubic hair. She pursed her lips. Foolish girl. She had a sense, once again, of the inevitability of everything, of playing a part in a script already written. Who was the author? How would the story end?

In a moment she pulled the blankets back up. She drew herself close to his naked body and ran her hand gently through the hair of his lower belly. After a while his breathing changed, grew stronger, though he was still mostly asleep. Magaly kissed him slowly on the lips and then his eyes flickered open. He immediately returned her kiss, their breath mingling and growing ragged together. When he began to stir, she firmly pushed him onto his back and then smoothly rolled on top of him. She teased him for a moment, refusing to let him enter her, holding herself above him so that his rigid member barely touched her. When he murmured in frustration, she slid languidly down upon him, eliciting a quiet moan. Then she made love to him in the morning light the way he had made love to her in the night. Afterwards, they slept again.

"Happy Hallowe'en," Westonfield said softly when he awoke two hours later and found Magaly looking at him. He reached out and ran his hand through her hair. He smelled her smell.

"Uh-huh," Magaly answered, looking into the face of the man she had seen shoot two human beings to death seventeen hours earlier. "It's late. One o'clock."

"I've got to call my kids," Westonfield muttered.

Magaly lay quietly for a while, watching his hand as it moved gently through her hair. "I can't let myself fall in love with you," she said.

Westonfield didn't look at her. He continued caressing her

hair. Then he said, "Love?"

"Yeah."

"What is it?"

"What is what?" Magaly asked.

"Love," Westonfield said. "What is it?"

Magaly breathed against her pillow, carefully considering her answer. "For a man?" she said. "I really have no idea. For a woman? Well, let's see. For me—for me, Bill—it's when this other life, this other person, is who's in my mind when I wake up in the morning, and when he's my last thought before I go to sleep at night. It's when I would rather have good fortune come to him than to me." She took his hand from her hair and placed it on her breast. "It's when you don't need to do something special to have fun with this person, when a walk together through new-fallen snow is better than— What did Scott Fitzgerald say? *A Diamond as Big as the Ritz.* That's what love is."

Westonfield came close, removed his hand from her breast, and kissed her nipple. "You forgot one thing," he said. "The last important part."

"Oh?"

"Yeah. The part where it all comes to an end."

"Must it?" Magaly asked.

"Sure."

"Why must it?"

"I don't know," Westonfield said. "But it always ends."

"The love ends? Or just the relationship?" Magaly asked impishly.

He smiled, kissed her deeply on the mouth, and said nothing.

* * *

Westonfield picked up his children when they got home from school at four o'clock. Millie continued to be cool. She said nothing about the events of the previous night, but he could see the front page of the *Detroit Free Press* spread out on the kitchen table, the headlines proclaiming the attack on the firemen. Tracey was delighted, anxious to meet Magaly, whom she had been told about. Fourteen-year-old Bill was grave, as was his wont, but his slate-grey eyes, like his father's, betrayed his happiness at seeing his old man. Tracey gave her father a wet kiss. Bill, Jr., shook his hand and grinned shyly when his dad hugged him.

When they arrived at Auburn, Tracey kibitzed up the sidewalk to the house, her Hallowe'en costume swinging in a plastic bag clutched in her hand. Billy followed his father deliberately to the door. Magaly rose from her chair in the living room to greet them. She had been nervous all morning, not knowing what to expect. Tracey made it easy. She walked up to Magaly and curtsied carefully. "Pleased to make your acquaintance," she said seriously. "My name is Morgan."

Magaly returned the curtsy smartly and said, "The pleasure is all mine." She bent down and kissed Tracey's cheek. Westonfield was right. She was easily the most beautiful little girl she had ever seen. Tracey sat on the couch without another word, watching her big brother.

Westonfield said, "Billy, this is Magaly Rodríguez, the lady that I've been looking after. Magaly, this is my son, Bill."

Billy held out his hand stiffly. He hadn't liked Susan Lawrence much, was uncomfortable with how different she and his mother were. He wasn't entirely sure what his father's relationship was with this woman, but in contrast to Tracey's perpetual ebullience, he was not enthusiastic. He shook Magaly's hand firmly. "Pleased to meet you."

Magaly was struck by how much he looked like his father. Westonfield had shown her photos and had remarked that his son favored him, but the resemblance extended beyond the basic features. The boy's walk had the same confident fluidity of his father's, despite his obvious shyness, and his eyes had the same presence. "I've heard so much about you, Bill," Magaly said. "I'm glad to finally meet you."

Billy smiled a small smile and said, "Me too."

"Well," Westonfield said, "We've got a big day ahead." He pointed to the kitchen. "Go check out what I've got for you, Morgan." He looked at Bill. "Go look, son."

Tracey bounced off the sofa and raced into the kitchen. Billy followed.

"Oh, my gosh!" Tracey shrieked. "They're the best punkins I ever saw! I love 'em, Daddy. Where did you get 'em?"

"From Charlie Brown's pumpkin patch, of course," Westonfield said. "That's where I always get them, isn't it?"

"'Course," Tracey said. "I forgot."

"What do you think, Bill?" Westonfield asked. "Are you ready to carve? I picked up three, like always. One for each of us. You want to show Magaly how good a carver you are?"

"Sure, Dad," Billy said, his face turning red, embarrassed that Magaly might think him immature.

Magaly followed them into the kitchen. She understood Billy's dilemma immediately. "Pumpkin carving is a real art, don't you think?" she said. "It goes back a couple thousand years, to when the Druids carved gourds to scare away evil spirits. Your father got only three, I'm afraid. Would you mind if you and I worked on one together, Bill? Your dad can help Tracey, if she'd like."

"Okay," Billy said. He looked at Magaly out of the corner of his eye. He had his doubts, but maybe she was all right after all.

"I know about the Druids," Tracey said. "They were Celts. They were our ancestors, weren't they, Daddy? They were the first Welsh people. We're Welsh, you know. They invented Hallowe'en. That's why I like it, and because I'm a witch. My mommie and daddy named me from Morgan Le Fey. Did you know that?"

Magaly laughed despite herself. "Yes, I did," she said. "Your father told me about your ancestors. I already knew about Hallowe'en, too, because I love it just like you. I'm so happy you're willing to share it with me this year."

Tracey beamed. "You're welcome," she said. She looked at her brother adoringly. "Don't worry about Billy. He's shy. But he isn't bad. I used to say he's bad, but I don't anymore."

"That's good," Magaly said. "Because I don't think he's bad, either. I think he's a fine young man. He's just like his father."

"That's what my mom says when she's mad at him," Tracey said.

"Oh, does she?" Magaly said. "Does she indeed?"

"She does indeed," Tracey said earnestly.

"I warned you about this one," Westonfield said.

"They're wonderful," Magaly said. "Both of them. And we're going to have a very good time together."

An hour later, deep into pumpkin carving, Magaly said to Billy, "I hear you're a baseball player."

"Uh-huh."

"Sorry to see the season end?"

"Sure."

"What do you play? What position?"

"I'm a pitcher."

"Really?"

"Yeah."

"Who do you play for?"

"The freshman team and summer intramural. 'F' League."

"He plays for varsity sometimes," Tracey said. "Even if he's still a little boy."

Billy blushed again. "Be quiet, Morgy. You don't know what you're talking about."

"Aw, Billy," Westonfield said. "She's just proud of you. Me, too. Tell Magaly."

Billy grimaced. "Well, freshmen aren't supposed to play varsity," he said. "It's a school rule. But they kind of bend the rules sometimes. I'm assigned to the freshman team but I relieve the starters sometimes in the varsity home games. Just a few innings."

"Yeah," Westonfield said. "ERA of 1.5 against kids three

and four years older than him!"

"No kidding," Magaly said. "That's great."

Billy shrugged.

"I was just sticking up for you," Tracey said, pouting.

"He knows it," Magaly said. "He knows, Morgan."

"Can you help me with the mouth?" Billy said suddenly, cradling the big orange pumpkin between his hands and studying the half-completed face. "That's the hardest part for me—the mouth. I can never decide whether to make him smile or frown. What do you think?"

Magaly examined the pumpkin. "Let's make him smile," she said. "There are already too many frowns in the world." She glanced at him and added, "Sometimes it's hard to tell—hard to tell if someone's smiling, I mean. Some folks smile on the inside. Some smile with their eyes. Did you ever notice that?"

Westonfield looked up.

"I think I know what you mean," Billy said. "I know people like that."

Magaly nodded. "Me, too."

"Me, too," Tracey said.

"So, who's your favorite ball player?" Magaly asked.

"I like the old timers best," Billy said immediately. "The ones who played a long time ago. Like the '27 Yankees and the '19 White Sox. Lou Gherig. Joe Jackson. But I guess my real favorites are the Negro League players from teams like the Pittsburgh Crawfords and the Philadelphia Giants. Cool Papa Bell. Josh Gibson. Judy Johnson."

"No kidding?"

"Yeah." He switched his attention from the pumpkin to Magaly. "Do you know about those guys?"

"A little bit," Magaly said. "Not nearly enough, Bill. But I love baseball. Who's your all time favorite?"

The fact that she said 'Bill' instead of 'Billy' was not lost on him. "I guess my favorite is Satchel Paige."

"Now that's a name I know."

"Yeah. He was so great—"

"Tell me."

"What do you wanna know?"

"Whatever you'd like to tell me. I'm all ears."

"Well, he was born in Mobile, Alabama, in 1906. He played in the Negro Leagues from 1924 to 1947. He went to the Majors in 1948 for the Cleveland Indians. He pitched for the St. Louis Browns from '51 to '53. He even pitched a little for the Kansas City Athletics in 1965, when he was fifty-nine years old."

"Wow!" Magaly said. "I don't know if I'm more impressed with how long he played baseball or by how much you know about him."

Billy looked at her seriously. "Satch won 104 games out of 105 games pitched in 1934. He pitched fifty-five no-hitters in his lifetime. Many good major leaguers never pitch one. They inducted him into the Hall of Fame at Cooperstown in 1971. His real name was Leroy. Leroy Paige. They wouldn't let him play in the Major Leagues until he was forty-one years old. On account of he was black."

Magaly set her carving knife down. "I know it," she said. "And what do you think about that?"

Billy pulled the pumpkin toward himself and looked at the toothy smile. He liked it. Magaly had completed the cut around the mouth she'd drawn and all he had to do was push the cut portion out of the shell with his fingers. As he did it, he thought about how he should answer her. After a while he said simply, "Satch is my hero. I guess I'm mad. I'll never forgive them for what they did."

Magaly leaned over and kissed him on the forehead.

* * *

They were cleaning up the mess when the telephone rang. It was Paul Randazzo. "Just calling with an update, Bill. Just like we figured, another blank wall. We found the shooters' car parked a block away from the warehouse. Registered to one of the dead men. Their names are Porfirio Pinzón and Gregorio

Puente. Mean anything to you?"

"Nope."

"Me or anyone else around here, either," Randazzo said. "They're both Cubans. No surprise there. Extensive out-of-state rap sheets. No surprise there, either. We're processing prints. That'll take a while. The ARs match the one you recovered on Merritt—from the Ohio burglary. It's our man, all right. Not a scintilla of evidence to point us toward the cocksucker's true identity, though. He's one smart, diabolical bastard, I'll tell you. He just sent us another message, Bill. One hell of a message. Poor Garvey. Did you know him?"

"Actually, I did slightly," Westonfield said. "I played cards with him a time or two at the old fireboat station years ago. I didn't recognize him right away with—you know. Good man."

"Yeah. Good man."

"Anything else?"

"Naw. That's it. Fuck it. Enjoy your couple of days off."

"I'll try. Thanks."

"How's that Maggie broad?"

"Okay."

"She seemed pretty damn tough last night. Hanging around you hasn't made her mean, has it?"

"I hope not."

* * *

At dusk they all went out trick-or-treating. Tracey ran ahead while her brother tried to keep up. Westonfield had assigned him the task of taking care of his sister and making sure she got up to the doors without being jostled by the older kids. As always, Billy took his job seriously. Despite being nearly perpetually aggravated by his sister, he worshipped her, and her excitement over the big night was contagious. He enjoyed it himself.

Magaly and Westonfield followed along. Westonfield updated Magaly on Randazzo's phone call.

"So now what?" she said.

"I don't know," Westonfield said. "You tell me. You're the official prognosticator."

"I don't feel him now," Magaly said.

"No," Westonfield agreed.

"Waning moon."

"Right, but as we found out last night, he has soldiers."

"I know," Magaly said. "But I think he's done for now—until the moon begins to grow again. You killed his people. You and Dale."

"He might have others," Westonfield said.

"I know, but he's made his point. He killed a fireman on Devil's Night, despite the much-ballyhooed dragnet. That's pretty heady stuff. The media are in a frenzy. He's getting his fifteen minutes of fame."

"Do you think that's what he wants?"

"That," Magaly answered, "and more."

"What else, ultimately. What?"

"You."

"Of course."

"Of course."

* * *

Back home, jack o'lanterns burning brightly in the windows, Tracey sorted her treasure trove of candy on the living room floor and Billy half-watched a 1950s horror movie. Westonfield and Magaly shared a beer and talked quietly.

Billy suddenly said, "Dad, I read in the paper about last night. About the fireman. Were you there?"

Westonfield looked at Tracey. She seemed oblivious. He nodded *yes*.

"What happened?"

"Not much more than what you saw in the paper, son," Westonfield said.

"I mean—did you have to shoot somebody?"

Magaly interjected, "How about if Billy and I go into the kitchen and talk about it, Bill? You and Morgan can stay out here and watch the movie and check out the candy. How's that?"

Westonfield looked at her for a moment, debating. Then he shrugged. "All right."

In the kitchen Billy said, "My dad doesn't talk about his job."

"No," Magaly answered.

"Do you know why?"

"Well, I'm not entirely sure," Magaly said. "But I know it's a hard job. He probably likes to leave it behind when he comes home."

"Oh..."

"Does that make you angry?"

"Sometimes."

"I suppose it does. Makes you feel left out, huh?"

"Yeah. A little."

"Your father loves you a lot."

"I know."

"All right, then," Magaly said. "I'll try to fill in some of the gaps. I'm no expert, but I'll do the best I can. What would you like to know?"

"I'd like to know what happened last night."

"There's a very dangerous man in the city right now, Bill. He's done some terrible things. Have you read about them in the paper?"

"Yeah."

"All right. It's your father's job to stop him. Find him and stop him."

"That's a pretty big job."

"Yes."

"Why did they give it to my dad?"

"Because they think he's the best one to do it."

Billy thought about that for a minute. "So what about last night?"

"Well, two men—not the one your father wants to find, but two men who might have worked with him—started a big fire, and when the firemen came... well, they shot one of the firemen. It was a terrible thing."

"Yeah. I think his name was Ben something."

"That's right. It was Ben Garvey. Your father and another policeman found the men where they were hiding, and the men began to shoot, so—"

"So my dad shot them."

"He had to."

"I suppose." His eyes were too sad for the eyes of a fourteen-year-old boy.

"It's true," Magaly said. "What would make you think it wasn't so, Bill?"

"Nothing," he said fervently. "I know my dad wouldn't hurt anybody unless he had to. Only—"

"Only..."

"Maybe he should get another job. So he doesn't have to do things like that anymore."

"Maybe," Magaly said.

"My mom says he pays too much attention to his job. She says he should do something else. She says he hurts the people around him on account of his work."

"She told you that, eh?"

Billy turned red. "Sort of. I shouldn't say."

Magaly smiled. "It'll be our secret. Just me and you."

"All right." A half-smile, exactly like his father's, flickered at the corner of his mouth.

"In a perfect world," Magaly said, "I'd have to say she's right. But you know what? Sometimes there are people who simply *need* to do what they do. It's a part of them, like arms and legs to the rest of us. And when the job they do is special, then despite the bad side, the rest of us are better for it. Understand? In the case of policemen, who could be better at catching bad guys than someone who knows all about bad guys? How good a baseball player would Satchel Paige have been if he hadn't loved baseball so much? Why did he keep on playing when white players who weren't half as good got all of the credit and most of the money? Because he loved the game." She reached out and brushed the hair back from the boy's forehead. "I would never come between you and your mom, Bill. I happen to know she's a very nice lady. In fact, I'll tell you a secret—your father loves her. He'll always love her, just like he loves you and Tracey. But don't be too hard on your dad. He tries hard. What did Satch say when they asked him if he was bitter about his treatment in the old days? Do you remember?"

"Yeah."

"Tell me."

"He said, 'Don't ever look back, because someone might be gaining on you.'"

"Correct," Magaly said. "That's one of the few things I knew for sure about Satchel Paige before you taught me. But that's like your father, you see. You wouldn't want him to look back, would you? To give up?"

"No."

"Of course not. And I'll tell you another secret. You don't know it yet, but you're just like him."

* * *

They were getting ready to put Tracey in bed when Jack Rourke knocked on the door. Magaly knew it was him when she heard his special knock—three loud raps, two soft, two loud, one soft. When Westonfield opened the door and Rourke stepped in, Tracey shrieked with delight and ran into his open arms. "Uncle Jack! Uncle Jack! Happy Hallowe'en!"

Rourke grabbed her under her outstretched arms, swept her into the air and hugged her close. Her legs, clad in fuzzy flannel pajamas with feet, encircled the broad girth of his belly. "How's my little princess?" he said. "How was the trick-or-treating? Got some good stuff for me?"

"'Course I do, Uncle Jack. I got your favorite. I got three

boxes of Good & Plenty. You can have 'em right now." She wriggled out of his arms and ran to the kitchen, returning in a moment with the boxes of candy. She gravely handed them to Rourke. When he reached for them she pulled them back. "First you have to do a trick," she said.

He pulled his face into a gargoylesque leer and bent down toward her. She shrieked again, really startled, and ran to her father. Westonfield, laughing, picked her up and Rourke quickly followed. "Aw, Trace," he said, "it's just me! I'm sorry. You said you wanted a trick..."

Tracey looked at him, her lower lip trembling. "You scared me, Uncle Jack," she said. "You scared me a whole bunch."

Rourke just stood there and looked helpless. Magaly came to him and gave him a kiss. She whispered in his ear that Tracey was so bright that she might have picked up some of what was happening. Billy came up and shook his hand warmly. He liked shaking his father's partner's hand because he shook it like a man, firm and long, not like some men who shook his hand differently because he was a boy. Jack gave him a wink.

When things settled down a little (it took Tracey about another minute to forgive Rourke), the adults sat drinking a beer. Jack had time for only one. He was on duty, working the Hallowe'en detail at the Fourth Precinct, but had slipped away for an hour to visit Westonfield. He knew that the kids would be there and always took great pleasure in seeing them.

Magaly talked to the children in the living room while Westonfield and Rourke updated each other on the latest information on the investigation. Both had talked to Randazzo. Nothing new in the last several hours. Fires were far fewer than the previous night, Rourke reported, and things were almost calm by contrast.

"Hopefully they got it out of their system," Westonfield said. "Maybe the blood of one fireman was enough to appease the bastards."

"I don't know," Rourke said. "As far as the regular arsonists are concerned, they're probably scared shitless they'll get caught by the great bogeyman. As far as the bogeyman himself—well, maybe one dead fireman's enough. On the other hand, the fact that you exterminated two of his *compañeros* may have proved to be rain on his parade." He chuckled. "What was the point of shooting them dead men after the fight was over, Bill? Dale Ward was so shook up down at Homicide afterwards that I had to help him take his peter out to piss. I made him promise not to tell about that. Anyway, he seemed a little better when I reminded him that mutilating a corpse was only a misdemeanor, and you fellas weren't likely to serve more than ninety days apiece."

"I appreciate your thoughtful crisis intervention, Jack." Westonfield mocked. "I know Dale will be the better for it. And tonight, you did a fine job with my daughter."

Rourke frowned. "Goddamnit, Bill! I didn't know she'd act like that. I adore that baby. I'll make it up to her."

Westonfield grinned. "Settle down, Jack. I know. This mess has got us all a little on edge." He took a sip of beer. "You did good last night. Another few seconds and we might have saved both of those men. You saved the one, anyway. I hate to think that if I'd kicked the door five seconds earlier, Garvey would be alive."

"There you go again," Rourke said. "Blaming yourself. You did good, too. Those scumbags were professionals. Cuban military. Special Forces. It's lucky they didn't make mincemeat out of both you and Ward and then eat Maggie for dessert."

"I suppose," Westonfield said.

"Damn straight," Rourke grunted, looking at his watch. "I gotta go." Before he left he took a cassette out of his jacket pocket and put it in the player in the living room. He picked up Tracey and held her in his arms, taking up a dance pose. He pushed the "play" button. It was *Big Town Boy*, by Shirley Matthews—Tracey's favorite. She giggled with delight as Rourke turned the sound up and swing-danced around the room with her. Rourke shouted to Magaly over the music, "Summer of '63!"

Magaly shouted back, "It's wonderful!" and meant it, though she'd never heard the song before. She stepped forward and joined in, astonished to discover that Rourke was an excellent dancer.

Westonfield and his son watched from their chairs. Like the carved pumpkins in the windows, they smiled with their eyes.

* * *

It took Tracey half an hour to calm down after Rourke left. Her father held her on his lap in the big easy chair. Billy was engrossed again with the movie, lying on the floor in front of the television because the sound was turned down low. Magaly quietly watched Westonfield rock his daughter to sleep. She lay face down on his chest, her eyes half-closed, the fingers of her right hand touching his cheek, slowly moving back and forth. Her breathing was slow, even, content. Once in a while, the fingers moved to her father's mustache and she traced little circles there with her index finger. At last she sighed, closed her eyes for good, and was asleep.

It seemed to Magaly that the mystery of William Westonfield was revealed before her, though it made little sense. That very morning she had pondered the meaning of making love to a man who had just killed other men. Now she watched him holding his daughter in a way that many less violent men would have found uncomfortable. For Bill it was as natural as brushing his teeth. He moved from one world to the other without noticeable effect or effort, out of some incomprehensible existential symbiosis. She smiled at him dreamily. When would the story end? Her heart told her soon. Her eyes strayed to the Ansel Adams calendar on the wall. Beneath *Moonrise Over Yosemite* her eyes ticked off the days until the next full moon. November 22nd. A Friday. According to legend, and according to Professor Saldívar, the *mayombero* could act any time the moon was waxing. That could be as soon as November 7th. But Magaly's intuition said that the evil one had played enough for a little while, that he would wait now until the moon was full and his powers were at their greatest. Then he would strike—in some unexpected, horrible way. She shuddered.

The pumpkins burned brightly in the windows, doing their ancient work of scaring away the wild spirits of the autumn night. The Westonfields, all of them witches, nested inside and waited while the dark storm gathered. Magaly wondered if even Bill would be strong enough to weather it. *Aguanilleo Zarabanda aribo.*

CHAPTER 27

Gabriel, the great *tata nkisi*, had accomplished much on Devil's Night. The next day, All Hallows Eve, he considered his accomplishments: one fireman dead, the television filled with vivid accounts of his death; the paper warehouse burned to the ground; his enemy Westonfield humiliated by the demonstration that the forces of Zarabanda could strike whatever the phase of the moon; the secrecy of his own identity maintained.

Yet he was dissatisfied, wary, troubled by the ease with which Porfirio Pinzón and Gregorio Puente had been dispatched. They were professional and competent compared to Tomás, the bungler, but they were dead. He could see their bullet-riddled bodies in his mind's eye, but he couldn't conjure the details of the deed on account of the irksome mist which continued to surround Westonfield. While the single fireman's death was undeniably a good thing, there should have been more. Had he been there personally, he felt sure he would have been able to kill at least four or five in a few seconds.

Also disconcerting was the fact that the beautiful Latina was assisting Westonfield. It was probably she who explained to them about the phases of the moon. What else had she told them? Certainly too much. Gabriel could read enough of her mind to know that she was romantically attracted to Westonfield. Of itself, this was of small concern, but why would a man like Westonfield complicate his work by involving himself with an arrogant *puta* like Magaly Rodríguez? He himself had never done such a stupid thing, and Westonfield did not appear to be stupid. He would have to deal with her sooner or later. Probably sooner rather than later.

The moon would begin waxing in just one week. This would give him more latitude in planning his actions. But, in truth, he was already tiring of the game. He longed to taste blood again. Not vicariously, as through the actions of Gregorio and Porfirio, but through of the deeds of his own hand. He needed to test his skills and his strength against this witch policeman, Westonfield. He longed for it the way other men longed for the carnal knowledge of women. He yearned to thrust his dagger into Westonfield's belly the way men thrust their cocks into women's bellies; he longed to see red blood erupt from the gaping knife-wound the way creamy semen spurts from the turgid *verga* at orgasm.

In the end, he decided to wait a while longer. Could not Gabriel, the greatest of *mayomberos* yet living, be a little patient? Also, this dangerous policeman would require some effort. Power and cunning would be necessary to overcome him. Why not wait until the full moon, when the magic powers of the faith would be at their zenith? Yes, he would wait until the full moon. Then he would strike the most fearful blow yet, an act so horrific as to turn the pundits to stone, to make tears run red from the eyes of the statues of the saints in front of the churches in the city!

So he waited, and the days passed in the planning of his ascendancy and revenge, always with the bitter knowledge that his enemies were walking unharmed and unhindered in the light of day. When the moon began to wax he felt stronger, alive, hyper-aware. He studied his foes one by one, rolling their qualities around in his seething mind like a terrier worrying a bone. With the single exception of Westonfield, he could see them all clearly now: the Mexican whore, the priest who looked like a rag doll, the fat partner. Some of them had been seen at the burial of the little blonde girl whose death had given him so much pleasure. He had sent an emissary to watch. The spy was successful, and reported back much that was useful. He laughed when he thought of his little arboreal assistant with the big tail and the great brown eyes.

But the terrible dreams! These were the most disquieting elements of all. In them, he was always at his altar preparing his *ndoki*, mixing the powders and oils he knew and loved so well. But there came a silver glow that began in a remote corner of the room. Or was it a corner of his mind? The glow was faint at first, barely discernable. But it grew slowly, flowing silver-white across the room, forcing the darkness back. The light was cold. Not the cold of death, of which he had no fear, but the cold of eternity—the cold that dwells amongst the stars. Before the light reached the altar, it always stopped. But then it changed, dancing about the room, a kaleidoscope. Then the light divided itself into beads of glittering silver, like liquid diamonds, sparkling and reflecting the light in a thousand facets. The light hurt his eyes, stabbing them like spears of ice. Then the beads began to take shape. One by one they gathered together, some large, some small, but all of them possessed of the same shimmering cold. In a while he perceived that the beads formed a sword, neither a rapier nor a stabbing sword, but a great broadsword, a claymore, the two-handed battle sword of the ancient Scots.

In the dreams Gabriel fell back before the altar and stared at the sword. But out of the sword came a voice. Like the light at first, the voice was barely perceptible. Then it grew stronger. But also like the light, it was cold and eternal, a cipher, a synthesis of the language of the invisible particles that flow on gossamer wings through space. And the voice said, "All things come alike to all: there is one event to the righteous, and to the wicked; to the good and to the clean, and to the unclean; to him that sacrificeth, and to him that sacrificeth not: as is the good, so is the sinner; and he that sweareth as he that feareth an oath." And when the voice uttered these words the earth shook, and the fabric of space was torn. Zarabanda screamed in his infernal pit, red pus flowing from his yellow eyes. Then the sword faded slowly away as though it had never been, and the voice was no more. Gabriel did not know what being spoke the words in the dreams, but he knew their origin. What did the dreamwords mean?

He began on Thursday, the seventh of November, when the

moon began to grow. He went out from his home and walked the streets. First he would need a sacrifice for his *ndoki*, the most powerful of all of the *ngangas*. What would he sacrifice? The usual offering was a black cat, but that wouldn't do this time. This was to be a titanic battle of polar forces. No, he would use a human being this time—a human child.

In the dark of the evening he went to a quiet neighborhood on the far west side of the city. It was far enough away from his own neighborhood to offer no evidence of his whereabouts, yet within the city limits of Detroit, so that they would know of a certainty who the perpetrator was. He knew many policemen lived there. He would seek the child of one of them. Would that not be a good start? These policemen were so stupid that it made him laugh. They always made an effort to maintain their privacy—they did not list their telephone numbers in the directories, they sent their children to private schools, they often wore civilian clothes back and forth to work instead of their uniforms. Yet many of them put police union stickers in the back windows of their automobiles. An associate had told Gabriel once that they did this to avoid parking tickets, believing that fellow officers would not ticket a vehicle with one of the stickers in the window. Gabriel wondered delightedly if, after the fact, the father of the child he was about to steal would think this ploy was worth it. He selected a house with two vehicles in the driveway, both of which had police stickers in the windows. There would be young children there because there was a swing set in the back yard and a tricycle in the garage. He waited, feeling. Yes. This one would be good. Then he left for the night.

He returned the next morning. As was usually the case, his intuition was correct. The policeman went to work, leaving the children home with their mother. He watched from a play-park across the street, strolling amongst the swings and slides and monkey bars. It was a sunny day, and unusually warm for early November, near fifty degrees. He sat for a while on a little plastic donkey set upon a coiled spring. It was only two feet above the ground and quite small, so he had to bring his knees up almost to his chest to ride it. He swayed to-and-fro on the little grey donkey for several minutes, holding onto the cracked and peeling ears for balance. The impudent ridiculousness of it amused him and made the time pass.

At noon the side door of the house opened and a woman dressed in a pink ski jacket emerged, followed by a little boy of about four. The woman immediately reentered the house, leaving her son to chase a swirling leaf around the side drive for a moment. Then the woman reemerged, pulling a baby carriage with her, holding the screen door open with her backside until she had maneuvered the carriage out the door. The woman closed the door, called her son to her, and walked down the driveway to the front sidewalk, pushing the carriage in front of her. The little boy skipped a few yards ahead, turning occasionally to see how far behind his mother was. Gabriel watched intently, but he couldn't see into the carriage.

He followed them around a corner along a hedgerow, willing himself to be invisible, willing them not to see him. They did not. When the woman got halfway down the hedgerow, the little boy ran ahead and darted around the end of the shrubs, out of sight, into the driveway of a small house. This neighbor had a certain reputation for oddness and the mother was concerned. She called her son to come back. No response—he was hiding around the corner, impishly waiting to scare her. She called again. No response. The woman felt a little panic. She looked around her. Seeing no one nearby, she trotted quickly up the sidewalk some sixty feet to the next driveway, calling her son's name anxiously, leaving the carriage on the sidewalk. She found him where he'd been hiding and pulled him out by the arm, scolding him for running ahead and for playing silly games. The woman was so relieved that her son was all right, and so intent on lecturing him, that she was nearly back to the place where she had left the baby before she realized the carriage was gone. At first she almost didn't credit her senses. She stopped and looked around as one stunned. She looked up and down the sidewalk. Nothing. She looked back the way she had come—she could see several blocks down. Nothing.

"Mommie," her son said, "where's Carrie?"

Pitifully, the woman ran back to the corner, looking first one way and then the other. Nothing. She stood rooted in place for a long moment, swiveling her head, expecting, miraculously, to see the carriage where only a moment before it had been invisible. Slowly at first, like a loon heard far across a lake at dusk, a keening erupted from the woman's throat. But the moan turned abruptly into a grief-stricken wail, the death-agony of a soul in hell. The little boy began to cry.

* * *

Night. His house. He took the baby from the corner where it lay sleeping and studied it. Pink. Weak. He felt only contempt. But he was thankful to Zarabanda that he had been so easily rewarded for his efforts. These policemen! What weaklings. He had set the big black cauldron full of water to boil on the stove an hour earlier. It was ready. He took the baby into the kitchen...

When he smelled the aroma of the boiling flesh he ejaculated, but his penis was still turgid. He laughed all the while. Then he let the kettle cool. He removed the child's bones and put them in a plastic bag, forking out a piece of tender meat when he was done, consuming it with relish, slurping the broth lustily. Then he took the bones to some woods he knew near Ann Arbor, and buried them in the soft earth beneath a white oak tree.

According to the dictates of the making of the *ndoki*, he retrieved them twenty-four hours later and returned them to his home. He went out into the night again, to a cemetery. Not Woodmere this time, lest the police be watching it, but to another in New Boston, to the south of the city. It was a huge place, well known to him. He worked hard all through the long night, ripping crypts from the walls of the mausoleum by mien strength and prying open the lids of seven coffins. He removed seven phalanges from the fingers of seven corpses, slipping them into the pocket of his jacket, leaving the ruined caskets where they lay upon the ground. Next he scraped some earth from the surfaces of seven new graves, placing it in a cloth bag he had brought for this purpose. Then he returned home again.

One more time he set the kettle to boil, returning the sanctified bones to the fetid stew. He tossed in raw garlic and red pepper. Next he sprinkled dark rum over the gurgling cauldron, saying a prayer of thanks and supplication to Zarabanda. Finally, he lit a fine Cuban cigar and smoked it for a while, his yellow-black eyes glazed over, watching the magic contents of the offering. After a while, he inhaled deeply, sucking the smoke of the cigar deep into his lungs. Then he leaned over and blew the smoke in a silver-grey cloud into the steam boiling off the kettle. He let it cool once again, taking the whole cauldron and its contents to the woods near Ann Arbor this time. He buried it in the same hallowed place he had buried the bones the night before. In yet another twenty-four hours he returned and disinterred it, carrying it contentedly home. The *ndoki* was completed. At last he was ready to strike.

CHAPTER 28

Dale Ward read the report a second time and set it down. "It's fucking crazy," he said. "Do you know these people, Bill? How's the mother?"

"I know Joe Santini a little," Westonfield said. "Never met his wife. Or his kids."

"You think the kid's dead?" Ward asked.

"Yeah," Westonfield answered simply. "I think the baby's dead."

"Aw, hell, I wouldn't be so sure," Ward protested wishfully, his mind unwilling to accept the horror of what might have occurred. "Maybe the kidnapper was some childless woman who wanted a kid of her own. You read about it in the paper sometimes. You know—a woman who can't have kids sneaks into a hospital and snatches a baby. That's bad enough, but at least then this kid would be alive."

"It was him," Westonfield said again.

"What makes you so sure?"

"It was him, Dale. Get over it. The baby's dead. He used it to make what Magaly calls a *ndoki*. It was only a few months old. I just hope it didn't suffer too much."

"What makes you so cocksure?" Ward repeated, folding his hands in his lap and putting his feet up on Rourke's desk at the Fourth Precinct. Sunlight streamed through the dirty window. It had been warm for three days. "As big as our case is, it's not everything. Other crimes don't stop on account of ours. This kidnapping could be anything." He took a deep breath, not really wanting to hear Westonfield's reasoning. "Take a look out that window, Bill. Let's go for a ride. Maybe it'll help you shake the blues."

"It's November the tenth," Westonfield said, dashing Ward's faint hopes for blissful ignorance. "The moon's been waxing for three days, Dale. He's ready now. He killed that baby for two reasons: to make his magic and to spite me." He looked out the window as Ward bade him, but he didn't see the same world Dale saw. He felt very old. "I want it to be over," he muttered. "I just want it all to end."

Ward stood up resolutely. "Let's get some air. It will do you good."

They found Magaly at the front desk, talking to Larry Runyon.

"We're going out for a spin, Maggie," Ward said. "Ready?"

"A spin to where?" Magaly asked. "How long you gonna be?"

"Not long," Ward said. "We're just going to drive around awhile."

"Sounds boring to me," Magaly said. "I'd rather stay and talk to Larry."

After twenty minutes in the car, most of it silent, both men lost in their own thoughts, Ward said, "I've been thinking about this girl a lot..."

Westonfield gave him a sidelong glance. "Oh?"

"The one that hit me in the back with the frozen rabbit."

"A story like that has a way of sticking with you," Westonfield offered. "I remember."

"Well, as I say, I've been thinking about her."

"Join the crowd," Westonfield said laconically.

Ward was puzzled. "You've been thinking about her, too?"

"No, Dale," Westonfield said, grinning, "I don't even know the girl, remember? What I mean is, I've also been thinking about the ladies."

"Oh."

"Do you love her?" Westonfield asked.

"Hell, I don't know," Ward said. "I think about her all the time."

"I believe you," Westonfield said. "But do you love her? They're not the same thing."

"Guess so."

"Rourke says I love them all forever."

"Love who?"

"My exes."

"Really," Ward said.

"That's what the man says."

"Exactly what does he mean?"

Westonfield's eyes ranged over the passing scene as he drove, seeing nothing, seeing everything. "I don't know," he said. "But that's what he says."

"Do you think he's right?" Ward asked.

Westonfield shrugged.

Ward was silent for a minute. "But this girl. I keep thinking of her," he said.

"Do you like it, Dale?" Westonfield asked. "That is, do you like it when you think about her?"

Ward considered his answer. He was never sure where Westonfield was coming from. "Sure," he said finally. "I like it fine."

Westonfield smiled cryptically. "Good. Sometimes it's its own reward, thinking about them."

"You're weird."

"I never heard that before."

"But I'm debating whether I want to get her back," Ward said. "I'm serious."

"So am I," Westonfield said. "What's to debate?"

"Well, we don't get along for one thing. She tried to kill me with my own rabbit."

"Then why do you want to be with her again?"

"Like I said, I think I love her."

"Well, maybe so, Dale," Westonfield said. "But I'd say, if I was to bet, that you're just filling in the gaps with what you *wish* was true, not what's true."

"You are so fucking weird."

"Christ, the girl tried to brain you."

"I know, but—"

"What I'm saying," Westonfield interjected, "is that now that it's over, maybe you're remembering the good parts over the bad parts. It could be you're filling in the blanks with what you'd *like* her to be. Be careful of idealizing her, Dale. We guys do that sometimes. Understand? We look at a girl, and where she's deficient, we simply fill in the gaps with our dreams. We paint them with a romantic brush, just like paint-by-the-numbers. Hell, if it ain't really there, we just add it on until we've got our ideal. Trouble is, when we do that, they're *not* our ideal. The only thing we've done is to play a trick on ourselves. We've made ourselves believe in someone who exists only in our minds." He reached over and patted Ward on the knee. "That's what I mean about just thinking about them. You're better off with your memories. You can't go back. You really can't."

Ward looked at him. "Do you love Magaly?"

To Ward's surprise—he expected silence, if not an outright rebuff—Westonfield said, "Sure I do."

A minute later Westonfield pulled to the curb in front of the Highwaymen motorcycle clubhouse at Livernois and Clayton. Even though it was early, several Harley-Davidson "hogs" were lined up in front. "Let's go in," Westonfield said.

Just as they were walking past the row of polished bikes, Westonfield stopped, studying them. He had one of those strangely placid looks on his face which Ward had learned meant nothing but trouble. When most men looked like that it meant they were content. When most men became angry, there was a fire in their eyes. But not Westonfield. Violence on his part was usually preceded by a strange, eery calm. As casually as if stepping on a bug he leaned back, raised his foot, and kicked one of the motorcycles over. Ward went pale, expecting a horde of pissed-off outlaw bikers to come storming out of the building. He eyed the fallen bike with consternation: the rear-view mirror was snapped off, the handlebars were twisted, the expensive paint job was gouged.

The door swung open and, not surprisingly, three burly, unshaven Highwaymen came out wearing their colors. Their eyes went first to the damaged motorcycle, then to the two policemen standing on the sidewalk. "What the fuck is goin' on here?" one of them said. He had shoulder length, strawberry-blonde hair, parted in the middle, and a long beard like ZZ Top.

Westonfield watched them silently.

The man took a step closer, intent on throttling the silent pair, when he took notice of the unmarked police car and then looked harder at Westonfield. "Oh," he said, "you're Westonfield, ain't you? I seen you around. What did you kick that bike over for? You don't have a right to do that. I know you're a cop, but you ain't got that kinda right. You can come on in and talk to us like we was men. We'll talk to you." The man was complaining, but to Ward's astonishment, he was clearly afraid. His lips were trembling. There were three of them, probably several more were in the clubhouse, but he was afraid. The biker motioned for the others to help him and they lifted up the bike, resetting the kickstand. "This cycle's fucked up pretty good," the biker said. "I'd like to know who's gonna pay for the damage."

Then several other equally scruffy Highwaymen emerged from the door. Ward reached for his radio to call for help, dreading the inevitable consequences even as he did so. What would his report say when it was all over? That they had been driving by and felt like destroying a motorcycle? But he was surprised again. Among the newcomers was a smallish, clean-shaven man with a florid complexion and freckles. He wore a black leather cap over his black hair, which, Ward noted, was shorter and neater than that of the other men. He had piercing green eyes. He ignored Ward and looked at Westonfield. "That's my bike, Bill," the man said in a thick Irish brogue. "Mine for sure. How come ye to do that?"

Westonfield started, looked hard at the man. "Well, I didn't know it was yours," he said, smiling one of those strange Westonfield half-smiles. They were the first words he'd uttered since he got out of the car. "I heard you were out of town, Bob."

The man studied Westonfield for another few seconds. Then he nodded cannily, a wisp of a smile flickering across his face in answer to Westonfield's. He went to his bike, whistled with disgust, and said, "Fucked it up pretty good, you Welsh bastard." He ran his hands over the scuffed paint, feeling the dents in the gas tank, clucking like a hen. Without taking his eyes off his motorcycle he said, "Who's the lad yer with?"

When Westonfield didn't immediately answer, the man looked up. "I say, who is he?"

"He's my new partner," Westonfield said, looking warily at the other bikers, who were milling around muttering. "I think it would be better if we got in off the street, don't you?"

"Suppose so," Bob said. "Let's go in. Bring yer wallet. I hope ye got paid today. Ye can even bring yer quiet partner along, if ye'd like." He looked sidelong at Ward, taking stock. "This one here ain't the man yer real partner is. Good Irishman, Jack."

Ward, true to his description, was silent.

* * *

When they walked out of the clubhouse an hour later, Ward said, "That was one hell of a strange way to set up a meeting."

"Was it?" Westonfield said.

"Seems to me."

"Well, it worked out all right."

"Guess so," Ward said. "If you call owing a motorcycle gangster five hundred dollars for screwing up his bike working out all right. Are you really going to pay him?"

"Sure I'm going to pay him," Westonfield said. "I screwed up his motorcycle."

"How do you know the guy?" Ward asked, changing his tack.

"He helped me out once."

"Oh?"

"A few years ago I was having a hard time with a crowd after a fight at one of the topless joints on Michigan. It was a hot summer night. Ol' Bob McMullen happened to come riding by on his hog. Can't say for sure why he did it, but he stopped to help. He jumped off his bike and waded right in. We've been half-assed friends ever since." After a moment Westonfield said, "I feel bad about his bike."

"What if the bike had belonged to somebody else?" Ward asked.

"Well, I guess he'd have a fucked up bike," Westonfield said.

Ward mulled it over. "Do you think he'll actually help you?"

"Why not?" Westonfield asked. "He helped me before."

"Right, but that was before you fucked up his motorcycle."

Westonfield looked at Ward with genuine incredulity. "What has that got to do with anything?" he asked.

* * *

Tracey loved to look at the collage of Thanksgiving scenes stapled to the bulletin board in her first grade classroom. The Pilgrims had funny hats and buckles on their shoes. Some of them sported guns—for hunting turkeys and deer, Mrs. Carmichael said—but the guns didn't look like the guns her father had. The Indians looked happy, smiles on their old-penny faces as they made offerings of vegetables and game to the hungry white people. Tracey wondered about the offerings. She didn't fully understand what took place between the people of the Old World and the people of the New, but she suspected that all had not been perfect between them, whatever the collage might suggest. Maybe the Indians didn't really like the white people very much. Maybe the offerings of food were meant only to make the strange new people believe that all was well—

then they wouldn't use their guns to hurt the Indians. The idea intrigued Tracey. She thought she would ask Mrs. Carmichael about it.

She was looking at the illustrations, pondering the truth about Indians and Pilgrims, when a sudden dread fell on her. She was sure a hand grasped her shoulder from behind. She spun around to see. Nothing. She looked toward the front of the class, but everything was as it should be. Mrs. Carmichael sat unconcernedly at her desk studying a book. She looked toward the back. The rest of the children were napping with their heads on their desks. She shivered. This was the second time this had happened. She went to Mrs. Carmichael, so quiet that her teacher didn't hear her approach. "Excuse me," she said softly.

Sharon Carmichael looked up, not at all surprised to see that it was the Westonfield girl. Tracey was far ahead of most of the other students and sometimes found naptime boring. She would occasionally even coax her teacher into lengthy private discourse. It wasn't entirely fair to the other children, monopolizing class time that way, but she saw no real harm in it. Besides, ever the teacher, she enjoyed her one-on-one chats with Tracey. The girl's intelligence and unassuming charm were endearing.

"Can I help you?" Mrs. Carmichael asked.

"I'm not sure," Tracey answered.

"Is something wrong?"

Tracey meant to tell her about the invisible hand, but balked when it occurred to her that Mrs. Carmichael would probably accuse her of having an overactive imagination. So instead she said, "It's about the Pilgrims and the Indians," and she told her teacher about her ideas.

"I see," Sharon Carmichael said. "Have you discussed this with your parents?"

Tracey shook her head.

Sharon Carmichael believed her. With any other child she would have attributed this sticky wicket to undue parental cynicism, but with Tracey that wasn't necessarily true—she was quite capable of applying her own shrewd analysis. "I think you're pretty clever," Mrs. Carmichael said. "But the Pilgrims and the Indians were friends at least *some* of the time. That's what matters, isn't it? Friendship?"

"I guess so," Tracey said.

"The thing is, honey, I think the ideas you have might be a little hard for the other students to understand."

"But I'm right, aren't I?"

Clearly, Tracey wasn't going to be so easily put off. Mrs. Carmichael thought for a minute and said, "A lot of smart people have studied these things, and you know what? I think you're right. The Pilgrims weren't always kind to the Indians. Sometimes there was fighting. And then the Indians did bad things, too. But I don't want you to dwell on it. That was a very long time ago, and now we know for sure that we're friends. See?"

Tracey nodded thoughtfully, thanked her, and returned to her seat. But she couldn't get rid of the feeling that something was wrong, something that had nothing to do with the first Thanksgiving. Even at lunch in the cafeteria she felt uneasy. She turned to her friend Jill who sat next to her eating a sandwich. "It felt like somebody touched me on my shoulder in class today," she ventured.

Jill rolled her eyes. "I bet it was Terry Fullbright. He thinks he's *so* funny. If Mrs. Carmichael catches him, he'll really be in for it. He'll have to stand in the corner forever. Terry's a poop."

"It wasn't Terry," Tracey said glumly.

Jill frowned. "Who was it then?"

"I don't know," Tracey said.

"You didn't see him?"

"No," Tracey said. "It wasn't anybody in our class. It was like somebody was grabbing me, but when I turned around nobody was there."

"Terry's fast," Jill reflected.

"It wasn't Terry," Tracey repeated. "He was sitting at his desk when the hand touched me. I looked real quick. It wasn't him."

Jill looked closely at her. "You think it was a ghost?"

"Maybe," Tracey said.

Recess followed lunch. It took place in the school parking lot which served as a playground. It was warm for the tenth of November and some sun filtered through the scattered clouds. A breeze sent brown leaves skittering across the play area. Tracey, Jill, and their friend Matilda stood together off to one side. According to rites established in times immemorial, the girls and boys segregated themselves. The girls skipped rope, played hopscotch, or stood chattering like birds in cliques. The boys played contact basketball or tossed rubber balls against the wall of the school while their chums ran the gauntlet. A few of the sturdier types secreted themselves on the grass behind a tree, engaging in a surreptitious game of mumblety-peg. Sharon Carmichael and two other teachers stood watch over their charges.

"Do you guys believe in ghosts?" Matilda asked. She had just been informed by Jill that Tracey thought a ghost had visited her in the classroom.

"I guess so," Jill said.

"Do you think a ghost touched you, Tracey?" Matilda persisted.

But Tracey was barely listening. She didn't particularly care whether her friends believed her or not. *She* believed that someone was there, and that was all that mattered. "Don't know," she said.

"You should tell Mrs. Carmichael," Jill opined.

"She wouldn't believe me," Tracey said.

"Maybe cuz you're making it all up," Matilda said accusingly.

"I'm not making it up."

Jill and Matilda looked at each other, then relented in unspoken agreement. The game was fun. It didn't matter if it was true.

Out of the corner of her eye Tracey became aware of a big

man standing on the sidewalk at the opposite end of the school. She noticed him because he looked out of place. He was too far away for her to tell much about him, but she could see that he was a black man. She felt somehow that he was watching her. She shaded her eyes with her hands and squinted hard, trying to see if she recognized him. She didn't. The other girls turned to look, but the man was gone. They saw nothing. Tracey couldn't have described what happened to him if she'd tried. One instant he was there, real as real, the next he simply melted away in a sort of glittering mist.

"What?" Jill said.

"What?" Matilda repeated, with considerable irritation.

"It was him," Tracey said. "It was the ghost."

"Where is he?" Jill demanded, looking down the length of the school. "I don't see no ghost."

"Way down there," Tracey insisted. "I saw him!"

"How come we didn't see him then?" Matilda asked, becoming a little less inclined to pursue the game.

Tracey didn't answer. The apparition both startled and scared her. Casting another wistful glance down the street, she protectively collected her two friends and moved toward the center of the playground. But only a few minutes later, her eyes were once again drawn away from the playground. The dark man stood watching, this time much closer. He was directly across the street. Tracey nudged Jill. "Look!"

Jill and Matilda saw him now. They could no longer doubt her. They turned back in shocked unison to proclaim their instant conversion, only to be met by yet another horror—Tracey's eyes had gone completely blank. There was no trace of recognition in them. Even worse, she began to walk slowly across the playground toward the ghost without a word. The girls tore themselves away from the terrifying tableau and fled to the monitors, screaming their heads off. Mrs. Carmichael looked up and saw Tracey walking stiffly toward the street. She ran toward her in near-panic, dropping her purse, spilling its contents in a cascade onto the pavement. She yelled Tracey's name and caught her by the arm just as she stepped off the curb. Tracey started as if awakened from a dream. "I'm okay!" she bawled through instant tears, but she couldn't say anything else. Sheer terror sucked the air out of her lungs. It seemed to her that the dark man wanted her to go with him, and when the other girls ran away, she had simply complied. Then, from another point of power, she felt the unexpected presence of her father—and he said *no*. This made the dark man angry. But her father stepped forward and the spell was broken. The dark man disappeared again on the mist. She was free.

Afterwards, the three little girls tearfully recounted to Mrs. Carmichael their story of the bogeyman. She scanned the area carefully for a long time while the girls hugged her skirt. She saw nothing save a small brown squirrel playing in a tree.

* * *

Millie Westonfield was drinking a cup of coffee in the teachers' lounge at the Livonia high school where she taught when a student assistant brought her a message. She had been thinking about her upcoming marriage to Derrick Sawyer, playing with the new name in her mind. *Millie Sawyer.* It sounded strange to her. She had been Millicent Westonfield for sixteen years, and now that name was going to cease to be. With the stroke of a pen, with an uttered phrase from a minister's lips, the person named Millie Westonfield would be gone forever. *There, you see!* she thought. *That's the effect the man has on you. Through sheer force of his personality you became bound to him, and you forgot about a time when you had never heard of a man named Bill Westonfield.* In fairness, she didn't have a sense that Bill wanted it that way, that he set out to dominate her life. In fact, when it happened, he probably found it to be a burden. Maybe an unbearable one. Hell, maybe that's why he left. Goddamn his devotion to himself, his obsession with duty and honor! Well, that wasn't completely fair, either, was it? He was a doting husband and father most of the time.

Thoughtful, sympathetic, strong. Always strong. His strength was so great that it made a mockery of hers, even if she, too, was strong. It was a strength reserved for—what? Only Bill knew the answer to that. Maybe even he didn't know. Anyway, that chapter in her life was over now. Over and done with. With Derrick she at least could make mistakes. She could be herself without fearing to fail in some way.

She buried her tumultuous thoughts and read the note: *Call Sharon Carmichael at Tracey's school at once.* A thrill of fear shot up her spine. Tracey's school never called. When she left for school that morning she'd been fine... Well, there was that episode yesterday, when Tracey had said someone was talking to her with foreign words from inside her own head. Considering the source, the statement wasn't all that unusual, and she had mostly dismissed it. She had absently jotted down the phonetic spelling of the strange words Tracey uttered and put the slip of paper into her purse. Maybe the "voice" had to do with something frightening Bill had said. She felt a flood of anger again, thinking that Bill might have stirred Tracey up to the point of being sick.

She picked up the telephone and dialed, waited impatiently for the school secretary to answer. After seven rings Nikki Pomeroy picked up the phone.

"Hello, Nikki, this is Millie Westonfield. I just received a message. Sharon Carmichael wanted to talk to me?"

"Oh, yes. Hi, Millie, Sharon will be right with you."

A ninety second wait. Finally, "This is Mrs. Carmichael."

"Hi, Sharon. Millie Westonfield."

"Oh, hello, Millie. Thanks for getting back to me. I'm sorry to bother you at work, but I decided I really should touch bases with you as soon as possible."

"Is Tracey all right?"

"She's fine."

"She hasn't been hurt? She's not sick?"

"No, she seems perfectly fine. We just had, well, a strange episode on the playground. Tracey and two other girls claim they saw a man watching them from down the street. Normally, I'd chalk it up to six-year-old imaginations. But the girls seem so adamant—especially Tracey."

"They say a man was watching them?"

"Tracey says he was a big black man. She says he was just standing there staring at her. I guess she pointed him out to the other girls, Jill Navarre and Matilda Jefferson. Jill and Matilda say they didn't see him at first. Tracey says he just disappeared. The girls moved to the middle of the playground where they would feel safer, but then the other girls saw him, too. It crosses my mind that it might have been Jill and Matilda's imaginations, fired up by Tracey's insistence at having seen the man. Tracey seemed to play it to the fullest, if playing she was. I caught her walking toward the street. If there *was* a man, maybe she was just curious to see who he was. I can't say for sure. Anyway, I looked up and down the street myself after the girls reported the incident to me, and I didn't see anything. Of course, if there actually was somebody there, he could have run away by the time I got there."

Millie was shocked. "Where is Tracey now? You're sure she's all right?"

"She's back in class, right as rain."

"Is she frightened?"

"She doesn't seem to be," Mrs. Carmichael said. "Frankly, I get the feeling it's almost an adventure to her. She says the man is a ghost."

"Are you absolutely sure that there was no prowler out on the street?" Millie asked.

"No, I'm not. But I doubt it very seriously. This is a good neighborhood, as you know. But with something like this, you can never say never. As I said, I looked. I didn't see anything unusual. I didn't see anyone out there. Would you feel better if I got Tracey out of class to come talk to you on the telephone?"

"Well, not as long as she seems all right."

"She does, and we'll watch her closely."

"Then I guess not. But you'll keep an eye out for strangers around school property?"

"We will. We've notified the janitor. He'll help us keep a lookout."

"Good, and you can be sure I'll give her a good talking-to tonight."

Millie finished the conversation and slipped the receiver into the cradle thoughtfully. It occurred to her that her first instinct might have been right. Could Bill's bizarre life finally have succeeded in damaging Tracey, causing emotional or behavioral problems at school? Tracey was always precocious, but this was too much—unless, that is, there actually *was* a stranger on the schoolgrounds. What about that horrific case of the baby stolen from the neighborhood where they used to live? It wasn't so very far from the school. The more she thought about it, the more she worried. She pulled her purse from beneath her chair and plopped it on the table, rummaging through it, looking for the slip of paper she had written on yesterday. She found it, opened it up, and studied it for a while. It seemed to be nothing but meaningless gibberish. Nevertheless, she reached for the telephone again and dialed another number.

The desk officer caught Westonfield just as he and Ward came walking back into the station. "Telephone, Sarge."

"Who is it?"

"Your ex."

Westonfield picked up the flashing extension on one of the telephones behind the desk. "Westonfield."

"Bill, this is Millie."

"What's wrong?"

"Sorry to bother you at work."

"It's all right. Is anything wrong?"

"I'm calling about Tracey—"

His heart was in his mouth.

"She's all right. She's in school," Millie said calmly. Then she told him about her conversation with Mrs. Carmichael.

Westonfield almost dropped the telephone. He screamed for Ward to get on another line to the Redford police and have them get units to Tracey's school. Their man was there. Oh, God, let there be time! He returned to Millie. "Where is she?" he shouted demonically.

"Bill, what's going on? I just said she's in school."

"I know she's in fucking school!" he yelled hoarsely. "Where is she *in* the school?" He was shouting so loud he doubted she could understand. "Millie," he repeated, barely mastering himself, "where *exactly* is she in the goddamn school?"

"She's in her class with Sharon Carmichael. And quit shouting at me! Her teacher says she's just fine. What on earth is going on?"

Faint hope flooded over him like a sheet of cold water. "Listen, Millie! Tracey is in terrible danger. Call the school right now. Tell them to take her to the office immediately. By herself. No other students. The Redford police are on the way. They'll know what to do. Do it now!" He slammed the phone down as he heard Ward screaming at the Redford police dispatcher to hurry.

Millie felt her life unraveling in one heartrending moment. Jesus, God in heaven, what was happening? She looked unseeingly at the strange words scrawled across the sheet of paper in her hand. Then the words came into focus. She read them aloud: *Aguanilleo Zarabanda aribo.*

Magaly had been talking to Larry Runyon in a small office behind the desk. When she heard the commotion, she ran out in time to see Westonfield and Ward run frantically around the corner of the desk and disappear down the corridor toward the garage. She followed, almost tripping over her own feet in her haste. "Wait a minute!" she shouted. "I'm right behind you."

The speedometer on the old unmarked Chrysler topped out at 110 miles an hour, stopped and jiggled in place, then crept up to 115. The whole car shuddered as Westonfield drove wildly northwest on the I-96 expressway toward Redford Township, the portable blue light blinking hypnotically on the dash, the siren shrieking in their ears. They covered the eighteen miles, most of it expressway, in just twelve minutes. When they barreled up, careening to a sliding halt in front of the school, Westonfield saw that three Redford police cruisers were already there, their lightbars flashing silently above the empty vehicles. Several uniformed policemen were walking along the sidewalks around the school, searching between the houses, up the driveways, and behind shrubbery.

He and Ward leaped from their car and raced toward the school, followed by Magaly. They slammed open the main door of the building and slid along the polished floor toward the administrative office. They burst past two uniformed cops who guarded the door, waving their badges—and there was Tracey, sitting calmly in a chair, talking to Mrs. Carmichael.

"Hi, Daddy," she said in surprise. "How come you're here?" Then she frowned. "Did I do something bad?" Westonfield swept her into his arms, hugging her close, nestling his nose into her hair, smelling her little girl smell. "No, baby," he said softly. "You haven't done anything wrong." Magaly walked in and instantly burst into tears. Then Tracey started to cry. The three of them stood in the office clutching each other for a long time.

Twenty minutes later Magaly handed Tracey over to Millie, who had just arrived. The women looked at each other, said nothing, but Tracey grinned impishly at them both. Westonfield was out with the Redford police, stalking up and down the sidewalks, examining every bit of tree fluff, every scrap of discarded Popsicle wrapper, and every twig he came across. The Detroit police crime lab evidence technicians were en route, and would be arriving shortly.

Magaly joined him. "Was he here?" she asked. "Was he here at the school?"

"I believe Morgan," he said. "But we haven't found a thing out here. I doubt if we will." He looked at her. "But you tell *me*. Was he?"

Magaly's eyes scanned the neighborhood. She closed her eyes, took a deep breath, let it out, stood very still. Then she said, "Yes, he was here. He stood where we're standing now. On this very spot. He was here. Watching."

Westonfield nodded. "But he could have grabbed my daughter, Maggie. He could have grabbed Morgan. Why didn't he?"

"Can't you see it, Bill?" she said wonderingly. "It was Tracey. She recognized him. She told her mother. She told her friends. And finally, even when he was here, she told her teachers. She saved herself, and maybe her friends, too. She beat him." Magaly smiled. "She's your daughter. She's a witch. What did you expect?"

"All right," Westonfield said, sparing a little grin, moving a strand of her hair away from her forehead as he loved to do. "Tracey beat him. Now what?"

An unpleasant, ethereal smell faintly teased at Magaly's nostrils. "I can smell him," she said. "I smell his foul stench. *Azúfre*. Can you smell it?"

"I smell it."

"He's been beaten here," Magaly said. "And he knows it, Bill. He'll be frustrated and he'll be afraid—maybe for the first time in his life. Now I think he'll wait. He'll wait for the full moon."

CHAPTER 29

Westonfield and Magaly lay warm together in bed, their limbs intertwined. It was ten o'clock in the evening on the twenty-first of November. Eleven days had passed since the harrowing incident at Tracey's school. Indian Summer had faded along with the intensity of the near-tragedy for them, and the weather had turned cold.

"I have to call Vickers," Magaly said lazily.

Westonfield squinted at her. Her face was close, and his near-vision was getting noticeably worse every year. He had to move his head back several inches in order to focus on her eyes. "Something I should know about?"

"No," she said, "just reporting in. I told you how nervous he gets when I don't call."

"I remember. You did update him on the baby's kidnapping and on the incident at Morgan's school…"

"Of course, but that was a week and a half ago," Magaly said. "The point is Herman knows about the killer's lunar cycle. He's probably as nervous as we are. Tomorrow's the full moon. He'll feel better if I contact him and just say nothing's going on."

"So call him," Westonfield said.

She threw back the covers and rolled over him to use the telephone on his side of the bed. As she reached for the receiver, Westonfield luxuriated in the feel of her warmth on his chest, her breasts dragging lightly across the hairs, tickling him. He cupped her right buttock in his hand, squeezed it gently.

Magaly made the call. As she had predicted, Vickers was as nervous as a cat. She reassured him that all was well, that he had been informed about everything of significance, and that, so far as she was aware, nothing had happened since the school incident of the tenth. He gave her a hard time over her choice of the word "significance." She should have known better. She assured him that she most definitely understood what the word meant, schmoozed him a little, and hung up.

She felt Westonfield's erect penis poking her belly. "What's this all about?" she asked, sliding next to him, kissing him and taking him into her hand.

"You," Westonfield whispered when she finished her kiss and moved her head back slightly. "It's about you."

An hour afterwards he lay gazing at the ceiling, morosely considering that it was the ceiling of a house that didn't belong to him. Then he looked into the eyes of a woman he wasn't married to. "Tomorrow is the last day," he said. "If we're right, that is. Truth be told, Maggie, I'm tired." His eyes traced the random patterns in the stucco paint on the ceiling. "My kids have been pulled out of school, getting tutored at home. Guards are with them everywhere. Me and my partner are split up. I'm living in this place that isn't home."

"Where is home?" Maggie asked. "Do you know where home is, Bill?"

"Not anymore," Westonfield answered.

"Me neither. We're stones doomed to roll, me and you. Carol Rourke said that to me—that I'm a stone doomed to roll. And look at you! You're not happy unless you're hanging over the edge of a cliff and an elephant's tromping on your fingers."

He grinned at her. "I suppose you're right."

"Of course, I'm right," she said. "But at least we have each other, fellow stone." She squeezed his penis.

The telephone rang. Magaly was still lying half across Westonfield so she grabbed the receiver. "This is Magaly. May I help you?"

There was a long pause on the other end, but Magaly could hear breathing. Then, "Is Bill there?"

Magaly didn't know the voice. "For you," she said, prying

Westonfield's fingers off of her butt and plopping the receiver into his hand.

"I like your ass better," he whispered to her. "Westonfield," he said louder into the phone.

"Bill..." said a man's voice. Familiar, but not immediately identifiable.

"Yes."

"This is McMullen."

"Who?"

"McMullen. Bob McMullen."

"Oh, Jesus! Hey, Bob, what's going on?"

"I've got the information ye wanted."

"What?"

McMullen was suddenly irritated. "Look, if this is a bad time—"

"No, Bob. It's not a bad time."

"Sounds like ye've got a lady over there," McMullen said with amusement.

"Yes I do," Westonfield said.

"Nice to have a lady, ain't it?"

"Yes."

"I remember yer wife, Susan. Very pretty woman."

"Yes."

McMullen chuckled. "Well, anyway, I found out where that fella lives."

Silence.

"Bill?"

Westonfield was stunned. "Sorry, Bob," he hissed. "You know where the son-of-a-bitch is? Right now?"

"Holy Mother o' God, man, I don't know if he's there this exact minute," McMullen said. "It ain't like I got a tail on him. I just happen to know where he's been hangin' his hat."

"I understand," Westonfield soothed. "Where, Bob?"

"On 31st. Just south of the I-94." He gave Westonfield the address.

"All right. Who gave this to you?"

"Are ye serious now, copper?"
"No."
"I didn't think so."
"Anything else?"
"What more do ye want, ye greedy sheep-shagger?"
"Nothing," Westonfield said.
"Well, there *is* a little more, whether ye want it or not," McMullen said, chuckling. "I got his name for ye. They say he goes by 'Gabriel.' Big black Cuban. Bad motherfucker. Gabriel. Very, very bad."
"Okay, Bob. And thanks! Thank you."
"Just don't get killed. Ye owe me big time for my bike, ye bloody Welsh bastard." He hung up.

Westonfield rolled over and looked into Magaly's eyes. "That was Bob McMullen. He just told me where Gabriel is."
"Who?"
"His name is Gabriel, Magaly—and I know where he is!"

She sat bolt upright, her breasts swaying, now unnoticed. "Gabriel," she said, the name sticking in her throat. "Yes. I can see that. The arrogant bastard."

Westonfield was puzzled. "What?"
"Gabriel was an angel, Bill. One of the most powerful. He was God's messenger. His pedigree is very confused in the mythology. But some say he was bad, fallen in some way, like Lucifer."
"You don't think it's his real name?"
"I don't know," Magaly said. "It could be. But there's a point to the name. You can bet on it. He loves to joke, doesn't he?"
"Yes."
"So maybe this is another joke."
"Well," Westonfield said, "maybe now the joke's on him. We know where he is, Maggie. If McMullen's information is correct, we've got him." He kissed her on the cheek and launched himself out of bed. There was a hell of a lot to do.

First he got on the telephone to Dale Ward in Trenton, told

him to get downtown immediately. Then he called Rourke at the Fourth Precinct, told him to stand by. Finally, he called Chief Milton Lucas's pager number. Lucas called back just as Westonfield was finishing getting dressed.

"Is this good information?" Lucas asked.

"Yes."

"You're sure?"

"Yes."

"All right, then," Lucas said. "Get with the Control Center. Find out who the on-call judge is. Let's get us a search warrant for the 31st address. You know the routine. Then call Identification and have 'em run this Gabriel every which way from Sunday. FBI. Immigration. Everything. I'll notify the Special Response Team, get 'em mobilized. We'll have everybody out to the Fourth Precinct within an hour. We should be able to hit the motherfucker within two hours. Okay?"

"I'll be there, chief. We'll be ready."

* * *

Westonfield and Magaly walked into the Fourth Precinct Power Shift office at 10:55 P.M. Rourke was waiting for them, eating a Payday candy bar, his feet propped up on his battered desk. "Hey, kids," he said, waving his hand like Buster Keaton. "Just finishing lunch."

"Where's Ward?" Westonfield asked as Magaly hugged and kissed Rourke.

"He's in the shithouse," Rourke said. "I think all the excitement's about to kill the boy."

"I hope a little diarrhea's all he's got to worry about," Westonfield said.

"SRT's forming up in the parking lot," Rourke said. "Lucas is here himself. So's your favorite commander. They're in her office. They told me to send you in when you got here." He grinned. "It gets better every fucking day, don't it?"

Westonfield nodded. "Yeah, it's great, Jack." He reached

into his pocket and retrieved a small bag of M&Ms. He tossed them to Rourke. "Here, in case you run low. By the way," he added, "Bob McMullen says hello. He likes you. Better than Ward, anyway. I knew you'd be flattered."

"Yes, I am flattered," Rourke said, tearing open the packet of M&Ms and immediately dipping in. "Bob is a no-account for sure, but at least he takes a bath once in a while. And he's an Irishman. Thanks for the M&Ms, Bill. I'll need all the energy I can muster for this clusterfuck we're about to get ourselves into." He looked at his watch. "You better get on down and talk to the chief and Doctor Ruth."

Westonfield looked at Magaly. "Keep this gluttonous maniac company for a while, okay? I'll go see what Lucas and Dillworth have cooked up. When Dale gets done puking, or whatever, tell him to have a seat 'til I get back." He went down the stairs.

When Westonfield was gone Rourke said, "He looks like shit."

"He's worried," Magaly said.

"Well, I know he's worried, Maggie. But, see, the man is always worried. It's his—I'm gonna scare you now—his *raison d'être*. He thrives on it. But this is different. Tonight he just looks like a truck ran over him."

Magaly knew that Rourke was right. "What does it mean?"

"Can't say, Maggie. The man makes no sense to anybody who's got sense." He chuckled, got to his feet, and hugged her close. "Help yourself to a coffee," he said. "You know where it is. I'm gonna go fetch Dale out of the shithouse before he drowns or something." He lumbered down the hall toward the bathroom.

Magaly plopped down at Westonfield's old desk and waited. After a moment, she got up again and went to the window, peering out into the artificially lit parking lot. She watched a dozen or more SRT officers, almost invisible in their black fatigues and jump boots, organizing equipment and loading it into two large blue assault vans. They looked very formidable, and she knew that they were among the best SWAT officers in the country, but somehow they seemed too organized, too modern, too well-equipped for the enemy they were about to face. The Cuban—no, he had a name, now—*Gabriel*, was a primal foe. He was not of this world. How do you fight magic and soul-storms with assault weapons? She watched the men silently for a long time, her trepidation growing by the minute. She had the feeling that something was going to go terribly, terribly wrong. The longer she watched, the more the feeling grew, until she went back to the desk and sat down again, shivering.

Rourke and Ward found her that way.

"Jesus," Rourke said, grabbing a chair, sliding it next to hers, and sitting down. "What's going on, sweetheart?"

"I think something bad is going to happen, Jack."

Rourke considered. "Well, he's a bad man, Maggie—this Gabriel. You know that as well as any of us. Lots can go wrong in situations like this. The sorry thing about it is you don't know 'til you know. That's the way it is. We found out where he might be. And we've got to go out and try to get him. There is just no other way to go about the business. Maybe we'll get him and maybe we won't." He looked at his watch. "In about another hour we ought to know." He leaned back and dumped the rest of the M&Ms into his mouth. "Damn, these little bastards are good," he said, leaning forward and hugging her again.

When Rourke went into the bathroom, Ward wasn't puking as had been anticipated. He was standing over one of the ancient porcelain sinks splashing water onto his pallid face. "You look worse than Westonfield," Rourke said.

"I feel worse than Westonfield," Ward said miserably, failing to appreciate Rourke's humor. He towel-dried his face, left the bathroom, and walked back down the corridor to the office. He looked at Magaly. She was one of the prettiest women he'd ever seen, yet, at the moment, he couldn't have cared less if she looked like a dead fish. For lack of anything better to say, he mumbled, "You look nice."

Rourke laughed.

"Thank you," Magaly said.

"Kid's insane," Rourke commented.

Then Westonfield came back.

"Well?" Rourke said.

Before Westonfield could answer, a patrolman came hurrying down the hall. "This is for you, Sarge," he said to Westonfield, handing him a thermofax. It was from "Needle Dick" Kearny, an old friend from "Ident," the Identification Section. Westonfield studied the page and sat down on Rourke's desk without looking where he was sitting. He knocked over a styrofoam cup of coffee. Even though it was his coffee that Westonfield had knocked over, Rourke studied the spreading brown liquid with indifference, making no move to wipe it up.

"Shit," Ward said, "you'd think a man would at least want to clean up a mess on his own desk."

"What do you think you're here for, kid?" Rourke said mildly, pointing to a roll of toweling on top of a nearby file cabinet. "I'm busy watching Bill think and read. It's all I can do to keep up with him. I have no time to engage in distracting housework."

Magaly fetched the toweling. She blotted up the coffee while Rourke looked at Westonfield and Ward glared malevolently at Rourke.

"This is on our boy," Westonfield said. "FBI file via U.S. Immigration. A name check on legal Cuban immigrants with the first or last name of Gabriel yields two hits. One is on an eleven-year-old boy. The other one is on a *Marielito* by the name of Gabriel Flores. Homestead, 1980. No file since then. No arrests, no warrants, no new information. He was born in 1959 in Campechuela." Westonfield looked up. "That makes him thirty-two. Sounds about right." He turned to Magaly.

Her eyes were open and looking at him, but they had turned inward. "It's him," she said mechanically. "Campechuela, by the Gulf of Guacanayabo. I know that town. I know it from my grandfather. There is a legend there. Stories of vampires, a great sorcerer, *palo mayombe*. It's him."

Rourke abandoned his recalcitrance of only a moment before, grabbed some toweling and wiped up a few drops of coffee that Magaly had missed.

Ward looked from one to the other and felt as if he needed to go to the bathroom again.

"It says here," Westonfield continued evenly, "that he's ex-military. Special Forces. That fits. He was also a member of an assassins' cult. No details on that, except that he has the image of a dagger tattooed on his dick." He looked at Magaly again. She was looking at the floor now. "Well?" he said.

"I told you, it's him," she said. "I told you."

Westonfield looked at her in silence for a moment. "Yes."

"Anything else?" Rourke ventured.

"Yeah," Westonfield said. "Nothing but a physical description, though, and the usual FBI number, SID number, and fingerprint classification." He threw the printout to Rourke and turned to a very pale Dale Ward. "He's six-feet-one. It says a hundred eighty-five pounds here. But that was eleven years ago. Hard to say now. Very dark complected. That fits everything we know."

"So what's the plan?" Ward asked.

Westonfield cocked his head oddly. "The plan is to kill him, isn't it?"

Ward swallowed hard.

Rourke slapped the fax on the table, lifted his leg, and farted.

Magaly fled to the bathroom. Ward decided it was an excellent idea, and went again.

Rourke said to Westonfield. "So it's him."

Westonfield ran his hand over the printout as if it were a talisman. "Yep."

"What did Thelma and Louise have to say?" Rourke referred to his meeting with Lucas and Dillworth.

"The usual raid parameters."

"Naturally."

"Naturally."

"I got a bad feeling," Rourke said.

"No shit," Westonfield said mildly.

"No, goddammit. I've got a bad feeling."

Westonfield shrugged. "Me, too."

"Well, what are we gonna do?"

"Go along with the program," Westonfield said. "Just hope this Gabriel's there. Hope we get lucky."

"Go along with the program," Rourke repeated.

"You know the neighborhood like the back of your hand. They want you to birddog it for them. The tac boys will do the door-kicking. Is that acceptable?"

"Do I have a choice?"

Westonfield grinned. "It's the program."

"What are you going to be doing?"

"I'll be there. On a scout. I'll take Ward with me."

Rourke frowned, hung his head.

"You all right?"

Rourke looked up. "No, Bill, I'm not all right. I don't like nothing about this situation. None of it. I don't like us not working together. Sure, we're all out there at the same time. But you know it's not the same. Ward's a good kid. He'll do what he has to do. And Maggie's the best broad I've ever seen when it comes to this kind of shit. But—well, it just ain't the same."

"We'll be together again soon enough," Westonfield said quietly. "You just be careful tonight, John Rourke."

Rourke made no comment. He opened his desk drawer and started hauling out extra ammunition. "Might need this," he said. "Remember the time you introduced me to Martha Reeves, Bill? When Martha and me and you and Dave Ruffin went out on the town? They couldn't believe it when we shot out a couple of street lights. That was so great," he said wistfully, looking at his partner again. "We sure had fun, Bill. Not just that time, but lots of times, didn't we?"

"We had fun," Westonfield said.

* * *

First in line in the caravan that snaked its way toward Gabriel Flores's hideaway on 31st Street were the two vans carrying the SRT teams. Next came Lucas and Dillworth. After that came Rourke and Bennie Adams. Westonfield and Ward were ensconced in the last car, with Magaly in her usual spot in the back seat. Ward said little, mostly because both Magaly and Westonfield were absolutely silent. Finally he asked, "How far is it?"

"Ten minutes," Westonfield said, his eyes remaining on the road. He didn't even glance toward Ward.

When it became clear that this would be all that was forthcoming, Ward added, "How is the operation going to go down?"

"I don't know," Westonfield said. "There are too many variables. The big-shots are going to treat it like a fucking narcotics raid."

"Is that a good idea?"

"You're asking me?" Westonfield replied sarcastically. "Hell, I'm just baggage. So are you."

Magaly leaned forward. "I'm worried about Jack."

Westonfield frowned.

"The whole situation's wrong, Bill. Can we back off, at least until you've had a chance to think it completely through?"

"What?"

Ward perked up, a little hopeful.

"Something's out of place," Magaly said. "Don't tell me you don't think so. You said it yourself. We're just baggage."

"Damn it," Westonfield said. "What are you getting at, Maggie?"

"I don't even think Gabriel's there."

Westonfield groaned. "Don't you think we should at least find out if he is?" he demanded. "It's out of our hands. The ball's rolling. We've got twenty cops out here."

"Maybe it's a trap," Magaly persisted.

"No," Westonfield said with finality. "I trust McMullen."

"Maybe Gabriel tricked him," Magaly said.

"Tricked him," Westonfield said, shaking his head.

"Yes, let himself be found." She looked at her watch. It was ten minutes past midnight. "It's the twenty-second of November now—the day of the full moon. It could be a part of his plan. Maybe he's found some way to end the game."

Westonfield considered it. "Even if you're right, what can we do? The SRT guys are good at what they do. They'll approach the house with all the caution they can muster. They'll move quickly. They'll cover all of the exits. They're wearing flak vests. Maggie, this is all we can do. If it's the end of the game, then so be it."

"What about Jack?" she said.

"What about him?" Westonfield demanded in frustration.

"I already told you," Magaly replied bleakly. "I'm worried about him." She slid back into her seat.

When they were less than half a mile from their destination, Westonfield suddenly slowed down and pulled to the curb. Directly ahead, Rourke and Adams took note and pulled over too. Westonfield waved them away when Rourke looked back through his rear window to see what was going on. Westonfield caught a glimpse of the knowing grin on his partner's face as it occurred to him that Westonfield was up to something. With a jaunty salute, Rourke sped away and disappeared into the night, seeking to catch up with the receding caravan.

Westonfield looked over his shoulder at Magaly, his eyes reflecting the yellow-pink light of the mercury vapor streetlight under which they'd stopped. "Suppose you're right," he said.

Magaly tilted her head. "Suppose I am."

"Remember the night of the shooting on Merritt Street, when I chased Gabriel down to the dead end? I sense him now, just like I did then. He's there. Yet he's *not* there. He's—" he went quiet and stared into the darkness ahead. He was silent for such a long time that Ward would have thought he'd fallen asleep if his eyes hadn't been open. Then Westonfield erupted in a rush, the triumph of revelation in his voice. "I got you, you dirty bastard!"

Ward's flashlight had slid onto the floor of the car, and when Westonfield yelled he banged his head on the dashboard. "Shit!"

"He's waiting," Westonfield bristled. "Like I said. Like on that night with Mejías. Like an evil, inhumanly patient spider. You're right, Maggie. I should have understood. He knows we're coming." He seized the microphone from the dashboard. "4-121 to SRT team leader..."

"Go ahead, 4-121," came the disembodied voice from the radio. "2100 here." It was Lucas.

"I'm a ways behind you, 2100. I think our subject may be outside of the residence, watching the show from a distance. Be ready for possible sniper activity."

"Uhhh... 4-121, what is the source of your information?"

Westonfield muttered under his breath. He vividly imagined Dillworth shaking her head in disgust. "I'm considering the Merritt incident, 2100. He was out in the dark watching us then. We can't be sure he's not doing it now."

"4-121, we can't sweep the area. The activity would only alert him."

"Affirmative, 2100. I'd like to hang back, cover your tails."

After a long pause, Lucas came back. "Affirm, 4-121. Let us know."

* * *

Gabriel was lying across his unmade lump of a bed, unable to sleep, thinking about his final plan. He had been trying to read the principals all evening, searching the undercurrents of the autumn air for signals. He read the fat policeman. He read the *puta*. There was little to be gleaned. This troubled him, because he knew they must be furiously searching for him—especially since the kidnapping of the baby, and since the failed attempt to steal the little witch. One day he would get Westonfield's daughter. He had often contemplated what he would do if she fell into his hands. Maybe he wouldn't kill her after all. Perhaps he would simply steal her and teach her the ways of *palo mayombe*. Could there be any sweeter revenge?

Then he felt it. He alerted like a jackal catching the scent of blood. He became a snuffling hound, actually raising his nose into the air. Ah! The mist was closer than it should have been, searching him out. He sampled the ether for a long moment. He savored its burnt-almond smell. Like cyanide. Like death. He moaned in ecstasy when he suddenly pierced the veil surrounding his enemy and beheld him. He knew there could be only one explanation for his success. Westonfield was close, and he was coming for him.

Gabriel had long prepared for this moment. It didn't take him long to complete the preparations. The explosives were set, his weapons ready, clean and oiled. He leaped from the bed and bounded about the dingy house, gathering his few possessions. Then he set the detonators and placed the radio transmitter in his duffel bag before carefully closing the rickety door. He walked quickly across the street into the vacant lot kitty-corner from his own house. He loved the darkness. He made himself ready at the back of the empty field, next to a dilapidated chain-link fence, sitting cross-legged on the cold ground. But he didn't feel cold.

* * *

The two vans of the SRT team came to a quiet stop a full block south of their target. Rourke guided his unmarked car to the curb behind them. Lucas and Dillworth were in front. The panel doors of the vans swung open and the fatigue-clad policemen, their faces hidden behind dark nylon masks, drifted out like a flow of black snow. The SRT commander formed his men into four units, two large and two small. The two larger units were the front and rear assault teams, the two smaller units were to cover the sides of the house. Then the whole team set out down the street, remarkably silent considering the amount of gear they carried.

Dillworth motioned to Rourke. "Stay with us," she whispered. "We'll stay right out front when the assault teams go in. Then we'll join them."

Rourke didn't like it. It seemed like Hollywood. This Gabriel was far too slippery. There had to be another way. Bill must know there was another way—that's why he was off doing whatever it was he was doing. But now Rourke was with a different partner, good guy that Benny was, and it didn't feel right. He felt as if he should say something to Dillworth or Lucas, but he couldn't think of anything that would make a difference. He held his tongue. He and Adams silently followed along toward the enigmatic horror up the street.

* * *

Westonfield cut one block east to 30th Street and then drove north with his lights out. When they were a block away he halted the scout car. Without a glance at Ward or Magaly he got out, softly pushing the door closed with the palm of his hand. He motioned for his companions to do the same. He looked toward 31st Street through the space between two houses and saw the black-clad SRT men proceeding rapidly forward. From experience, he knew they would approach the house almost at a trot and move in quickly, limiting any chance for the target to escape or prepare a defense. He spotted Rourke and Adams bringing up the rear, knowing Jack must be thoroughly mortified.

"Come along, Dale," he said. "I want to see how the place looks from up this way." Then he turned to Magaly, who was looking with trepidation up the street. "Come on, Maggie. It's just a little ways. From where we'll be, you should be able to see it go down."

"I'm worried about Jack," she said. She sounded like a lost girl.

Westonfield grimaced and said nothing, pacing quickly away up the sidewalk. At his direction, Ward caught an address. They were only ten or twelve houses south of where the 31st Street address should be. After another fifty yards Westonfield stopped, motioning silently for them to stop too. In the dim light, Ward marked how Westonfield's head lifted and canted to one side, bringing his prominent Welsh nose into dark relief. He was intently examining a vacant lot that lay just ahead, on their left, exactly between themselves and where Gabriel's house ought to be. He stood that way for a full minute.

* * *

Rourke stood poised with Adams, Dillworth, and Lucas in the front yard of the darkling house they would in seconds descend upon with a vengeance. All of the houses on the block were dark, but Gabriel's seemed in some way possessed of a preternatural absence of light, a kind of bleakness of the spirit that Rourke sensed for the first time. He had heard Westonfield and Magaly talk about Gabriel in metaphysical terms many times, but had never really understood until now. A gloom lay about the old house like a fog. It effused an earthy smell of blood, mold and old wood. It was the smell of death. As the SRT units rushed into their preassigned positions around the house, Rourke, Adams, and the two executives secreted themselves as best they could behind two big trees in the front yard. The SRT commander looked over at Lucas, anticipating the go-ahead. Lucas gave one last look around the area. All seemed well. Satisfied, he nodded. The team commander silently dropped his upraised arm.

* * *

Magaly suddenly, insanely, walked away toward Gabriel's house, muttering something about helping Jack Rourke, saving him from hellfire. Ward was astounded to observe that

Westonfield didn't appear to be surprised. He merely hissed for him to grab her and keep her away from the shooting. Before Ward could even fashion a response Westonfield was gone, vanished into the darkness of the vacant lot that had become the focus of his attention. *Aguanilleo Zarabanda aribo.*

Ward was completely torn. He knew he needed to do exactly what Westonfield told him to do. That was the one rule, the cardinal rule, that Westonfield always said would keep him alive. Yet he yearned mightily to stay with his partner. Among policemen, there was no greater instinct. On the other hand, he needed to keep Magaly safe. But here she was, wandering into danger like some kind of crazy zombie. He supposed she'd finally broken down under the strain. He cursed a murderous oath and ran after her. Even as he did so he knew he'd made the right decision. Westonfield could at least fend for himself. Magaly could not.

Magaly wasn't sure what happened, but when she came to her senses she found herself emerging from an alley onto 31st Street. She could see the house almost straight ahead. Even if it hadn't been surrounded by black-uniformed policemen she would have known that it was Gabriel's house. It was the place that had haunted her dreams since childhood, the abode of the devil.

Rourke couldn't believe it. He had been thinking about Carol, and how he could make it all up to her, when he saw Magaly step from the shadows and start across the street. Then Dale Ward ran willy-nilly from between the houses and started for Magaly. At that precise moment the SRT commander dropped his hand and the rams swung violently against both doors. The last thing Jack Rourke saw was the face of Magaly Rodríguez smiling at him. Then the world erupted in white light. The roar was deafening, but he didn't hear it. He, and Bennie Adams, and Ruth Dillworth, and Milton Lucas, and all of the SRT team were blasted to their elemental atoms in an instant of flame and smoke.

* * *

This is how it should be, Westonfield thought as he slunk stealthily forward. *This is how it should be.* He knew Gabriel was here, in this very field. Now it was just the two of them. He prayed that Jack and Magaly would be all right, but he couldn't dwell on it. He needed to draw on every bit of training, every bit of skill, and every bit of instinct gleaned from twenty-three years on the street to deal with the killer. Then the thought struck him like a thunderbolt. Gabriel wasn't going to snipe at the assault team. That's what Magaly had meant about hellfire. He wasn't going to shoot them. He was going to blow them up!

Even as Westonfield reached for his radio to warn them, the darkness to the west was rent by a volcano of fire and noise, the concussion rocking him backward. But in the sudden light there was Gabriel, silhouetted against the night like the Whore of Babylon, no more than thirty yards away, his arms outstretched in triumph. Westonfield did not wait. He pulled his weapons, one in each hand, and stepped forward.

* * *

Gabriel watched in fascination as the events unfolded before him like a stage play. There they were, as he knew they would be, all dressed up in their fancy uniforms and with all of their gear. He watched them swarm around his house like black bees. They actually believed they could catch him. No matter, they would be dead very soon. There was the fat policeman, the one who had tackled the fireman who was already dead. Fool. But where were the rest? Westonfield was very close. The strange mist was virtually on top of Gabriel now, mingling curiously with his own. He had never felt this sensation before. It was at once pleasurable and painful—*as when a whore gets raped*, he thought. He desperately wanted to kill a few with the rifle he cradled in his arms, but decided he would wait and do the thing as he had planned it.

He steadied the transmitter in his hand, waiting breathlessly for the right moment. There! The tactical commander raised his arm. When it came down, they would move in, break his doors down, and storm into the house. The arm dropped. The ram in front swung back and crashed into the door with a hollow boom. The black bees swarmed into the house. Gabriel pressed the button and hell came to earth. He forgot himself in a moment of wild triumph and abandon. Even as he leaped up, setting his AR-15 aside, throwing his arms into the blue-black sky, glorying in the wash of the blast, he became aware of Westonfield in the darkness behind him.

* * *

In the bare half-second after Gabriel seized the sky in exaltation, Westonfield saw the demon become aware of him. When the light from the explosion winked out, Gabriel went down and rolled to the left, grabbing up his rifle as he tumbled. Westonfield anticipated where Gabriel would land and fired into the dark. He emptied the magnum in three seconds. He instantly brought up the Sig with his left hand and fired again, adjusting a second time for where he thought Gabriel might be. He fired eight shots, spacing them carefully. Then he thrust the Smith, still in his right hand, into its holster, switched the Sig to his right hand, and resumed fire, emptying the magazine.

Somehow, even as the gunfire reverberated in his ears, Westonfield knew that Gabriel had been hit badly. So many thoughts crowded his mind in that instant that he nearly dissolved into helplessness. Had Magaly survived the explosion? What about Jack? No. Jack was gone. He knew Jack must be gone. Then he felt the bullet strike him, hard, like a sledge in the chest. He went down, flat on his back. Oh, Christ! He held the Sig above his prone body and struggled to drop the empty magazine from the weapon and insert a new one. He did it. Two more bullets zipped over his body, followed by the reports. Judging by the muzzle flashes, he knew that Gabriel was no more than thirty feet away, also down. He pointed the Sig again and lined up the blue dots of the Tritium night sights in a row on the shadow that must be Gabriel. He fired again, a full magazine, the empty casings flying from the ejection port straight up into the darkness. A few came down upon his own body, tinkling metallically.

For a few seconds Westonfield heard nothing. Then he heard the sound of ragged breathing and a curse in Spanish. He heard the sound of a person moving, and then he saw a shadow move, and then an apparition rose up from the damp grass and glided away like a limping soldier. Westonfield ran his hands over his chest. He felt the small hole in his shirt, on the far left side. His hand came away sticky. Hard to say how bad it was, but the spreading numbness wasn't a good sign. Mercifully, he felt no pain. He knew that would come later. He struggled to his feet and staggered after his quarry.

Westonfield knew that Gabriel must have been hit many times, yet still his prey went on, back to the alley and then north toward the I-94 expressway. The light grew as they approached the illuminated ribbon of the service drive. At last Westonfield could see Gabriel before him, not more than fifty yards ahead, loping along crazily, half hopping, half dragging his ruined leg behind him. It occurred to Westonfield that he might try to shoot him in the back, but he knew that at that distance his aim would be too unsteady. He followed as best he could.

Gabriel reached the service drive, zigzagged like an overzealous mime across it, and disappeared over the steep embankment. When Westonfield reached the lip he looked cautiously over. Gabriel was lying sprawled on his back, six feet from the highway, staring back up at him. It was one o'clock in the morning, so only a few cars and trucks roared by, oblivious to the scene that unfolded off to the side of the road. Westonfield saw no sign of the AR-15. Gabriel must have left it in the field. He staggered down, watching him carefully, struggling for breath, finding it increasingly difficult to get enough air into his lungs. Blood welled over his belt buckle, collecting and then spilling onto his pants, dripping down his leg.

At last Westonfield stood over his great enemy, a foe whose name he had learned only that day. The devil lay still, riddled by so many bullets he looked not much different from Porfirio and Gregorio at the paper warehouse. His eyes were orbs of black ink, the dilated pupils surrounded by irises the color of mustard.

An eternity passed as the two men stared into each other's eyes.

"My friend," Gabriel said at last in Spanish, the words coming through ragged gasps. "We finally meet." He spat a mouthful of blood, and whispered, "I wish I had killed you."

Westonfield thought of the unspeakable crimes Gabriel had committed against Katy Marroquín, how he had come so close to stealing his own daughter. "You killed Jack Rourke," he moaned in bewilderment, weaving unsteadily on his feet.

Gabriel was nearly beyond speech now. He gestured feebly, nodding his head 'yes' slightly, a hint of a smile coming to his bloody lips.

"Why?" Westonfield implored, his tongue thick in his mouth, his voice cracking. "Why?"

Gabriel's eyes traced their way with satisfaction over Westonfield's riven body, saw the blood dripping copiously from the trouser cuff. His smile widened.

Westonfield slid the revolver from its holster, pointed it unsteadily at Gabriel's chest, and pulled the trigger. *Click.* Empty. He dropped the Smith to the ground, retrieved the Sig, pointed it, pulled the trigger. *Click.* Also empty. He felt frantically in his pockets for another magazine or loose cartridges for the magnum. Nothing. He must have lost them all in the gunfight in the field, the same way Gabriel had lost his rifle. Tears of frustration dripped down onto Gabriel, little silver drops adorning the pools of blood. The world began to spin and Westonfield wobbled drunkenly on his feet.

All the while Gabriel looked up at him, seeming more amused than hateful. Westonfield looked again into the depths of his eyes, finding there only a dark riddle and the reflection of his own face.

Marshalling his last shred of strength, Gabriel whispered again, "Because I'm like *you*." He would have laughed if he could. "I'm just like you."

Then the devil's eyes went to his own waist and rested on a sheathed knife there. He glanced at Westonfield meaningfully, and then looked again at the knife.

Westonfield's arterial wound bled freely now, his blood mingling with Gabriel's into a slick of liquid copper. He collapsed to his knees, eyes half-closed. With a Herculean effort, he drew Gabriel's long dagger from its sheath and placed it over the devil's heart. As he leaned over to thrust the glittering blade home, his shirt parted and Gabriel caught a glimpse of the Saint Michael's medal dangling there. He nodded in approbation.

Westonfield half thrust and half fell across him, the razor-sharp dagger slicing neatly through the bone and into Gabriel's beating heart.

A while later the police found them there, stiff in death, Westonfield draped horizontally across Gabriel like a fallen beam.

EPILOGUE

It took a long time for Magaly to write about the events in Detroit in the fall of 1991. There were wounds to close. There was healing to be done. She went back to New York—to her friends, her job, her life. Vickers was patient. He knew she had a special talent and that it only needed time to bear fruit. He knew that one day the story would come out and flow onto paper like the *sangría* she loved.

The impetus came one day in the autumn, almost a year later, as she crossed the street right in front of the *Harper's* office. It was a rainy day and a lone beat policeman was doing his best to sort out an automobile accident. Traffic was heavy, the road was blocked, and the line of blocked cars grew longer by the minute. Tempers flared, and when the policeman finally got the damaged cars out of the roadway, a Jaguar roared out of its lane and through a puddle of water, splashing it in a cascade onto the policeman. The Jag disappeared down the street, its business-suited driver shouting an obscenity at the hapless cop.

Magaly felt a rage rise within her of almost maniacal proportions. Shaking with indignation, she ran to the policeman, who was trying to wring dirty water from his uniform. Preoccupied as he was with getting doused, he didn't see her coming. She took him by the arm. Startled, he looked down into her eyes. The only thing Magaly could think to do was to reach out with her hand and touch his face. She didn't say a word for a long moment, just stood there in the street, touching his face and looking into his oddly familiar eyes. He smiled, embarrassed, muttering that he was all right. Magaly smiled back. The cop thought it was the most beautiful smile he had ever seen.

A month later, the story for *Harper's* was nearly complete. It lacked only the last few lines. Magaly sat at the computer in her new office overlooking Central Park. The visage of Bill Westonfield rose before her unbidden as it did sometimes. Then she typed: "It's like Father Lewandowski told me last October. We offer up our big city cops to keep the devil at bay. Then we go about our business, secure in the knowledge that the lives of the protectors we've condemned will placate the gods of chaos. We give no more thought to them than a *mayombero* gives to a dead chicken. Burnt offerings."

She sighed a long sigh, pushed her chair back and looked out the window, off into the grey New York sky.

The End

BURNT OFFERINGS

by

Charles W. Newsome

Available at your local bookstore or use this page to order.
--1-932581-34-0- Burnt Offerings - $19.00 U.S

Send to: Trident Media Inc.
              801 N. Pitt Street #123
              Alexandria, VA 22314
Toll Free # 1-877-874-6334
Please send me the item above. I am enclosing
$_____(please add $4.50 per book to cover postage and handling).
Send check, money order, or credit card:

Card #_____ Exp. date _____

Mr./Mrs./Ms._____
Address_____
City/State_____Zip_____

Please allow four to six weeks for delivery.
Prices and availability subject to change without notice.

Printed in the United States
26582LVS00002B/37-342